Acclaim for Scott Smith's

A SIMPLE PLAN

"The year's finest literary shivers. . . . A beautifully-controlled piece of writing." —*Entertainment Weekly*

"Each character flaw fits seamlessly into place. Each power play and change of circumstance is timed to perfection. . . . Recalls *The Treasure of the Sierra Madre*, the better work of Jim Thompson (*The Grifters*; *After Dark, My Sweet*) and Thomas Berger's tales of small-town souls who succumb to murderous mayhem." —*The Boston Globe*

"It is remarkable to read such a terrifying work expressed in such a seductively reasonable voice." —*The Washington Post*

"An absolute corker. Noir with nuances. Pounce!" —*Daily News*

"Like watching a train wreck. There is nothing to be done, but it is impossible to turn away. . . . Smith is to be lauded for his elegantly unsettling descriptions of violence and especially for taking an uncompromising approach to his material." —*Chicago Tribune*

"Astonishing." —*Vanity Fair*

"Expertly crafted . . . will make you feel like an unindicted co-conspirator. To say more about the plot would ruin the pleasure of reading the book for yourself." —*People*

"A seamless, unpretentious thriller." —*New York* magazine

"Absorbing. . . . Straightforward, engaging; its characters and relationships ring true. . . . An enjoyable chronicle of crime."
—*The Plain Dealer*

"Scott Smith's first novel is that rare and satisfying combination: a compulsive thriller which also happens to be a beautifully-written original work of art."
—Robert Harris, bestselling author of *Fatherland*

"Offers plenty of thrills." —*Newsday*

"You're likely to be riveted by this unusually accomplished debut." —*Glamour*

Scott Smith

A SIMPLE PLAN

Scott Smith was educated at Dartmouth College and Columbia University. He lives in New York City.

ALSO BY SCOTT SMITH

The Ruins

A SIMPLE PLAN

A SIMPLE PLAN

A NOVEL BY

Scott Smith

VINTAGE BOOKS
A DIVISION OF RANDOM HOUSE, INC.
NEW YORK

FIRST VINTAGE BOOKS EDITION, OCTOBER 2006

The Library of Congress has cataloged the Knopf edition as follows:
Smith, Scott, 1965 July 13–
A simple plan : a novel / by Scott Smith.
p. cm.
1. Young men—Fiction. 2. Murderers—Fiction. 3. Treasure-trove—Fiction. 4. Guilt—Fiction. 5. Larceny—Fiction. 6. Wealth—Moral and ethical aspects—Fiction. I. Title.
PS3569.M5379759 S57 1993
813'.54—dc20 92-42478

Vintage ISBN-10: 0-307-27995-2
Vintage ISBN-13: 978-0-307-27995-8

Book design by Virginia Tan

www.vintagebooks.com

Printed in the United States of America
10 9 8 7 6 5 4

FOR MY PARENTS,
WITH SPECIAL THANKS TO ALICE QUINN,
GAIL HOCHMAN, VICTORIA WILSON,
AND ELIZABETH HILL

No man chooses evil because it is evil; he only mistakes it for happiness, the good he seeks.

—MARY WOLLSTONECRAFT

A SIMPLE PLAN

I

My PARENTS died in an automobile accident the year after I was married. They tried to enter I-75 through an exit ramp one Saturday night and crashed head-on into a semi hauling cattle. My father was killed instantly in the wreck, decapitated by the hood of his car, but my mother, miraculously, survived. She lived for a day and a half more, hooked up to machines in the Delphia Municipal Hospital, her neck and back broken, her heart leaking blood into her chest.

The semi driver came through it all with only a few minor bruises. His truck had caught fire, though, barbecuing the cattle, and after my mother died he sued my parents' estate for damages. He won the suit but got no material satisfaction from it: my father had mortgaged his farm to the hilt and was teetering on the edge of bankruptcy when he died.

My wife Sarah's pet theory was that he'd committed suicide, driven to it by the embarrassing proliferation of his debts. I argued with her at the time, though not very wholeheartedly. In hindsight, you see, it seems that he may've made certain preparations. A week before the accident, he came by my house in his pickup, its truck bed packed with furniture. Sarah and I had no use for any of it, but he was insistent, threatening to head straight for the dump if we didn't accept the entire load, so I helped him carry it, piece by piece, down to the basement. After he left us, he drove over to my brother Jacob's apartment and gave him the pickup.

There was also his will, the first clause of which was an injunction upon Jacob and me that we swear orally, in each other's presence, to visit his grave every year, without fail, on his birthday. It continued from there, a bizarrely elaborate document, pages and pages, going through the old farmhouse room by room, bequeathing each object to us by name, no matter how trivial or inconsequential—a shaving kit, a broom, and an old Bible for Jacob; a broken blender, a pair of work boots, and a black stone paperweight in the shape of a crow for me. It was pointless, of course, wasted effort. We had to sell everything of any value to pay the debts he'd left behind, and the things of no value we had no use for. We had to sell the farm, too, our boyhood home. A neighbor bought it, grafting it to his own land, absorbing it like a giant amoeba. He knocked down the house, filled in the basement, and planted a soybean field on the lot.

My brother and I had never been close, not even as children, and the gap between us only grew wider as we got older. By the time of the accident, we had very little except our parents left in common, and their sudden deaths eased whatever weight this might've normally held.

Jacob, older than I by three years, had dropped out of high school and lived alone in a small apartment above the hardware store in Ashenville, the town in which we were raised, a tiny crossroads marked with a flashing yellow light, as rural as rural gets in northern Ohio. He worked on a construction crew in the summer and survived off unemployment benefits through the winter.

I'd gone to college, the first in my family to do so, graduating from the University of Toledo with a bachelor's degree in business administration. I'd married Sarah, a classmate of mine, and moved to Delphia, thirty miles east of Ashenville, just outside of Toledo. There we bought a three-bedroom, unabashedly suburban house—dark green aluminum siding and black shutters, a two-car garage, cable TV, a microwave, the Toledo *Blade* delivered with a soft thump to our doorstep every evening at dusk. I commuted back to Ashenville each weekday, to the feedstore there, where I worked as assistant manager and head accountant.

There was no animosity between Jacob and me, no bad blood, we simply weren't comfortable around each other, had difficulty finding things to say, and made little attempt to hide it. More than once, coming out onto the street after work, I saw him dodge into a doorway to avoid meeting me, and each time I felt more relief than pain.

The one tie we did have, after our parents' accident, was the keeping of our promise to our father. Year after year on his birthday we'd repair to the cemetery and stand in stiff, awkward silence beside the grave site, each waiting for the other to suggest that a proper amount of time had passed, so that we could part and slip back into our separate lives. It was a depressing way to spend an afternoon, and we probably would've given it up after the very first time had we both not felt that we'd be punished somehow if we did, cursed from beyond the grave for our failure to stand by our word.

Our father's birthday was December 31, the last day of the year, and the visit gradually took on a ritualized aspect, like any other event during the holiday season, a final hurdle to cross before reaching the new year. It became, essentially, our chief time to interact. We'd catch up on each other's lives, talk about our parents or our childhood, make vague promises to see each other more often, and leave the cemetery with the clean feeling of having rather painlessly fulfilled an unpleasant duty.

This went on for seven years.

ON THE eighth year, December 31, 1987, Jacob picked me up at my house. He came around three-thirty, a half hour late, with his dog and his friend Lou in his truck. They'd been ice fishing together, their chief activity in the winter, and we had to drop Lou off on the other side of Ashenville before proceeding to the cemetery.

I never liked Lou, and I don't think he ever liked me. He used to call me Mr. Accountant, saying it in a way which seemed to imply that I ought to be embarrassed by my occupation, ashamed of its conventionality and stability. I was peculiarly intimidated by him, though I could never discern exactly why. It certainly wasn't his physical presence. He was a short, balding man, forty-five years old, just beginning to put on weight in the gut. His blond hair was thin, wispy, so that you could see his scalp beneath it, pink and chapped looking. He had crooked teeth, and they gave him a slightly comical quality, a mock toughness, making him look like some two-dimensional disreputable character out of a boy's adventure book—an old boxer, a street thug, an ex-con.

As I came down the walk, he climbed out of the pickup to greet me, so that I'd have to sit in the middle of the seat.

"Howdy, Hank," he said, grinning. Jacob smiled at me from behind the wheel. His dog, a big, overgrown mutt, mostly German shepherd, but with some Labrador thrown in on top, was in the back. It was a male dog, but Jacob had named him Mary Beth, after a girl he'd dated in high school, his first and only girlfriend. He referred to him as a "she," too, as if the dog's name had blinded him to his gender.

I climbed in, Lou pulled himself up behind me, and we backed our way down my driveway to the street.

My house was in a small subdivision called Fort Ottowa, after a frontier outpost whose inhabitants had frozen to death in a blizzard sometime before the start of the Revolution. It was farmland, unrelentingly flat but made over to look like it wasn't. The roads curved around imaginary obstacles, and people constructed little hills in their front yards, like burial mounds, covering them with shrubbery. The houses up and down the street were tiny, each one built right up against the next—starter houses, the realtor had called them—full of newly married couples on their way up in the world, or retirees on their way down, the former planning careers and babies and moves to nicer neighborhoods, the latter waiting for their savings to disappear, their health to suddenly worsen, their children to send them away to old-age homes. It was a way station, a rung near the bottom of the ladder.

Sarah and I, of course, belonged to the first group. We had a nest egg, an account gathering interest in the Ashenville Savings Bank. Someday soon we were going to move away, take a step up in the world, the first of many. That was the plan, at least.

Once beyond my neighborhood, we headed west, away from Delphia, and as we did the curving streets, the clustered groupings of two-story houses with circular driveways and swing sets and picnic tables rapidly dissolved away behind us. The roads straightened themselves, becoming narrower in the process. Snow blew across them in places, moving snakelike, in long, thin, dusty lines, piling up along their edges. Houses strayed from one another, separated by whole fields now rather than simple squares of grass. Trees disappeared, the horizon widened, and the view took on a windswept look, a white-gray barrenness. We passed fewer and fewer cars.

It was an uncomfortable ride. Jacob's truck was eleven years old, and there was nothing about it that did not show its age. At one time it had been painted a bright tomato red, my brother's favorite color, but it was faded now to a scablike burgundy, its sides pockmarked with rust. Its shocks were shot, its heater erratic. The rear window was missing, replaced by a sheet of plastic. The radio was broken, the windshield wipers torn off, and there was a hole the size of a baseball in the floor. A steady stream of cold air blew in through this, shooting straight up my right pant leg.

Jacob and Lou talked about the weather as we drove, how

cold it had been lately, when it would snow next, whether or not it had rained on the previous New Year's Eve. I kept silent, listening. Whereas I normally felt merely awkward alone with Jacob, when I was with him and Lou together I felt both awkward and excluded. They had an aggressively private way of interacting; their language was coded, intimate, their humor schoolboyish and obscure. Lou would say "pineapple," with an extra stress on the "pine," or Jacob would moo like a cow, and they'd both immediately tumble into laughter. It was bewildering—I could never escape the feeling that they were constantly making fun of me.

We passed a frozen pond, with skaters on it, children in bright jackets shooting back and forth. Dark, weathered barns dotted the horizon. It never ceased to surprise me: we were ten minutes away from my house and already surrounded by farms.

We drove south of Ashenville, skirting the town, keeping it just out of sight beyond the horizon, taking State Highway 17, ruler straight, until we hit Burnt Road. We turned right there, heading north, then left onto Anders Park Road. We crossed a long, low cement bridge over Anders Creek, plowed snow piled thickly over its railings, making it look fake, like something from a Christmas story, a cookie-dough bridge.

Beyond the creek was Anders Nature Preserve, a thickly wooded square of land that hovered at the right-hand edge of the road for the next two miles. It was a park, run by the county. There was a small pond at its very center, stocked with fish and surrounded by a mown field. People came out from Toledo during the summer to picnic there and play games, to throw Frisbees and fly kites.

The place had originally been the private estate of Bernard C. Anders, an early automobile magnate from Detroit. He'd bought the land in the 1920s and built a large summer house on it, the stone foundations of which were still visible beside the pond. When he died, during the Depression, the estate passed to his wife. She moved into the house year-round and lived there for the next four decades, finally leaving it only to be buried. She and Bernard had produced no children, so she chose to bequeath the land to the county, on the condition that they make it into a nature preserve and name it after her husband. It was an unusual place for a park, out in the middle of nowhere, surrounded on four sides by working farms, but the county, with an eye on state tax credits for parkland, accepted. The house was razed, picnic tables carted in, hiking trails cut, and Anders Nature Preserve was created.

We'd gone about a mile past the bridge, halfway down the southern edge of the park, when a fox sprinted in front of us.

It all happened very quickly. I saw a flash of movement off to the left, coming out of the snow-covered field, had just enough time to focus in on it, see that it was a fox, a large, reddish one, sleek and healthy, a dead chicken hanging from its jaws, and it was in front of us, shooting across the road, its body taut, hugging the ground, as if it thought it might sneak by unseen. Jacob slammed on the brakes, too hard, and the truck went into a skid, its rear end coming out to the left, its front bumper sliding right, digging with a loud, raking sound into the snow at the edge of the road. There was the crystalline popping sound of a headlight shattering; then the truck slammed to a stop. We were thrown forward, and the dog came flying in through the plastic rear window, tearing it, his legs scrambling in panic. He was there in the cab for just a moment—I felt his fur, cold against the back of my neck—then he was gone, back out the hole he had made, over the side of the truck, and into the woods after the fox.

Jacob was the first to speak. "Fuck," he said softly. "Fuck, fuck, fuck."

Lou giggled a little at that and pushed open his door. We

climbed out onto the road. The imploded headlight was the only damage, and we stared at it for a bit, forming a semicircle around the front of the truck.

Jacob tried calling the dog. "Mary Beth!" he yelled. He whistled shrilly.

No one seeing us standing there would've ever recognized us as brothers. Jacob took after our father, while I took after our mother, and the difference was dramatic. I'm brown haired, brown eyed, of medium height and build. Jacob was several inches taller than me, blue eyed, with sandy blond hair. He was also a fat, fat man, immensely, even grotesquely overweight, like a caricature of obesity. He had big hands, big feet, big teeth, thick glasses, and pale, doughy skin.

We could hear the dog barking. He was getting farther and farther away.

"Mary Beth!" Jacob yelled.

The trees were fairly thick here, standing close together—maples, oaks, buckeyes, sycamores—but there was relatively little undergrowth. I could see the fox's tracks winding their way in and around the trunks, disappearing into the distance. Mary Beth's paw prints ran parallel to them, a little darker in the snow, wider and rounder, like a trail of hockey pucks beneath the trees. The ground was perfectly flat.

We listened to the dog's barking grow fainter and fainter.

On the other side of the road was a field, smooth with snow. I could see tracks there, too, coming toward us from the far horizon, perfectly straight, as if the fox had been walking along one of the field's furrows, masked from view by the snow. In the distance, a little toward the east, I could make out Dwight Pederson's farm—a stand of trees, a dark red barn, a pair of grain silos, and a two-story house that looked gray against the snowy landscape, though I knew it was actually light blue.

"It had one of Pederson's chickens," I said.

"Stole it." Lou nodded. "Broad daylight."

Jacob whistled for Mary Beth. After a while it seemed like he'd stopped moving away. The barking neither decreased nor increased in volume. We listened to it, tilting our heads toward the woods. I was getting cold—there was a stiff wind cutting across the road from the field—and I was eager to climb back inside the truck.

"Call him again," I said.

Jacob ignored me. "She's treed it," he said to Lou.

Lou's hands were deep in the pockets of his jacket. It was an army surplus jacket, white for camouflage in the snow. "That's how it sounds," he said.

"We'll have to go in and get her now," Jacob said.

Lou nodded, took a wool hat from his pocket, and pulled it down over his pink skull.

"Call him once more," I said, but Jacob ignored me again, so I tried calling the dog myself.

"Mary Beth," I yelled. My voice came out pitifully thin in the cold air.

"He's not coming," Lou said.

Jacob shuffled back to the truck and opened the driver's side door. "You don't have to go, Hank," he said. "You can wait here if you want."

I didn't have a hat with me, and I wasn't wearing boots—I hadn't planned on hiking through the snow—but I knew that both Jacob and Lou expected me to stay behind, expected me to wait like an old man in the truck, and I knew that they'd joke about it while they made their way off through the trees and tease me when they returned.

So, against my will, I said, "No, I'll go."

Jacob was leaning into the truck, fiddling around in the space behind the seat. When he emerged he was holding a hunting rifle. He took a bullet out of a little cardboard box and loaded it into the gun. Then he put the box back behind the seat.

"There's no reason," he said. "You'll just be cold."

"What's the rifle for?" I asked. Out of the corner of my eye, I could see Lou grinning.

Jacob shrugged. He cradled the gun in his arms, flipped the collar of his jacket up around his ears. His parka was bright red and, like all his clothes, a size too tight for him.

"It's posted land," I said. "You can't hunt here."

Jacob smiled. "It's compensation: that fox's tail for my broken headlight." He glanced toward Lou. "I'm only taking one bullet, like the great white hunter. That seem fair to you?"

"Perfectly," Lou said, drawing out the first syllable so that it sounded like "purrrr."

He and Jacob both laughed. Jacob stepped awkwardly up onto the snowbank at the side of the road, balanced there for a second, as if he might fall backward, then gathered himself and lumbered down into the trees. Lou followed right behind him, still giggling, leaving me alone on the road.

I hesitated there, wavering between the twin sins of comfort and pride. In the end it was pride and the thought of Lou's snickering that carried the day. With something bordering on revulsion, I watched myself climb up over the bank and set off through the snow, hurrying lest they get too far ahead.

THE SNOW was shin deep in the woods, and there were things hidden beneath its smooth surface—the trunks of fallen trees, stones, broken branches, holes, and stumps—which made the going much harder than I'd anticipated. Lou led the way, spry, scurrying ratlike between the trees, as if he were being chased. I followed directly in his tracks, and Jacob brought up the rear, a good ways behind us, his face turning a brilliant pink, just a shade lighter than his jacket, with the effort of moving his huge body forward through the snow.

The dog's barking didn't seem to get any closer.

We continued on like this for about fifteen minutes.

Then the trees suddenly thinned, and the land dropped away before us into a wide, shallow bowl, as if, millions of years before, a giant meteorite had landed there, carving out its impression in the earth. Parallel lines of stunted, sickly looking trees transversed the hollow—they were apple trees, the remains of Bernard Anders's orchard.

Lou and I stopped on the edge of the bowl to wait for Jacob. We didn't talk; we were both out of breath. Jacob shouted something through the trees at us, then laughed, but neither of us understood him. I scanned the orchard for the dog, following his paw prints with my eyes. They disappeared in the distance beneath the trees.

"He's not in there," I said.

Lou listened to the dog's barking. It still seemed very far away. "No," he agreed. "He isn't."

I made a complete circle of the horizon with my eyes, taking in both the orchard and the woods behind us. The only thing moving for as far as I could see was Jacob, working his way aggressively through the snow. He still had another fifty yards to go and was progressing at a pathetically slow rate. His jacket was unzipped, and even at that distance I could hear the tortured sound of his breathing. He was using his rifle like a cane, digging its butt into the snow and pulling himself forward by its barrel. Behind him, he'd cut a wide swath of deep, messy tracks, so that it looked as if he'd been dragged through the woods against his will, struggling and kicking the entire way.

By the time he reached us, he was soaked with sweat, his skin actually steaming. Lou and I stood there watching him try to catch his breath.

"Christ," he said, gasping, "I wish we'd brought something to drink." He took off his glasses and wiped them on his jacket, squinting down at the ground as if he half-expected to find a pitcher of water sitting there in the snow.

Lou waved his hand in the air like a magician, snapped his

fingers over the right-hand pocket of his jacket, then reached in and pulled out a can of beer. He popped its top, slurped the foam from the lid, and, smiling, offered it to Jacob.

"Always be prepared," he said.

Jacob gulped twice at it, pausing in between to catch his breath. When he finished, he returned the can to Lou. Lou took a long, slow swallow, his head tilted back, his Adam's apple sliding up and down the wall of his throat like a piston. Then he held the can out toward me. It was a Budweiser; I could smell its sweetish scent.

I shook my head, shivering. I'd started to sweat hiking through the snow, and now, standing still, my damp skin was becoming chilled. The muscles in my legs were trembling and jumping.

"Come on," he said. "Have a sip. It won't hurt you."

"I don't want any, Lou. I'm not thirsty."

"Sure you are," he prodded. "You're sweating, aren't you?"

I was about to decline again, this time more forcefully, when Jacob interrupted us.

"Is that a plane?" he asked.

Both Lou and I glanced into the sky, searching the low clouds for movement, ears keyed for the hum of an engine, before realizing that he was pointing down into the orchard. We followed his finger to the very center of the bowl, and there, nestled among the rows of stunted apple trees, hidden almost completely by its covering of snow, was indeed a tiny single-engine airplane.

Lou and I reached it first, side by side.

The plane was resting perfectly flat on its belly, as if it were a toy and a giant hand had reached down out of the sky to set it there, snug beneath the branches of the trees. There were remarkably few signs of damage. Its propeller was twisted out of shape, its left wing was bent back a bit, tearing a tiny hole in the fuselage, but the land itself was relatively unmarked; there were no upturned trees, no jagged, black gashes in the earth to reveal its path of impact.

Lou and I circled the wreck, neither of us approaching close enough to touch it. The plane was surprisingly small, no bigger really than Jacob's truck, and there was something fragile about it: it seemed far too tiny to support the weight of a man in the air.

Jacob came slowly down into the orchard. The snow had settled more deeply here, and he looked like he was wading or shuffling toward us on his knees. Off in the distance, Mary Beth continued sporadically to bark.

"Jesus," Lou said. "Look at all these birds."

At first I didn't see them—they were so still in the trees—but then suddenly, as soon as I saw one, they all seemed to jump out at me. They were everywhere, filling the entire orchard, hundreds and hundreds of black crows perched motionless on the dark, bare branches of the apple trees.

Lou packed some snow into a ball and tossed it at one of them. Three crows lifted into the air, completed a slow half circle over the plane, and settled with a soft fluttering onto a neighboring tree. One of them cawed, once, and the sound of it echoed off the shallow sides of the bowl.

"It's fucking spooky," Lou said, shivering.

Jacob came up, huffing and puffing. His jacket was still unbuttoned, his shirttails hanging out. He took a few seconds to catch his breath.

"Anybody inside?" he asked.

Neither of us answered him. I hadn't even thought about it, but of course there had to be someone inside—a pilot, dead. I stared uneasily at the plane. Lou threw another snowball at the crows.

"You haven't checked?" Jacob asked.

He handed his rifle to Lou and lumbered up to the plane. There was a door in its side, just behind the damaged wing. He grabbed its handle and gave it a tug. The plane made a loud creaking sound, metal pushing against metal, and the door swung open about five inches, then stopped. Jacob tugged again, putting his weight into it, and got another inch and a half. Then he grabbed the edge of the door with both hands and pulled so hard that the whole plane rocked back and forth, dislodging its shell of snow, revealing the shiny silver metal beneath, but not moving the door at all.

Emboldened by his aggressiveness, I approached the plane more closely. I tried peering in through the windshield but could make nothing out. The glass was spiderwebbed with a tiny, intricate matrix of cracks and frosted over with a thick sheet of ice.

Jacob kept tugging at the door. When he stopped, his breath was coming hard and fast again.

Lou stood a little ways off. He looked like a sentry, with Jacob's rifle cradled in his arms. "It's jammed, I guess," he said. He sounded relieved.

Jacob peered in through the crack he'd made, then pulled his head back.

"Well?" Lou asked.

Jacob shook his head. "Too dark. One of you'll have to go in and check it out." He took off his glasses and wiped at his face with his hand.

"Hank's the smallest," Lou said quickly. "He'll fit the easiest." He winked at Jacob, then grinned toward me.

"I'm smaller than you?"

He patted his little stomach, the beginning of his paunch. "You're thinner. That's what counts."

I looked toward Jacob for help but immediately saw that there'd be none forthcoming. He had a toothy smile on his face, his dimples cutting into his cheeks.

"What do you think, Jacob?" Lou asked.

Jacob started a little laugh but then stopped. "I can't imagine you fitting, Lou," he said seriously. "Not with that gut of yours." They both turned to look at me, straight-faced.

"Why go in at all?" I asked. "What's the point?"

Lou started to grin. A handful of crows flapped heavily into the air, changing trees. It seemed like the whole flock was watching us.

"Why not just get the dog," I said, "then go into town and report this?"

"You scared, Hank?" Lou asked. He shifted the rifle from one arm to the other.

I watched myself cave in, disgusted by the spectacle. I heard a voice in my mind very clearly analyzing the situation, saying I was acting like a teenager, doing something pointless, even foolish, to prove my courage to these two men, neither of whom I respected. The voice went on and on, reasonable, rational, and I listened to it, agreeing with everything it had to say, while I strode angrily around the plane to its open door.

Jacob stepped back to give me room. I stuck my head inside the doorway, let my eyes adjust to the darkness. It seemed even tinier inside than it had outside. The air felt warm, and humid, too, like in a greenhouse. It gave me an eerie feeling. A thin stream of light entered from the tear in the fuselage and shot across the cabin's darkened interior, like a weak flashlight beam, forming a tiny crescent moon against the opposite wall. The rear of the plane was almost completely dark, but it appeared to be empty, a bare metal floor growing narrower and narrower the farther back it went. Just inside the doorway was a large duffel bag lying on its side. If I'd reached in with my hand, I could've grabbed it and dragged it out.

Toward the front, I could see two seats, gray with the

light filtering in through the ice-covered windshield. One of them was empty, but there was a man's body slouched in the other, his head resting against the control panel.

I pulled my head out of the doorway.

"I can see him from here."

Jacob and Lou stared at me. "Is he dead?" Jacob asked.

I shrugged. "We haven't had snow since Tuesday, so he's been out here for at least two days."

"You aren't going to check?" Lou asked.

"Let's just get the dog," I said impatiently. I didn't want to go into the plane. It seemed stupid of them to make me.

"I think we ought to check." Lou grinned.

"Come on, Lou. Cut the crap. He can't be alive."

"Two days isn't that long," Jacob said. "I've heard of people surviving stuff longer than that."

"Especially in the cold," Lou agreed. "It's like keeping food in the refrigerator."

I waited for the wink, but it didn't come.

"Just go in and check him out," Jacob said. "What's the big deal?"

I frowned, feeling trapped. I stuck my head back inside the plane for a second, then pulled it out again. "Can you at least scrape the ice off the windshield?" I asked Jacob.

He gave a deep, theatrical sigh, more for Lou's benefit than mine, but nevertheless shuffled off toward the front of the plane.

I started to squeeze my way in through the doorway. I turned sideways and slipped my head and shoulders inside, but when I got to my chest, the opening seemed suddenly to tighten, gripping me like a hand. I tried to pull back, only to find that my jacket and shirt were snagged. They bunched up under my armpits, exposing the skin above my pants to the cold air.

Jacob's bulk darkened the windshield, and I heard him start to scrape at the ice with his glove. I watched, waiting for it to get lighter, but nothing happened. He started to pound—dull, heavy thuds that echoed through the plane's fuselage like a heartbeat.

I exhaled as far as possible and lunged forward. The doorway's grip moved from my sternum to just above my navel. I was about to try again, thinking that one more push would do it, that I could get in, examine the dead pilot, and get out as quickly as possible, when I saw a curious thing. The pilot appeared to be moving. His head, resting against the dashboard, seemed to be shaking ever so slightly back and forth.

"Hey," I whispered. "Hey, buddy. You all right?" My voice echoed off the plane's metal walls.

Jacob continued to pound against the glass. Thump. Thump. Thump.

"Hey," I said, louder, slapping the fuselage with my glove.

I heard Lou move closer in the snow behind me.

"What?" he asked.

Jacob's hand went thump, thump, thump.

The pilot's head was motionless, and suddenly I wasn't so sure. I tried to squeeze forward. Jacob stopped pounding.

"Tell him I can't get it off," he yelled.

"He's stuck," Lou said gleefully. "Look at this."

I felt his hands grab me just above the waist. His fingers dug in, a rough attempt at tickling. I kicked out with my right leg, hitting air, and lost my footing in the snow. The doorway's grip held me up. Lou's and Jacob's laughter came filtering inside, muted and far away.

"You do it," Lou said to Jacob.

I was pushing and pulling now, not even sure which way I wanted to go, just trying to get free, my feet digging into the snow outside, the weight of my body rocking the plane, when there was a sudden flash of movement up front.

I couldn't tell what it was at first. There was the sense of the pilot's head being tossed to the side, then something exploding upward, rising and pounding frantically against the inside of the windshield. Not exactly pounding, I realized slowly, but fluttering. It was a bird, a large black crow, like the ones sitting in the apple trees outside.

It came off the windshield and settled on the rear of the pilot's seat. I watched its head dart back and forth. Carefully, noiselessly, I tried to work my way backward out of the doorway. But then the bird was airborne again; it smacked once into the windshield, bounced off, and flew straight at me. I froze at the sight of it, simply watched it come, and only at the very last moment, just before it hit me, pulled my head down into my shoulders.

It struck me in the exact center of my forehead, hard, with what felt like its beak. I heard myself cry out—a short, sharp, canine sound—pulled back, then forward, somehow broke free from the doorway, and fell into the plane's interior. I landed on the duffel bag and didn't try to get up. The bird returned toward the front, bounced off the windshield, flew back toward the now open doorway, but veered to the right before reaching it, shooting up toward the jagged little hole in the fuselage. It perched there for a second, then wormed its way through like a rat and disappeared.

I heard Lou laugh. "Holy shit," he said. "A fucking bird. You see that, Jake?"

I touched my forehead. It was burning a little, and my glove came away bloody. I slid off the duffel bag, which was hard and angular, as if it were full of books, and sat down on the floor of the plane. A rectangle of light from the open doorway fell across my legs.

Jacob stuck his head inside, his body blocking the light.

"You see that bird?" he asked. I could tell he was smiling, even though I couldn't make out his face.

"It bit me."

"It bit you?" He didn't seem to believe me. He waited there a moment, then pulled his head away from the door. "The bird bit him," he said to Lou. Lou giggled.

Jacob darkened the doorway again. "You all right?"

I didn't respond. I was angry at both of them, felt that none of this would've happened if they hadn't pressured me into going inside. I moved in a crouch toward the front of the plane.

I could hear Lou's voice, faintly. "You think birds carry rabies or anything?"

Jacob didn't answer him.

The pilot was dressed in jeans and a flannel shirt. He was a small, thin man, young, in his twenties. I came up behind him and tapped him on the shoulder.

"You alive?" I whispered.

His arms hung down at his sides, his fingertips just barely brushing the floor. His hands were swollen, impossibly large, like inflated rubber gloves, their fingers curling slightly inward. His shirt sleeves were rolled up, and I could see the hair on his forearms, dark black against the ghostly whiteness of his skin. I grasped his shoulder and pulled him away from the dashboard. His head fell back heavily against the seat, and I flinched at the sight of it, jerking myself up and banging my own head against the plane's low metal ceiling.

His eyes had been eaten out by the bird. Their dark sockets stared at me, his head rolling a bit to the right on his neck. The flesh around his eyes had been chewed completely away. I could see his cheekbones, white in the dim light, pale and translucent, like plastic. There was a bloody icicle coming out of his nose. It hung all the way down to the base of his chin.

I stepped back, fighting a surge of nausea. Yet even as I did so I felt myself strangely drawn forward. It was something like curiosity, but stronger: I felt an absurd desire to take off my gloves and touch the man's face. It was a powerful, morbid pull, and I had no name for it, but I fought it, taking another step back, then another, and by the time I made my fourth step, the feeling was gone, replaced only by revulsion. The pilot's face stared after me as I retreated toward the doorway.

From a distance its expression looked beseeching, mournfully so, like a raccoon's.

"What the fuck're you doing?" Jacob asked. He was still in the doorway.

I didn't answer him. My heart was beating thickly in my temples. I stumbled against the duffel bag, turned and kicked it ahead of me toward the doorway. It was surprisingly heavy, as if it were full of dirt, and its weight brought back my initial wave of nausea.

"What's the matter?" Jacob asked. I shuffled toward him, pushing the bag across the floor. He backed away.

When I got to the door, I set my shoulder against it and—using my increased leverage—managed to creak it open another three inches. Jacob and Lou watched me, their faces curious, wavering between amusement and apprehension. The day seemed brighter than it had before, but it was just my eyes. I squeezed the duffel bag through the door, then followed it out into the snow.

"You're bleeding, Hank," Jacob said. He raised his hand to his own forehead, turned toward Lou. "That bird bit him."

Lou scrutinized my forehead. I could feel a little line of blood running down into my left eyebrow. It was cold against my skin.

"It ate out his eyes," I said.

Jacob and Lou stared blankly at me.

"The bird. It sat in the pilot's lap and ate out his eyes."

Jacob grimaced. Lou gave me a skeptical look.

"You can see his skull," I said. "See the bone." I crouched down, scooped up some snow, and held it, burning, against my forehead.

The wind had picked up a little, and the apple trees in the orchard were swaying in it, creaking. The crows on their branches had to lift their wings every now and then to keep their balance. The light was beginning to fade and, with it, whatever warmth there had been to the day.

I took the snow away from my forehead. It was light brown with blood. I removed my glove and touched the cut with my finger. It was cold from the snow, and tender. There was a bump rising up, as if a marble or a tiny egg had been planted just beneath my skin.

"You've got a little bump," Jacob said. His rifle was slung over his left shoulder; his jacket was buttoned up.

Lou crouched down beside the duffel bag. It was closed with a tightly knotted drawstring, and he had to take off his gloves before he could undo it. Jacob and I watched him work at it. When he got it loose, he opened the bag.

As he looked inside, his expression went through a remarkable transformation. There was an initial hint of perplexity, his eyes opening wide, as if trying to focus better, his eyebrows rising slightly; but this was followed quickly by signs of excitement and amusement, his face flushing a deep crimson, his lips pulling back in a smile to reveal his crooked teeth. Watching him, I felt sure that I didn't want to know what the bag contained.

"Holy fucking shit," he said. He reached inside and hesitantly touched whatever was there, a petting motion, as if it were alive and he was afraid it might bite.

"What?" Jacob asked. He moved heavily toward Lou through the snow.

With a sinking sensation, remembering the bag's weight, I decided suddenly that it must be a body, or parts of a body.

"It's money," Lou said, smiling up at Jacob. "Look." He leaned the bag forward.

Jacob bent over and squinted at it, his mouth dropping open. I looked, too. It was full of money, packets held together with thin paper bands.

"Hundred-dollar bills," Lou said. He took one of the packets out, held it up in the air before his face.

"Don't touch it," I said, rising to my feet. "You'll get fingerprints on it."

He glanced sourly at me but returned the packet to the bag. Then he put his gloves back on.

"How much do you think is here?" Jacob asked. They both looked toward me, deferring to my accountant's knowledge.

"Ten thousand to a packet," I said. I measured the bag with my eyes, tried to guess how many packets could fit inside. "It's probably close to three million dollars." I said this without really thinking. Then, when I thought about it, it seemed absurd. I didn't believe it.

Lou picked up another packet, this time with his gloves on.

"Don't touch it, Lou," I said.

"My gloves are on."

"The police'll want to get prints from the packets. You'll smudge any that are already there."

He frowned but dropped the packet back into the bag.

"Is it real?" Jacob asked.

"Of course it's real," Lou said. "Don't be stupid."

Jacob ignored him. "You think it's drug money?" he asked me.

I shrugged. "It's from a bank." I gestured toward the bag. "That's how they sort money. A hundred bills to a packet."

Mary Beth appeared suddenly on the opposite rim of the orchard, working his way down through the snow toward the plane. He looked dejected, as if we'd let him down by not joining in on his pursuit of the fox. We all watched him approach, but no one commented on his return. One of the crows cawed at him, a warning cry, and it hung for a second, sharp and clear in the crisp air, like a note from a bugle.

"This is crazy," I said. "That guy must've robbed a bank."

Jacob shook his head in disbelief. "Three million dollars."

Mary Beth came around the front of the plane, wagging his tail. He gave us a sad, tired look. Jacob crouched down and patted absentmindedly at the dog's head.

"I suppose you're going to want to turn it in," Lou said.

I looked at him, shocked. Up till that point I hadn't even considered that we had an option. "You want to keep it?"

He glanced toward Jacob for support, then back at me. "Why not each keep a packet? Ten thousand dollars apiece, and turn the rest in?"

"For starters, it's stealing."

Lou gave a quick snort of disgust. "Stealing from who? From him?" He waved toward the plane. "He won't mind."

"It's a lot of money," I said. "Somebody knows it's missing, and they're looking for it. I guarantee that."

"You're saying you'd turn me in, if I took a packet?" He picked one of the packets out of the bag, held it out toward me.

"I wouldn't have to. Whoever's looking for it knows how much is missing. If we hand it in a little short and you start spending hundred-dollar bills around town, it won't take them long to figure out what happened."

Lou waved this aside. "I'm willing to take the risk," he said, flashing a smile from me to Jacob. Jacob smiled back.

I frowned at them both. "Don't be stupid, Lou."

Lou continued to grin. He slipped the packet into his coat, then picked a second one out of the bag and handed it to Jacob. Jacob took it but couldn't seem to decide what to do with it. He crouched there, his rifle in one gloved hand, the money in the other, looking expectantly at me. Mary Beth rolled in the snow at his feet.

"I don't think you'd turn me in," Lou said. "And I know you wouldn't turn your brother in."

"Get me near a phone, Lou, and you'll see."

"You'd turn me in?" he asked.

I tried to snap my fingers, but with gloves on they didn't make any sound. "Like that."

"But why? It's not like it'd harm anyone."

Jacob was still crouched there, the money in his hand. "Put it back, Jacob," I said. He didn't move.

"It's different for you," Lou said. "You've got your job at the feedstore. Jacob and I don't have that. This money'd matter to us."

His voice had edged itself toward a whine, and, hearing it, I felt a revelatory flash of power. The dynamic of our relationship had shifted, I realized. I was in control now; I was the spoiler, the one who would decide what happened to the money. I smiled at Lou.

"I'd still get in trouble if you took it. You'd fuck up, and I'd be considered an accomplice."

Jacob started to stand up, then crouched back down again. "Why not take all of it?" he asked, looking from Lou to me.

"All of it?" I said. The idea seemed preposterous, and I started to laugh, but it made my forehead ache. I winced, probing at the bump with my fingers. It was still bleeding a little.

"Just take the bag," he said, "leave the dead guy in there, pretend we were never here."

Lou nodded eagerly, pouncing on the idea. "Split it three ways."

"We'd get caught as soon as we started spending it," I said. "Imagine the three of us suddenly throwing hundred-dollar bills around at the stores in town."

Jacob shook his head. "We could wait awhile, then leave town, start up new lives."

"A million apiece," Lou said. "Think about it."

"You just don't get away with something like that." I sighed. "You end up doing something stupid, and you get caught."

"Don't you see, Hank?" Jacob asked, his voice rising with impatience. "It's like this money doesn't even exist. No one knows about it but us."

"It's three million dollars, Jacob. It's missing from somewhere. You can't tell me no one's searching for it."

"If people were searching for it, we would've heard by now. There would've been something on the news."

"It's drug money," Lou said. "It's all under the table. The government doesn't know about any of it."

"You don't—" I started, but Lou cut me off.

"Jesus, Hank. All this money staring you right in the face. It's the American dream, and you just want to walk away from it."

"You work for the American dream, Lou. You don't steal it."

"Then this is even better than the American dream."

"What reason would you have for turning it in?" Jacob asked. "No one's going to get hurt by our taking it. No one's going to know."

"It's stealing, Jacob. Isn't that enough?"

"It's not stealing," he said firmly. "It's like lost treasure, like a chest full of gold."

There was some sense in what he was saying, I could see that, yet at the same time it seemed like we were overlooking something. Mary Beth made a whimpering sound in the snow, and Jacob, without taking his eyes off my face, began to pet him. The crows sat quietly in the surrounding trees, hunch shouldered against the cold, like miniature vultures. Darkness was falling quickly all around us.

"Come on, Hank," Lou said. "Don't fuck this up."

I still didn't say anything—I was hesitating, wavering. As much as I delighted in my power over Lou and Jacob, I didn't want to do something I'd later regret merely to contradict them. Without even realizing it, without even intending to do it, I began searching for a way to take the packets. And it was like magic, too, like a gift from the gods, the ease with which a solution came to me, a simple plan, a way to keep the money without fear of getting caught. I could just sit on it, hiding it away until the plane was discovered. If someone found the wreck and there was no mention of a missing three million dollars, I'd split it up with Lou and Jacob and we could go our separate ways. But if, on the other hand, it seemed like someone knew the money was missing, I'd burn it. The duffel bag and the packets themselves would be the only evidence that could be held against me. Up until the very instant I gave Lou and Jacob their shares, I'd be in complete control. I could erase my crime at a moment's notice.

Looking back on it now, after all that's happened, it seems insane with what little fear I picked this path. It took me perhaps twenty seconds, a third of a minute's worth of debate. For a brief instant I was in complete control, not only of the money's destiny but also of my own, and Jacob's, and Lou's, yet I was utterly unconscious of this, had no feel for the weight of my decision, could not sense how, within the next few seconds, I was going to set into motion a series of events that would radically transform each of our lives. In my ignorance, my choice seemed straightforward, unambiguous: if I were to give up the duffel bag now, it'd be an irrevocable step—I'd hand it over to the sheriff, and it'd be gone forever. My plan, on the other hand, would allow me to postpone a decision until we had more information. I'd be taking a step, but not one that I couldn't undo.

"All right," I said. "Put the money back."

Neither of them moved.

"We're keeping it?" Lou asked.

"I'm keeping it."

"You're keeping it?" Jacob said. "What do you mean, you're keeping it?"

"This is what we're doing. I keep it for six months. If no one comes looking for it during that period, then we'll split it up."

Jacob and Lou stared at me, taking this in.

"Why do you keep it?" Lou asked.

"I'm the safest. I have a family, a job. I've got the most to lose."

"Why not split it up now?" he asked. "We each sit on our own shares?"

I shook my head. "This is how we're doing it. If you don't want it like this, we can turn it in now. That's the choice I'm offering you."

"You don't trust us?" Jacob asked.

"No," I said. "I guess I don't."

He nodded at that but didn't say anything.

"They'll discover the plane before six months is up," Lou said. "Spring'll come and somebody'll find it."

"Then we'll see for sure if anyone knows there was money on it."

"And if someone knows?" Jacob asked.

"Then I'll burn it. The only way we'll keep it is if there's absolutely no chance of getting caught. As soon as it seems like we might be in trouble, I'll get rid of the money."

"You'll burn it," Lou said, disgusted.

"That's right. Every last bill."

Neither of them spoke. We all stared down at the duffel bag.

"We don't tell anyone," I said. I looked at Lou. "Not even Nancy." Nancy was Lou's live-in girlfriend. She worked in a beauty parlor over in Sylvania.

"She's got to know eventually," he said. "She's gonna wonder where all my money's coming from."

"She can know when we decide that it's safe to keep it. Not a moment sooner."

"Then the same thing holds for Sarah," he said.

I nodded, as if this went without saying. "We'll continue to live like normal. I'm just asking you to hold off for six months. It'll be there, waiting for you. You'll know it's there."

They were both silent, thinking.

"All right?" I asked. I looked first at Lou, then at Jacob.

Lou was scowling at me, as if he were angry. He didn't say anything. Jacob shrugged, hesitated a second, then nodded. He dropped his packet back into the bag.

"Lou?" I said.

Lou didn't move. Jacob and I stared at him, waiting. Finally, with a grimace, as if it pained him to do it, he pulled the wad of money from his jacket, stared at it for a moment, and then, very slowly, slid it into the bag.

"We count it before you take it," he said, his voice low, almost a growl.

I smiled at him, even grinned. It seemed funny that he didn't trust me.

"All right," I said. "That's probably a good idea."

2

IT WAS getting dark now, so we decided to return to the truck and count the money there. As we hiked back toward the road, Jacob and Lou started talking about what they were going to do with their newfound wealth. Jacob wanted a snowmobile, a wide-screen TV, a big fishing boat that he'd name *Hidden Treasure*. Lou said he was going to invest half his share in the stock market and spend the rest on a beach house in Florida with a deck, a hot tub, and a wet bar. I just listened, wanting all the time to warn them not to make plans, that we might not be able to keep it, but for some reason remaining silent.

Lou and I carried the duffel bag together, walking sideways, each of us holding an end, and it slowed us down enough for Jacob to keep up. Jacob talked the whole way, chattering like a child. You could feel his excitement—it was something palpable; he exuded it like a scent.

The temperature began to drop as soon as the sun went down, glazing the surface of the snow into an icy skin, which we broke through each time we took a step. There was very little light beneath the trees. Branches seemed to jump out at us as we walked, appearing suddenly from the darkness directly before our faces, making us duck and weave as we moved forward, like a trio of boxers.

It took us nearly thirty minutes to reach the road. When

we got there, Jacob put his rifle back behind the truck's front seat and started searching for his flashlight, while Lou and I emptied the money onto the tailgate. We were both a little stunned, I think, at the number of packets that spilled from the bag, mesmerized by the sight of so much wealth, and that's probably why we didn't notice the sheriff's truck until it was almost upon us. Perhaps if we'd seen it earlier, if we'd made out its headlights when they were still hovering on the edge of the horizon, two yellow pinpricks moving slowly toward us, I would've acted differently. I would've had time to think things through, to consider my options with a little more care, so that when the truck finally got close enough for me to make out the bubble light on its roof, I might've decided to tell Sheriff Jenkins about the plane. I could've shown him the money, explained how we were just about to call him up on the CB, and, by doing that, I would've ended the whole thing right then and there, would've handed it to the sheriff in a nice, tidy bundle, disposing of it before it had a chance to unravel and entangle us all.

But it didn't happen like that: the truck was no more than two hundred yards away when we noticed it. We heard it first, heard its engine, the crunch of its tires against the frozen road. Lou and I looked up at the same time. A half second later Jacob pulled his head from behind the seat.

"Shit," I heard him say.

Without thinking, acting purely on instinct, like an animal burying its store of food, I slammed shut the tailgate. The money tumbled out across the truck bed, the packets making a soft thumping sound against the metal floor. We'd dropped the duffel bag to the ground after we'd emptied it, and I bent to pick it up now. I draped it across the money, covering it as best I could.

"Go up front with Jacob," I whispered to Lou. "Let me do the talking."

Lou shuffled quickly away, his head bowed. Then the

sheriff was there, his brakes squeaking as he came to a stop on the opposite side of the road. He leaned across the seat to roll down the window, and I stepped out to greet him.

Technically Carl Jenkins wasn't really a sheriff, though that's what everyone called him. Sheriff was a county position, and Carl worked for the town. He was Ashenville's only policeman, a position he'd held for nearly forty years. People called him Sheriff simply from a lack of any other possible title of respect.

"Hank Mitchell!" he said as I came toward him, his whole face smiling, as if he'd been driving along just now hoping he'd run into me. I didn't know him that well; we were no more than nodding acquaintances, but I always felt like he was sincerely pleased to see me. I think he made everyone feel that way, even strangers; he had that quality about him, a disarmingly unguarded avuncularity, a smile that caught you by surprise.

He was a small man, shorter than I. His face was perfectly round, with a wide, shiny forehead and a small, thin-lipped mouth. There was an air of properness about him, an elegance: his khaki uniform was invariably perfectly pressed, his nails clipped, his thick white hair combed and carefully parted. He smiled often and always had a clean, freshly scrubbed smell about him, a sweetish mixture of talcum powder and shoe polish.

I stopped a few feet short of his truck.

"Engine trouble?" he asked.

"No," I said. "Dog trouble." I felt remarkably calm. The money was just a small thought in the very back of my head. I could tell he wasn't going to get out of his truck, so I knew we wouldn't have a problem. I told him about the fox.

"He treed it?" Carl asked.

"We thought so, but we didn't get more than a hundred yards into the park before he came running back."

Carl peered at me over the rim of his half-raised window,

a look of concern on his face. "What happened to your head?"

I touched the bump with my hand, then waved out toward the woods. "Walked into a branch," I said. It was the first thing I thought of.

He continued to stare at me for another second or so, then glanced off toward Jacob and Lou. They'd both given him a wave when he pulled up, but now they'd climbed inside Jacob's truck. Their faces were close together, practically touching, and they were talking in what I could only call a conspiratorial manner. Lou was speaking, gesturing excitedly with his hands, and Jacob was nodding at what he said. Mary Beth was sitting on Jacob's lap, staring out the window at us.

"They been drinking?" Carl asked quietly.

"Not yet," I said. "Jacob and I were at the cemetery this afternoon."

"The cemetery?"

I nodded. "Visiting my parents' graves. This is the day we always do it."

"New Year's Eve?" His face lit up. He seemed to enjoy the idea of this.

"I took the day off," I said.

Carl reached forward and flicked a switch on the dashboard, turning the truck's heater to high. There was a warm, rushing sound inside the cab. "Is Jacob still out of work?" he asked.

"He's looking," I lied, feeling the usual flood of embarrassment I experienced whenever my brother's joblessness became a topic of conversation.

"Lou working?"

"No. I don't think so."

Carl shook his head sadly, staring across the road at them. "That's a shame, isn't it? Two grown men, both eager for work. This country . . ." He trailed off, seemingly lost in thought.

"Well," I started, "we should probably—"

"Lou used to coach baseball," Carl said, cutting me off. "At a boy's camp up in Michigan. Used to be one hell of a shortstop. You know that?"

"No," I said. "I'd never heard that before."

"You wouldn't guess it looking at him now. But there was a time . . ."

Jacob's truck made a creaking sound as he pushed open his door. Carl fell silent, and we both watched my brother squeeze himself out onto the road and lumber toward us.

"Hello, Jacob," Carl said. "I was beginning to think maybe you were trying to avoid me."

Jacob smiled sheepishly. It was his usual expression when approaching figures of authority. As soon as I saw it, I remembered it from our childhood. It was how he'd looked when a teacher called on him in school.

"I was just cold," he said. "I wanted to get in the truck and warm up a bit."

"Hank tells me you two were visiting your parents' graves today."

Jacob glanced at me, then gave Carl a hesitant nod.

"That's a good thing," Carl said, "a real good thing. I hope my kids do the same for me when I'm gone."

"My dad made us," Jacob said. "It was in his will."

Carl didn't seem to hear him. "I remember your father," he started, but then seemed immediately to think better of it, as if suddenly unsure that it was actually our father he remembered and not some other deceased native of Ashenville. He shook his head. "A good man," he said. "An exceptionally good man."

Neither Jacob nor I could come up with a way to respond to that. There was a moment's silence, which Jacob ended finally by saying, "You tell him about the plane?"

I looked at him in shock. He had a big grin on his face, his fat cheeks ridged with dimples, his lips pulling back to show his teeth. He glanced toward me, and, for a second, I was afraid he might even wink.

"What's this?" Carl asked. He looked from Jacob to me.

"Hank and I were driving by here on Tuesday, this exact same stretch of road, and we thought we heard a plane going down."

"A plane?"

Jacob nodded. "It was snowing pretty hard, and we couldn't be sure, but it sounded exactly like a plane having engine trouble."

Carl stared at him, eyebrows raised, waiting. I tried to think of something to say, some way to change the subject, but nothing came. I stood there, angrily willing Jacob to shut his mouth.

"There haven't been any reports of a missing plane?" he asked.

"No," Carl said slowly, drawing it out, as if to show that he was thinking while he talked, taking what Jacob had told him seriously. "Can't say I've heard anything like that." He glanced at me again. "You just heard an engine? No crash?"

I forced myself to nod.

"Could've been anything then. A motorcycle, a snowmobile, a chain saw." He waved across the fields toward the southeast. "Maybe it was something Dwight Pederson was tinkering with."

We all turned and stared at the Pederson place. There were lights on in the downstairs windows, but the barn and outbuildings were lost in the darkness.

"If you do hear anything," Jacob said, still wearing his clownish smile, "you should give us a call. We could show you where we were."

"I'm sure it would've been reported by now," Carl said. "Planes don't just drop out of the sky without people noticing them missing."

I looked at my watch, trying to cut things off before Jacob had a chance to say anything more. "You're probably eager to get home, Carl. It's after five."

He shook his head, sighing. "I've got a late one tonight, New Year's Eve and all. Apt to be some drinkers out driving." He looked at Jacob. "I trust you won't be one of them."

Jacob's smile faded from his face. "No. You don't have to worry about me."

Carl stared at him for a second, as if expecting him to say something more. Then he turned toward me. "How's Sarah getting along? She must be about due, if I'm not mistaken."

"End of January," I said. My wife was eight months pregnant with our first child.

"You'll have to wish her a happy new year from me," Carl said. He began to roll up his window. "And tell Lou not to be so shy next time. I won't bite."

CARL drove off while we were climbing into the truck. He continued westward, away from Ashenville.

"Just drive for a bit, Jacob," I said. "Don't follow him. Head back toward town."

Jacob started the engine. It took him a while to turn around on the narrow road.

"Go slowly," I said. I was afraid that some of the packets might blow out of the truck bed if we went too fast.

Nobody spoke until we were on our way. Then, as we were crossing the bridge over Anders Creek, I said, "Whose idea was that? To ask him about the plane?" I leaned forward so I could see both of them. Lou was sitting in the center, with the dog in his lap. He had his arms around him, hugging him to his chest. Neither of them answered me.

"Was it yours, Lou?" I'd meant to question them calmly, to rationally show them the danger of what they'd done, but my voice betrayed me, coming out tight and full of anger.

Lou shrugged. "We thought it up together."

"Why?" I asked.

"So we could find out if anyone was looking for the plane," Jacob said. His voice sounded triumphant, as if he felt he'd outwitted me. "And not only that, but now if someone does come looking for it, Carl'll call us first. That way we won't be surprised."

"You've just decided to steal three million dollars, and the first thing you do is interrogate the sheriff about it. Doesn't that seem even the slightest bit foolish to you?"

"We found out that no one's looking for it," Jacob said. "We never would've known that if we hadn't asked."

"It was stupid, Jacob. If they find the plane now, and they realize that the money's missing, he's going to know right off who took it."

"But that's the beauty of it. There's no way we'd have mentioned it to him if we were the ones who took the money."

"Promise me you won't do anything like this again."

He smiled at me. "Don't you see how sneaky it is? Our asking him about the plane puts us on his side."

"It was a risk," I said. "It was stupid."

"But it paid off. We found out—"

"This isn't a game, Jacob. We've committed a crime. We could go to jail for what we've done tonight."

"Come on, Hank," Lou said. "No one's going to send us to jail for this. None of us has records, we aren't criminals. Anyone would've done what we did."

"You're saying we didn't commit a crime?"

"I'm saying they wouldn't send us to jail for it. Even if they convicted us, we'd get a suspended sentence."

"Especially if we hadn't spent any of the money yet," Jacob said. "I think—"

"I don't care what you think," I said, my voice rising toward a shout. "If I feel like you're taking unnecessary risks,

I'll burn the money." I looked from Jacob to Lou. "Do you understand?"

Neither of them said anything.

"I'm not going to jail because of something stupid you two idiots have done."

They both stared at me, shocked by my outburst. Mary Beth made a whimpering sound in Lou's arms. I looked out the window. We were on Burnt Road, moving south, surrounded by fields.

I took a deep breath, tried to calm myself down. "I just want you to be careful," I said.

"We'll be careful, Hank," Jacob said quickly. "Of course we'll be careful."

Lou didn't say anything, but I could sense him, even with my head turned toward the window, grinning at Jacob.

"Stop the truck," I said. "We can count it here."

JACOB pulled off onto the edge of the road, and we climbed outside into the cold. We were about three miles west of town. Snow-covered fields lined either side of the road, and there were no houses in sight, no lights of any sort. If a car had approached us from either direction, we would've been able to see it for nearly a mile before it reached us.

Jacob and Lou counted the money; I stood behind them with a flashlight. Mary Beth remained inside the empty cab, sleeping on the seat. They organized the packets into stacks; each stack was ten packets high. It seemed to take forever to count them. I divided my attention equally between the piles of money and the surrounding horizon, alert for approaching lights.

The night was very quiet. The wind hissed across the empty fields; the snow made an occasional creaking sound as it settled alongside the road; and over it all, soft but insistent, came the steady shuffling hush, like cards being dealt at a casino, of Jacob and Lou counting the packets into piles.

When they finished, there were forty-four stacks lined up one after the other along the truck's tailgate. It was $4.4 million.

It took a little while for this to sink in. We stood there, gazing at the money. Lou counted the stacks again, touching the top packet of each one with his forefinger.

"How much is that apiece?" Jacob whispered.

I had to think for a second. "Almost a million and a half."

We continued to stare at the money, stunned.

"Put it away," I said finally, shivering in the cold. I handed Jacob the duffel bag and watched it grow solid as he slowly refilled it.

When all the money was inside, I took it back to the cab.

Lou lived southwest of Ashenville, in the opposite direction from me, and we drove there first. It was getting colder and colder; a fretwork of ice was forming along the edge of the windshield. The torn rear window flapped in the wind, sending a steady stream of frigid air pulsing through the cab. Mary Beth rode in the back, huddled halfway into the truck, right up against our necks, so that I could hear him breathing in my ear. The bag of money was resting on the floor, wedged tightly between my legs. I held the top shut with my hand.

It was quarter till seven by the time we reached Lou's.

Nancy's car was in the yard, and there were lights on in the house. It was a large, run-down farmhouse, ancient, one of the oldest surviving homes in the area. Lou and Nancy rented it from Sonny Major, whose grandfather had once owned all the surrounding fields, growing corn and cabbage in them; he'd been one of the region's gentry in the high days before the Depression. Things had gone downhill since then. Sonny's father had sold nearly all the land over the years, except for two thin strips along the road. One of these supported the farmhouse; the other, a smaller plot about three quarters of a mile to the south, had a tiny, rusted-out house trailer on it. Sonny lived in the trailer, alone, within sight of the house he'd grown up in. He called himself a carpenter but survived chiefly off the money he made from Lou and Nancy's rent.

Jacob parked in the driveway, leaving the engine on. Lou opened the door and climbed outside, hesitating for a second before shutting it.

"I was thinking we might each take a packet now," he said. "Just to celebrate with." He smiled at me.

I slid over toward the door, keeping the duffel bag between my legs. Mary Beth climbed in through the window, his fur smelling fresh and cold. He shook himself and then sat down on the seat, leaning up against Jacob. Jacob put his arm around the dog.

"Forget about the money, Lou," I said.

He wiped at his nose with his hand. "What do you mean?"

"Nothing's going to change in your life for the next six months," I said.

Jacob patted Mary Beth's side, a hollow sound. There were trees clustered around Lou's house, huge ones with thick, gray trunks rising up tall against the blackness of the night sky. They were swaying a little in the wind, their branches clicking together. Down the road Sonny's trailer was completely dark. He wasn't home.

"All I'm asking for—" Lou started, but I shook my head, cutting him off.

"You aren't hearing me, Lou. What I'm saying is, don't ask."

I leaned over and pulled shut the door. He stared at me for a moment, through the window, then exchanged a quick glance with Jacob before turning and walking slowly up his driveway.

. . .

IT TOOK forty minutes to drive from Lou's house to mine. Jacob and I covered much of this distance in silence, sunk in our own private thoughts. I replayed my encounter with Carl. I'd lied to him; it'd come easily, naturally, and I was surprised by this. I'd never been successful at deceit before. Even as a child I couldn't lie; I hadn't had the self-confidence for it—the essential calmness—and had always ended up either giving myself away or breaking down and confessing. As I reviewed my talk with Carl, though, I could find no weak points, no holes in my story. Jacob had overstepped, it was true, asking about the plane, but I realized now that what he'd said wasn't as compromising as it had originally seemed. Perhaps, as he claimed, it might even help us.

I hardly thought of the money. I hadn't yet allowed myself to begin considering it as my own. It was too vast a sum for me to personalize; it seemed abstract, a mere number, nothing more. I felt an edge of lawlessness, it's true—a cool, cocky feeling rippling with a terrible fear of getting caught—but it stemmed more from my mendacity with Carl than from any understanding of the magnitude of our theft.

Jacob had pulled a candy bar from the glove compartment and was chewing at it while he drove. The dog sat on the seat beside him, his ears erect, watching him eat. We were on Highway 17 now, making our way into the outskirts of Delphia. Trees were springing up alongside the road, houses beginning to cluster into subdivisions. The traffic slowly thickened. I was almost home.

The thought came to me suddenly, in a little jolt of panic, that if we were to be caught, it would be because of Lou.

"Lou'll tell Nancy, won't he?" I said to Jacob.

"Will you tell Sarah?" he asked.

"I agreed not to."

Jacob shrugged, took a bite from his candy bar. "Lou agreed not to tell Nancy."

I frowned, dismayed. I knew that I was going to tell Sarah

about the money as soon as I got home—I couldn't imagine not telling her—and this knowledge seemed to confirm my reservations about Lou. He'd tell Nancy, and one of them would screw it up.

I reached over and adjusted the rearview mirror so that I could look at my forehead. Jacob turned on the dome light for me. When I touched it, the bump felt smooth and hard, like a pebble. The skin directly above it was shiny and taut, while the area around it was taking on a purplish tint, a painful-looking darkness, as blood coagulated within the damaged tissue. I licked the thumb of my glove and briefly tried to clean the wound.

"How do you think that thing knew he was in there?" Jacob asked.

"The bird?"

He nodded.

"It's like a vulture. They just know."

"Vultures see you, though. They see you crawling in the desert. That's how they know you're dying, if you're crawling or just lying there. That thing couldn't see inside the plane."

"Maybe it smelled him."

"Frozen things don't smell."

"It just knew, Jacob," I said.

He nodded, three short, quick movements of his head. "That's right," he said. "That's exactly my point." He took another bite of his candy bar, then fed the last little bit to Mary Beth. The dog seemed to swallow it without chewing.

When we pulled into my driveway, I sat there for a few seconds before climbing out, staring off through the windshield. The house's front light was on, illuminating the trees in the yard, their branches glistening with ice. The living-room curtains were drawn, and there was smoke coming from the chimney.

"You and Lou going out tonight?" I asked. "Celebrating the new year?"

It was cold in the truck; I could see our breath in the air, even the dog's. The sky outside was cloudy, starless.

"I suppose."

"With Nancy?"

"If she wants."

"Drinking?"

"Look, Hank. You don't have to be so hard on Lou. You can trust him. He wants this just as bad as you—more so, probably. He's not going to mess it up."

"I'm not saying I don't trust him. I'm saying he's ignorant and a drunk."

"Oh, Hank—"

"No, hear me out." I waited until he turned to face me. "I'm asking you to take responsibility for him."

He put his arm around the dog. "What do you mean, responsibility?"

"What I mean is, if he fucks up, it's your fault. I'll hold you to blame."

Jacob turned away from me and looked outside. All up and down the street my neighbors' windows were full of light. People were finishing their dinners, showering, dressing, busily preparing for their New Year's celebrations.

"Who takes responsibility for me?" he asked.

"I do. I'll look after the both of us." I smiled at him. "I'll be my brother's keeper."

It came out like a joke, but I only half meant it that way. All through our childhood our father had told us how we ought to take care of each other, how we couldn't depend on anyone else. "Family," he used to say, "that's what it always comes down to in the end: the bonds of blood." Jacob and I had never managed to pull it off, though; even as children we were always letting each other down. Because of his weight, he'd been mercilessly teased at school and was constantly getting into fights. I knew that I was supposed to help him, that I ought to be jumping to his defense, but I could never figure out a way to do it. I was weak, small for my age, a thin, bony kid, and I'd just stand with everyone else, in a tight circle around my brother and his tormentors, watching, in absolute silence, while he was beaten up. It became the template for an interaction that we'd ceaselessly repeat as we aged: Jacob would fail somehow, and I—feeling impotent and embarrassed and unworthy—would do nothing but observe.

I reached over the dog's head and punched Jacob lightly on the shoulder, feeling silly doing it, an awkwardly forced attempt at fraternal camaraderie. "I'll take care of you," I said, "and you'll take care of me."

Jacob didn't respond. He just watched me open the door, pull the duffel bag out of the truck, and, straining, hoist it over my shoulder. Then, as I was picking my way carefully up through the snow to the house, he reversed down the driveway and drove off.

I ENTERED quietly, setting the bag inside the hall closet, on the floor toward the back. I draped my jacket across its top.

There were sliding doors on either side of the entranceway; the one on the right led to the dining room, the one on the left to the living room. Both were closed now. The dining room's was rarely open; except for the extremely sporadic occasions when we had company over, we always ate in the kitchen. The living room's, on the other hand, was closed only when we had a fire going.

Straight ahead, the entranceway divided into a flight of stairs on the left and a long, narrow hallway on the right. The stairs led to the second floor, the hallway to the kitchen at the rear of the house. Both of these were sunk in darkness.

I slid open the door to the living room. Sarah was in there, reading in a chair beside the fire. As I entered, she looked up: a tall, thin-boned woman with dark blond, shoulder-length hair, and large, brown eyes. She had some lipstick on, a bright shade of red, and her hair was pulled away from her face with a barrette. Both things—the lipstick and the barrette—made her seem younger, more vulnerable, than she really was. She was wearing her bathrobe, a huge tent of white terry cloth with her initials sewn in blue thread above her heart, and its folds masked the distension of her abdomen somewhat, making it look like she merely had a pillow resting on her lap. Beside her, on the table, was a half-finished bowl of cereal.

She saw me looking at the bowl. "I got hungry," she said. "I wasn't sure when you'd be back."

I went over to kiss her on the forehead, but just as I was bending down, she cried, "Oh!" grabbed my hand, and placed it on her stomach beneath the robe. She gave me a dreamy smile. "Feel it?" she asked.

I nodded. The baby was kicking. It felt like an erratic heartbeat, two firm thrusts and then a softer one. I hated when she made me do this. It gave me an uneasy feeling, knowing that something was alive inside her, feeding off her, like a parasite. I pulled my hand away, forced a smile.

"Do you want dinner?" she asked. "I could cook us an omelet." She waved toward the back corner of the room, where an open doorway led into the kitchen.

I shook my head. "I'm all right."

I sat down in the chair on the other side of the fireplace. I was trying to decide on the best way to tell her about the money, and as I attempted to work my way around this, it suddenly came to me that she might not approve; she might try to make me give the money back. This idea led me to a disturbing revelation. I saw for the first time how much I actually wanted the money. Up till then—with Jacob and Lou—I'd always been the one threatening to relinquish it, and this had allowed me to nurture the illusion that I was relatively disinterested in its fate: I would keep it, but only if certain rigorous conditions were met first. Now, confronted with the possibility of being forced myself to give it back, I understood how artificial those conditions really were. I wanted the money, I realized, and I'd do almost anything to keep it.

Sarah sat there, the book in her lap. She had her hand on her belly, the dreamy look on her face. She came out of it slowly.

"Well?" she asked. "How did it go?"

"It was all right," I said. I was still thinking.

"You spent all this time at the cemetery?"

I didn't answer her. The room was dark, except for the fire and the little lamp on the table beside her chair. There was a miniature grandfather clock on the mantelpiece and a bearskin rug on the floor before the hearth, both wedding gifts from my parents. The rug was fake, a storybook bear with perfect, glass-marble eyes and white plastic teeth. On the opposite wall was a window-size mirror in a wooden frame. Its surface reflected the room back at me so that I could see myself in it, along with Sarah and the fireplace.

Sarah leaned toward me in her chair. "What happened to your forehead?"

I touched my bump. "I banged it."

"Banged it? On what?"

"Sarah," I said. "I'm going to give you a hypothetical situation, okay? Like a game."

She set her book face-down on the table beside her and picked up the bowl of cereal. "All right."

"It's a thing of morals," I said.

She took a spoonful of cereal, then wiped her mouth with the back of her hand, getting lipstick on it.

"Let's say you were out walking and you found a bag of money."

"How much money?"

I pretended to think. “Four million dollars.”

She nodded.

“Would you keep it, or would you turn it in?”

“It’s somebody else’s money?”

“Of course.”

“So it’d be stealing to keep it?”

I shrugged. That wasn’t the direction I wanted her to move in.

She barely even seemed to think about it. “I’d turn it in,” she said.

“You’d turn it in?”

“Of course. What would I do with four million dollars? Can you see me bringing home that much money?” She laughed, slurped loudly at another spoonful of cereal.

“But imagine all the stuff you could do with four million dollars. You could start a whole new life.”

“It’s stealing, Hank. I’d end up getting caught.”

“What if you were sure you wouldn’t get caught?”

“How could I be sure of that?”

“Maybe you knew no one was looking for it.”

“But how would I explain my change in lifestyle? My fancy clothes, my trips to the Caribbean, my jewelry, my minks? People would start asking questions.”

“You’d move away. You’d go somewhere where people didn’t know you.”

She shook her head. “I’d always be worried about getting caught. I wouldn’t be able to sleep at night.” She stared down at her fingernails. They were painted bright red, the same color as Jacob’s jacket. She wiped at the lipstick on her hand. “No. I’d turn it in.”

I didn’t say anything. Sarah lifted her cereal bowl to her mouth and sipped the milk from it. She watched me over its rim.

“You’d take it?” she asked, her face half hidden by the bowl.

I shrugged. I bent over and untied one of my shoes.

She set the cereal bowl down. "It seems to me like it'd be an awful lot of trouble."

"Let's say you got rid of the problem of getting caught." I made a cutting motion with my hand. "There's absolutely no way it'll happen."

She frowned. "Whose money is it?"

"What do you mean? It's yours."

"But who am I stealing it from?"

"A drug dealer. A bank robber."

"If it were a bank robber, it'd be the bank's money."

"All right, then it's a drug dealer."

"Oh, Hank," Sarah said. "You just want me to say I'd take it."

"But isn't it conceivable that you might?"

"I'm sure that in some situations I'd think twice before turning it in."

I didn't know what to say to that. It wasn't at all what I had hoped for.

She glanced toward me. "Why're you asking me this?"

I decided suddenly that I'd made a mistake. Hypothetically, I realized, I wouldn't have taken the money either. I got up and walked back toward the hallway.

"Where are you going?" she called after me.

I gave her a little wave with my hand. "Wait."

I went to the hall closet and took the bag out from underneath my jacket. I dragged it behind me, across the hallway's tiled floor and into the living room. Sarah had the book open in her lap again, but she closed it when she saw me with the bag.

"What—?" she started.

I brought it right up in front of her, loosened its drawstring, and, with a dramatic flourish, emptied it at her feet.

The money fell into a large pile, packets sliding out across the bearskin rug.

She stared down at it, shocked. She set her book on the table. Her mouth opened, but she didn't say anything.

I stood in front of her, holding the empty bag. "It's real," I said.

She continued to stare at it. She looked pained, as if she'd just been struck in the chest.

"It's all right," I said. I stooped down, like I was going to start putting the money back, but instead I just touched it with my hand. The bills felt cool against my fingertips, their paper soft and worn, like cloth. They were old, their edges a little tattered, and I thought of all the hands they must've passed through already before reaching my own—millions of different people, in and out of wallets and purses and vaults, so that they could end up here, finally, spread out in a pile across my living-room floor.

"You took it from the feedstore?" she asked.

"No. I found it."

"But it's somebody's. They have to be looking for it."

I shook my head. "Nobody's looking for it."

She didn't seem to hear me. "It's four million dollars?"

"Four point four."

"You found it with Jacob?"

I nodded, and she frowned.

"Where?"

I told her about the fox and Mary Beth, about the hike into the park and our discovery of the plane. When I told her about the bird, she squinted at my forehead, a pained, sympathetic look coming over her face, but she didn't say anything.

After I finished, we sat for a bit in silence. I picked up a packet and held it out toward her. I wanted her to touch it, to see what it felt like, a dense little brick of money, but she wouldn't take it.

"You want to keep it, don't you?" she asked.

I shrugged. "I guess so. I mean, I don't see why we shouldn't."

She didn't say anything. She put her hands on her stomach and stared down at it, a distracted look on her face. The baby was kicking.

"If we keep it," I said, "we'll never have to worry about money again."

"We don't have to worry about money now, Hank. You've got a good job. We don't need this."

I stared into the fire, thinking about that. It was dying down, the flames flickering low. I got up and added another log.

She was right, of course: we couldn't claim—as Jacob and Lou probably did, and as my parents might've had they lived long enough to join us in our present situation—that the money was something we needed, something we couldn't live without. Our life wasn't a struggle in that way. We were solidly middle class; when we worried about the future, it was not about how we were going to feed ourselves, or pay our bills, or educate our children, it was about how we'd manage to save enough for a larger house, a better car, more complicated appliances. But just because we didn't need the money didn't mean we couldn't want it, couldn't see it as a salvation of a different sort, and put up some struggle to keep it.

I'd gone to college to become a lawyer, only to give it up when I hadn't gotten the grades. Now I was an accountant in the feedstore of my hometown, the same town I'd spent all my childhood vowing to escape. I'd settled for something less than I'd planned on when I was younger and then convinced myself that it was enough. It wasn't, though; I saw that now. There were boundaries on Sarah's and my life, limits to what we could do and where we could go, and the pile of money lying at my feet illuminated them, highlighted the triviality of our aspirations, the bleakness of our dreams. It offered us a chance at something more.

I tried to find a way to communicate this to Sarah.

"My job's never going to amount to much," I said, pushing at the fire with the poker. "I'll be manager someday, after Tom Butler dies or retires, but he's not much older than me, so neither of those'll happen very soon, and by the time they do, I'll be an old man myself."

I'd thought this several times over the previous few years, a gray, depressing probe into the future, but I'd never spoken it out loud before, and I was astonished to hear myself do so now. It was as if someone else had uttered the words; I had to pause a moment to let them sink in.

Sarah nodded, her face calm, expressionless, and I got a further shock from that: she wasn't surprised by what I'd said. She'd already known the extent of my possibilities at the feed-store as well as I had. I waited for her to say something, to protest in some way, but she didn't.

"Think of the life we could give the baby," I whispered. "The security, the privilege."

I glanced over at her, but she wasn't looking at me. She was looking down at the packets. I continued to poke at the fire.

"It's lost money, Sarah. Nobody knows anything about it. It's ours if we want it."

"But it's stealing. If you get caught, you'll go to jail."

"Nobody gets hurt by our keeping it. That's what makes it a crime, isn't it? People getting hurt?"

She shook her head. "It's a crime because it's against the law. It doesn't matter whether anybody gets hurt or not, you'll still get arrested. I'm not going to be left bringing up a child all by myself because you've done something stupid and ended up in jail."

"But we can do it for the right reasons," I said. "We can do it so that something good comes from it." I was beginning to flounder. I wanted the money, and I wanted her to want it too.

She sighed, as if in disgust. When she spoke again, her voice rose a step. She was becoming angry. "I'm not worried about the morality of it, Hank. I'm worried about getting caught. That's what's real; the rest is just talk. If you get caught, you'll go to jail. I'd let you keep it if there wasn't that risk, but there is, so I won't."

I stopped short at this, startled. I'd assumed from the beginning that any reluctance I'd encounter on her part about keeping the money would stem from moral grounds. It had given me a helpless, fatalistic feeling—I knew that there was no way to argue against something like that—but now I saw that it was much simpler. She wanted to keep the packets, but she was afraid of getting caught. I should've realized this from the beginning, too. Sarah, above all else, was a pragmatist—it was the quality I loved best in her—she dealt with things at their most basic level. For her, a decision to keep the money would be predicated on two simple conditions. The first—which I'd already dealt with—was an assurance that no one would be hurt by our actions; the second was that we wouldn't get in any trouble. Everything else, as she'd said, was just talk, a distraction from what mattered.

I told her about my plan.

"The money's the only evidence that we've committed a crime," I said. "We can sit on it and see what happens. If someone comes searching for it, we'll just burn it, and that'll be that."

She pursed her lips. Watching her, I could see that I'd gained a foothold.

"There's no risk," I said. "We'll be in complete control."

"There's always a risk, Hank."

"But would you do it if you thought there wasn't?"

She didn't answer me.

"Would you?" I pressed.

"You've already left a lot of clues."

"Clues?"

"Like your tracks in the snow. They lead in from the road, right to the plane, and then back out again."

"It's supposed to snow tomorrow," I countered triumphantly. "They'll be gone by tomorrow night."

She half-nodded, half-shrugged. "You touched the pilot."

I frowned, remembering Jacob asking Carl about the plane. It was starting to seem stupid again, rather than clever.

"If they suspect you for any reason," Sarah said, "they'll be able to figure out that you were there. All they need is a single follicle of hair, a half-inch thread from your jacket."

I lifted my hands in the air, palms up. "But why would anyone suspect me?"

She answered quickly, though she didn't have to. I knew what she was going to say. "Because of Jacob and Lou."

"Jacob's all right," I said, not sure if I really believed it. "He'll do whatever I say."

"And Lou?"

"As long as we have the money, we can control Lou. We'll always be able to threaten that we'll burn it."

"And after we divide the money?"

"He'll be our risk. He'll be what we have to live with."

She frowned, her forehead wrinkled in thought.

"It seems like a small price to pay," I said.

She still didn't say anything.

"We can always burn the money, Sarah. Right up to the very last moment. It seems silly to give it up now, before anything's even gone wrong."

She was silent, but I could see that she was coming to a decision. I returned the poker to its stand, then went back and crouched down over the packets. Sarah didn't look at me. She was staring at her hands.

"You have to go back to the plane," she said, "and return some of it."

"Return it?" I didn't understand what she meant.

"Just part of it. You'll have to go early tomorrow morning, so when it storms later it'll cover your tracks."

"We're keeping it?" I asked, a little thrill of excitement running over my body.

She nodded. "We'll put five hundred thousand back, and keep the rest. That way when they find the plane, they'll assume no one has been there yet."

"That's an awful lot of money."

"That's how much we're leaving."

"It's half a million dollars."

She nodded. "It'll bring us down to an even three-way split."

"So would two hundred thousand."

"That's not enough. Five hundred is perfect. No one would walk away from that much money. It'll put us beyond suspicion."

"I don't think—" I started, but she cut me off.

"It's five hundred thousand, Hank. Either that or we give it all back."

I glanced up at her, surprised at the forcefulness of her tone.

"Greed is what'll get us caught," she said.

I considered that for a moment; then I acquiesced. "All right," I said, "it's five hundred thousand."

I counted out fifty packets right then and there, as if afraid she might change her mind. I stacked them up at her feet, like an offering at an altar, and put the rest into the duffel bag. Sarah sat in her chair, watching me work. When the bag was full, I pulled its drawstring tight, closing it, and smiled up at her.

"Are you happy?" I asked.

She made a noncommittal gesture with her hand, as if she were flicking away a fly. "We can't get caught," she said. "That's the important thing."

I shook my head, leaning forward across the bag to take her hand. "No," I said. "We won't."

She frowned down at me. "You promise you'll burn it if things get out of hand?"

"That's right," I said. I pointed toward the fireplace. "I'll burn it right here."

I HID the bag of money beneath our bed, pushed all the way back against the wall, with two empty suitcases jammed in after it, masking it from view.

We stayed up late, watching a New Year's show on TV. When the orchestra played "Auld Lang Syne," Sarah sang along, her voice high and tremulous, but hauntingly pretty. We drank sparkling cider, nonalcoholic, because of the baby, and clinked glasses at the stroke of midnight, wishing each other the best for the coming year.

Before we went to sleep, we made love—gently, slowly—Sarah crouched over me, the weight of her belly resting flat upon my stomach, her breasts hanging full and heavy in the darkness above my face. I cupped them carefully in my hands, squeezing her nipples between my fingertips until she moaned softly, a low, animallike sound coming up from deep inside her chest. Hearing her, I thought of the baby, pictured it rocking within her, enclosed in a watery bubble, waiting to be born, and the image gave me a strange, erotic thrill, sent a shiver running across the surface of my skin.

Afterward Sarah rested beside me on her back, holding my hand to the tautness of her belly. We were underneath the blankets; I was pressed up tight against her. The room was cold. Ice was forming along the edges of the windowpanes.

I listened to the sound of her breathing, trying to guess whether she was asleep yet. It was slow and steady, which made it seem like she might be, but there was a tenseness about her body, as if she were listening very hard for something to happen. I caressed her stomach, a light, feathery touch. She didn't react.

I was starting slowly to slip into sleep myself, thinking of the bag of money sitting right beneath us on the floor, and of the dead pilot out in his plane in the darkness, with the ice and the orchard full of crows, when Sarah turned her head and whispered something at me.

"What?" I asked, struggling back awake.

"We should just burn it, shouldn't we?" she said.

I raised myself on my elbow, looked down at her in the darkness. She blinked up at me.

"People don't get away with things like this," she said.

I lifted my hand off her belly and brushed the hair from her face. Her skin was so pale, it seemed to glow. "We'll get away with it," I said. "We know exactly what we're doing."

She shook her head. "No. We're just normal people, Hank. We aren't sneaky, we aren't smart."

"We're smart," I said. I brushed my hand across her face, making her shut her eyes. Then I laid my head down beside her on her pillow, snuggling up against her warmth. "We won't get caught."

I'm not sure if I actually believed this: that we were unassailable. Certainly I must've been aware even then of the dangers of our course, must've felt some fear when I stopped to consider all the difficulties yet to be overcome. There were Jacob and Lou and Carl and the plane and a hundred other ways that I could only guess at through which trouble might come and find us. On the most basic level I must've been scared simply because I was committing a crime. It was something I'd never even considered doing before, something far enough beyond my realm of experience to give me a lost feeling in and of itself, even without the fear of punishment that hung all about it like an aura. But I don't think these thoughts weighed on me then as much as they do now, in hindsight. I think I was happy then; I think I felt safe. It was New Year's Eve. I was thirty years old, contentedly married, with my first child soon to be born. My wife and I were lying curled up in bed together, having just finished making love, and beneath us, hidden away like the treasure it was, sat $4.4 million. Nothing had gone wrong yet; everything was still fresh and full of promise. I can look back now and say that in many ways this was the absolute apogee of my life, the point to which everything before led upward, and from which everything after fell away. I don't think it was possible at that moment for me to believe we could ever be punished for what we'd done: our crime seemed too trivial, our luck too great.

Sarah was silent for a long time. "Promise me," she said finally, taking my hand and placing it back on top of her stomach.

I tilted my head and whispered in her ear, "I promise we won't get caught."

Then we went to sleep.

3

I AWOKE around eight the next morning. Sarah was already out of bed; I could hear her showering in the bathroom. I huddled there beneath the covers, warm, still a little sleepy, and listened to the pipes creaking under the pressure of the water.

The pipes in my parents' house had made a similar sound whenever someone opened a faucet. As a child, Jacob had told me that there were ghosts within the walls, moaning, trying to escape, and I'd believed him. One night my mother and father had come home, drunk, and started dancing in the kitchen. I was six, maybe seven years old. Roused by the noise, I arrived just in time to see them, wrapped in each other's arms, trip over a chair, my father's head knocking a fist-size hole in the wall as he went down. Terrified, I rushed into the room with a wad of newspaper, to patch the hole before the ghosts could escape, and at the sight of me—a scrawny, nervous kid in pajamas, my hair tousled with sleep, frantically jamming paper into the wall—my parents broke into hysterical laughter. It was my first memory of embarrassment, of being ashamed, but thinking back on it that morning I felt no bitterness toward them, only a curious sort of nostalgia and longing. I missed them, I realized, still half asleep, my mind wandering, half-dreaming, so that, as I thought of them, they somehow usurped Sarah's and my places—my mother, young, pregnant, was washing herself in the bathroom while my father waited beneath the covers, the shades pulled down, the room dim, listening to the pipes softly creak behind the wall above his head.

That was how I always tried to think of my parents, as young—like Sarah and me—with their life together just beginning. It was more invention than recollection: I hadn't been born very long before things started to fall apart, so the memories I retained of my parents, the real ones, the ones that came floating up unbidden, were from when they were already aging, both of them drinking too much, the farm slipping away behind their backs.

The last time I saw my father alive, he was drunk. He'd called me at the feedstore one morning, his voice sounding shy and embarrassed, to see if I could stop by sometime and take a look at his accounts. I consented gladly, feeling a little shy myself, but flattered, too, because he'd never really asked me for help before.

I drove out to the farm that evening, straight from work. My father had a little study that opened directly off the kitchen, and there, on the folding card table he used as a desk, I spent the next fifty minutes disentangling his finances. He kept track of his bills in a huge leather-bound ledger. The book contained a mess of hastily scrawled numbers, columns merging one into the other, computations scribbled illegibly in the margins. He'd written most of the notations in ink, so when he made a mistake—which appeared to have been quite often—he had to cross it out rather than erase it. Even through this morass of disorder, though, it was instantly clear to me that my parents were about to lose their farm.

I'd known they were in trouble, had known it for as long as I could remember, but I'd never imagined that things could get this far out of hand. They owed money to just about everyone—the electric, phone, and water companies, the insurance company, the doctor, and the government. It was lucky they didn't have any livestock, because then they would've owed Raikley's, too. They owed money for repairs on their combine, for fuel and seed and fertilizer. Those were just bills, though: they were bad to get behind on, and my parents would've had to pay them eventually, but they weren't how you lost your farm. It was the bank that would take your property, and it was to the bank that my father owed the bulk of his money. He'd overborrowed and mismanaged. He'd mortgaged his home, mortgaged his land, and now, in a matter of weeks, he was going to lose them both.

I worked for a while before I said anything, organizing numbers into coherent columns, separating his debits from his assets, adding everything up. My father sat behind me on a stool, watching over my shoulder. They'd already eaten dinner, and he was drinking now, whiskey out of a juice glass. The study door was open, and through it we could hear my mother washing dishes in the kitchen. When I finally put down my pencil and turned around to face my father, he smiled at me. He was a large, heavyset man, with a good-sized paunch, and blond, balding hair. His eyes were pale blue, small in his face. They leaked little strings of tears when he drank too much.

"Well?" he asked.

"They're going to foreclose you," I said. "I don't imagine they'll give you much past the end of the year."

I could tell that he'd been expecting me to say this—he had to have known, the bank must've been threatening him for months, but I think he'd been hoping I'd find some loophole, something he was too uneducated, too unfamiliar with the intricacies of accounting, to see for himself. He got up from his stool, went over to the door, and shut it. Then he sat back down.

"What can we do?" he asked.

I lifted my hands into the air. "I don't think we can do anything. It's too late."

My father considered that, frowning. "You're telling me you did all that adding and subtracting, and you still can't figure out a way to help us?"

"You owe a lot of people money, Dad. There's no way you can pay them all back, and when you don't, they'll take the farm."

"They aren't going to take the farm."

"Have you talked with the bank? Haven't they—"

"Banks." My father snorted. "You think I'm going to give up this place to a bank?"

It was then that I realized he was drunk—not seriously drunk, just enough so that he could feel the alcohol running warmly through his veins, like a soporific, deadening his perceptions, enervating his reactions.

"You don't have a choice," I said, but he waved me aside.

"I got plenty of choices," he said. He stood up, set his glass down on the stool. "All you're looking at is those numbers, but that's not half the story."

"Dad," I started, "you're going to have to—"

He shook his head, cutting me off. "I don't have to do anything."

I fell silent.

"I'm going to bed," he said. "I was just staying up because I thought you'd be able to figure out how to get them off my back."

I followed him from the room, trying to think of something to say. There were things they'd have to be considering now, not the least of which was finding someplace new to live, but I couldn't imagine a way to bring this up. He was my father; it seemed like I could only insult him by offering advice.

My mother was still out in the kitchen. The dishes were

all done now, and she was cleaning one of the counters. I think she must've been waiting for us to finish, because she dropped her sponge and came right over when we emerged. My father went straight past her, heading toward the stairs, and I started to follow him.

"No, Hank," my mother whispered, stopping me. "He'll be all right. He just needs some sleep."

She took me by the elbow, pulled me off toward the front door. She was small, but strong, too, and when she wanted you to do something, she let you know. Right now, she wanted me to go home.

We talked for a moment in the entranceway before I left. It was drizzling out, cold. My mother turned on the porch light, and it made everything look shiny.

"You know?" I asked her.

She nodded.

"Have you talked about what you're going to do?"

"We'll manage," she said quietly.

Her composure, coupled with my father's denial, was giving me a panicky feeling in my chest. It didn't seem like they had any understanding for the magnitude of their trouble. "But this is bad, Mom," I said. "We're going to have to—"

"It'll be all right, Hank. We'll weather it through."

"Sarah and I can give you a few thousand. We could maybe take out a loan, too. I can talk to somebody down at the bank."

My mother shook her head. "Your father and I are going to have to make a few sacrifices is all. But we can do that. You don't have to worry." She smiled, turned her cheek toward me for a kiss.

I kissed her, and she opened up the screen door. I could see that she didn't want to talk about it, that she wasn't going to let me help. She was sending me away.

"Careful of the rain," she said. "It'll make the pavement slick."

I ran through the drizzle to my car. As I climbed inside, the porch light flicked off behind me.

I called my father the next morning, from my office. I wanted him to come into town and go to the bank with me, so that we could have a talk with the manager, but he refused. He thanked me for my concern, then told me that if he wanted my help, he'd ask for it. Otherwise I should assume he had everything under control. Having said that, he hung up the phone.

That was the last I ever spoke to him. Two days later, he was dead.

SARAH turned off the shower, and—as if to fill the sudden silence—a voice whispered in my head: *you forgot to go to the cemetery.*

It was New Year's Day, which meant that Jacob and I had let a year pass without visiting the graves. I considered this, debating its importance. It seemed to me that the thought behind the ritual, the simple act of remembrance, was more important than the visit itself. I could see nothing that was gained by our actual presence at the cemetery. Besides, it was only a matter of a single day. We could go this afternoon, twenty-four hours later than we'd promised. I was sure that, considering the circumstances, our father would forgive us our tardiness.

But then, at the same time, I realized that much of the visit's importance came through its strict observance, the fact that we were forced to put aside a specific afternoon each year, block it off from any outside interference, and devote it to the memory of our parents. The minor inconvenience of it was exactly what gave it its weight. The new year was a boundary, a deadline we'd let pass.

I began to consider several possible forms of penance for

this transgression, all of them revolving around an increased number of trips to the grave site in the coming year, and was up to twelve, one each month, when Sarah reappeared from the bathroom.

She was naked except for a yellow bath towel wrapped around her head. Her breasts had become so full that they looked comical on her tiny frame, like something a pubescent boy might draw. Her nipples were a brilliant crimson, two scabs against the bloodless white of her skin. Her belly hung low and heavy, and she cradled her hands beneath it while she walked, as if it were a package she was carrying, rather than a natural distension of her body. She looked awkward, clumsy. It was only at rest that she had any grace, holding her eight months' weight with a peculiar stateliness, an animallike elegance. I watched her waddle to the windows and, one at a time, pull open their shades.

The room filled with gray light. The sky was cloudy, cold looking, the trees beyond the glass dark and bare.

My eyes were partly closed; Sarah glanced toward the bed but didn't seem to realize I was awake. She unwrapped the towel from her head, bent over, and rubbed at her hair. I watched her, her body framed against the window and the winter sky beyond.

"We forgot to visit the cemetery," I said.

She looked up, startled, her body still bent partly over. Then she went back to rubbing her hair. She worked vigorously at it; I could hear the sound of the cloth against her scalp. When she finished, she straightened up and wrapped the towel around her chest.

"You can do it this afternoon," she said. "After you go back to the plane."

She came over and sat on the edge of the bed, her legs spread wide, her weight resting behind her on her hands. I sat up, so I could see her better. She looked at me and put her hand over her mouth.

"Oh, God," she said. "You're all bloody."

I reached up and touched my bump. It was virtually gone, but I could feel a wide swath of caked blood arcing out from it across my forehead.

"It bled during the night," I said.

"Does it hurt?"

I shook my head, probing the wound with my fingertips. "It feels like it's almost gone."

She nodded but didn't say anything.

"Think if it'd hit me in the eye," I said.

Sarah examined my forehead, but with a distracted expression on her face. I could tell she was thinking of something else.

"You ought to tell Jacob you're going back to the plane," she said. "Maybe have him come with you."

"Why?"

"It just seems smart. Last thing we need is for him or Lou to drive by and see your car sitting next to the park. They'll start thinking something's going on, that you're trying to trick them."

"They wouldn't see the car. I'll be there and back before either of them is even out of bed."

"It's just being careful, Hank. That's what we have to be from now on. We have to be thinking ahead all the time."

I considered that for a moment, then nodded halfheartedly. Sarah watched me closely, as if waiting for me to argue. When I didn't, she gave my leg a squeeze beneath the covers.

"We aren't going to tell him about putting the money back, though," she said. "You'll have to hide it under your jacket and go into the plane by yourself."

"You're saying he'd go back and steal it?"

"Maybe. Jacob's human. It'd be a perfectly natural thing to do. Or tell Lou about it. I know Lou would do it." She brushed at her hair with her hand. Wet, it looked darker than it actually was, almost brown. "This way we don't have to worry about it. We can just know it's there, and that if it's there, we're safe."

She rubbed my foot. "Okay?"

I nodded. "Okay."

Smiling, she slid up the bed toward me, leaned forward, and kissed me on my nose. I could smell her shampoo, something lemony. I kissed her back on the mouth.

I GOT UP to shower, and Sarah, wearing a dark green maternity dress, disappeared downstairs to fix us breakfast.

I turned on the water to let it heat up, then went to the mirror and inspected my forehead. In its exact center was a small hole, no bigger than an acne scar. Dried blood spiraled out from it, highlighting it like the target on a bull's-eye.

I stared at myself until the mirror began to fog over, cleaning some of the blood away with my thumb, then stripped out of my pajamas. I felt bloated, hazy, as if my body knew that it was New Year's Day and thus automatically assumed that I was hung over.

As I was preparing to climb into the shower, I noticed there were no towels in the bathroom. When I opened the door to go get one, I found Sarah crouched with her back to me by the bed, the duffel bag resting beside her on the floor, packets of money spread out across the carpet.

She looked up as I came into the room, glancing over her shoulder with what seemed like a guilty smile. Seeing it appear on her face, I felt a flicker of suspicion move through my body, like a shiver. I knew immediately that it was unwarranted, knew that it was merely my surprise at finding her in the bedroom with the money when I thought she was downstairs in the kitchen, and I instantly felt as if I'd wronged her somehow, falsely accusing her of a misdeed.

"I need a towel," I said. I stood perfectly still in the

doorway—naked, and feeling foolish because of it. I'd never liked walking around undressed, not even in front of Sarah. My body—its physical presence, the space it took up, the color of its skin—embarrassed me. Sarah was just the opposite. On especially hot summer days, she liked to lounge bare skinned around the house.

"Oh, Hank," she said, "I'm sorry. I meant to get you one." She didn't stand up.

She was holding a packet of money in each hand. I started to take a step toward the hall but then stopped. "What're you doing?" I asked.

She nodded toward the duffel bag. "I wanted to make sure it wasn't in order."

"In order?"

"If it was from a bank robbery, the serial numbers might've been in order. We couldn't spend it then."

"Are they?"

She shook her head. "It's all old."

I stared down at the packets spread out across the floor. They were organized very neatly, stacked into piles of five. "You want me to help put it back?" I asked.

"No," she said. "I'm counting it."

"Counting it?"

She nodded.

"But we already did that. Jacob and Lou and I counted it last night."

She gave me a little shrug. "I wanted to do it too," she said. "It didn't seem real unless I did it myself."

When I got out of the shower, Sarah was back downstairs. I could hear her banging things together in the kitchen. I crouched by the bed and checked beneath it, moving one of the empty suitcases aside. The duffel bag was there, safe, pushed up against the wall, looking exactly as I'd left it the night before.

I slid the suitcase back into place, dressed quickly, and hurried downstairs for breakfast.

AFTER we finished eating, I called Jacob and told him that we had to go back to the plane.

"Back to the plane?" he asked. He sounded groggy, barely awake.

"We have to make sure we didn't leave anything behind," I said. I was in the kitchen. Sarah was at the table, knitting a sweater for the baby and listening to our conversation. The money I'd counted out the night before was stacked beside her.

"What could we've left behind?" Jacob asked.

I could picture him in my mind, lying on the bed in his little apartment, still dressed in the clothes he'd worn last night, fat, unshaven, the covers wadded into a dirty knot at his feet, the shades pulled, the room smelling stalely of beer.

"We weren't careful," I said. "We have to go back and look things over."

"You think you left something?"

"Lou left his beer can."

My brother's voice took on a tired, exasperated tone. "His beer can?"

"And I moved the pilot. We have to put him back like he was."

Jacob sighed into the phone.

"I think I might've bled a little onto the plane's floor, too."

"Bled?"

"From my forehead. They can tell things from blood. It's worse than fingerprints."

"Jesus, Hank, nobody's going to notice a couple drops of blood."

"We can't take the chance."

"I'm not going to walk all the way—"

"We're going back," I said loudly. "We're not going to fuck this up because you're too lazy to do it right." My voice came out even angrier than I'd intended it to, and it had an immediate effect on both my listeners. Sarah glanced up, a startled look on her face. Jacob fell into silence.

I smiled reassuringly at Sarah, and she went back to her knitting. "I'll pick you up," I said to Jacob. "And after we're through we can stop by the cemetery."

He made a low groaning sound, which solidified slowly into speech. "All right," he said.

"In an hour."

"Should I call Lou?"

I debated for a second, watching Sarah work at the little yellow sweater. I had no desire to spend the morning in Lou's presence, especially not a hung over Lou. "No," I said. "There's no reason for him to come."

"But I can tell him we're going?"

"Of course," I said. "We're all in this together. Last thing we want now is to start keeping secrets from each other."

WE COULDN'T figure out how to hide the money on me so that Jacob wouldn't notice it. There were fifty packets; it was like trying to conceal fifty small paperback books on my body. We filled my pockets, jammed bills up my sleeves, in my socks, under my waistband; but after a while certain areas of my body started swelling suspiciously, looking weighted down, stuffed, and there were always a few packets left over that we couldn't find a place for.

"I don't think it's going to work," I said finally.

We were in the kitchen still. I had my jacket on, was starting to get hot, frustrated. The packets stuffed into my clothes made me feel heavy; every movement was awkward, like a robot's. We were both wearing gloves.

Sarah was standing a few feet away from me, looking me

up and down. It was obvious from her expression that she didn't approve of what she saw. "Maybe you could just carry it in a bag."

"A bag?" I said. "I can't carry it in a bag. What would I tell Jacob?" I unzipped my jacket, and three packets fell out, slapping to the floor in quick succession. I watched her squat down to pick them up.

"Maybe we should put less back," I said.

She ignored me. "I know what we'll do," she said. Then she turned and walked rapidly from the room.

I waited in the kitchen for her, like a burly scarecrow, my arms extended stiffly away from my sides. When she came back, she had a little knapsack in her hand.

"It's for carrying the baby," she said. She held it up in front of me. It was made of purple nylon, with a picture of a cartoon dinosaur on its front. Sarah seemed very pleased with it. "I got it out of a catalog."

I took off my jacket, and we hung the knapsack over my shoulders, loosening its straps until it rested snugly against my stomach. Sarah wrapped the money in a plastic garbage bag—so that I'd have something to leave it in when I reached the plane—then stuffed the bag inside the pouch. After she finished, I zipped up my parka. There was a definite bulge around my abdomen, but the jacket's bulk obscured it.

"You look a little fat," Sarah said, patting me on the belly. "But Jacob'll be the last one to comment on that."

"I look pregnant is what I look like," I said. "I look like you."

ASHENVILLE was a small, ugly town, just two streets really, Main and Tyler, with a blinking yellow light to mark their intersection. Each of the four corners formed by this junction supported one of the tiny municipality's essential institutions—the town hall, Raikley's Feedstore, St. Jude's Episcopal Church, and the Ashenville Savings Bank. The rest of the town, a motley group of one- and two-story structures, splayed out around these four establishments, straggling off along either side of Tyler and Main: the post office, the volunteer fire department, a small grocery store, a gas station, a pharmacy, a diner, a hardware store, a laundromat, two taverns, a hunting goods store, a pizza place.

There was a gray uniformity about the buildings, a seemingly universal dilapidation that inevitably depressed me whenever I saw them. Paint peeled from their clapboard sides in huge barklike strips, as if they were molting; cracked windowpanes were covered over with yellowed newspapers; gutters sagged; shutters banged in the wind; and giant black gaps dotted the rooftops, marking the blank spaces left by stormblown shingles. It was a poor town, a farm town which had seen its greatest days sixty years ago, in the decade before the Depression, a town whose population had steadily decreased in every census since 1930, and which clung now, leechlike, to the land around it, sucking out only enough sustenance to maintain its tenuous hold there, hunched over, careworn, dying.

It was nine-thirty by the time I pulled up in front of the hardware store, above which Jacob lived. Ashenville was quiet, its sidewalks virtually empty. The pale, cloud-filtered light gave it a tired, pallid quality, as if, like many of its inhabitants, it was hung over, entering the new year on wobbly legs, a dry, sticky taste in its mouth. Christmas decorations clung to the light poles lining the street—green, red, and white tinselly creations: snowmen, Santas, reindeer, candy canes, looking old and limp, beaten down, like things you might see at a garage sale.

Jacob was waiting on the street with Mary Beth, leaning against a parking meter. I was relieved to see him there; it meant I didn't have to enter his apartment, something that always oppressed me, highlighting as it did his material failure in the world. Jacob lived in squalor: it was a poor person's apartment, badly lit and grimy, full of broken-down furniture and leftover food, and the thought of him waking and eating and sleeping there infused me with a disagreeable mixture of pity and contempt.

I'd tried on several occasions to help Jacob, but it never worked. The last time had been seven years before, just after our parents' accident. I'd offered him a part-time job at the feedstore, driving a delivery truck. It was something that, when we were children, had been done by a semiretarded man, a slow-moving giant with mongoloid features who spoke a high-pitched language full of nods and giggles that no one could understand. That was years ago, and I'd forgotten all about it, but Jacob hadn't. He was insulted, angry, as mad at me as I'd ever seen him. For a moment it even seemed like he was going to hit me.

"I just want to help you," I'd said.

"Help me?" he asked, sneering. "Leave me alone, Hank. That's how you'll help. Just stay the fuck out of my life."

And so that, essentially, was what I'd done.

Jacob shoved Mary Beth into the backseat of the station wagon, then climbed in beside me, breathing loudly through his open mouth, as if he'd just sprinted up a flight of stairs. He had a Styrofoam cup full of coffee, and after he shut the door he pulled something wrapped in a greasy paper towel from his jacket pocket. It was a fried-egg sandwich, liberally ketchuped, which he immediately began to eat.

I eased out onto the road, appraising his condition. He was wearing his red jacket, and its bright color highlighted the wanness of his face. He hadn't shaved; his hair was greasy and uncombed. The lenses of his glasses were speckled with dirt.

"You went out with Lou last night?" I asked. I could feel the baby bag hanging like a large, heavy football against my stomach. My jacket was bunched up over it, touching the edge of the steering wheel. It felt obvious to me, absurdly so, and I had to resist the temptation to look down.

Jacob nodded, his mouth jammed full of toast and egg and ketchup.

"Have fun?" I asked.

He nodded again, wiping his lips with the back of his hand.

"Where'd you go?"

He swallowed, took a sip of coffee from the Styrofoam cup. I noticed that there was no steam coming off it; it was cold. The thought of this made me feel a little sick.

"The Palace," he said. "In Metamora."

"You and Lou and Nancy?"

He nodded, and we drove for a while in silence. Mary Beth rode with his head sticking over into the front seat, resting next to Jacob's shoulder. We were outside of town now, moving west. In the distance, swaybacked, its roof caving in, was an old, brown barn, a handful of holsteins clustered around its rear. The day was still and gray, neither particularly cold nor warm, the temperature hovering just below the freezing mark. If it were to snow, as it was forecasted to, it would be wet and sloppy.

I cleared my throat, was about to speak, but then didn't. Jacob finished his sandwich. He balled up the paper towel and set it on the dashboard. I eyed it with distaste.

I had something I wanted to ask him but sensed that he would take it wrong. Finally I just did it. "You think Lou told Nancy?" I asked.

He shrugged. "Leave him alone," he said.

I glanced across at him, trying to read his expression, but he was turned away, staring out the window at the passing fields, a sullen set to his shoulders.

I braked the car, pulling over to the side of the road. Mary

Beth skidded, legs flailing, to the floor behind us. "He told her, didn't he?"

We were somewhere near where we'd counted the money the night before. There were no houses in sight, no cars. The land was treeless and white.

Jacob turned from the window. His face looked tired, creased. "Come on, Hank. Let's just get there and do this."

I put the car in park. The dog scrambled back up onto his seat, whimpering. We both ignored him.

"He'll have to tell her someday, won't he?" Jacob asked. "How's he going to take his share without telling her?"

"You're saying she knows?" I asked. I took a deep breath. My voice sounded panicked, even to myself.

"You're trying to tell me you didn't say anything to Sarah?"

"That's right."

He watched me, as if waiting for me to change my mind.

"Did he tell her or not?" I asked.

He continued to stare at me. He seemed to consider something for a second but then put it aside. He turned back toward the window.

"I don't know," he said.

I waited. Of course Lou has told her, I thought. Just like I told Sarah. And Jacob knows about both of us. I considered briefly the importance of this, that Jacob had lied to me, that I in turn had lied to him, and that we each knew the other was lying. For a second it almost seemed funny, and I smiled.

Jacob waved down the road. "Come on," he said tiredly. "Let's get this over with."

WE APPROACHED the nature preserve from the same direction we had the day before, coming across the low cement bridge over Anders Creek, then down past Dwight Pederson's farm along the park's southern edge. There was a dog sitting at the end of Pederson's driveway, a large collie, and it barked at us as we drove by, a deep, full-chested sound. Mary Beth barked back, high-pitched, startling us, and then, tail up, turned to watch the collie recede through the rear window.

I parked next to the gouge Jacob's truck had left in the snowbank the day before and shut off the engine. I was appalled at the marks we'd left on the place. Our tracks moved off from the road, cutting a giant, ragged gash straight into the woods. Anyone driving by would've noticed them immediately. To the left the fox's tracks trailed across the field toward Pederson's farm, a string of tiny black dots in the snow, straight and precise. I followed them with my eyes.

"You're going to park here?" Jacob asked. "Right out in the open?"

I considered this briefly. He was right, of course, but I could think of no alternative. "You see a hiding place somewhere?" I said.

"We could drive around to the park entrance, bring the car inside."

I shook my head; this was something I'd already debated and put aside. I listed off my reasons now, one at a time. "The gate'll be locked," I said, "the road inside won't be plowed, and we'd probably get lost if we tried to find the plane without having our tracks to lead us to it."

Jacob glanced back toward the bridge. "It just seems like a risk, leaving it out like this."

"We left your truck here yesterday."

"Yesterday we didn't know what was in there."

"It's okay, Jacob. We'll do it quickly. In and out in a flash."

"Maybe we should just blow it off."

I noticed that he was sweating profusely, a hangover sweat, pungent smelling, like overripe fruit. He wasn't worried about someone seeing the car, I realized; he was worried about the hike into the park.

"You drank too much last night," I said. "Didn't you?"

He ignored my question. He wiped his face on the sleeve of his jacket, and it left a dark spot on the fabric. "My truck yesterday," he said, "your car today. It might start people wondering."

I unhooked my seat belt, preparing to climb from the car, and as I did so, I felt the bag of money resting heavily against my gut. It'd be easier, I saw suddenly, if he didn't come. I turned to look at him. He had ketchup smeared across his chin.

"This is what we'll do," I said. "You'll stay here. I'll go in, straighten things out at the plane, and come back as quick as I can. If anyone drives by while I'm gone, you can pretend you're fixing something with the car."

"And if they stop to help?"

"You talk to them."

"Talk to them? What the fuck am I supposed to talk to them about?" His voice came out thin and tight sounding. I couldn't tell whether it was from fatigue or disgust.

"Tell them it's okay. Tell them you've got it fixed."

"And what about the tracks?" He waved off into the woods.

"I'll bring the dog with me," I said. "If anybody asks, you can just say Mary Beth ran off, and Lou and I went in after her."

"We'll end up getting in trouble if someone comes by. They'll remember we were here when they finally discover the plane."

"It'll be spring before anyone finds the plane. No one's going to remember our being here after all that time."

"What if the sheriff comes by again?"

I frowned. I'd forced myself to forget about Carl. "He won't come by," I said, with exaggerated self-confidence. "He had to work late last night. I guarantee you he's still in bed."

"And if he isn't?"

"If he comes by, you can tell him we lost something here last night. Tell him I dropped my hat in the woods and wanted to come back to search for it."

"Yesterday you yelled at me for taking risks. This seems like more of a risk than what I did."

"It's a necessary risk, Jacob. There's a difference."

"I don't see what's so necessary about it."

I shrugged, feigning indifference. "If you want, we can just burn the money right now. It'll save me the hike."

"I don't want to burn the money, I want to leave."

"I'm going in there, Jacob. You can either stay here and stand guard, or come along with me."

There was a long pause while he looked for a way out. He didn't find one. "I'll stay here," he said.

I put on a wool hat, the same dark blue as my jacket and gloves. Then I took the keys from the ignition and shoved them into my pocket.

MARY BETH ran on ahead as I moved into the woods, disappearing through the trees, then came galloping back, the tags on his collar jingling, his fur dusted with snow. He made a few tight circles around me and sprinted off again. I strode after him, feeling good, the cold air invigorating me, waking me up.

It took me about fifteen minutes to reach the rim of the orchard, and I paused there for a moment, surveying the scene. The plane sat in the middle of the shallow bowl, its metallic skin looking burnished, like silver, amidst the dark branches of the apple trees. Our tracks surrounded it, black holes in the snow.

A wind came up, making a rushing sound through the trees around me, and it carried with it a subtle wetness, a sense of imminent change. I glanced at the sky. It was a deep, slow-moving gray, full of the promise of snow.

The crows were still in the orchard. I didn't notice them

from the rim of the bowl, but as I started down into it, they suddenly seemed to be everywhere, moving restlessly from tree to tree, cawing incessantly, as if they were arguing with one another.

I moved toward the wreck, my hand cupped against my stomach, supporting the weight of the baby pouch. The dog followed at my heels.

The plane's door was hanging open, exactly as we'd left it. I could see the mark the duffel bag had made in the snow when I'd pushed it out, a long, shallow trough. Mary Beth circled the wreck, sniffing the air.

I stuck my head in through the doorway, allowed my eyes a moment to adjust to the lack of light, then squeezed my whole body inside. I was hurrying, thinking about Jacob sitting out on the road in my car, and of all the possibilities for things going wrong because of that, when I felt the same unnatural warmth on my face I'd noticed the day before, the same heavy stillness to the air, and the memory of the bird shot through my mind.

I crouched on the floor, right where the duffel bag had been sitting, rested my hand against the wall to keep my balance, and peered toward the pilot.

He was in his seat, in the same position I'd left him the previous afternoon. His head was leaning back, staring upside down toward the rear of the plane, his arms thrown out, crucifixlike, to either side. His face was wearing the same mournful expression—the white rings of bone around his eyes making them seem clownishly grief-stricken; the bloody icicle coming out of his nose and protruding up past his open mouth; the tip of his tongue—swollen and dark—sticking out between his lips.

I slapped my hand against the plane's fuselage.

"Hey!" I yelled. "Get out of here!"

My voice echoed back at me. I listened to it, waiting. Mary Beth approached the open doorway, sniffing loudly. He made a little whining sound but didn't stick his head inside. There was no sign of movement from the front.

"Hey!" I yelled again. I stomped my boot against the floor.

I waited, but nothing happened. Finally, satisfied that I was the only living thing in the plane, I stood up, scanning the floor to see if I'd dripped any blood the day before. Finding none, I started to inch my way toward the front. I unzipped my jacket as I went.

I came up quietly behind the pilot, walking in a slight stoop, trying to decide where I should plant the money. I'd planned to just lay it on the copilot's seat, but now I saw that this wouldn't work—it would've fallen off in the crash. I'd have to put it at the dead man's feet, stuff it up tight against the nose of the plane.

I unzipped my jacket and removed the money from the knapsack. I wiped the garbage bag with my gloves, to erase any fingerprints, then crouched down and slid it forward along the floor. I pushed it past the two seats, past the pilot's boots, all the way up to the front of the plane. My back started to sweat while I worked, a cold, clammy feeling. I was holding my breath, and it made me dizzy.

When I'd jammed the money in as far as it would go, I stood up, grasped the pilot by his shoulders, and eased him forward. He bent at his waist with surprising ease, his feet sliding backward along the floor. At the last second his head rolled forward on his neck, landing on the plane's control panel with a smacking sound, like a bat hitting a ball. The bloody icicle broke, fell to the floor, and shattered.

I took a deep breath, and stepped back. I straightened my body until the top of my hat touched the plane's metal roof; then I held myself there, thinking, checking things off in my head. I'd looked for blood, I'd planted the money, I'd repositioned the pilot. There was nothing left to do.

I zipped up my jacket, turned, took a single step, and froze. There were two birds sitting just inside the open doorway, watching me. It was the strangest thing—I seemed to think of them before I actually saw them, their images floating across my mind as I turned my body, two shadows emerging from the plane's darkness to confront me. It was eerie; it was as if I'd willed them into being.

I stared at them. They didn't move.

I waved my arms. "Scat!" I yelled.

One of the birds edged toward the doorway. The other remained where it was.

Very slowly, I took a step forward. The first bird shuffled quickly to the door. It stopped on the threshold to watch me, its plumage shiny in the light streaming in from the orchard. The second bird lifted its wings, as if to threaten me. It moved its head from side to side on its shoulders. Then it stretched its neck and cawed. The sound ricocheted off the walls. When it died down, the bird settled its wings back into its body and took a tentative step toward me.

"Out!" I yelled.

The first bird gave a little cry and disappeared with a quick hop through the doorway. I could hear the push of its wings as it flew away. The other bird simply sat there, turning first one eye toward me, then the other.

I stepped forward, stomping my boot against the floor.

The bird shuffled backward, away from the door. It lifted its wings again.

I watched it, waiting. "I'm leaving," I said, like an idiot. I took two shuffling steps forward, closing in on the door.

The bird retreated, sinking into the darkness at the rear of the plane, its wings still raised. I had to move at a stoop, my shoulders hunched over, my boots making a rough, scraping sound against the floor.

When I reached the door, I went out backward, so I

wouldn't have to take my eyes off the crow. It raised its wings a little higher, turned its head to watch me disappear.

"I'm leaving," I said again, squeezing myself out into the snow.

Outside, the world seemed brighter, just as it had the day before. I leaned my shoulder against the door and, straining, pushed it shut. It swung closed with a violent metallic shriek.

Mary Beth had disappeared. I followed his tracks with my eyes. The trail headed off toward the road. I called his name, twice, halfheartedly, then gave up, assuming that he was already back at the car with Jacob.

As I started up the gentle slope away from the wreck, I sensed that there was something different about the orchard, something besides the illusory change in light, but it wasn't until I reached the bowl's rim that I realized what it was. It was a snowmobile, a low, whining hum hanging beelike in the air around me. It was coming from the direction of the road.

I paused, my body tense, listening, trying to decide what it meant. The wind had died down, the day felt warmer, and when I glanced at the sky I saw that, rather than thickening toward the predicted storm, it was actually clearing. I could even make out a large patch of blue to the south.

The snowmobile's buzz slowly gained in volume, far away still but moving closer. The crows in the orchard called loudly back and forth to one another.

I took one last look at the plane, glinting dully in the bottom of the hollow, then turned and started back toward the road at a run.

I STRAINED to listen for the snowmobile while I ran, but I couldn't hear it. The sounds of my breathing, of my arms rubbing against my jacket, my boots slapping down into the snow, and the trees flashing quickly by, all hid the hum of its engine. The footing was slick, my boots heavy, and I tired quickly. I slowed to a walk after a few minutes, when I was still only halfway back to the road. As soon as I ceased to run, I heard the engine. It was close now. It sounded as if it were right in front of me, just out of sight through the trees. I could hear Mary Beth barking. I listened, walking for about twenty yards to let my heart slow down a bit, then took a deep breath and started to run again.

I saw the car first, my dark green station wagon pulled off at the side of the road. It appeared like a shadow before me, suddenly materializing between the trunks of the trees. Then there was my brother, standing in front of it like a giant red beacon. Next to him was a smaller man, and beneath this man, between his legs, was the snowmobile, its engine idling now, spitting out a dense cloud of light gray smoke.

The man was tiny, old, dressed in an orange hunting jacket. It was Dwight Pederson—I recognized him immediately. He had a rifle slung over his shoulder.

When I saw who it was, I dropped back to a walk. I still had about thirty yards to go before I reached the road, but I realized instantly that whatever damage Jacob had managed to produce through talking to the old man would only be increased by my sprinting frantically up to them out of the woods. I had to go slow now, react rather than act. I put my hands in my pockets and carefully picked my way toward them through the trees, trying to appear calm, in control, casual.

Pederson saw me first. He stared at me, seemingly uncertain who I was, then raised his hand halfway up his body in greeting. I waved back, smiling. Jacob was talking very fast. I couldn't hear what he was saying, but it looked like he was arguing with the old man. He was making a cutting motion in the air with his arm and shaking his head. When he saw Pederson wave at me, he threw a panicked look into the woods but didn't stop talking. Pederson seemed to be ignoring him. He gunned the snowmobile's engine, then said something short to Jacob and pointed down at the snow in front of them.

What happened next happened very quickly.

Jacob took a step toward the old man, reared back, and gave him a wide, swinging blow to the side of his head. Pederson fell sideways, his body collapsing onto the edge of the road, absolutely lifeless, his left leg still draped partway over the seat, his rifle slipping from his shoulder. Jacob lost his footing on the follow-through, tumbled over the back of the snowmobile, and landed directly on top of the old man.

Mary Beth started to bark.

Jacob struggled to raise himself off Pederson's body. His gloves slipped in the snow; he couldn't seem to regain his feet. He'd lost his glasses when he fell, and, still lying there, he patted his hands around him in the snow until he found them. Then he put them on and started struggling upward again. When he finally made it to his knees, he paused, resting for a moment before, with what looked like a superhuman effort, he rose to his feet.

The snowmobile's engine continued to idle, a deep, steady rumble. The dog cautiously approached Jacob from the center of the road. He gave his tail a slow, hesitant wag.

Jacob stood there, motionless. He touched his face with his glove, took his hand away to stare at it, then put it back.

All this time, I hadn't moved. I'd stood there frozen, watching in horror. Even now I only partly shook myself free. I took a single step toward the road.

Jacob leaned back and kicked the old man. He kicked him twice, with all his strength, once in the chest and once in the head. After that he stopped. He put his hand up to his face and turned to look toward me.

Mary Beth started to bark again.

"Oh, Jacob," I said, very quietly, as though speaking to myself. Then I began to run, moving quickly through the snow toward my brother.

. . .

JACOB stood there, his glove covering his mouth and nose, watching me approach.

The snowmobile's engine was making a coughing sound, threatening to stall, and the first thing I did when I reached the road was bend down and turn it off.

Jacob was crying. This was something I hadn't seen since we were children, and it took me a second to accept that it was actually happening. He wasn't sobbing, wasn't weeping, there was nothing violent or dramatic about it, he was simply seeping tears; they moved slowly down his cheeks, his breath coming a little more quickly than usual, coming with a certain shakiness to it, a trembling and hesitation. His nose was bleeding—he'd banged it falling on top of Pederson—and now he was pinching his nostrils shut between two of his fingers.

I glanced down at the old man. He was lying on his side, his left leg still propped up on the snowmobile's seat. He was dressed in jeans and black rubber boots. His orange jacket was hitched up around his waist; I could see his belt, thick and dark brown, and above it an inch of thermal underwear. Jacob had knocked off his hat when he hit him, revealing a sparse head of long, gray hair, dirty looking, oily. An orange wool scarf covered most of his face. I could see where Jacob had kicked him, right above the left ear. There was a dull red scrape there, around which his skin was already beginning to darken into a bruise.

Mary Beth stopped barking finally. He came up and sniffed at Jacob's boots for a second, then moved off into the center of the road.

I crouched over Pederson's body. I took off my glove and held my hand against his mouth. He didn't seem to be breathing. I put my glove back on and stood up.

"He's dead, Jacob," I said. "You've killed him."

"He was tracking the fox," Jacob said, stuttering a bit. "It's been stealing his chickens."

I rubbed my face with my hand. I wasn't sure what I ought to do. "Jesus, Jacob. How could you do this?"

"He would've gone right by the plane. He would've found it."

"It's all over now," I said, feeling my chest begin to tighten in anger. "You've ruined it for us."

We both stared down at Pederson.

"They're going to send you to jail for this," I said.

He gave me a panicked look. His glasses were wet from the snow. "I had to do it." He sobbed. "We would've been caught."

His eyes glittered, small and wild in the white, doughy expanse of his face; his cheeks were damp with tears. He was terrified, bewildered, and, seeing him like that, my anger collapsed, immediately replacing itself with a rush of pity. I could save him, I realized, my older brother, I could reach down and pluck him out of this trouble, and in the process I'd save myself, too.

I glanced quickly up and down the road. It was empty.

"Have any cars gone by?" I asked.

He didn't seem to understand. He took his hand away from his nose, wiped at the tears on his cheeks. Blood was smeared across the skin above his upper lip, giving him a comical appearance, as if he were wearing a fake mustache.

"Cars?" he said.

I gestured impatiently at the road. "Have any passed? While I was in the park?"

He stared off into the distance. He thought for a second, then shook his head. "No. Nothing." He put his hand back over his nose.

I glanced across the road, toward Pederson's farm. The house was very small and far away. I thought I could see smoke rising from its chimney, but I couldn't tell for sure. The snowmobile's tracks headed off straight down the center of the field, running parallel to the fox's.

"What do we do now?" Jacob asked. He was still crying a little, and he turned away from me, pretending to stare at Mary Beth, to hide it. The dog was sitting in the middle of the road.

"We'll make it look like an accident," I said. "We'll drive him away from here and make it look like a snowmobile accident."

Jacob gave me a frightened look.

"It's all right," I said. "We can get away with this." For some reason seeing him panic made me all the more calm. I felt confident, completely in control.

"They'll follow the tracks," he said. "They'll come here and they'll see our tracks and they'll follow them to the plane."

"No. A storm's coming." I waved at the sky, which, despite what I was saying, was continuing to clear. I ignored this, bullying my way forward. "Any minute now it'll start snowing, and all of this'll be covered up."

Jacob frowned, as if ready to disagree, but he didn't say anything. He brought his hand back up to his face, and I saw the blood smeared on his glove.

"You didn't get blood on him, did you?"

"Blood?"

I crouched beside Pederson, inspecting his clothes. There was a dark brown smear on the shoulder of his jacket. I scooped up a handful of snow and rubbed at the stain. Only a little bit came off.

Jacob watched me, a look of resignation on his face. "It's not going to work, Hank," he said. "We're going to get caught."

I continued to rub at the blood. "This isn't a big deal. It's not something people'll notice."

He held his hand out in front of him, stared down at his glove. "You said it's worse than fingerprints," he said, his voice taking on a quickness, a jagged quality.

"Jacob," I said firmly. "Calm down." I stood up and touched him on his arm. "All right? We can do this if we stay calm."

"I killed him, Hank."

"That's right," I said, "but it's done. Now we have to deal with it. We have to cover it up so you don't get caught."

He shut his eyes. He put his hand back over his nose.

I realized that I had to get him away. I pulled the car keys out of my pocket. "You're going to take Mary Beth and drive back to the bridge." I waved down the road toward Anders Creek. "I'll meet you there."

He opened his eyes, bewildered. "At the bridge?"

I nodded. "I'm going to drive Pederson there on the snowmobile. We'll push him over the edge, make it look like he drove off by accident."

"It'll never work."

"It'll work. We're going to make it work."

"Why would he be down at the bridge?"

"Jacob," I said. "I'm doing this for you, all right? You've got to trust me. Everything's going to be okay." I held out the car keys in the palm of my glove. He stared at them for several seconds; then he reached out and took them.

"I'm going to drive through the park," I said. "Out of sight from the road. You'll get to the bridge before me, but I don't want you to stop. I want you to drive by and then circle back. I don't want people to see you sitting there."

He didn't say anything.

"Okay?"

He took a deep breath, letting it out slowly, and wiped at his cheeks. The car keys jingled in his hand. "I just don't think we'll get away with it."

"We'll get away with it."

He shook his head. "There's so much to think about. There's all this stuff we probably haven't even noticed yet."

"Such as?"

"Stuff we're not counting on. Stuff we're missing."

I was growing impatient. Time was slipping by. Any moment a car might appear on the horizon, driving toward us. If we were seen here like this, everything would be lost. I took Jacob by the elbow, guiding him toward the station wagon. I sensed that if I could get him moving, everything would be all right. We stepped out onto the road. The dog rose to his feet and stretched.

"We aren't missing stuff," I said. I tried to smile reassuringly at him, but it felt like it came out pleading. I gave him a little push forward.

"Just trust me, Jacob," I said.

IT WAS perhaps ten seconds after Jacob started the car and drove off, as I was turning toward Pederson to pick him up and set him on the snowmobile, that the old man let out a long, agonized moan.

He was still alive.

I stared down at him in shock, my head swimming. He kicked his leg a little, and it slipped off the snowmobile onto the ground. His boot made a heavy thumping sound when it landed. I glanced down the road. Jacob had disappeared.

Pederson mumbled something into his wool scarf. Then he groaned again. One of his gloves flexed into a fist.

I stood there, bent at the waist, my mind racing. With frightening clarity, I saw two paths opening up before me. Taking one of them, I'd be able to finish it right here. I'd get Pederson up on the snowmobile, drive him back to his house, and call Carl. I'd have to tell him everything, and give the money back. If I did that, if I were totally honest, and Pederson survived his beating, I knew I'd have a good chance at escaping a jail sentence. But Jacob wouldn't. Carl would send somebody down to the bridge to pick him up. He'd be charged with assault and battery, or attempted murder. He'd go to jail, probably for a long time. And the money would be gone.

Then, of course, there was the other path. It was already prepared for, already halfway trodden upon. I had the power to save Jacob, save the money. And in the end, I suppose, that was why I did it: because it seemed possible, it seemed like I wouldn't get caught. It was the same reason I took the money, the same reason I did all that follows. By doing one wrong thing, I thought I could make everything right.

Pederson groaned. He seemed to be trying to lift his head.

"I'm," he said very distinctly, but nothing more. He clenched his fist again.

I stooped down beside him. It was an ambiguous motion: someone watching us from a distance might've assumed that I was trying to help the old man.

His scarf was wrapped tightly around the bottom half of his face. His eyes were closed.

When I'd seen Jacob hit him, it had happened so quickly that it seemed natural to me, predictable. I'd been surprised, but not shocked. I'd accepted it immediately. Jacob, I said to myself, has killed him. In my mind at that instant Pederson had been dead. And that's what I told myself now as I crouched over his body. *He's already dead*, I said. *He's already dead.*

At first I'd planned to hit him again, like Jacob had, perhaps in the throat. For some reason I thought of the throat as a particularly vulnerable spot on the body. But looking at his neck, I saw his bright orange scarf, and the sight of it changed my mind.

I glanced up and down the road, to make sure no cars were coming, then leaned forward, took the scarf in my hand, balled it up a bit, and pressed down firmly against his mouth. With my other hand I pinched shut his nostrils.

Looking back now, it seems as though there ought to have been something more, some impediment or compunction, a barrier to struggle through. I would've expected at the very least a sense of terror, an atavistic revulsion, a realization that what I was doing was unequivocally wrong, not simply because the society of which I was a member called it such but because it was murder, a primal crime. There was nothing like that, though. And perhaps this shouldn't be surprising—perhaps it's romantic to expect that epiphanic realization, that sudden sense of fate's diverging pathways as one hesitates between them, choosing. In real life the immensity of such moments must almost always slip by unnoticed, as it did for me, something to be added later, in hindsight, but buried until then beneath the incidental details—the feel of Pederson's scarf through my glove, the worry that I was squeezing his nostrils too tightly, that I might be bruising them, and that this might be discovered in an autopsy.

I didn't feel evil. I felt nervous, scared, nothing more.

He struggled very little. He moved his hand once, a wiping motion across the ground, as if he were trying to erase something, but that was all. His eyes stayed shut. There was no noise, no death rattle, no final groan. I held the scarf there for a long time. The sky had cleared enough now for the sun to come out, and it warmed my back. I could see a cloud shadow moving slowly along the edge of the field across the road. As I watched it pass, I started to count. I counted very slowly, pausing before each number, concentrating on the sounds they made in my head. When I reached two hundred, I let go of the scarf, took off my glove, and felt carefully for the old man's pulse.

There was nothing there.

I RODE east through the nature preserve, keeping the road just out of sight to my right. I reached the pond after a minute or so. It was frozen solid. Picnic tables were scattered haphazardly about its border. Everything was covered with snow.

Past the pond, the woods were thicker, and I had to choose my route with more care, winding in and out between matted tangles of underbrush. The branches of the trees scraped against my jacket, as if they were trying to stop me, hold me back.

Pederson's body straddled the seat in front of me, slouched forward like the pilot's in the plane. I had to press right up against his back to reach the controls.

I tried to occupy my mind solely with thoughts of my plan. I sensed a danger in circling back to what had happened already that morning, sensed that doing so would only lead to confusion and anxiety, that the safest path was forward, where things could still be changed.

The bridge would be plowed and salted, I knew; there would be a thick bank of snow along either edge. If Pederson had wanted to cross without damaging his snowmobile's treads on the cement, he would've had to have ridden along one of these banks—banks that were just wide enough to support his machine and just high enough to crest the top of the guardrails.

People would wonder what he was doing there, why he'd decided to cross the bridge, but it wouldn't be enough to make them suspicious. It would be a mystery, something they'd shake their heads over, nothing more. Unless, of course, the plane were discovered before it snowed. There would be the snowmobile's tracks then, the footprints leading into the park. There would be signs of a scuffle alongside the road.

I glanced up at the sky. It was continuing to clear with a startling rapidity. There was a wide expanse of blue now, sun streaming down through the branches of the trees, the air cold and crisp. What clouds remained were fair-weather clouds, white and fluffy. There was no sign of impending snow.

The closer I got to the edge of the park and the bridge beyond it, the harder I had to work to keep my mind fixed on my plan. Other thoughts crept in. It began with the physical sensation of Pederson's body against my chest. His head was nestled beneath my chin. I could smell his hair tonic through his hat. His body itself was compact, dense. It didn't feel at all like I would've expected it to. It felt like it ought to be alive.

And as soon as I thought this—that Pederson was dead, that I had killed him, smothered the life out of him with my own hands—my heart fluttered heavily up into my throat. I realized that I'd crossed a boundary, done something abhorrent, brutal, something I never would have imagined myself capable of. I'd taken another man's life.

This thought bewildered me, set my mind tumbling backward and forward, rationalizing, justifying, denying, and it was only with an extreme effort of will that I regained control. I shut myself down, pulled back, forced my mind to concentrate on nothing except what was going to occur in the next fifteen minutes. I continued on toward the eastern edge of the park, my arms supporting Pederson's body, guiding the snowmobile through the trees, half my brain occupied with thoughts of the bridge and Jacob and the sheriff, the other half desperately trying to fight off a strange, horribly threatening sensation—that I was doomed now, trapped, that the rest of my life would pivot somehow off this single act, that in trying to save Jacob, I'd damned us both.

THE PARK'S southeast corner went right up to the foot of the cement bridge.

I paused at the edge of the woods, making sure no one was in sight. The creek was about fifteen yards wide here. It was frozen solid, the ice covered with a thin layer of snow.

Pederson's farm was behind me, down the road. There were fields across the creek, empty to the horizon. Jacob hadn't arrived yet.

I eased the snowmobile out alongside the road, the engine rumbling beneath me. I looked to the east, then back to the west. There were no cars in sight. I could see the old man's house now, just visible around the edge of the trees. It was closer than I'd thought. I could make out its windows, could see the collie sitting on the top step of its porch. If someone had been standing there watching, they'd have been able to see me, too.

I gunned the engine, maneuvering the machine up onto the bank of plowed snow, moving slowly along it until I reached the center of the bridge. There was a ten-foot drop there from the roadway to the ice. The guardrail was buried in snow.

I put Pederson's hand on the throttle, adjusted his body in the seat, sliding him back a bit, planting his boots on the footrests. I slung his rifle over his shoulder, pulled his hat down on his ears, wrapped his scarf tightly around his face. The motor coughed a little, stuttering, and I gave it some gas.

I glanced up and down the road again. There were no cars, no movement whatsoever. The collie was still sitting on Pederson's porch. It would've been impossible to tell, of course, whether someone was watching from a window there, but I quickly scanned them all the same. They reflected the sky back at me, the bare branches of the trees surrounding the house. I turned the snowmobile's skis toward the creek and eased it slowly forward, until it hung partway over the ice, balancing on the edge of the snowbank.

I tried to think if I was forgetting something, shutting my eyes, but my mind refused to help me. I could think of nothing.

The collie barked, once.

I stepped down onto the roadway, braced my feet against

the pavement, and pushed the snowmobile forward with my shoulder. It went over with surprising ease. First it was there, and then it was gone. There was a tremendous crash when it hit the ice, and the engine shut itself off.

I climbed back up onto the bank to see.

The snowmobile had rolled over in midair, landing on Pederson, crushing him beneath its weight. The ice was cracked, but not collapsed, forming a bowl-shaped depression around the old man and his machine. The creek was seeping slowly in, covering his body. His hat had fallen off again, and his gray hair floated out away from his head in the icy water. His scarf was tight around his face, clinging to it like a gag. One of his arms was pinned beneath the snowmobile. The other was thrown palm upward to the side, as if he'd died struggling to free himself.

JACOB arrived a few minutes later, from the east. He slowed the car to a stop beside me, and I climbed inside. As we sped away, I glanced back at the bridge. The old man's body was just visible beneath it, a splash of orange on the ice.

We drove by the Pederson place for the second time that day. The collie barked at us again, but Mary Beth, lying curled up in a ball on the backseat, didn't seem to notice. I'd been right earlier, there was smoke coming out of the chimney. That meant the old man's wife was there, sitting beside a fire in the parlor, awaiting his return. The thought of this made my chest tighten.

When we passed the spot where the fox had crossed the road, I heard Jacob give a sharp intake of breath.

"Jesus," he said.

I looked out the window. There were tracks everywhere—the fox's, the dog's, Jacob's, Lou's, mine. There was a gash in the snowbank from Jacob's truck and, crossing the road, tread marks from Pederson's snowmobile. It was a mess, the whole thing, impossible to miss. The tracks seemed to converge as they disappeared into the woods, as if to form an arrow, pointing straight toward the plane.

Jacob started to cry again, very softly. Tears rolled down his face, and his lips began to quiver.

When I spoke, I made my voice sound very calm. "It's all right," I said. "It's going to snow. As soon as it snows, that'll all be gone."

Jacob didn't say anything. He started making hiccoughing sounds in his chest.

"Stop it," I said. "It's working out. We're getting away with it."

He wiped at his cheeks. The dog tried to lean over the seat and lick his face, as if to comfort him, but Jacob pushed him away.

"Everything's okay," I said. "As soon as it snows, everything'll be okay."

He took a deep breath. Then he nodded.

"You can't react like that, Jacob. The only way we'll get caught is if we fall apart somehow. We have to stay calm."

He nodded again. His eyes were red and puffy.

"In control."

"I'm just tired, Hank," he said. His voice was rough, barely more than a whisper. He looked out the window, blinked his eyes. His nose had stopped bleeding, but he hadn't wiped off the dark smear from above his mouth. It gave his face the look of a fat Charlie Chaplin.

"I was up too late last night, and now I'm tired."

I HAD Jacob drive us all the way around the park. We headed back toward town along its northern edge, on Taft Road.

The nature preserve looked exactly the same on this side as it had on the other. It was just woods—sycamores, buckeyes, maples, a few evergreens, the occasional white curve of a birch. Some of the pines were still dusted with snow from

Tuesday's storm. There were birds every now and then, flashes of movement among the bare branches, but no signs of any other wildlife, no rabbits or deer, no raccoons or possums or foxes. It seemed strange to think that the plane was in there—the bag full of money, the dead pilot—and that beyond the wreck, on the other side of the park, was Pederson, whom I'd smothered, lying there in the icy water of Anders Creek.

I'd never pictured Jacob and myself as men capable of violence. My brother had gotten into fights at school, of course, but always because he'd been trapped, teased to the point where he had no choice but to lash out. He wasn't articulate enough to use his tongue, so he used his feet and hands instead, but the result was just as pitiful. He never really learned how to fight, never managed even an imitation of the true pugilist's desire to cause pain: no matter how overwhelmed with rage, he always appeared to be holding himself back, as if afraid to hurt his antagonists, and it made his fury seem farcical, make-believe, like something out of a silent movie. He'd flail clumsily at them, open fisted, as though he were swimming, tears streaming down his face, and they'd laugh at him, calling him names.

In our hearts, we were both products of our father's temperament, a man so pacifistic he refused to raise livestock—no cattle, no poultry, no swine—because he couldn't bear to see them slaughtered. Yet somehow, together, we'd managed to kill a man.

When we reached Ashenville, Jacob pulled to a stop in front of his apartment. He put the car in park but didn't turn off the ignition. Most of the town was closed for New Year's. There were only a few people on the street, hurrying somewhere private, heads tucked low against the cold. A wind had come up, and it blew things across the road. The sky was perfectly clear now; sunlight danced off of the hardware store's plate-glass window and made the pavement sparkle. It had turned into a beautiful winter day.

Jacob didn't get out. He stared blankly past the windshield, as if he wasn't sure where he was. He touched the bridge of his nose with his fingertips.

"I think I broke it," he said.

"You didn't break it," I reassured him. "It's just bleeding."

He still looked scared, shaken up, and it was beginning to worry me. I didn't want to leave him like this. I reached across the seat and turned off the engine.

"You know what I thought of?" I asked. "Right when you hit him?"

He didn't answer me. He was still probing at his nose.

"I thought of you getting into a fistfight with Rodney Sample." I tapped my head with my hand. "I had this instant flash of it inside my brain, an image of you swinging at him and falling down."

Jacob didn't say anything.

"How old were you then? You remember?"

He turned and gave me a distracted look. He had his gloves on again. The right one was stained dark with blood; there was a dime-size spot of dried egg yolk on its forefinger.

"Rodney Sample?"

"In gym class. You swung at him, and you both fell down."

He nodded but didn't say anything. He gazed down at his gloves, noticed the egg yolk. He lifted his hand and licked at it, then wiped it on his pant leg.

"We're in it now," he said, "aren't we?"

"Yes." I nodded. "We are."

"Jesus." He sighed, and then it seemed, for a moment, as if he were about to cry again. He wrapped his arms around his stomach and, rocking a bit, started to scratch at his elbows.

"Come on, Jacob. Pull yourself together. What's done is done."

He shook his head. "I killed him, Hank. They're gonna do an autopsy, and then they'll know."

"No," I said, but he ignored me.

"It's easy for you to be calm. It's not you that they'll send to jail." He was taking deep breaths now, panting.

"You didn't kill him," I said, surprising myself. He was scaring me with his panic; I was trying to calm him down.

He glanced at me, confused.

I realized immediately that I didn't want to tell him what I'd already begun to. I tried to backtrack. "We both killed him," I said. I looked out the window at the street, hoping he'd let it go. But he didn't.

"What do you mean?" he asked.

I attempted a smile. "Nothing."

"You said I didn't kill him."

I stared at him, trying to work it through in my mind. Since we were children I'd known that I couldn't depend on him—he'd be late, he'd forget, he'd let me down out of laziness or ignorance—so of course I should've known better. But he was my brother; I wanted to trust him. And, though I could sense that there was a danger in it, I saw that there might be a benefit, too. I'd saved him; it seemed like he ought to know about it. It would put him in my debt.

"He was still alive when you left," I said. "I didn't realize it till I went to pick him up, and by then you were already gone."

"I didn't kill him?" Jacob asked.

I shook my head. "I smothered him with his scarf."

It took a while for my brother to absorb this. He stared down at his lap, his head tucked into his chest, so that the skin beneath his chin piled up into a rippling series of folds.

"Why?" he asked.

The question caught me by surprise. I looked at him closely, trying to analyze what had prompted me to do it. "I did it for you, Jacob. To protect you."

He shut his eyes. "You shouldn't have done it. You should've let him live."

"Christ, Jacob. Didn't you hear me? I said I did it for you. I did it to save you."

"Save me?" he asked. "If you'd let him live, it would've just been me beating him up. We could've turned in the money, and it wouldn't have been that bad. Now it's murder."

"All I did was finish what you started. We did it together. If you hadn't done your part in the first place, I never would've had to do mine in the second."

That silenced him. He took his glasses off, cleaned them on his jacket, and then put them back on.

"We're going to get caught," he said.

"No, Jacob, we aren't. We've done it, and we're going to get away with it. The only way we'll get caught is if you break down and attract attention."

"I'm not going to break down."

"Then we aren't going to get caught."

He shrugged, as if to say, "We'll see," and we watched a little boy ride by on a bicycle. He pedaled right down the center of the street, struggling against the wind. He had a black ski mask on, and it made him look threatening, like a terrorist.

"Are we going to tell Lou?" Jacob asked.

"No."

"Why not?"

I felt something shift and settle heavily into place when he asked this. The word *accomplice* floated up from somewhere in my mind, and for perhaps the first time in my life I understood what it meant. It was a powerful word; it connected people, bound them to one another. Jacob and I had committed a crime together, and our fates were now inextricably intertwined. That Jacob appeared to be more frightened at present than I was by what we'd done meant nothing.

Our power was equal; we were in each other's hands. If he was too shaken to understand that at present, he wouldn't be for long.

I turned toward him. "Why would you want to tell Lou?"

"It just seems like he ought to know."

"This is a bad thing, Jacob. This is something we could spend the rest of our lives in jail for."

He shut his eyes again.

"Promise me you won't tell him," I said.

He hesitated, staring down at his gloves. Then he shrugged. "All right."

"Promise me."

He sighed, looked past me out the window. His pickup was parked across the street. "I promise I won't tell Lou," he said.

We fell silent after that. Jacob seemed like he was about to get out of the car, but then he didn't.

"Where'd you hide the money?" he asked.

I gave him a sharp glance. "In the garage," I lied.

"In the garage?"

"I thought Sarah might find it if I hid it in the house."

He nodded, waited a moment, as if trying to think of something further to say. Then he reached over and opened the door. The dog sprang to his feet behind us.

"We forgot to visit the cemetery," I said.

Jacob looked at me with a tired expression, his lips edging into a sneer. "You want to go now?"

I shook my head. "I'm just saying we forgot."

He made a deprecatory gesture with his hand. "That's about the least of our problems, isn't it?" he asked. He didn't wait for my answer. He just heaved himself up to his feet, whistled for Mary Beth, and—when the dog scrambled over the back of the front seat and out onto the pavement—swung the door shut behind him.

. . .

SARAH heard me come home and called me upstairs. I found her in the bedroom, the shades pulled, the light dim. She was just settling in for a nap, lying on her back beneath the covers, her hair pinned in a bun on top of her head.

I sat down beside her, on the edge of the mattress, and began to recite the morning's events. I started from the beginning, letting the story unfold, leaving its climax, the encounter with Pederson, to fall, bombshell-like, in its proper place. Sarah rolled onto her side, shutting her eyes, the covers pulled up to her chin. She didn't react to what I said; she simply lay there, her lips frozen into a sleepy smile. I wasn't even sure that she was listening.

But then, just as I was describing my exit from the plane, she lifted her head a little and opened her eyes.

"What about the beer can?" she asked.

She'd caught me off guard. "The beer can?"

"Lou's beer can."

I realized that I'd forgotten to look for it. I'd meant to do it after I planted the money, but then the two crows had appeared, flustering me.

"I didn't find it," I said, hedging.

"You looked?"

I paused, considered fibbing, but my hesitation eliminated the need for it.

"You forgot," she said, her voice heavy with recrimination.

"I didn't see it. It wasn't near the plane."

She lifted herself into a sitting position. "If they find it," she said quickly, "they'll know someone's been there."

"It's just a beer can, Sarah. No one's going to notice it."

She didn't say anything. She was staring down at the bed. I could see that she was becoming angry: her lips were locked tightly over her teeth, and it seemed like she was clenching the muscles in her forehead.

"They'll assume it was dropped last summer," I said. "By someone picnicking in the orchard."

"They can run tests to see how long it's been there. They can tell by how much it's rusted."

"Come on, Sarah. They aren't going to run any tests." I was stung by her tone of voice. It seemed to imply that I'd made a grave and unforgivable error. She thought I'd acted foolishly.

"They'll find Lou's fingerprints on it."

"He was wearing gloves," I said, straining to remember if this was true. "It's just a beer can lying out in the woods. Nobody's going to think twice about it."

"They will, Hank. If there's even the slightest suspicion that any of the money's been taken, they'll search every inch of the orchard. And if they find the beer can, and they find Lou's fingerprints on it, they'll track us down."

I thought about that. I was hurt by her anger and had a vague desire to hurt her back. I knew that she was blowing things out of proportion, but at the same time I saw that she was probably justified in her fear. We'd left something behind: small as it was, it still had the potential to become a clue, a little piece of evidence to indicate our presence.

"We might as well just burn it," she said.

"Come on, Sarah."

She shut her eyes and shook her head.

"We aren't going to burn it," I said.

She didn't say anything. She smoothed the cover out across her belly, a sulky look on her face, and, watching her, I realized suddenly that I wasn't going to tell her about Pederson. I was surprised by this, jolted. We'd never kept secrets from each other, had always confessed everything. But I knew I wasn't going to tell her this, not here, not now. Perhaps I would sometime in the future, in ten or twenty years, when we were living happily off the money, when what I'd done had been justified, upheld by what had come after. I'd tell her then how I'd saved us from discovery, how I'd taken it upon myself, alone, to protect her and our unborn child from harm. She'd be shocked at my bravery, at the way I'd kept it to myself all those years, and she'd forgive me everything.

The truth was, I was afraid of what she'd think of me. I was terrified of her judgment.

"Your forehead looks better," she said, not looking at me. It was an effort at rapprochement.

I touched my forehead. "It doesn't hurt anymore," I said.

Then we sat in silence. Sarah dropped back onto her pillow, rolling toward me. I didn't look at her. I was waiting for her to say that she was sorry. If she had I might've told her, but she didn't, and finally I gave up.

"Go on," she whispered.

"That's it," I said. "I shut the door and hiked back through the woods to the road. Then we came home."

It didn't snow all afternoon. I moved restlessly about the house, glancing now and then through the windows at the sky. I turned on the radio every hour and listened for the weather. The forecast was for snow, heavy at times, lasting through the afternoon and into the evening, but by dinnertime there wasn't a cloud in sight, and when the sun finally set, a brilliant sea of icy white stars appeared in the sky, blinking down through the darkness at the earth.

Pederson's accident made the local news. Sarah and I saw it on TV before dinner. They had a shot of the bridge, taken sometime that afternoon. The snowmobile was still in the water, half submerged, the old man's hat floating beside it, but his body had already been retrieved. There were tracks up and down the creek's bank, so that you could imagine the scramble to pull him out, the panic and flurry fueled by the illusory hope that he might not yet be dead.

The newscaster said the body had been found by a passing motorist, shortly before noon. There was no mention of foul play, no indication that anything suspicious had been discovered. In the background I could see the sheriff's truck, pulled off onto the edge of the road, its lights flashing. Carl was standing beside it, talking to a tall, thin man in a bright green down vest, perhaps the unnamed motorist. In the very corner of the screen, off in the distance, I could see Pederson's house. There were three or four cars in the yard, friends come to comfort the widow.

Sarah didn't comment on the report. All she said was, "That's sad, on New Year's Day and all." She didn't seem to realize how close the creek was to the nature preserve.

I went to bed sunk in a deep depression.

I'd killed a man. There it was, every time I turned back to look—it was something I had done. In my heart I felt unchanged, the same man I'd always been, but in my head I knew I was different now. I was a murderer.

And then there was Sarah. I hadn't told her the truth. It was the first major lie ever to come between us. I realized, too, that with the passing of time it would only grow more difficult to tell her. My fantasy of confessing in twenty years was just that, a fantasy. Each moment I spent in her presence without telling her was a continuation, a reaffirmation of the original lie.

I drifted into sleep that night with my arm draped across her belly. If the baby were to kick, I'd be able to feel it in my dreams. But my last waking thoughts were not of the infant, or of Sarah, or of the money. My last waking thoughts were of Jacob. I closed my eyes and saw the look of panic on his face as he stood over Pederson's body, believing that he'd killed him, and in my chest, as my breathing deepened into sleep, I felt a surge of warmth, the same wave of pity for him I'd felt when I'd seen the tears glistening on his cheeks. But it wasn't just for Jacob now, this warmth and pity—it was for myself, too, and Sarah, and the baby, and Pederson, and Pederson's widow. I felt sorry for everyone.

. . .

IN THE morning I could tell just from the light in the bedroom that it was snowing. It was dim, gray, with a sense of movement to it, and a silence. I slipped out of bed and crossed quietly to the window. Giant, wet flakes were floating down out of the sky, spinning, swirling, sticking to whatever they touched. It had obviously been snowing for most of the night. The tracks in the yard were filled in, the branches of the trees bowed down toward the earth. Everything, the whole world, was white with it, covered up, hidden, buried.

4

MY OFFICE window faced directly south, out the front right-hand corner of Raikley's Feedstore, toward St. Jude's Episcopal Church across the street. I was there at my desk on Wednesday, the sixth of January, eating a powdered donut with a cup of lukewarm coffee, when a handful of darkly clothed men and women emerged from the church's side door and made its way slowly across the gravel parking lot, through the chain-link gate of the tiny cemetery, to the dark black gouge of a freshly dug grave forty yards beyond.

It was Dwight Pederson's funeral.

There were six cars in the parking lot, including the silver hearse pulled up right next to the cemetery's gate. It was a small gathering; Pederson had been something of a loner; he hadn't had that many friends. I could pick out his widow, Ruth, as she made her way back toward the grave. The priest clung to her arm, diminutive, his shoulders bowed, his left hand clutching a Bible to his chest. I could see only the very edge of the grave; the rest was hidden behind the church. The crowd of mourners arranged itself around its border.

St. Jude's bell began to toll.

I finished my donut, then got up and took my coffee to the window. The cemetery, perhaps a hundred yards away, was far enough in the distance that I couldn't identify the people around the grave. Some of them were hidden behind the church; the others, heads bowed, bodies muffled against the cold, were faceless, like strangers, though I must've known most of them. They would've been people I passed on the street in town, people I knew stories about, comic anecdotes, gossip.

I watched as they bowed their heads, then lifted them, saying something in unison before bowing again. I could see Ruth; her back was turned to me. She didn't lift her head with the others; she kept it bowed. I suppose that she was weeping. The priest was hidden from view.

I remained at the window until the service was over and the people began to make their way slowly back toward the parking lot. I watched them, counting under my breath. There were seventeen in all, including the driver of the hearse and the priest. They'd given up their morning to honor the memory of Dwight Pederson and express their grief over his death. They all believed that he'd died accidentally, a freak tragedy, pinned beneath his snowmobile in six inches of icy water, his leg and two of his ribs broken, his skull cracked, struggling vainly to free himself from the suffocating grip of his woolen scarf.

Only Jacob and I knew the truth.

Things were going to get easier from here on out, I knew. With each passing day there would be less and less anxiety about what I'd done. Pederson was buried, eliminating the threat of something being discovered in an autopsy; the plane was covered with snow, the tracks around it erased forever.

Perhaps the greatest relief of all, though, was that I still thought of myself as a good man. I'd assumed that what had happened at the edge of the nature preserve would change me, affect my character or personality, that I'd be ravaged by guilt, irreversibly damaged by the horror of my crime. But nothing changed. I was still who I'd always been. Pederson's death was just like the money; it was there whenever I thought about it, but then when I didn't, it was gone. It made no difference to my life in a day-to-day sense unless I called it up myself. The key was not to call it up.

I believed that what I'd done on New Year's Day was an anomaly. I'd been forced into it by extraordinary circumstances, circumstances far beyond my control, and now the whole thing seemed remarkably understandable to me, even forgivable.

But was it? If there was an anxiety which plagued me at that time, it had nothing to do with being caught, nothing to do with the money or the memory of my crime. It had to do with Sarah. Would Sarah understand what I had done?

I could feel a draft coming through the window. There was a plastic sheet of insulation sealing its outside frame, but it was torn and flapped loosely in the wind. I watched the mourners talk for a bit in the parking lot. They clustered around Ruth Pederson, hugging her one after the other. The men shook one another's hands. Finally they all climbed into their cars, pulled out of the parking lot, and started slowly down Main Street toward the western edge of town.

They were going back to the Pedersons': I could imagine it well enough. They'd eat lunch around a big wooden table in the kitchen—casseroles and three-bean salads, cold cuts and potato chips. There would be warm drinks—tea, coffee, hot chocolate—in Styrofoam cups and for dessert they'd have Jell-O, carrot cake, chocolate chip cookies. Ruth Pederson, changed now out of her black dress, would sit at the head of the table. She'd watch the others eat, making sure that everyone had enough. People would hover around her, speaking softly, and she'd smile at what they said. Everyone would go out of their way to help clean up, washing dishes and putting them back in the wrong cabinets. Then, as the afternoon wore on into evening, the light fading westward toward the nature preserve, they'd slip off one by one into their own lives, until at last Ruth was left all by herself in the empty house.

I could picture this in my mind—could see her sitting there, the house sunk in shadows, the guests gone, their well-meaning tidiness leaving her nothing to busy herself with except her grief—but, though I knew that I ought to, I felt no remorse at the image, no guilt, only an abstract sort of empathy, distant and subdued. I'd taken her husband from her; it was not something I would've thought I could ever live with. Yet, there I was.

I pulled shut the blinds, finished my coffee, dropped the empty cup into the wastebasket. Then I sat down at my desk, turned on the little light there, pulled a pen from my shirt pocket, and set to work.

ON MY way home from the feedstore that night, I took a long detour, so that I could drive by the nature preserve. I circled above it, then came in from the west, moving slowly along the park's southern border. It was just beginning to get dark, and I drove with my high beams on, scanning the edge of the road for our tracks. There was nothing there; all the signs of our passage, even the gouge Jacob's truck had cut into the snowbank, had been erased.

When I drove by the Pederson farm, I could see several lights shining through the windows of the house. The collie was sitting on the porch. It didn't bark this time though; it simply stared at my station wagon, its ears erect, its thin, angular head rotating slowly on its shoulders as the car drifted past down the road toward the bridge over Anders Creek.

A FULL week passed. I spoke twice with Jacob on the phone but didn't see him. We talked only briefly, both times about Pederson, reassuring each other as to the success of our cover-up. I didn't speak to Lou at all.

Thursday afternoon I was working in my office when Sarah appeared. Her face was flushed from the cold, making her look angry, and there was a busyness about her—her eyes shifting rapidly from spot to spot, her hands reaching up to touch now her hair, now her face, now her clothes—which told me that something bad had happened. I stood up quickly, came out from behind my desk, and helped her take off her jacket. Beneath it she was wearing one of her maternity dresses—a fleet of tiny sailboats floating across a sea of pale blue, cheap-looking fabric. The dress molded itself to the swollen dome of her belly. I couldn't help but stare at it; it reminded me of some giant fruit. There was a baby inside her: whenever I saw her now, the thought jarred me, gave me an uneasy feeling in my own stomach.

Sarah dropped heavily into the armchair beside my desk, the chair customers sat in when they came to ask me for an extension on their bills. Her hair was pinned up around her head, and she was wearing dark red lipstick.

"Lou's told Nancy," she said.

I went over and shut the office door. Then I sat down behind my desk.

"I saw her at the grocery store," Sarah said. "I came in to buy some applesauce, and I was digging through my purse for a coupon I'd cut out of the paper when she came up behind me and asked why I was bothering with it."

"With the coupon?"

Sarah nodded. "She said with our New Year's present I shouldn't have to worry."

I spread my hands out across the desk, frowning.

"She said it right in front of the cashier. Like she was commenting on the weather."

"What did you say?"

"Nothing. I pretended I didn't understand."

"Good."

"But she knew. She could tell I understood what she was talking about."

"We couldn't really expect Lou not to tell her, could we?"

"I want to burn it."

"I mean, she had to find out sooner or later."

"We've made a mistake, Hank. Admit it. We're in over our heads."

"I think you're overreacting," I said. I leaned forward to take her hand, but she pulled it away. I stared across the corner of the desk at her. "Come on, Sarah."

"No. We're going to get caught. I want to burn it."

"We can't burn it."

"Don't you see, Hank? How it's going to get out of hand? It was all right when just the four of us knew. But everyone feels like they can tell someone else. There're five of us now. Pretty soon there'll be more. It'll just keep growing like that until we get caught."

"We can't burn it," I said again.

"It's a small town. It won't take that long. We have to stop it while we still can."

"Sarah," I said slowly. "It's not as simple as it was at first."

She started to protest, but then she saw my face. "What do you mean?" she asked.

"Do you remember seeing the story about Dwight Pederson on the news? The old man whose snowmobile went into the creek?"

She nodded. "On New Year's Day."

"He didn't die accidentally."

Sarah didn't seem to understand. She gave me a vacant stare.

"He saw Jacob and me at the nature preserve, and we killed him." Saying this, I felt a weight shift from my shoulders. Without having planned it, I was confessing. I was coming clean.

Sarah sat there, trying to grasp it.

"You killed him?" she asked. Her face had a strange look to it. It wasn't horror, which was what I'd dreaded most; it was something closer to fear—apprehension tinged with perplexity—and beneath it all, just the slightest hint of disapproval, sitting there like a seed, waiting to learn more before it sprouted and grew. Seeing it, I hesitated, and then, without even thinking, so that when I heard myself speak I was astonished by the words, I began to lie again.

"Jacob did it," I said. "He knocked him off his snowmobile and kicked him in the head. Then we took him down to the bridge and made it look like an accident."

My confession lay between us, stillborn, draining blood onto the papers scattered across my desk.

"Jesus," Sarah said.

I nodded, staring down at my hands.

"How could you let him do that?" she asked. She said it, I could tell, not out of admonition but merely from curiosity. I didn't know how to answer her.

"Couldn't you have stopped him?"

I shook my head. "It happened so fast. He just did it, and then it was over."

I glanced up at her, met her eyes. I was relieved by her look; it was calm. There was no horror in it, no grief, simply confusion. She didn't understand what had happened.

"He was tracking the fox," I said. "If Jacob hadn't killed him, he would've found the plane, and seen our tracks around it."

Sarah considered that for a moment. "We can still burn the money," she said.

I shook my head again. I wasn't going to do that. I'd killed for the money; if I were to give it up now, it would mean that I'd done it for nothing. The crime would become senseless, unforgivable. I understood this but knew I couldn't say it to her. I frowned down at my desk, rolled a pencil slowly across its surface beneath the palm of my hand.

"No," I said. "We aren't going to burn the money."

"We're going to get caught," she said. "This might be our last chance." Her voice rose as she spoke, and I glanced toward the door. I held my finger to my lips.

"If we burn it," she whispered, "Jacob'll be all right. There'll be no motive, no reason to connect us with Pederson. But if we wait to get caught, Carl might put things together."

"We're okay," I said calmly. "We're not in any danger. And if it begins to look like we're in danger, we can just burn the money then. It's still the only evidence to show that we've committed a crime."

"But now it's not just stealing, it's murder."

"We're the only ones who know about this, Sarah. Us and Jacob. It's our secret. There's no reason for anyone else to suspect a thing."

"We're going to get caught." She sank backward into her chair, her hands on her stomach.

"No," I said, with more conviction than I felt. "We aren't. No one else is going to know. Not about Pederson, and not about the money."

Sarah didn't say anything. She seemed close to tears, but I could tell that, at least for the moment, I'd held her off. She was going to let things stand as they were; she was going to wait and see what happened. I got up from my chair and moved around the desk to her side. I touched her hair, then bent down and hugged her. It was a graceless movement: she was sitting slouched away from me, her belly protruding between us, and I had to lean over the arm of the chair to reach her, but it had the desired effect. She let her head fall toward my shoulder, reached her arms up around my back.

My phone started to ring. It rang five times and then stopped.

"I promised you, Sarah, didn't I? I promised I wouldn't let us get caught."

She nodded her head against my neck.

"And I won't," I whispered. "I'll talk to Lou about Nancy. It'll be okay. Just wait it out, and it'll be okay."

THAT NIGHT, as the feedstore was closing, I heard Jacob's voice in the lobby, arguing with the cashier. I got up quickly and moved to the doorway of my office.

Jacob was standing at the checkout counter, his jacket zipped up to his throat. He was gazing beseechingly at Cheryl Williams, a squat, thickly rouged older woman who was a part-time cashier. Cheryl was shaking her head.

"I'm sorry, Mr. Mitchell," she said. "I just can't do that. You'll have to go across the street to the bank."

"Come on, Cheryl," Jacob pleaded. "They're closed."

"Then you'll have to wait till the morning."

"I can't wait till the morning," he said, his voice rising. "I need it now."

There was something about how he was standing, some visual clue in the way his feet were positioned beneath the bulk of his body which made me sure suddenly that he'd been drinking.

"Jacob," I said, cutting off Cheryl's reply.

They both turned toward me at the same time, identical expressions of relief on their faces.

"She won't let me cash this," Jacob said. He had a check in his hand, and he waved it at Cheryl.

"We're not a bank," I said. "We don't cash checks."

Cheryl, who'd gone back to counting out for the day, let a smile slip quickly across her face.

"Hank—" Jacob started, but I cut him off.

"Come into my office," I said.

He walked across the lobby to my office, and I shut the door behind him.

"Sit down," I said.

He lowered himself into the same armchair Sarah had sat in earlier that afternoon. It made a creaking noise beneath his weight.

I went to the window and opened the blinds. The sun was nearly set. Lights were coming on in the town. The church and cemetery were already submerged in darkness.

"You've been drinking," I said, not turning from the window. I heard him stir uncomfortably in his chair.

"What do you mean?"

"I can smell it. It's not even five o'clock, and you're already drunk."

"I had a couple beers, Hank. I'm not drunk."

I turned from the window, leaned back on the sill. Jacob had to twist around in the armchair to see me. He seemed awkward, embarrassed, like a child called to the principal's office.

"It's irresponsible," I said.

"I really need the money. I need it tonight."

"You're worse than Lou."

"Come on, Hank. I had two beers."

"He's told Nancy, hasn't he?"

Jacob sighed.

"Answer me."

"Why do you keep harping on that?"

"I just want to know the truth."

"But how would I know that?"

"I want to know what you think."

He frowned, slouching into the chair. He wasn't looking at me. "She's his girlfriend," he said. "They live together."

"You're saying he told her?"

"If Lou asked me whether or not you'd told Sarah, I'd say—"

"Has Lou asked you that?"

"Come on, Hank. I'm just trying to show you that it's only me guessing. I don't know anything for sure."

"I'm not asking what you know. I'm asking what you think."

"Like I said, she's his girlfriend."

"That means yes?"

"I guess so."

"And do you remember what we said? How you're responsible for him?"

He didn't answer.

"If he screws this up, it's your fault. You'll be the one I'll blame."

"It's not like—"

"I'll burn the money, Jacob. If I think you two're going to screw this up, I'll just burn it."

He stared down at his check.

"You better straighten him out, and you better do it quick. You tell him that he's responsible for Nancy, just like I'm telling you you're responsible for him."

Jacob looked up at me, thinking. He worked his tongue along his teeth, sucking, as if he were trying to clean them. His forehead, wide and low, was spattered with pimples. His skin was greasy; it glistened in the light from my desk lamp.

"It's like a food chain," he said. "Isn't it?"

"A food chain?"

He smiled. "Lou's responsible for Nancy, I'm responsible for Lou, you're responsible for me."

I thought about this; then I nodded.

"So in a way," Jacob said, "you're responsible for all of us."

I couldn't think of anything to say to this. I stepped away from the window, walked over to my desk, and sat down behind it. "How much is the check for?" I asked.

He glanced at the check in his hand. He was still wearing his gloves. "Forty-seven dollars."

I reached across the desk and took it from him.

"What's it for?"

"It's from Sonny Major. I sold him my ratchet set."

I scanned the check, then handed it back to him along with a pen. "Sign it over to me."

While he signed it, I removed two twenties and a ten from my wallet. I gave them to Jacob in exchange for the check.

"You owe me three dollars," I said.

He put the money in his pocket, seemed to think about getting up, but then decided against it.

He glanced at my forehead. "How's your bump?" he asked.

I touched it with my finger. All that was left was a tiny scab. "It's healed."

He nodded.

"Your nose?" I asked.

He wrinkled his nose, inhaled through it. "Fine."

After that we sat in silence. I was preparing to stand up and guide him toward the door when he asked, "You remember Dad breaking his nose?"

I nodded. When I was seven, our father had bought a mail-order windmill, to help irrigate one of his fields. He'd almost finished putting it together, was up on a ladder tightening a bolt, when a sudden gust of wind set the contraption's aluminum sails spinning. Our father was hit in the face, knocked off his ladder to the ground. Our mother had seen it all from the house, and—since he'd remained on his back for a moment, his hand clamped on his head, rather than instantly regaining his feet—she'd run to the phone and called an ambulance. Ashenville had a volunteer fire department, so it was our father's friends who came rushing out to the farm, and they kidded him about it for years. Our father never forgave her for the embarrassment.

"That windmill's still up," Jacob said. "You can see it from the road when you drive by."

"It's probably the only thing he ever built that actually worked," I said.

Jacob smiled—our father's inadequacy as a handyman had been one of our family's running jokes—but when he spoke again his voice came out sounding mournful, full of loss and regret.

"I wish they were still around," he said.

I looked up at him then, and it was as if a curtain were being dragged back from a window, giving me a sudden glimpse into the depths of my brother's loneliness. Jacob had been much closer to our parents than I had. He'd lived at home up until the year before the accident, and even after he moved out, he still spent most of his time there, doing chores, talking, watching TV. The farm had been his refuge from the world. I had Sarah, and now a baby coming, but Jacob's family was all in the past. He didn't have anyone.

I tried unsuccessfully to think of something to say. I wanted to reach out in some way, to tell him something reassuring, but I couldn't find the proper words. I didn't know how to talk to my brother.

Jacob broke the silence finally by asking, "What do you mean, blame me?"

I realized with a little jolt of panic—a jolt that instantly subverted whatever empathy I'd been feeling for him before he'd spoken—that if I wanted to control Jacob, I needed to offer some concrete threat rather than the simple, abstract idea of blame. It took me only a second to come up with one: it was the obvious choice, the only thing I really had that I was sure would frighten him.

"If we get caught because of Lou," I said, "I'll tell about Pederson. I'll say you murdered him, and that all I did was help you cover it up."

He stared at me. He didn't understand.

"I'll say I tried to stop you, but you pushed me aside and killed him."

Jacob seemed genuinely shocked by this. When he spoke, he had to search for his words. "You killed him, Hank," he said.

I shrugged, lifted my hands. "I'll lie, Jacob. If we get caught because of Lou, I'm going to make you pay."

He grimaced, as if he were in pain. His nose was running, and he rubbed at it with his glove, then wiped his glove on his pants. "I don't want to be responsible for him," he said.

"But that was the deal. That was what we agreed upon."

He shook his head. The folds of flesh beneath his chin, white and marbled, continued to tremble for a second after he stopped. "I can't control him."

"You have to talk with him, Jacob."

"Talk with him?" he asked, his voice exasperated. "Talking's not going to keep him from doing stuff."

"Threaten him," I said.

"With what? You want me to tell him I'll beat him up? Say I'll burn his house down?" He gave a snort of disgust. "Threaten him."

We both fell silent. I could hear people moving about in the lobby, getting ready to head home for the night.

"I don't want to be responsible for him," Jacob said.

"Then I guess we have a problem."

He nodded.

"Perhaps," I said, "we ought to just burn it."

It was only a bluff, I didn't mean it, and Jacob didn't respond to it. He stared down at my desk, his forehead creased. I could tell that he was struggling to think.

"Lou's not going to get us caught," he said.

"That's right. Because you're not going to let him."

Jacob didn't seem to hear me; he was still lost in thought. When he finally spoke, he did so without glancing up at me. "And if it looks like he is, he could always just get into an accident."

"An accident?"

"Like Pederson."

"You mean we could kill him?" I asked, appalled.

He nodded, staring down at my desk.

"Jesus, Jacob. He's your best friend. You can't be serious."

He didn't answer me.

"The big-time murderer," I said.

"Come on, Hank. I'm just—"

"Ice him, right? Grease him." I sneered, my voice rising to mimic his own. " 'He could always just get into an accident.' Who do you think you are, Jacob? A gangster?"

He wouldn't look at me.

"You make me sick," I said.

He sighed, frowning.

"How did you want to do it?" I asked. "Did you have a plan?"

"I thought we could make it look like a car accident."

"A car accident. That's brilliant. And how were you going to manage that?"

He shrugged.

"Maybe put him in his car and push him over the bridge into Anders Creek?" I asked.

He started to say something, but I didn't let him.

"We were lucky with Pederson. Everything worked in our favor. That's not going to happen again."

"I was just thinking—"

"You aren't thinking anything. That's the problem. You're being stupid. Remember how you felt out by the park? You were crying. You were bawling like a baby. You want to go through that again?"

He didn't answer.

"Look out the window," I said. "Look across the street, at the cemetery."

He looked toward the window. It was completely dark now; we couldn't see outside anymore. The glass reflected my office back in at us.

"They buried Dwight Pederson last week. He's out there because of you, because you were greedy and you panicked. How does that make you feel?"

I stared across the desk at him until he looked me in the eye. "If I hadn't done it," he said, "he would've found the plane."

"You should've let him find it."

Jacob gave me a perplexed look. "You killed him," he said. "You could've saved him, but you didn't."

"I killed him to save you, Jacob. It was either him or you, and I chose you." I paused. "Maybe I made a mistake."

He didn't seem to know how to respond to that. He continued to gaze at me, the same confused expression on his face.

"But I'm not going to do it again," I said. "Next time I'll give you up."

"I can't be responsible for him," Jacob whispered.

"Just talk to him. Tell him I'll burn the money if I think he's screwing things up."

He stared morosely down into his lap, and I noticed for the first time that he was beginning to get a bald spot. It startled me. If he had lost some weight, he would've looked exactly like our father had at the time of his death. He looked beaten down, defeated.

"I wish we could just split the money up right now," he said. "Split it up and run away."

"That's not what we planned, Jacob."

"I know." He sighed. "I'm just saying what I wish."

THE NEXT day was Friday. That evening, during dinner, Sarah asked me if I'd talked with Lou yet.

I shook my head. "Jacob's going to do it."

We were eating spaghetti, and Sarah was in the midst of helping herself to seconds. "Jacob?" she asked. She held the serving spoon poised in midair, pasta dangling off it toward her plate. She was wearing a dark blue dress. In the brightly lit kitchen it made her face look wan and anemic.

I nodded.

"Shouldn't you do it yourself?"

"I thought it'd be better if he did it. Lou'll listen to Jacob. He won't listen to me."

She finished serving herself and set the pot down in the center of the table. "Are you sure Jacob realizes how serious this is?"

"I scared him a bit," I said.

Sarah glanced up at me. "Scared him?"

"I said I'd tell about Pederson if we were caught because of something Lou did."

"And?"

"At first he panicked a little, but I think it's going to work." I smiled. "He even suggested that we kill Lou."

She seemed unimpressed by this. "How?" she asked.

"How what?"

"How did he want to kill him?"

"He wanted to make it look like a car accident."

Sarah frowned. She picked her fork up, twirled some spaghetti onto it, then stuck it into her mouth, chewed, and swallowed. "I don't think you should threaten Jacob," she said.

"I wasn't threatening him. I was trying to wake him up."

She shook her head. "If Jacob can think about plotting with you against Lou, then it'll be just as easy for him to plot with Lou against us."

"Jacob's not going to plot against us," I said, as if the idea were absurd.

"How can you be sure?"

"He's my brother, Sarah. That counts for something."

"But who's he closer to, you or Lou? Lou's more of a brother to him than you are."

I considered that. It was true, of course. "You're saying Jacob would try to kill me for the money?"

"I'm saying don't scare him. All you'll end up doing is forcing him into Lou's arms. They don't have families like you. They could just walk in here, shoot you, take the money, and run off."

"The money's hidden. They don't know where it is."

"Let's say they came in here with a gun, held it to your head, told you to show them where it was."

"They'd never do it."

"Let's say they held the gun to me." She patted her stomach. "Held it right here."

I pushed the spaghetti around my plate with my fork. "I can't really imagine Jacob doing that, can you?"

"Can you imagine him killing Pederson?"

I didn't answer. Here was another opening; I sensed it beckoning to me, and I hesitated. It would merely be a matter of speaking, no more than a few words, a simple declarative sentence. I sat there for perhaps thirty seconds, staring across at Sarah, trying desperately to survey all the possible consequences, both of speaking and of keeping silent, but they evaded me, hovering just beyond the edge of my vision, so when I finally made my choice, I did it blindly.

"Can you?" she prodded.

"Jacob didn't kill Pederson," I said, and, as in my office the day before, there was the sudden lightening of confession. I shifted my body in the chair, searched Sarah's face for a reaction.

She stared across the table at me, expressionless. "You told me—"

I shook my head. "He knocked him out, and we thought he was dead. But when I picked him up to set him on his snowmobile, he let out a moan, and I had to finish him off myself."

"You killed him?" she asked.

I nodded, a great wave of relief rolling over my body. "I killed him."

Sarah leaned across the table. "How?"

"I used his scarf. I smothered him."

She touched her chin with her fingertips, shocked, and for a brief moment her face seemed to open, so that I could look inside and watch my words slowly taking hold. I saw bewilderment there, a quick flicker of fear, and then a glance at me that had something like repulsion in it, a glance that put a distance between us, pushing me away. For an instant she was frightened, but then, as quickly as it had come, it passed; her face closed, and she brought me back.

"Why didn't Jacob do it?" she asked.

"He was already gone. I'd sent him off to meet me at the bridge."

"You were alone?"

I nodded.

"Why didn't you tell me before?"

I struggled for a truthful answer. "I thought it might frighten you."

"Frighten me?"

"Upset you."

Sarah didn't say anything. She was following some thought inside her head, rearranging things to fit this new scenario, and it gave me a panicky feeling to watch her, as if she were hiding herself from me, pretending to a composure that she didn't really feel.

"Does it?" I asked.

She looked at me for a second, but only halfway, with her

eyes and nothing more. Her mind was still somewhere else. "Does it what?"

"Upset you?"

"It's . . . ," she started. She had to concentrate to find a word. "It's done."

"Done?"

"I don't think I would've wanted you to do it, but now that it's happened, I can understand why."

"But you wish I hadn't?"

"I don't know," she said. Then she shook her head. "I guess not. We would've lost the money. Jacob would've been arrested."

I thought about this for a second, searching her face for some further reaction. "Would you've done the same thing? If you'd been there instead of me?"

"Oh, Hank. How could I . . ."

"I just want to know if it's possible."

She shut her eyes, as if attempting to imagine herself crouched over Pederson's body, his scarf balled up in her hand. "Maybe," she said finally, her voice a whisper. "Maybe I would've."

I couldn't believe this, refused to, and yet, even as I did so, sensed that it might be true. She might've killed him just like I had. After all, would I have imagined Jacob knocking Pederson down, kicking him in the chest and head? Or, more to the point, would I have imagined myself smothering the old man with his scarf? No, I thought, of course not.

I saw with a shudder that not only couldn't I predict the actions of those around me, I couldn't even reliably predict my own. It seemed like a bad sign; it seemed to indicate that we'd wandered, mapless, into a new territory. We were as good as lost.

"Jacob doesn't know?" she asked.

I shook my head. "I told him."

Sarah winced. "Why?"

"It seemed like he was falling apart. He was crying. I thought it'd be easier on him if he knew that we shared the blame."

"He's going to use it against you."

"Use it against me? How could he use it against me? If one of us is going to get in trouble, we both will."

"Especially if you threaten him. He'll go to Lou, and they'll use it to plot against us."

"This is paranoia, Sarah. This isn't real."

"We're keeping secrets from Jacob, aren't we?"

I nodded.

"And you and Jacob are keeping secrets from Lou?"

I nodded again.

"Then why can't you believe that he and Lou are keeping secrets from us, too?"

I didn't have an answer for that.

LATE IN the evening, around eleven, Sarah's stepmother, Millie, called, long distance from Miami. Sarah's mother and father, like mine, were both dead. Her mother had died when Sarah was very young, her father right after she and I were married.

Millie had become Sarah's stepmother when Sarah was still in her early teens, but they'd never been very close. The last time they'd seen each other was at my father-in-law's funeral. They talked once a month on the phone, though, a ritual that they both participated in seemingly more out of a sense of familial obligation than from any desire to speak with each other.

Sarah had grown up in southern Ohio, just across the river from Kentucky. Millie had been a nurse in the hospital where Sarah's mother died, slowly, of leukemia. That's where she'd met Sarah's father. She was originally from West Virginia and, even after a full decade in Miami, had a slight southern accent, which Sarah picked up from her whenever they talked.

Their calls were long collective monologues—Millie drawled on about the mundane activities of her small coterie of friends, bemoaned the increasing decrepitude of Miami in general and her apartment complex in particular, and ended with an irrelevant anecdote or two from Sarah's father's life. Sarah talked about her pregnancy, about me and the cold weather we'd been having, about things she'd read recently in the paper or seen on TV. They never asked each other questions; there was very little interaction between them at all. They talked at each other for twenty minutes, and then, as if they'd agreed beforehand upon a mutually acceptable time limit, said good-bye and hung up.

Tonight Millie called just as we were getting into bed. When I realized who it was, I whispered to Sarah that I was going downstairs to get a snack. I didn't like being in the room with her when she talked on the phone; it made me feel like I was eavesdropping.

In the kitchen, I poured myself some milk and made a cheese sandwich. I ate standing up at the counter, in the dark. Through the side window, ten yards away across a thin strip of lawn, was my next-door neighbor's house, a mirror image of my own—everything exactly the same, but reversed. A TV was on in the master bedroom; I could see its bluish flickering through the upstairs window, like light reflected off a pool.

I stood there in the darkness for several minutes, finishing my sandwich, while I reviewed my earlier conversation with Sarah. I was relieved by the calmness of her reaction to my confession, immeasurably so. I'd been worried that what I'd done would frighten her, that she'd treat me suddenly as some sort of psychopathic monster, but nothing of the sort had happened. There was no reason for it to have, I saw now—just as I still looked upon myself as a good man despite my crime, Sarah did too. We had our entire past together to weigh against this one anomaly. There'd been that initial shock, of course—I'd seen it—that flash of fear and repulsion, but in a matter of seconds she'd filed it away somewhere, pragmatic as always, and resigned herself to what had happened. It's done, she'd said and then moved forward, focusing on the future rather than the past. Her concerns were simply practical—whether or not Jacob knew of the crime and what effect this would have on our relations with him and Lou. She was imperturbable, a rock. If all else failed, I realized, standing there in the kitchen, she'd be the one who'd carry us through.

Next door, the television flicked off, and the house went dark. I set my empty glass in the sink.

On my way upstairs I noticed that the dining-room door was partway open. I flipped on the light, peeked inside. There were papers scattered across the wooden table, magazines and brochures.

Upstairs I could hear Sarah's voice, talking on the phone. It sounded soft, muffled, as if she were speaking to herself. I slid the dining-room door open all the way and stepped inside.

I approached the table hesitantly, as if I were afraid Sarah might hear me, though that wasn't a conscious thought. I scanned its surface. There were all sorts of brochures, at least thirty, probably more, travel brochures with pictures of tanned women in brightly colored bikinis, of families skiing and riding horses, of men on tennis courts and golf courses, of tables laden with exotic food. "Welcome to Belize!" they read, "Paris in the Spring!" "Crete, Island of the Gods!" "Come Sail the Pacific with Us!" "Nepal, the Land Time Forgot!" Everything was shiny, slick looking; everyone was smiling; all the sentences ended in exclamation points. The magazines—*Condé Nast Traveler, Islands, The Caribbean, The Globetrotter's Companion*—were exactly the same only larger.

There was a notebook off to the side, folded open, with Sarah's handwriting in it. At the top of the page was written "Travel." Below it were listed the names of cities and countries around the globe, each one numbered, apparently in order of preference. The first one was Rome, the second Australia. On the facing page was another list, this one headed "Things to Learn." Below it were listed such things as sailing, skiing, scuba diving, horseback riding. It was a very long list, reaching to just above the bottom of the page.

These were Sarah's wish lists, I realized with a pang; this was what she dreamed of doing with the money. My eyes ran up and down the pages: Switzerland, Mexico, Antigua, Moscow, New York City, Chile, London, India, the Hebrides. . . . Tennis, French, windsurfing, waterskiing, German, art history, golf. . . . The lists went on and on, places I'd never heard her mention, ambitions I'd never dreamed she had.

Ever since I'd met her, I'd thought of Sarah as more confident and decisive than myself. She'd been the one to ask me out on our first date; she'd been the one to initiate our first sexual encounter; she'd been the one to suggest that we get engaged. She'd picked the wedding date (April 17), planned the honeymoon (a ten-day trip to Naples, Florida), and decided when we'd begin trying to have a baby. It seemed like she always managed to get what she wanted, but I realized now, standing there looking down at the magazines and brochures scattered across the table, that she hadn't really, that behind her facade of assertiveness and drive there must lay an enormous reservoir of disappointment.

Sarah had received a B.S. in petroleum engineering from the University of Toledo. When I first met her, she was planning on moving down to Texas and landing a high-paying job in the oil industry. She wanted to save up her money and buy a ranch someday, a "spread" she called it, with horses and a herd of cattle and her own special brand, an *S* embedded within a heart. Instead, we got married. I was hired by the feedstore in Ashenville in the spring of my senior year, and suddenly, without really choosing it, she found herself in Delphia. There weren't many openings in northwestern Ohio for someone with an undergraduate degree in petroleum engineering, so she ended up working part-time at the local library. She was a trouper; she always made the best of things, yet there had to be some regret in all this; she had to look back every now and then and mourn the distance that separated her present existence from the one she'd dreamed of as a student. She'd sacrificed something of herself for our relationship, but she'd never attracted attention to it, and so it had seemed natural to me, even inevitable. It wasn't until tonight that I saw it for the tragedy it was.

Now the money had arrived, and she could begin to dream again. She could draw up her wish lists, page through her magazines, plan her new life. It was a nice way to envision her—full of hope and yearning, making promises to herself that she felt certain she could fulfill—but there was also something terribly sad about it. We were trapped, I realized; we'd crossed a boundary, and we couldn't go back. The money, by giving us the chance to dream, had also allowed us to begin despising our present lives. My job at the feedstore, our aluminum-siding house, the town around us—we were already looking upon all that as part of our past. It was what we were before we became millionaires; it was stunted, gray, unlivable. And so if, somehow, we were forced to relinquish the money now, we wouldn't merely be returning to our old lives, starting back up as if nothing of import had happened; we'd be returning having seen them from a distance, having judged them and deemed them unworthy. The damage would be irreparable.

"Hank?" Sarah called from upstairs. "Honey?" She was off the phone.

"Coming," I yelled. Then I flicked off the light and quietly slid the door shut behind me.

. . .

SATURDAY afternoon, just as Sarah and I were finishing lunch, the doorbell rang. It was Jacob; I found him waiting on the front porch, dressed, to my surprise, in gray flannel slacks and a pair of leather shoes. It was the first time since our parents' funerals that I'd seen him in anything but jeans or khaki work pants, and it startled me a bit, set me off my guard, so that it took me another moment or so to notice the even more drastic change in his appearance—his lack of hair. Jacob had gone to the barber and gotten a crew cut; his hair had been clipped back tight against his scalp, so that now his head seemed too large for his body, seemed to hover like an overinflated balloon above his shoulders.

He stood there, watching me, waiting for my reaction. I smiled at him. Despite the obvious tightness of his pants, despite the way his brown shoes clashed with his blue socks, he seemed pleased with himself, pleased with how he looked, and that wasn't something that happened very often. It gave me a warm feeling toward him, made me want to compliment him.

"You got your hair cut," I said.

He smiled shyly, touched his head with his hand. "Just this morning."

"I like it," I said. "It looks good."

He continued to smile, glancing away now, embarrassed. Across the street one of the neighbor's kids was smacking a tennis ball against his garage door with a hockey stick. The ball was wet, and every time it hit the door, it left a mark. Mary Beth was watching him from the truck.

"You have time to talk?" Jacob asked.

"Sure." I opened the door wide. "You eat lunch yet? I could fix you a sandwich."

He glanced past me into the house. He was shy around Sarah—shy around women in general—and always tried to avoid coming inside when she was around. "I thought maybe we could go for a drive," he said.

"We can't talk here?"

"It's kind of about the money," he whispered.

I stepped down onto the porch, pulling the door shut behind me. "What's wrong?" I asked.

"Nothing's wrong."

"Is it about Pederson?"

He shook his head. "It's just something I want to show you. It's a surprise."

"A surprise?"

He nodded. "You'll like it. It's a good thing."

I stared at my brother, debating for a moment, then pushed the door back open. "Let me get my jacket," I said.

AS SOON as I got into the truck, I asked him what was going on, but he wouldn't tell me.

"Just wait," he said. "I have to show you."

We drove west out of Delphia, toward Ashenville. At first I thought we were going back to the nature preserve, but then we took a left onto Burnt Road rather than a right, and headed south. It was a cold, sunny day. The snow on the fields had an icy crust to it, and no matter where you looked it seemed to sparkle. It wasn't until we were almost there, turning off onto the dirt road that had once led to our driveway, that I realized Jacob was taking me to our father's farm.

I stared through the window at the fields as the truck slowed to a stop. I hadn't been out to the farm in years, and I was startled to see it now, shocked by how little still remained to show me that it had once been my home. The house and barn and outbuildings had been dismantled and carted away, the basement filled in and seeded over. The huge circle of shade trees that had once marked the boundary of our front yard had been chopped down and sold for lumber. The only vestige of our family's presence on the land was our father's windmill, which still stood—at a slight angle now—about a quarter mile to the west.

"Do you come by here a lot?" I asked Jacob.

He shrugged. "Sometimes," he said. He was staring out toward where our house was supposed to be. You could see for more than a mile, and all of it was the same. With the flatness and the snow covering everything, it was hard to keep your eyes from wandering; there was nothing to pick out and focus on over anything else. It was like looking up into the sky.

"Do you want to get out?" Jacob asked.

I didn't, but it seemed like he did, so I said, "Sure," and pushed open my door.

We hiked straight into the field, along where we guessed our gravel driveway had once run. Mary Beth bounded ahead of us through the knee-deep snow, pausing now and then to sniff at things we couldn't see. We stopped about a hundred yards in from the road, when we reached the place where our house had once stood. We may've had the wrong spot; there were no clues to help us orient ourselves, no hearthstone or pump handle, not even a slight depression in the earth to mark the filled-in basement. It was just like everything else around it. The windmill stood off to the left in the distance, looking derelict and disused. There was a little breeze coming down out of the north, and when it gusted, it spun the windmill's sails. They creaked as they lurched into motion, like an old rocking chair, but the sound took a second to reach us, and by the time we turned to look, the sails had stopped.

Jacob was trying to guess where things had stood—the barn, the tractor shed, the grain bins, the metal hut our father had used to store seed. He rotated on his heels, pointing out the different spots. His leather shoes were wet from the snow.

"Jacob," I said finally, interrupting him. "Why'd you bring me here?"

He grinned at me. "I've decided what I'm going to do with my share of the money."

"And what's that?"

"I want to buy back the farm."

"This farm?"

He nodded. "I'm going to rebuild the house, the barn, everything just like it used to be."

"You can't do that," I said, appalled. "We have to leave."

The dog was digging in the snow at our feet, and Jacob watched him for a moment before answering. Then he looked up at me. "Where am I going to go, Hank?" he asked. "It's different for you guys. You've got Sarah, and Lou's got Nancy, but I don't have anyone. You want me to just drive off all alone?"

"You can't buy the farm, Jacob. Where would you say you got your money?"

"I thought we could tell people that Sarah had come into an inheritance. Nobody around here knows anything about her family. We'll say that you guys bought the farm before you left, and set me up to run it."

I stared off around us at the empty fields, at our tracks running crookedly back through the snow to the road, and tried to imagine my brother staying here, rebuilding the house, putting up fences, planting crops. I couldn't believe that it would ever happen.

"I thought you'd be happy," he said. "It's our farm. I'm going to bring it back."

I frowned at him. He was wrong: I was anything but happy. The farm was something I'd been running away from all my life. For as long as I could remember, I'd seen it as a place where things broke down and fell apart, where nothing ever worked out as planned. Even now, looking out at the vacant space that had once held my home, I was filled with an overwhelming surge of hopelessness. Nothing good had ever happened here.

"It's so hard, Jacob," I said. "Do you realize that? You don't just buy a farm, you have to work it. You have to know about machines and seed and fertilizers and pesticides and herbicides and drainage and irrigation and the weather and the government. You don't know about any of that. You'd end up just like Dad."

As soon as I said it, I realized I'd been too harsh. I could tell just from the way my brother was standing that I'd hurt him. His jacket was hitched up, his shoulders hunched, his hands sunk deep in the pockets of his flannel pants. He wasn't looking at me.

"I was supposed to get the farm," he said. "Dad had promised it to me."

I nodded, still ashamed by what I'd said. Our father had wanted one of us to be a farmer, the other to be a lawyer. I'd done better in school, so I was the one they sent to college. We'd both failed him, though; neither of us had managed to live up to his dreams.

"I'm asking for your help," Jacob said. "I've never done it before, but I'm doing it now. Help me get the farm back."

I didn't say anything. I didn't want him to stay here after we split up the money—I knew that only bad would come of it—but I couldn't find a way to tell him this.

"I'm not asking for any money," he said. "I just want you to tell people in town that Sarah's come into an inheritance."

"You don't even know if Muller would sell it to you."

"If I offer him enough money, he'll sell it."

"Can't you buy a different farm? Something out west, where people don't know us?"

Jacob shook his head. "I want *this* farm. I want to live here, where we grew up."

"What happens if I refuse to help?"

He considered that briefly, then shrugged. "I don't know," he said. "I guess I'd try to think up another story."

"But don't you see the danger, Jacob? How your remaining here would be a threat to all of us? The only way we'll really be safe is if everyone disappears."

"I can't leave," he said. "I don't have any place to go."

"You've got the whole world. You can settle anywhere you want."

"This is where I want to go." He stamped his shoe in the snow. "Right here. Home."

Neither of us spoke for nearly a minute after that. Another breeze came up, and we stared out toward the windmill, but it didn't move. I was working up my confidence to say no to Jacob, to tell him that it would never work, when—perhaps sensing what I was about to do—he allowed me a way out.

"You don't have to decide now," he said. "I just want you to promise me you'll consider it."

"All right," I said, grateful for the reprieve. "I'll think it through."

IT WASN'T until after he'd dropped me off, as I was opening my front door, that I realized why he'd dressed up and gotten his hair cut before he came to see me. He'd done it to impress me, to make himself look mature and responsible, to show me that—if he were only given the chance—he could play the part of an adult just as well as I. The thought of this, of him shining those shoes in his grungy apartment, of him squeezing his legs into those uncomfortable pants, tightening his belt, pulling up his socks, and then standing for a few moments before the bathroom mirror to appraise the result, filled me with a horrible feeling of wretchedness for myself and Jacob and the way we were to each other. It made me want to give him the farm.

I knew that this would never happen, though, even as I yearned for it, and when I talked it over with Sarah later that afternoon, she agreed.

"He's got to leave, Hank," she said. "There's no way he

can stay." We were in the living room, sitting in front of the fire. Sarah was knitting again, and her needles clicked away while she talked, as if they were translating what she said into Morse code. "You have to make him understand that."

"I know," I said. "I just couldn't do it while we were out there. I'll tell him on Monday."

She shook her head. "Don't tell him until you have to."

"What do you mean?"

"The more time we let pass, the less important it'll seem to him."

I could see what she was saying; she was scared of antagonizing him, of forcing him into Lou's arms. I thought for a moment of arguing with her, telling her that we had no reason to fear Jacob, that he was my brother and we could trust him, but I realized that I had no means to convince her of this, no solid, objective evidence to demonstrate his allegiance. So all I said was, "I wish we could give it to him."

The needles stopped clicking, and I felt Sarah glance at me across the hearth. "He can't stay here, Hank. It'd be like leaving a giant clue behind."

"I know. I'm just saying I wish I could help him somehow."

"Make him promise to leave, then. That's how you'll help him."

"But what will he do, Sarah? Have you thought about that? He's got nowhere to go."

"He'll have a million dollars. He'll be able to go wherever he wants."

"Except here."

"That's right." She nodded. "Except here."

The needles started up again.

"I've always felt bad toward Jacob," I said, "even when we were little. I've always felt like I was letting him down."

"It's not like he's done all that much for you over the years."

I waved this aside. She didn't understand what I was talking about. "I used to look up to him," I said. "Until I went off to school and saw him teased by the other kids for his weight. Then I was embarrassed, ashamed that he was my brother. I started to look down on him, and he knew it. He could sense the change."

Sarah's needles went click, click, click. "That's natural," she said. "You were just a child."

I shook my head. "He was this shy, anxious kid."

"And now he's a shy, anxious adult."

I frowned at her. I was trying to express how I felt toward my brother, trying to give her some hint of the despair that had washed over me earlier that afternoon, after he'd dropped me off.

"Did you know that he was a bed wetter?" I asked.

"Jacob?" Sarah smirked at the idea.

"In seventh grade he began losing control of his bladder every night. It lasted all through the winter and into the spring. My mom used to set her alarm clock so that she could wake him in the middle of the night, get him up, and take him to the bathroom, but it didn't work."

Sarah continued her knitting. She seemed like she wasn't really paying attention.

"Toward the end, I told one of my friends about it, and pretty soon everyone knew. Everyone in the whole school."

"Was Jacob mad?"

"No. He was just ashamed, but that made it worse. He didn't even tell our parents about it, so I never got in trouble." I paused, thinking about this. "It was the cruelest thing I've ever done."

"That was ages ago, Hank," Sarah said. "I bet he doesn't even remember anymore."

I shook my head. I shouldn't have tried to speak about it, I realized: it hadn't come out right, I hadn't said what I meant.

What I meant was that I wanted to help my brother, to do something good for him, to make his life better than it was. But I couldn't find a way to say this.

"It doesn't matter what he remembers," I said.

LATE that night I woke to the sound of a car's engine idling in our driveway. Sarah was on her back beside me, breathing deep and slow. The only light in the room came from the digital alarm clock, a pale green glow floating out across the night table and settling softly onto the blanketed bulk of her pregnant body.

It was quarter till one. Outside, the car's engine shut itself off.

I slipped out of bed and padded to the window. The sky was clear. A half moon, pale yellow, almost white, hung at its very center. Stars shone through the branches of the trees, bright and precise. The snow in the front yard sparkled with their light. At the bottom of the driveway, parked with its nose facing the house, was Lou's car.

I glanced quickly at Sarah, who continued her steady, muted breathing; then I tiptoed across the room and out into the hallway.

As I headed down the stairs, I heard a car door squeak open. After a moment, it squeaked shut again, slowly, quietly.

At the front door I peeked through the slit window. Lou was making his way carefully up the driveway. He was wearing his white camouflage jacket and walking like he was drunk. I wasn't sure, but it looked like there was someone waiting in the car. As I watched, Lou veered off toward the garage.

The garage was attached to the left side of the house. I couldn't see the front of it, and when Lou got near it, he disappeared from sight.

I didn't have any weapons in the house. All I could think

of were the knives in the kitchen, and I didn't want to leave the window to go get one.

He spent a long time by the garage. The doors were unlocked, but there was nothing in there for him to steal. I stared at his car. There was definitely someone waiting there, maybe even two people.

The miniature grandfather clock in the living room ticked loudly through the silence, punctuating it, seeming to draw it out.

I considered briefly turning on a light, trying to scare them away, but I didn't do it. I just peered out the window, shivering in my pajamas and bare feet, and waited for Lou to reappear.

When he finally did, he headed not for his car but straight toward my front door.

I stiffened, took two steps back into the entranceway.

Lou climbed up onto the porch, his boots making a hollow sound against the wood, a pair of drumbeats. He tried the door, jiggling the knob, but it was locked. Then he knocked, very softly, tapping with his glove.

I didn't move.

He knocked again, louder, with his fist, and—remembering Sarah asleep above me—I stepped forward and unlocked the door.

I opened it just a crack and peered outside.

"What're you doing, Lou?" I whispered.

He gave me a big, jagged-toothed smile. His eyes seemed to twinkle. "Mr. Accountant!" he said, as if he were surprised to see me.

I frowned at him, and his expression changed quickly in response, instantly becoming serious, somber.

"Hank," he said. "I'm here to make a tiny withdrawal." Then he giggled, unable to hold it back. He wiped his mouth with his glove. I could smell the alcohol on his breath.

"Go home, Lou," I said. "Turn around and go home." A steady stream of cold air came in through the open doorway and poured across my bare feet, making them ache.

"It's freezing out, Hank," he said. "Invite me in."

He pressed his body up against the door, and—when I involuntarily retreated—stepped inside. He shut the door behind him, a big grin on his face.

"I've decided it's time to split it up, Hank. I want my share." He rubbed his gloves together and glanced around the entranceway, as if he were expecting the duffel bag to be just sitting there, right out in the open.

"The money's not here, Lou."

"Is it in the garage?"

"Even if it were here, I wouldn't give you any."

He reared back in indignation. "Just because you have it doesn't mean it's yours. Part of it's mine." He tapped his finger against his chest.

"You made an agreement," I said sternly.

He ignored me. He leaned to the side and looked down the hallway into the kitchen. "Is it in the bank?"

"Of course not. It's hidden."

"I just need some cash, Hank. I need it right now."

"The only way we keep the money is if we stick to the agreement."

"Come on, Mr. Accountant," he said, his voice soft and insinuating. "Be a sport."

"Who's in the car?"

"In the car?"

"Waiting for you." I gestured past the front door.

"Car's empty. It's just me."

"I saw someone in the car, Lou. Is it Nancy?"

He smiled a little. "You been watching me all this time?" He seemed to find this funny, and his smile deepened.

"Nancy and who else?" I asked. "Is Jacob there?"

Lou shook his head. "Just Nancy." He paused and then,

when he saw me frown, smiled again, like a child caught in a fib. "Nancy and Sonny," he said.

"Sonny Major?" I asked, surprised. I hadn't thought that they were friends.

He nodded. "He came over for the rent, and Nancy and me invited him out." His grin stretched into a leer. "That's why I need the money, Mr. Accountant. I'm taking my landlord out drinking."

"You tell them about the plane?"

He snorted with disgust. "Course not. I told them you owed me some money."

I frowned. The house made a creaking sound around us in the darkness, settling into its foundation.

"All I'm asking for is what's rightfully mine," he said. He wobbled a bit back and forth on his feet, and, watching him, I felt an overwhelming wave of impatience. I wanted him to leave. I wanted him to leave immediately.

"It doesn't even have to be all of it," he said. "Just give me one of the packets. I can come back later for the rest."

I spoke very slowly, keeping my voice low and quiet. "If you ask me again," I said, "I'll go and burn the money first thing tomorrow. Is that clear?"

He snickered at that. "Bluff," he whispered. "B-L-U-F-F."

"Call it then. See what happens."

He snickered again. "I know a secret, Mr. Accountant. Jacob told me a little secret."

I stared at him.

"I know what happened to Dwight Pederson."

I stiffened, just for a moment; then I stopped myself. I stayed surprisingly calm. My mind was thinking very quickly, darting this way and that, but my body didn't betray it. Jacob had told him about Pederson: I was stunned, I hadn't expected this at all.

Lou grinned at me. I forced myself to look him directly in the eyes. "Dwight Pederson?" I said.

His smile widened, taking up his whole face. "You killed him, Mr. Accountant. You and Jacob."

"You drink too much, Lou. You don't know what you're saying."

He shook his head, still smiling. "I'm not going to let you burn the money. It'd be like stealing from me. I'll tell if you do it."

The clock in the living room chimed the hour, a single, deep toll. After it died away, the hallway seemed darker and quieter than before.

I put my hand against Lou's jacket, right at the center of his chest. I exerted no pressure; I simply rested my palm there. We both looked down at it. "Go home, Lou," I whispered.

He shook his head again. "I need the money."

I stepped over to the hall closet. I felt around inside my jacket until I found my wallet. I took two twenties from it and held them out to him.

He hardly even glanced at them. "I want one of the packets," he said.

"They aren't here, Lou. I've hidden them away from the house."

"Where?"

"Take the twenties." I shook them at him.

"I want my share, Hank."

"You'll get it this summer, like we agreed."

"No. I want it now."

"You aren't listening to me, Lou. I can't give it to you. It's not here."

"I'll come back in the morning then. We can go get it together."

"That's not what we agreed on."

"Be a shame if someone wrote a note to the sheriff, saying there might be something a little suspicious about Dwight Pederson's accident."

I gave him a cold stare. I was overcome by a desperate desire to hurt him. I wanted to take my fist and smash his crooked teeth down the back of his throat. I wanted to break his neck.

"Take the twenties," I said.

"I mean, he just drove off that bridge? You believe that?" Lou shook his head in mock disbelief. "Seems pretty strange to me." He paused, grinning. "Weren't you two out that way on New Year's morning?"

"You'd never do it."

"I'm desperate, Hank. I'm broke, and I owe people money."

"If you turned us in, you'd lose it all."

"I can't wait till summer. I need it now."

"Take the twenties," I said. I held the bills out toward him.

He shook his head. "I'm coming back in the morning. I need at least a packet."

I began to panic, but only briefly. Then I saw a way out. "I can't go in the morning," I said. "It's a day's drive away. I can't go until after Sarah has the baby."

Lou didn't seem to know if he should believe me. "A day's drive?"

"It's at a storage place up in Michigan."

"What the fuck is it doing up in Michigan?"

"I didn't want it near us. In case we came under suspicion for some reason. I wanted it far away."

I could see him debating inside his head. "When's she supposed to have it?" he asked.

"In a couple weeks."

"And we'll go then?"

"Yes," I said. I just wanted him to leave.

"You promise?"

I nodded.

"And we'll split it up?"

I nodded again. "Take the twenties," I said.

He looked down at the money. Then he took it and shoved it into his jacket pocket. He smiled at me. "Sorry to wake you," he said. He backed away, two unsteady steps toward the door. I opened it for him, and, when he was out on the porch, shut and locked it behind him.

I watched him through the window, watched him stand there on the front step, take the twenties from his pocket, and slowly inspect them before he set off, weaving a bit, down the driveway to his car.

When he opened the car door, the dome light flashed on for a second, and I saw two people inside. In the front seat was Nancy, smiling up toward him. In the back, lost in shadow, was a second person. At first I assumed it must be Sonny Major. But then, just as Lou shut the door behind him and the light flicked off, I had an instant's tremor of doubt. Sonny Major was a tiny man, smaller than Lou. The man in the rear of the car had looked large, even huge. He'd looked like Jacob.

I watched the car roll down the driveway. They were out on the street before Lou turned on his headlights. I waited there, my feet numb against the cold wooden floor, until the sound of the car's engine faded away and the house, once again, descended into silence.

I tried briefly to think of what I ought to do, but I couldn't come up with anything. All I could think was that things had gotten out of hand. I was in trouble now, and there seemed to be no way out of it.

When I turned to go back to bed, I found Sarah, wrapped in her white terry cloth robe, staring down at me like a ghost from the shadows at the top of the stairs.

We talked right there, on the stairs. I climbed up to her and we sat down beside each other in the darkness, on the next-to-last step, like two children.

"You heard?" I asked.

Sarah nodded. She rested her hand on my knee.

"All of it?"

"Yes."

"Jacob told Lou about Pederson."

She nodded again, giving my knee a little squeeze. I put my hand on top of hers.

"What are you going to do?" she asked.

I shrugged. "Nothing."

"Nothing?"

"Keep the money. Wait it out."

She leaned away from me. I could feel her looking at my face. I stared down toward the front door. "You can't do that," she said. Her voice, without rising at all, nevertheless had taken on a subtle urgency. "If you don't give it to him, he'll tell."

"Then I'll give it to him."

"You can't. He'll get us caught. He'll start spending it everywhere, attracting attention."

"All right, then I won't. I'll call his bluff."

"But he'll tell."

"There's nothing else I can do, Sarah," I said, my voice rising with frustration. "Those are my two options."

"Burn the money."

"I can't. Lou'll tell about Pederson. I'll end up getting charged with murder."

"Blame it on Jacob. If you turn in the money and promise to testify against him, they'll grant you immunity."

"I can't do that to Jacob."

"Look what he's done to you, Hank. This is all his fault."

"I'm not going to do that to my own brother."

I could hear Sarah's breathing; it was coming fast and shallow. I squeezed her hand.

"I don't think he'll tell," I said. "I think if we stand firm, he'll wait till summer."

"And if he doesn't?"

"Then we're in trouble. That's the risk we take."

"You can't just sit back and wait for him to turn you in."

"What do you want me to do? You want me to kill him? Like Jacob said?"

She waved this aside, frowning. "All I'm saying is that we have to do something. We have to find some way to threaten him."

"Threaten him?"

"It's a power thing, Hank. We were controlling him by keeping the money, but now he's controlling us. We have to think of a way to regain control."

"Things'll only get worse if we threaten him. It's like upping the ante; all he'll do is throw in another chip."

"You're saying you want to give up?"

I took my hand away from hers and rubbed my face with it. All around us, the house was absolutely quiet, as if it were listening. "I just want to keep doing what we planned," I said. "I want to wait till summer."

"But he'll tell."

"He won't gain anything by telling. He knows that. The money'll be gone if we go to jail."

"He'll do it out of spite. He'll do it just because you don't follow his orders."

I shut my eyes. My body was beginning to ache with fatigue. It wanted to return to sleep.

"I don't think you understand how serious this is, Hank."

"We should go back to bed," I said, but Sarah didn't move.

"You're at his mercy now. You'll have to do whatever he tells you."

"I still have the money. He doesn't know where it is."

"Your leverage came from the threat of burning it. That's gone now."

"I shouldn't have told Jacob."

"You know Lou. He'll use it against you for all it's worth."

"I can't believe he did this to me."

"Even if we make it through to the summer and split up the money, he'll always have this to threaten you with. He'll wait ten years, until he's spent his share, then he'll track us down. He'll blackmail us. He'll send you to jail."

I didn't say anything. I wasn't thinking about Lou; I was thinking about Jacob.

Sarah took my hand again. "You can't let him do that. You have to take control."

"But there's nothing we can do. You keep talking about threatening him, but how're we going to do that? We don't have anything to threaten him with."

She didn't say anything.

"Is there something you want me to do?" I asked. "Do you have a plan?"

She stared at me, hard, and for a second I thought she was going to say she wanted me to kill him, but she didn't. She just shook her head. "No," she said. "I don't."

I nodded. I was about to stand up, to head back to the bedroom, when she grabbed my hand and held it to her stomach. The baby was kicking. I felt it beneath my palm, something dark and mysterious, the warm softness of her body pushing up forcefully against my skin. It went on for several seconds.

"It'll be all right," I whispered, when it was finally finished. "Trust me. We'll see it through."

It was the type of thing people always say when they're trapped in untenable situations; I realized that as soon as I began to speak. It was like what my mother had said to me the last time I'd seen her, something both false and brave, an aversion of the eyes and a closing of the ears, a denial of the peril we were in. It was a bad sign, that I felt the need to say it, and I could tell by the way Sarah kept my hand pressed against her belly, her grip tight and insistent, that she knew it, too. We were in trouble; we'd started something dangerous together, full of naive self-confidence and assurance, and now we were watching it slip out of our control.

"I'm scared, Hank," she said, and I nodded.

"It'll be all right," I whispered again, feeling foolish this time. But there was nothing else to say.

I WAS up early the next morning. I dressed in the hallway and brushed my teeth downstairs so I wouldn't wake Sarah. In the kitchen I made myself some coffee, and while I drank it I read yesterday's newspaper.

Then I drove over to Jacob's.

I parked across the street from his apartment, right behind his pickup. It was a beautiful morning, cold, crisp, cloudless. Everything looked clean, scrubbed—the striped vinyl awning of the grocery store, the parking meters' silver pillars, the flag snapping in the wind above the town hall. It was still early, a little before eight, but Ashenville was already wide awake, the street active with people coming and going, newspapers folded under their arms, cups of coffee steaming in their mittened hands. Everyone seemed to be smiling.

Jacob, as I'd expected, was asleep when I arrived. I had to pound, wait, and then pound again before I heard him shuffling slowly toward the door. When he finally got there, he seemed displeased to find me standing outside. He leaned against the doorjamb for a moment, squinting at the light from the hallway, a look of profound disappointment on his face. Then he grunted hello, turned, and stumbled back into the apartment's dim interior.

I stepped inside, shutting the door behind me. It took a few seconds for my eyes to adjust to the lack of light. His apartment was cramped, airless. It was just a big, square, carpetless room. Off to the left was a door leading to a tiny bathroom. Next to it, running the entire length of the apartment, was a two-foot-deep recess cut into the wall. This was Jacob's kitchen. There was a bed, a table with two chairs, an old, broken-down couch, a television set. Dirty clothes were strewn across the couch; empty beer bottles dotted the floor.

It stank of poverty. Every time I saw it, it made me sick.

Jacob returned to the bed, collapsing on his back. The bedsprings moaned beneath his weight. He was dressed in a pair of long johns and a T-shirt. The thermal underwear clung grotesquely to the soft thickness of his thighs. There was a good three inches of skin showing beneath the bottom of his shirt. It was fat—white, rippled, malleable. It seemed obscene to me. I wanted him to cover himself with a blanket.

I went over and pulled open the blinds on the two windows, filling the room with sunlight. Jacob shut his eyes. The air was thick with dust, sifting slantwise through the light like miniature snow. I considered briefly the possibility of sitting down, eyed the couch with distaste, and decided not to. I leaned back against the windowsill and folded my arms across my chest.

"What'd you do last night?" I asked Jacob.

Mary Beth was on the foot of the bed, his head resting on his paws, one ear cocked, one eye open, watching me.

Jacob, eyes shut, shrugged. "Nothing." His voice was gritty with sleep.

"You go out?"

He shrugged again.

"With Lou?"

"No." He coughed, cleared his throat. "I've got a cold. I didn't go out."

"I saw Lou," I said.

Jacob pulled a blanket over himself and rolled onto his side, his eyes still closed.

"He came by the house."

Jacob opened his eyes. "And?"

"Nancy was with him, and somebody else. I thought it might've been you."

He didn't say anything.

"Were you there? In the car?"

"I told you." His voice sounded as if he felt picked on. "I didn't see Lou last night. I'm sick."

"That's the truth?"

"Come on, Hank." He rose up on his elbow. "Why would I lie to you?"

"Was it Sonny?"

"Sonny?"

"Sonny Major. Was it him in the car?"

"I don't know. How would I know that?" He put his head back down on the pillow, but he was fully awake now. I could tell it from the sound of his voice.

"Are they friends?"

"Sure. He's his landlord."

"They go out together?"

"I don't know," Jacob said tiredly. "Why not?"

"Does he know about the money?"

"The money?"

"Yes," I shouted, exasperated. "Has Lou told him about the money?"

Someone banged against the wall next door, and we both froze.

After a moment, Jacob sat up in bed. He dropped his legs over the edge, leaned forward with his forearms resting on his knees. I stared at his naked feet. I was always shocked by their size. They looked like two raw chickens.

"You've got to relax, Hank. You're getting paranoid. Nobody knows but us and Nancy and Sarah."

"Sarah doesn't know."

He looked up at me, then shrugged. "Us and Nancy then. That's it."

The dog climbed out of bed, stretched, then walked across the floor toward the bathroom. He disappeared inside and started to drink loudly from the toilet. We listened until he stopped.

"I killed Pederson for you, Jacob," I said.

He straightened up. "What?"

"I killed him for you."

"Why the fuck do you keep saying that? What does that mean?"

"It means I put myself at risk for you, and you turn around and betray me."

"Betray you?"

"You told Lou where I hid the money."

"Hank, what the fuck's going on with you today?"

"He knew it was in the garage."

Jacob was silent. The dog came walking back out of the bathroom, his nails clicking against the tiled floor.

"You never said I shouldn't," Jacob mumbled.

Very quietly, I said, "You told him about Pederson."

"I didn't . . ."

"You betrayed me, Jacob. You promised me you wouldn't tell."

"I didn't tell him anything. He's just guessing. He did the same thing to me."

"Why would he've guessed something like that?"

"I told him how we went back to the plane that morning. He'd just seen about Pederson on the news, and he said, 'Did you kill him?' "

"And you denied it?"

He hesitated. "I didn't tell him."

"Did you deny it?"

"He guessed, Hank," Jacob said, his voice impatient, put upon. "He just knew."

"Well that's great, Jacob. Because now he's using it to blackmail me."

"Blackmail you?"

"He says he'll tell if I don't give him his share."

Jacob thought about that. "Are you going to do it?"

"I can't. He'd start spending hundred-dollar bills all over town. He'd get us caught just as quick doing that as he would by telling Carl about Pederson."

"You really think he'll tell?"

"Do you?"

Jacob frowned. "I don't know. Probably not. It's just that he's been gambling lately, so he's short on money."

"Gambling?"

He nodded.

"Where's he been gambling?" For some reason the idea seemed absurd to me.

"In Toledo. At the racetrack. He's lost some money."

"A lot?"

Jacob shrugged. "A bit. I'm not sure exactly."

I rubbed my face with my hands. "Shit," I said. Then I turned to the window. There was a pigeon sitting outside on the ledge, puffed up against the cold. I tapped the glass with my knuckles, and it flew away. Its wings flashed in the sunlight.

"Do you see what's happening, Jacob?" I asked.

He didn't say anything.

"Lou can send us both to jail now."

"Lou's not going to—"

"And we can't control him. Before, we could threaten to burn the money, but now we can't. He'll tell if we do."

"You never would've burned it, Hank."

I waved this aside. "You know what the problem is? The problem is, you think you can trust him. He's your best friend, so you think he won't betray you."

"Come on. Lou's just—"

I shook my head. "You don't have any distance on this. You're too close to see what he's really like."

"What he's really like?" Jacob asked incredulously. "And you think you're going to tell me that?"

"I can tell you—"

He cut me off, his voice rising with anger as he spoke. "He's my best friend, Hank; you know nothing about him. You've seen him drunk a few times, so you think you know him, but you don't. You can't tell me anything."

I turned to face him. "Can you guarantee that he won't turn us in?"

"Guarantee?"

"Will you write up a confession, saying you killed Dwight Pederson all by yourself, sign it, and give it to me to keep?"

He threw me a frightened look. "A confession? Why would you want that?"

"To show the police if Lou were to tell on us."

Jacob was speechless. He seemed mortified by the idea, which was exactly what I'd hoped for. I didn't really want a confession; I was just trying to scare him, trying to shock him out of his complacency.

"It's your fault, Jacob, our being in this mess. You're the one who told him."

Jacob didn't say anything. I waited a moment, then turned back toward the window.

"Now Lou's asking me for something I can't give him," I said. "And when I refuse to do it, he's going to tell. He's going to send us to jail."

"Come on, Hank. You're the one that's going to end up getting us caught. You're getting all worked up over—"

"I came here this morning," I said, not turning from the window, "to find out whose side you're on."

"Side?"

"You have to choose."

"I'm not on any side. You both keep talking about sides . . ."

"Lou talks about sides?"

He ignored my question. "I'm on both your sides. We're all together. That was the plan."

"If you had to pick a side—"

"I'm not going to pick a side."

"I want you to pick one, Jacob. I want to know: Lou, or me?"

Behind me I could sense his confusion, his panic. The mattress creaked as he shifted his weight.

"I'm . . ."

"Pick one."

There were perhaps ten full seconds of silence. I waited through them, holding my breath.

"I'd pick you, Hank," he said then. "You're my brother."

I rested my forehead against the windowpane. The glass was cold; it made my skin ache. Out on the street, right below me, an old man dropped his newspaper, and it flung apart in the wind. A passing couple helped him gather it back together, and they talked for a bit, the old man nodding vigorously. "Thank you," I saw him say as they parted. "Thank you."

Mary Beth made a yawning sound, and I heard my brother start to pet him.

"Don't forget it, Jacob," I said, my breath steaming the glass in front of me. "Whatever else happens, don't forget it."

Tuesday afternoon there was a knock on my office door. Before I could say anything, it creaked open, and Lou stuck his head through. He smiled at me, showing his teeth. They looked like a rodent's, sharp, yellow.

"Hey, Mr. Accountant," he said. Then he stepped inside, shutting the door behind him. He came all the way up to my desk but didn't sit down. He had on his white jacket, a pair of work boots. His face was pink from the cold.

This was the moment I'd been dreading for the past three

days, but now that it had finally arrived, I experienced no fear, no anger. I simply felt tired.

"What do you want, Lou?" I sighed. I knew that whatever it was, it probably wasn't something I could give him.

"I need some money, Hank."

That was all he said. He didn't issue any threats, didn't mention Pederson or Jacob, but I could feel it hanging in the air between us, like a scent.

"I already told you—" I started, but he cut me off with a wave of his hand.

"I'm not asking for that," he said. "I'm just asking for a loan."

"A loan?"

"I'll pay you back as soon as we split up the money."

I frowned. "How much?"

"I need two thousand," he said. He tried smiling at me but seemed immediately to sense that it was a bad idea and gave it up.

"Two thousand dollars?" I asked.

He nodded somberly.

"Why would you need that much money?"

"I've got debts."

"A two-thousand-dollar debt? To who?"

He didn't answer me. "I need the money, Hank. It's real important."

"Gambling debts?"

He seemed to flinch a little, surprised perhaps that I knew about the gambling, but then he managed a smile. "Lots of debts."

"You've lost two thousand dollars?"

He shook his head. "A bit more than that." He winked. "This is just good-faith money, to hold people off till I get my split."

"How much did you lose?"

"All I need is two thousand, Hank."

"I want to know how much you lost."

He shook his head again. "That's not really your business, Mr. Accountant, is it now?" He stood there in front of me, patient, immovable, his hands in the pockets of his jacket.

"It's not like I carry that much money around with me," I said. "I can't just reach into my desk and hand you two thousand dollars."

"There's a bank across the street."

"I need time," I said. "You'll have to come back at the end of the day."

AFTER he left, I went over to the bank and withdrew two thousand dollars from Sarah's and my account. I brought it back to my office, sealed it in an envelope, and dropped it into my top desk drawer.

I tried to do some work, but the day was shot; I couldn't concentrate on anything. I doodled in the margins of letters. I read a hunting magazine someone had left in my office.

I knew that giving him the envelope would commit me to splitting up the money. It was the only way he'd ever be able to repay me. I understood this but tried to pretend that it was irrelevant. What I told myself I was doing was buying time. I knew there had to be a way out, and I was sure that I could find it, if I only had a little space in which to concentrate. I needed to think; I needed to work things through.

Lou came back just before five, knocked on my door, and entered again without my calling him in.

"You get it?" he asked. He seemed to be in a great hurry. It made me move very slowly.

I reached over, slid open the desk drawer, and took out the envelope. I set it on the edge of my desk.

He stepped forward to take it. He ripped open the flap and counted the bills, his lips moving over the numbers.

Then he smiled at me. "I really appreciate this, Hank," he said, as if I'd done it voluntarily.

"I'm not going to give you any more," I said.

He counted the bills again, seemed to do some sort of computation in his head. "When's Sarah due?"

"The twenty-fourth."

"Next week?" His face brightened.

"Next Sunday."

"And then we'll get the money?"

I shrugged. "I'll need a few days, for things to settle down. And we'll have to do it on a weekend. I can't take off from work."

Lou started backing toward the door. "You'll call me?" he asked.

"Yes." I sighed. "I'll call you."

I didn't tell Sarah about any of it.

THE DAYS passed one after the other. The twenty-fourth came and went. During all that time I neither saw nor spoke with either Jacob or Lou. Sarah talked incessantly about the coming birth. She didn't mention Lou or Nancy at all.

At night I would lie in bed and count off the people who knew. I'd test them in my head for weakness, picture each of them turning me in, trying to double-cross me, rob me, hurt me. I started to dream about it—Lou beating me with a rolling pin; Jacob coming at me with a fork and knife, wanting to eat me alive; Nancy kissing Sarah, then whispering in her ear, "Poison him. Poison him. Poison him."

I'd wake in the middle of the night and picture Lou's beer can lying in the snow at the edge of the orchard, imagine someone from the FBI picking it up with a pair of rubber gloves, dropping it into a plastic bag, sending it off to the lab. Or I'd think of Carl, sitting in his office in Ashenville, waiting, when the wreck was finally discovered, to tie together

Jacob's report of a downed plane with the appearance the next day of Dwight Pederson's lifeless body.

They'd exhume the corpse, they'd dig it up, they'd study it and pick it apart, and then they'd know.

But, strangely, nothing happened. The money sat undisturbed in its bag beneath the bed. No one seemed to suspect me of anything. No one seemed to be plotting against me. Lou left me alone. And, gradually, I began to resign myself to what my life had become. I could live with my anxieties, I realized. They were finite. Any day now the baby would be born. I'd call Lou's bluff, brave it out. In the spring the plane would be discovered. A few months after that we'd split up the money and move away.

Then it would all be over.

Early in the morning on Thursday, January 28, just as I was preparing to leave for work, Sarah went into labor. I rushed her to the hospital, fifteen minutes away on the other side of Delphia, and there, at 6:14 that evening, she gave birth to a baby girl.

5

I BROUGHT Sarah and the baby home four days later. The baby was healthy, pink. She weighed nine pounds even, had rolls of fat beneath her chin and pudgy little hands attached to her arms.

Driving home, we decided to name her Amanda, after Sarah's paternal grandmother.

I was stunned at how dirty the house had become in Sarah's brief absence. It embarrassed me that I hadn't been able to keep it clean on my own. There were dirty dishes piled in the sink, newspapers scattered about the rooms, a thick clot of hair in the bathtub drain.

I ushered them straight upstairs, to the bedroom. I put Amanda in her crib, which I'd set up beneath the window. Sarah watched me from the bed. The crib was the same one my father had dropped off at our house the week before his accident. It had been Jacob's and mine when we were infants; our father had built it himself.

I went downstairs and fixed Sarah some tea and toast. I brought it to her on a tray, and we talked while she ate. We talked about Amanda, of course—about the sound she made when she was hungry, the way she jerked her leg if you touched the sole of her foot, the pale, limpid blue of her eyes. We talked about the hospital—about the mean night nurse whose shoes had squeaked like they were full of water as she made her rounds through the darkened hallways; the nice morning nurse who'd spoken with a lisp and so tried to avoid saying Sarah's name; the doctor with the gap between his teeth who kept referring to Amanda as a he.

I stood over the crib through all of this, watching the baby sleep. She was on her back, her head turned toward the window, her eyes tightly shut, as if she were squinting at the sky. She held her hands in loose fists up beside her shoulders. She was very still. I kept wanting to touch her and make sure that she was alive.

Sarah finished her tea and toast. She talked and talked, as though she'd spent the past four days storing up things to tell me. I smiled and nodded, urging her along until she suddenly interrupted herself.

"Is that Jacob?" she asked, and I looked out the window.

My brother's truck was rattling into the driveway.

I GREETED him at the door and invited him in, but he said he didn't have time. He'd brought a gift for the baby, something wrapped in pink tissue paper, and he handed it over to me quickly, as if carrying it embarrassed him.

"It's a teddy bear," he said. He'd left his truck running. The dog was sitting in the passenger seat, watching us. He barked once, at me, and his nose banged against the window, leaving a wet smear along the glass.

"Come see her," I said. "Just quickly. She's upstairs."

Jacob shook his head, took a step back, as if he were afraid I might pull him in. He was on the very edge of the porch. "No," he said. "I will later. I don't want to bother Sarah."

"It's no bother," I said. I shifted the teddy bear from one arm to the other.

Jacob shook his head again, and there was an awkward silence while he searched for something to say before he left.

"You decide on a name yet?" he asked.

I nodded. "Amanda."

"That's nice."

"It's after Sarah's grandmother. It's Latin. It means worthy of being loved."

"That's real nice," Jacob said. "I like it."

I nodded again. "You sure you won't come up?"

He shook his head. He stepped off the porch, but then he stopped. "Hank," he said. "I wanted to . . ." He faded off, glanced toward the truck.

"What?"

"Can I borrow some money?"

I frowned, shifting the teddy bear back to my other arm. "How much?"

He put his hands into his coat pockets, stared down at his boots. "Hundred and fifty?"

"A hundred and fifty dollars?"

He nodded.

"Why do you need that much money, Jacob?"

"I got to pay my rent. I'll get my unemployment check next week, but I can't wait that long."

"When would you pay me back?"

He shrugged. "I was sort of hoping you could just take it out of my share of the money."

"Are you even trying to find a job?"

He seemed surprised by the question. "No."

I tried unsuccessfully to keep my voice free from judgment. "You're not even looking?"

"Why should I look for a job?" He lowered his voice into a whisper. "Lou told me you agreed to split up the money."

I stared down at his chest, considering this. I saw fairly clearly that I couldn't tell him I wasn't going to give them their shares until the summer—he'd tell Lou, and I wasn't ready for that. But if I wanted to pretend otherwise, then I had no reason not to loan him the money. Behind him his truck rumbled and coughed in the driveway, spitting out clouds of bluish smoke. All up and down the street my neighbors' houses were absolutely quiet, as if abandoned, their windows blank. It was trash day, and plastic garbage cans lined the curb.

"Wait here," I said. "I've got to go upstairs and get my checkbook."

SARAH unwrapped the teddy bear while I stood at my dresser and wrote out Jacob's check. The baby was sound asleep in her crib.

"It's used," Sarah whispered, a note of disgust running through her voice.

I went over to look at the bear. There was nothing obviously wrong with it—no stains or holes, no missing eyes or protruding hunks of stuffing—but it had an undeniably rumpled look. It was old, used. It had dark brown fur, almost black, and a brass key inserted in its back.

Sarah wound the key. When she let it go, music came out of the bear's chest, a man's voice singing: "*Frère Jacques, Frère Jacques/Dormez-vous? Dormez-vous?*" As soon as I heard it, I realized why the bear looked so old.

"It was his bear," I said.

"Jacob's?"

"When he was little."

The music continued, sounding flat and far away beneath the teddy bear's fur:

Frère Jacques, Frère Jacques,
Dormez-vous? Dormez-vous?
Sonnez les matines. Sonnez les matines.
Ding, dang, dong. Ding, dang, dong.

Sarah held the bear up in front of her, reappraising it. The music gradually slowed—each note drawing itself out as if it would be the very last—but it didn't stop.

"I guess it's sweet of him, isn't it?" she said. She sniffed at the bear.

I took the tissue paper and shoved it into the wastebasket beside the bed. "I wonder where he's kept it all these years."

"Is he coming up?"

"No," I said, moving toward the door. "He's in a rush."

Sarah started to wind up the bear again. "What's the check for?"

"Jacob," I said, over my shoulder. I was stepping out into the hallway.

"He's borrowing money?"

I didn't answer her.

THE BABY started to cry as I made my way back up the stairs. She began softly—something between a suppressed cough and a squawking sound like a bird might make—but just as I entered the bedroom, she suddenly, as if at the twist of a knob, increased her volume to a full-blown wail.

I lifted her from the crib and carried her to the bed. She started to cry even harder when I picked her up, her whole body tensing beneath my hands, her face going a brilliant crimson, as if she were about to pop. I was still surprised by her weight; I hadn't thought a baby could be so heavy, and there was a peculiar denseness about her, too, as if she were full of water. Her head was huge and round; it seemed to take up half her body.

Sarah extended her arms toward me, lifting the baby from my hands, a pained expression on her face.

"Shhh," she said. "Amanda. Shhh."

The teddy bear was sitting beside her, its back to the headboard, its little black paws reaching out, as if it also had wanted to comfort the crying infant. Sarah held Amanda in the crook of her arm and with her free hand unbuttoned her pajama top, exposing her left breast.

I turned away, walked back toward the crib, and looked out the window. I was still embarrassed by the sight of Sarah nursing Amanda. It gave me a creepy feeling, the thought of the baby sucking fluid out of her. It seemed unnatural, horrid; it made me think of leeches.

I gazed down at the front yard. It was empty: Jacob and his truck had disappeared. The day was still, beautiful, a postcard of winter. Sunlight shimmered off frozen surfaces; the trees laid thick, precise shadows across the snow. The gutters on the garage were swaybacked with icicles, and I made a mental note to knock them off the next time I went outside.

When my eyes strayed upward from the icicles, they discovered, on the very peak of the garage, the dark outline of a large black bird. My hand moved involuntarily toward my forehead.

"There's a crow on the garage roof," I said.

Sarah didn't respond. I massaged the skin above my eyebrows. It was perfectly smooth; the bump had left no scar. The baby was making a cooing sound behind me while she nursed, steady and insistent.

After a minute or so Sarah called my name. "Hank?" she said softly.

I watched the crow hop back and forth along the garage roof's snowy peak. "Yes?"

"I thought up a plan while I was in the hospital."

"A plan?"

"For making sure Lou doesn't tell."

I turned to face her. My shadow, framed in the window's square of sunlight, fell gigantically across the bedroom floor, my head looking monstrous on my shoulders, like a pumpkin. Sarah was bent over Amanda, smiling in an exaggerated manner—her eyebrows raised high on her forehead; her nostrils flared; her lips parted, showing her teeth. The baby ignored her, frantically sucking at her breast. When Sarah turned toward me, the smile dropped from her face.

"It's kind of silly," she said, "but if we do it right, it might work."

I came over and sat at the foot of the bed. Sarah turned back to Amanda, stroked the baby's cheek with her fingertips.

"Yes," she whispered. "You're a hungry little girl, aren't you?" Amanda's lips worked eagerly at her nipple.

"Go on," I said.

"I want you to tape him confessing to Pederson's murder."

I stared at her. "What're you talking about?"

"That's my plan," she said. "That's how we're going to keep him from turning you in." She grinned at me, as if she were very pleased with this idea.

"Is this supposed to be funny?"

"Of course not," she said, surprised.

"Why would he confess to something he didn't do?"

"You and Jacob invite him out for drinks; you get him drunk; you take him back to his house, and you start joking about confessing to the police. You take turns pretending to do it—you first, Jacob second, Lou last—and when Lou does it, you tape him."

I assumed that there had to be something logical embedded within what she'd just proposed, and I tried for the next moment or so to find it.

"That's insane," I said finally. "There's no way it would work."

"Jacob helps you. That's the key. If Jacob eggs him on, then he'll do it."

"But even if we could get him to say it—and I doubt we could—it wouldn't mean anything. No one would ever believe it."

"That doesn't matter," she said. "We just need something to scare him with. If we tape him saying it, and we let him hear it, there's no way he'll turn you in."

Amanda finished nursing. Sarah took a dish towel from the night table and draped it across her shoulder. Then she picked up the baby and began to burp her. She pulled her pajama top back across her breast but didn't button it. They were the pajamas I'd given her for Christmas. She hadn't fit into them then—her stomach had been too large—so this was the first time I'd seen them on her. They were flannel, white with little green flowers. I could remember buying them at the mall in Toledo, could remember wrapping them in a box on Christmas Eve and then her opening them the next morning, holding them up against her swollen belly, but it all seemed as though it had happened ages ago. We'd come so far since then, so much had happened—I'd lied, stolen, murdered—and now that past, so close in a purely temporal sense, was utterly irrecoverable. It was a terrifying thing to recognize, the gulf that separated the two of us then—opening our presents together on the floor beneath the tree, a fire burning on the hearth—from the two of us now, sitting here in our bedroom, plotting how to blackmail Lou and frighten him into silence. And we'd crossed it not in any great leap but in little, nearly imperceptible steps, so that we never really noticed the distance we were traveling. We'd edged our way into it; we'd done it without changing.

"All you have to do is get him to understand that you and Jacob could claim he killed Pederson just as easily as he could claim you did it. If you make him think that Jacob would side with you, he'll never risk bringing in the police."

"This is dumb, Sarah."

She glanced up from the baby. "What harm could come from trying it?"

"Jacob won't want to help."

"Then you'll have to make him. It won't work without him."

"He'd be betraying his best friend."

"You're his brother, Hank. He'll do it if you show him how important it is. You just have to get him so he's as scared of Lou as we are." She glanced up at me, pushed her hair away from her face. There were hollows beneath her eyes, dark, bruised-looking circles. She needed to sleep. "It won't end when Lou has his money. He'll be hanging over us for the rest of our lives. The only way it'll stop is if we can make him fear us as much as we fear him."

"You're saying the tape'll make him fear us?"

"I know it will."

I didn't say anything. I still couldn't imagine Lou confessing to killing Pederson, not even in jest.

"We should at least try, Hank, shouldn't we? We can't lose anything by trying."

She was right, of course, or at least it seemed as if she was. But how could I have known then all the loss to which her simple plan would ultimately lead? I could see no risk: if it worked, it would save us, and if it didn't, we'd just be right back where we started.

"All right," I said. "I'll talk to Jacob. I'll see if I can get him to do it."

I TOOK the next day off so I could help Sarah with the baby.

In the afternoon, while the two of them were napping, I slipped out and bought a tape recorder. I went to Radio Shack, in Toledo. I told the salesman that I needed something tiny and uncomplicated. It was for dictation, I said, for recording business letters while I drove to and from work. He sold me one that was a little smaller than a deck of cards. It fit snugly, almost invisibly, into my front shirt pocket, and its record button was extra large, so that you could feel it through the fabric and know which one to press without taking it out to look.

Sarah and the baby were still asleep when I got home. I checked on them quickly, then went into the bathroom and practiced turning the tape recorder on and off in front of the mirror. I did it over and over again—a slow, casual gesture—

my right hand scratching briefly at my chest, my palm holding the machine in place while my index finger pushed down the button. It looked good, I thought; it was something Lou would never notice.

Later, after Sarah woke up, I tried it out on her. She was in bed, with Amanda in her arms.

"What's the first thing you're going to buy with the money?" I asked, and when she glanced up at me, I scratched at my chest, turning on the tape recorder.

She bit her lip, debating. In the silence, I could just barely make out a soft humming sound coming from my pocket.

"A bottle of champagne," she said. "Good champagne. We'll drink it, get a little tipsy, and then we'll make love on the money."

"On the money?"

"That's right." She smiled. "We'll spread it out across the floor, make ourselves a bed of hundred-dollar bills."

I took the tape recorder from my pocket and rewound it to the beginning. "Look what I bought," I said. I handed it to Sarah.

"Does it work?"

I grinned. "Press the play button."

She found the button, pushed it in.

"A bottle of champagne," her voice began, the words emerging one after the other with incredible clarity. "Good champagne. We'll drink it, get a little tipsy . . ."

THURSDAY evening, around five-thirty, I telephoned Jacob from the feedstore and suggested we visit the cemetery together, finally fulfilling our obligation to the ghost of our father. He declined at first, saying he was busy, but eventually I managed to badger him into it. We agreed to meet at quarter till six, on the street in front of Raikley's.

By the time I emerged from the feedstore, he was already

waiting for me on the sidewalk with Mary Beth. He looked even more overweight than normal, his face puffy, swollen. His jacket was so tight that he couldn't drop his arms to his sides. He kept them extended, away from his body, like an overstuffed doll. The sun had set, and it was dark out. The streetlights cast weak circles of pale yellow light across the pavement at regular intervals along the road. A few cars moved by, and down in front of the pharmacy a cluster of teenagers loitered, talking and laughing loudly. Other than that the town was quiet.

Jacob and I crossed the street toward St. Jude's, stepped up onto the opposite sidewalk, and moved into the parking lot. Our boots crunched in the gravel. Mary Beth jogged on ahead of us toward the cemetery.

"I've been thinking about the money," Jacob said, "and I think maybe we were fated to get it."

"Fated?" I asked.

He nodded. He was eating a hunk of chocolate cake wrapped in a piece of aluminum foil, taking great bites out of it as we walked, and he had to wait, chewing and swallowing, before he could speak.

"There are so many things that might've gone some other way," he said. "If it'd just been chance, then it never would've happened. It's like it was meant to, like we were chosen."

I smiled at him. It seemed like a romantic idea. "What things?"

"Everything." He listed them off on his fingers. "If the plane had flown another mile, it would've crashed out in the open and been discovered right from the start. If the fox hadn't crossed exactly in front of us, and we hadn't crashed, and Mary Beth hadn't been there or hadn't jumped from the truck and chased it, and the fox hadn't run right next to the plane, we never would've found it. If you'd left the bag inside after checking on the pilot, we would've come into town and told the sheriff without even knowing about the money. It just goes on and on."

We'd reached the cemetery's chain-link gate now, and we stopped there, as if hesitant to go inside. The gate was merely ornamental; it blocked the path but nothing more. There was no fence attached to it. Mary Beth sniffed at it for a moment, lifted his leg briefly against its supporting post, then stepped off the path and entered the cemetery by himself.

"But why is that fate?" I asked Jacob. It seemed more like luck to me, and it was a little frightening to hear him list off all the things that had gone our way. I couldn't escape the thought that everything balances out in the end: if it was luck that was bringing us through our present difficulties, it was bound to turn on us before we were through.

"Don't you see?" he said. "It's too arbitrary to be just chance. It seems like there has to be something determining it, a plan helping us along."

"God's?" I asked, smiling. I waved at the church.

He shrugged. "Why not?"

"And what about Pederson? Was that part of this grand plan?"

He nodded emphatically. "If he'd come at any other time that day, he would've found the plane. There would've been our tracks. We would've been caught."

"But why have him come at all? If you were the one making the plan, wouldn't you have just omitted him?"

He thought about that, finishing off his cake. He licked at the aluminum foil a few times, then balled it up and tossed it into the snow. "Maybe it's important for something which hasn't happened yet," he said, "something we don't know about."

I didn't say anything. I'd never heard him attempt to philosophize before. I wasn't sure what he was getting at.

"It's going on right now, too, I bet," he said. "Things are

happening in just the right sequence, one after the other, falling into place so that it all works out for us."

He grinned at me. He seemed to be in an exceptionally good mood, and for some reason this irritated me. It reeked of complacency. He had no concept of the trouble we were in.

"You're happy we found the money, then?" I asked.

He hesitated, as if confused by the question. He seemed to think that there was a trick embedded in it. "Aren't you?"

"I'm asking you."

He waited a second, then nodded. "Definitely," he said, his voice serious. "Without a doubt."

"Why?"

He answered quickly, as if this were something he'd already considered many times. "I can get back the farm now."

He looked at me when he said it, to see my response, but I kept silent, my face expressionless. In a few minutes I was going to ask him to betray his only friend: it didn't seem like the right moment to inform him that he couldn't remain in Ashenville.

"And I can have a family," he went on. "I wouldn't have before. I need to find someone like Sarah, and—"

"Like Sarah?" I asked, startled.

"Someone aggressive. You needed that, too. You were too shy to find someone on your own; she had to come and get you."

I was a little bewildered to hear him say this, but at the same time I recognized it as true. I nodded at him, prodding him on.

"Without the money," he said, "no one was ever going to come and get me. I'm fat"—he patted at his stomach—"and poor. I was going to grow old and be alone. But now that I'm rich, all that'll change, someone'll come get me for the money."

"You want someone to love you just for your money?"

"I've never had anyone, Hank. All my life. If I can get someone now, I'm not going to care why she's with me. I'm not proud."

I leaned against the cemetery gate, watching him tell me this. His face and voice were very serious. This wasn't modesty or self-deprecatory humor; there was no sense of irony whatsoever. It was the truth, cold and shiny as a bone freshly stripped of its flesh: this was how Jacob saw his life.

I didn't know how to react. I stared down at his massive boots for a moment, embarrassed, then said, "Whatever happened to Mary Beth?"

He adjusted his glasses on his nose, squinted past me into the cemetery. "She's in there."

"She's dead?"

"Dead?" he said. "What do you mean? She was just here, you saw her."

"Not the dog. Mary Beth Shackleton, from high school."

Jacob frowned. "She's married, I think. Last I heard she'd moved to Indiana."

"She liked you without the money, didn't she?"

He laughed, shaking his head. "I never told you the truth about that, Hank. I was always too ashamed." He didn't look my way while he spoke; he stared off beyond me into the cemetery. "She dated me as a joke. It was a bet she made with some of her friends. They all chipped in and bet her a hundred dollars that she wouldn't go steady with me for a month. So she did."

"You knew this?"

"Everybody did."

"And you went along with it?"

"It wasn't as bad as it seems. It was mean of her to do, but she did it in a nice way. We never kissed or touched or anything like that, but we walked around a lot together, and talked, and when the month was up she still stopped to say hello to me when we passed, which she didn't have to do."

I was shocked. "And you named your dog after her?"

He shrugged, smiling strangely. "I liked the name."

It was absurd, of course, the whole thing. I felt sorry for him, and ashamed.

A car honked somewhere farther down in town, and we both paused, listening. The night was very quiet. The dog had reappeared out of the cemetery and was sitting now beside the gate.

"I'm thirty-three," Jacob said, "and I've never even kissed a woman. That's not right, Hank."

I shook my head. I couldn't think of anything to say.

"If my being rich'll change that," he said, "then fine. I don't care if it's just for the money."

We fell silent after that. Jacob had spoken too much; we both seemed to sense this. An awkwardness hung about us like a mist, so thick that we could hardly see each other through it.

I unlatched the gate, and we passed into the cemetery. Mary Beth bounded off ahead of us.

"Sort of spooky, isn't it?" Jacob asked, his voice loud, brave, a bulldozer straining to push his embarrassment aside. He made a moaning sound, like a ghost, then laughed, short and sharp, trying to twist it into a joke.

But he was right; it was spooky. The church was dark, empty; the sky clouded over, its stars hidden, its moon just a vague shimmer above the horizon. What little illumination there was to guide our way drifted in from the surrounding town, entering the cemetery weakly, more glow than light, not strong enough even to pull shadows from our bodies. The darkness among the graves was so complete it was like something liquid; walking through the gate, I felt as if I were descending into a lake. I watched Mary Beth disappear ahead of us, leaving only the sound of the tags on his collar, clinking lightly together whenever he moved, to prove that he was there at all.

We found our parents' graves by memory rather than sight. They'd been buried in the very center of the cemetery, just to the right of the path. When Jacob and I got there, we stepped off into the snow and stood before the tombstone. It was just a simple square of granite, serving as marker for both of them. Etched into it were the words

JACOB HANSEL MITCHELL	JOSEPHINE McDONNEL MITCHELL
December 31, 1927–	May 5, 1930–
December 2, 1980	December 4, 1980

Twofold is our mourning

Below this were two blank spots, sanded smooth. These were for Jacob and me: our father had bought four plots before he died, to ensure that we might all be buried together one day.

I stood perfectly still before the grave, staring intently at the stone, but I wasn't thinking about our parents, wasn't remembering their presence, or grieving for their loss. I was thinking instead about Jacob. I was searching for a way to enlist his aid in our plot against Lou. That was why we were at the cemetery tonight: I was reminding him of the bond we shared as brothers.

I waited several minutes, letting the silence build around us. I was wearing my overcoat, a suit and tie, and the cold bit at me, the wind pressing through my pant legs like an icy hand, firm, insistent, as if it wanted me to step forward. My eyes moved furtively from the stone to the dark shape of the church, then sideways toward Jacob, who stood beside me, swaddled in the tightness of his jacket—silent, massive, immovable—a giant red Buddha. I wondered briefly what he was thinking about, standing there so still: perhaps some private memory of our parents, or of Mary Beth Shackleton, or of the mysteries of fate, and the gift it'd brought him, the doors it promised to open now, finally, when his life already seemed so far along. Perhaps he wasn't thinking of anything at all.

"Do you miss them?" I asked.

Jacob answered slowly, as if rousing himself from sleep. "Who?"

"Mom and Dad."

There was a brief silence while he thought this over. I could hear the packed snow beneath his boots creaking as he shifted his weight from foot to foot.

"Yes," he said, his voice sounding flat in the cold air, honest. "Sometimes."

When I didn't say anything, he went on, as if to explain himself. "I miss the house," he said. "I miss going over there on the weekends to eat dinner, and then sitting around afterwards to play cards and drink. And I miss talking with Dad. He was someone who listened when I spoke. I don't know anyone like that anymore."

He fell silent. I could tell that he wasn't quite through, though, so I just stood there, staring up at the sky, waiting for him to go on. Off to the west, above the church's spire, I could see the blinking lights of two planes moving slowly toward each other. For a second it looked like they were about to collide, but then they passed. It was only a trick of perspective; up in the air they were miles apart.

"Dad would've understood what we're doing," Jacob said. "He knew the importance of money. 'It's all that matters,' he used to say, 'the blood of life, the root of happiness.' "

He glanced toward me. "Do you remember him saying stuff like that?"

"Only toward the end. When he was losing the farm."

"I kept hearing him say it, and it seemed so simple that I never really listened. It wasn't until just recently that I began to understand. I thought he was talking about how you can't eat without money, or buy clothes, or keep warm, but that's not it at all. He was talking about how you can't be happy without money. And not a little money either, not just enough to get by; he meant a lot of money. He was talking about being rich."

"They were never rich," I said.

"And they were never happy, either."

"Never?"

"No. Especially not Dad."

I tried quickly to retrieve an image of my father happy. I could picture him laughing, but it was drunken laughter, shallow, giddy, absurd. I couldn't come up with anything else.

"And they got sadder and sadder as their money ran out," Jacob said, "until finally, when it was gone, they killed themselves."

I glanced at him, startled. Suicide had always been Sarah's theory; I'd never heard my brother even consider it before.

"You don't know that," I said. "They were drinking. It was an accident."

He shook his head. "The night before it happened, Mom called me on the phone. She said she just wanted to say good night. She was drunk, and she made me promise her that I'd get married someday, that I wouldn't die without having had a family of my own."

He paused, and I waited, but he didn't go on.

"And?" I asked.

"Don't you see? She'd never called me before. That was the first and only time. Dad was the one who always made the calls. She telephoned me that night because she knew, because they'd just finished planning it out, and she realized she wouldn't see me again."

I tried quickly to analyze what he'd just told me, to search for holes. I didn't want to believe him. "They would've done it differently if they were committing suicide," I said. "They wouldn't have driven into a truck."

He shook his head. He'd already thought this through on

his own; he could anticipate my questions. "They had to make it look like an accident. Dad knew we'd need his life insurance to cover all his debts. It was the only way he could think to pay them off. The farm was mortgaged—they had nothing left of any value except their lives."

"But they could've killed the truck driver, Jacob. Why wouldn't they just've driven into a tree?"

"Driving into a tree still looks like suicide. They couldn't risk that."

I tried to imagine our parents sitting in the darkness at the bottom of the exit ramp, waiting for a pair of headlights to appear before them, and then, when they finally did and my father shifted into first, their final hurried words to each other, things they'd planned out earlier that day, assertions of love, the last parts of which would be lost in the rumble of the approaching truck, the horribly impotent screech of brakes before the impact. I balanced this image against another, the one I'd held in my head for the past seven years, that of them drunk, laughing, the radio thumping out music, a window down to let in a cold rush of air and the accompanying illusion of sobriety, the two of them oblivious of their error until that final, irrevocable moment when the truck loomed before them, impossibly large, its huge mass of metal towering over the hood of their car. I tried to decide which I preferred—their knowledge or their ignorance—but they both seemed too pitiful, too sad, for me to accept. I didn't know which to choose.

"Why didn't you tell me this before?" I asked.

Jacob took several seconds to search for an answer. "I didn't think you'd want to know."

I nodded; he was right. Even now I didn't want to know, didn't want to pick through what he'd just said, to weigh its various particulars and decide if I believed them. An onslaught of conflicting emotions swept over me—jealousy that our mother had contacted Jacob that last night rather than myself; surprise that he'd managed to keep the whole thing so secret from me for all this time; grief over the possibility that our parents—good, hardworking people—could've been driven by their need for money to such a hopeless act, literally sacrificing their lives and risking that of an innocent bystander to save themselves and their children from their debts.

Jacob started to stamp his feet, trying to stay warm. I could tell that he wanted to leave.

"Jacob," I said.

He turned toward me, looked me in the face. "What?"

Mary Beth moved around us in the darkness, clinking, like a tiny ghost wrapped in chains.

"Sarah knows about the money. I had to tell her after Lou came looking for it."

"That's all right," he said. "She's probably the safest of us all."

I shrugged. "The thing is, she's terrified of Lou. She's scared he'll end up getting you and me put in jail for killing Pederson." I waved off to the left, toward Pederson's grave. Jacob followed my gesture with his eyes.

"Lou's okay," he said. "He just wants to make sure you give him the money. Once you do that he'll leave you alone."

"I'm not going to give him the money. Sarah and I talked about it, and we agreed we shouldn't."

Jacob stared at me for several seconds, pondering the implications of this. "Then I guess we'll see if there's anything behind his bluff."

I shook my head. "It's not going to come to that. We're going to do something first."

He glanced at me, a quizzical look on his face. "What do you mean?"

I told him about Sarah's plan. He listened all the way to the end, his shoulders hunched in his jacket, his hands sunk deep in its pockets.

When I finished, he asked, "Why're you telling me this?"

"I need your help," I said. "It won't work unless you help."

He scuffed at the snow with his boot, frowning. "I don't think I want to do it. Lou isn't a danger."

"He is a danger, Jacob. He always will be."

"It's not like—"

"No," I said, "think about it. Even if I were to give him his split, it wouldn't stop. There's no statute of limitations on murder. Ten years from now, when he's wasted his share, he'll be able to track you down and blackmail you with what he knows."

Jacob didn't say anything.

"Are you willing to live with that?" I asked. "Year after year, just waiting for him to come and find you?"

"He wouldn't do that."

"He's already done it to me. He's done it twice. I'm not going to let him do it again."

Mary Beth reappeared from the darkness, wagging his tail, his breath coming fast and hoarse, as if he'd been chasing something. He jumped up on Jacob, and Jacob pushed him down.

"You had your chance, Jacob. You were responsible for him, and you let it get out of hand. Now I'm going to take responsibility."

"You're blaming me?"

"He found out about Pederson through you, didn't he? That's what got us into this position."

"I didn't tell him about Pederson." It seemed very important to him that I believe this, but I ignored it. "If it's anyone's fault," he said bitterly, "it's yours. You were the first one to act suspicious. You soured all our relations with it. Lou's only acting like you expected him to right from the start."

I turned to face him. I could tell from the tautness of his voice that I'd hurt his feelings. "I'm not blaming you, Jacob.

I'm not saying it's anybody's fault. It just happened, and now we have to deal with it." I smiled at him. "It's fate, maybe."

He frowned down at the grave.

"It's either this or burn the money."

"You're not going to burn the money. That's an empty threat."

It was true, of course, and I nodded. "It's not that big of a deal, Jacob. It's not like I'm asking you to kill him."

He didn't respond to that. He flipped up the collar of his jacket so that it covered the lower half of his face, then turned from the grave and glanced back across the parking lot toward Main Street. I followed his gaze. I could see Raikley's from there, could see my office window. I could see the town hall, the post office, the grocery store. Everything was quiet.

"I need your help," I said.

"I can't trick him like that. He'd never forgive me."

"He's going to be drunk, Jacob. He's not going to remember how it happened." I realized as soon as I said it that this was the hook I needed. It wasn't the idea of betraying Lou that bothered my brother, it was Lou's knowing about it. "You can pretend to be surprised if you want," I continued quickly, reeling him in, "like you didn't know about the tape recorder. You can pretend that it was all my doing, that I was tricking both of you."

Jacob debated for a second. "It would only be a threat?" he asked. "We'd never actually use the tape?"

I nodded. "It's just to make sure he doesn't turn us in." I could tell he was wavering, so I put my finger on the scale. "You told me that if it came down to it, and you had to make a choice, you'd choose me."

He didn't say anything.

"It's come down to it now, Jacob. Are you going to stand by your word?"

He was silent for a long time, watching me. The dog rolled in the snow at his feet, grunting, but we both ignored him. Jacob wrapped his arms around his stomach, stared down at our parents' headstone. My eyes had adjusted to the darkness, and I could make out his face now, could see his eyes behind his glasses. He looked cold and anxious. Finally he nodded.

I tried to think of something to say, something reassuring.

"Why don't you come for dinner tonight?" I asked him, surprising myself. "Sarah's cooking lasagna." Even now I'm not sure why I said it, whether it was out of pity for him or fear that if he were to go home alone that night he might call Lou and warn him about our plot.

Jacob continued to stare down at the grave. I could see what was happening inside him: his core passivity, his traditional mechanism for dealing with stress, was rising to the surface, and I knew now that if I could just keep ahold of him, I'd be able to make him do whatever I wanted. I took a step toward the parking lot. Mary Beth came up out of the snow, ears erect. He wagged his tail, thumping it against Jacob's pants.

"Come on," I said. "She uses Mom's recipe. It'll be just like old times." Then I put my hand on his arm and turned him back toward the path.

SARAH was in the kitchen when we got home.

"Jacob's come for dinner," I yelled as we stepped into the entranceway.

Sarah leaned out through the doorway to give us a wave. She was wearing an apron and had a metal spatula in her hand. Jacob, looking large and sheepish, returned her wave, but he was a second too late: she'd already disappeared back into the kitchen.

I took him upstairs to the bedroom. Mary Beth followed at our heels. The room was dark, the curtains pulled. When I flicked on the light, I saw that the bed was unmade. Sarah, though she'd recovered with remarkable rapidity from her delivery, was still a little run-down, and she'd spent much of the previous six days prone beneath the sheets, the baby sleeping at her side.

I shut the door behind us, guided Jacob toward the night table. I sat him down on the edge of the mattress, then picked up the phone, carefully untangled its cord, and placed it in his lap.

"Call Lou," I said.

He stared at the phone. It was an old one, black plastic with a rotary dial. He didn't seem to want to touch it. "Now?" he asked.

I nodded. I sat down beside him, leaving about a foot of space between us. We were on my side of the bed, facing the windows. The sound of pots clinking together came faintly up the stairs. Mary Beth moved about the room, sniffing. He inspected first the bathroom, then the crib. When he reached the bed, he stuck his head beneath it. I pushed him away with my foot.

"That was our crib," I said to Jacob. I pointed toward the crib. "Dad built it."

Jacob seemed unimpressed. "What do I say?" he asked.

"Tell him I invited you two out for drinks tomorrow night, to celebrate Amanda's birth. Tell him I'm buying."

"What about the money?"

I debated this for a second. "Tell him I agreed to split it up," I said, thinking it might lower Lou's guard. "Tell him we'll get it next weekend."

Jacob shifted his weight, and the phone wobbled in his lap. He set one of his hands on top of it. "Have you thought about the farm yet?" he asked.

I stared at him. I didn't want to talk about the farm right now. Mary Beth jumped onto the bed and settled down behind Jacob, right up against his back. He put his head on my pillow.

"Not really," I said.

"I was kind of hoping you would've made a decision by now."

He was going to trap me into it, I realized suddenly; he was going to make the farm his price for Lou's betrayal. The teddy bear was lying on the floor beside the bed, and—to fill the silence that my reluctance to answer created—I picked it up and wound its key. Its music started to play. The dog lifted his head to watch.

"Jacob," I said, "are you blackmailing me?"

He gave me a startled look. "What do you mean?"

"Are you saying you won't help me unless I promise you the farm?"

He thought about it; then he nodded. "I guess so."

The bear sang, *"Dormez-vous? Dormez-vous? Sonnez les matines. Sonnez les matines."*

"I do something for you," Jacob said, "then you do something for me. That's fair, isn't it?"

"Yes," I said. "I suppose that's fair."

"So you'll help me get it back?"

The bear's music gradually slowed. I waited until it stopped, until the room was absolutely still, and then—knowing full well that I was making a promise to my brother that I never intended to fulfill—I nodded.

"I'll do whatever you ask me to," I said.

As Sarah and I were putting dinner on the table—lasagna, garlic bread, and salad—Jacob excused himself to go to the bathroom. The bathroom was down the front hallway, beneath the stairs, and I followed him with my eyes as he lumbered out of the kitchen. I watched him until he disappeared inside.

"He's going to do it?" Sarah whispered, gesturing with her knife toward the bathroom. We were standing over the table together, Sarah cutting the bread while I poured out two glasses of wine. Sarah was drinking apple juice with her meal; until she finished nursing, she wasn't allowed to have any alcohol.

"We just called," I said. "We're picking up Lou tomorrow at seven."

"Did you listen to their conversation?"

I nodded. "I sat right next to him."

"He didn't give him any hints?"

"No. He said exactly what I told him to."

"And he doesn't mind doing it?"

I hesitated before I answered, and Sarah glanced up at me. "He made me promise to help him buy back the farm."

"Your father's farm?"

I nodded.

"I thought we already agreed—"

"He didn't give me a choice, Sarah. It was either that or he wouldn't help us."

The toilet flushed, and we both looked toward the hallway. "But you're not really planning on letting him stay, are you?" she asked.

The bathroom door opened, and I turned from her, taking the jug back toward the refrigerator.

"No," I said, walking away. "Of course not."

Amanda was sleeping in the family room, in her Portacrib. Sarah brought her out for Jacob to see before we ate. He didn't seem to know how to act around the baby. He blushed when Sarah made him take her in his arms and held her out, away from his body, as if someone had spilled something on her and he was afraid to get himself dirty. She started to cry a little as soon as he took her into his hands, and Sarah had to soothe her, whisking her quickly back to the family room.

"She's so tiny," Jacob mumbled, as if he hadn't expected this. That was all he could think to say.

It was a peculiar dinner. At first it appeared that only Sarah would manage to enjoy herself. She looked pretty, alluring, and seemed to know it. Her body was already reclaiming the tightness it had lost in her pregnancy, and though I knew that she must have been exhausted—the baby had not let her sleep for more than four hours straight since they'd returned from the hospital—she still looked vibrant, healthy. She rubbed my calf with her foot while we ate.

Jacob, in his shyness around her, focused on his food. He ate rapidly, gorging himself, his forehead breaking out into a sweat. Everything about him hinted at his social discomfort—he exuded it like a miasma—and after a while it began to feel contagious. I, too, started having difficulty finding things to say, started overthinking before I responded to his or Sarah's questions, so that my answers came out sounding unnaturally terse and formal, as if I were angry with them and afraid to show it.

It was the wine that saved the evening. Sarah seemed to sense it first: each time Jacob or I emptied a glass, she stood up and refilled it for us. I'm not a drinker—I've never enjoyed the disinhibiting effect of alcohol, that gradual slipping of self-control—but tonight it worked exactly as I'd always been told it was meant to, as an anodyne, a lubricant, a builder of bridges. The more I drank, the easier it became for me to talk with Jacob, and the more he drank, the easier it became for him to talk with Sarah.

My inebriation, as it grew, filled me with an unexpected feeling of hope. It was a physical sensation, something warm and liquid that spread outward from my chest—from my heart, I remember thinking—to the tips of my fingers and toes. I began to wonder if my brother was not so unreachable as I'd always imagined. Perhaps it was still possible to reclaim him, to invite him into my family and bind him to my heart. He was across the table from me now, saying something to Sarah, almost flirting with her, in fact, but shyly, like a child with a teacher, and at the sight of it I felt a surge of love for the two of them, an overwhelming desire to make things come out right. I would help Jacob buy some land out west, I decided, in Kansas or Missouri; I'd help him set it up just like our father's farm, help him build a replica of the house we'd been raised in, and it would be a place to which Sarah and Amanda and I could return over the years, a respite from our travels across the globe, a surrogate home for us to leave and then come back to, bearing gifts for Jacob and his family.

I watched them talk and laugh with each other, and though I knew I was drunk, sensed it in everything I said and did and thought, I still couldn't help but believe that everything was going to be okay now, that it was all going to work out exactly as we planned.

As we were finishing dinner, the baby started to cry. Sarah took her upstairs to nurse while I did the dishes. By the time she returned—having put Amanda to sleep in her crib—I'd finished, and Jacob was in the bathroom again.

We'd decided to pass the evening playing Monopoly. Sarah began laying out the board on the kitchen table while I sponged down the counter. I'd stopped drinking toward the end of the meal, and now the wine was settling on me like a heavy cloak, so that everything I did seemed to require more effort than it ought to. I was beginning to think that what I wanted to do was go upstairs and fall asleep.

When I finished with the counter, I went over to the table and sat down. Sarah was dealing out the money. She went in ascending order—ones, fives, tens, twenties, fifties. When she got to the hundreds, she glanced up at me, smiling mischievously.

"You know what we should do?" she asked.

"What?"

She flicked her finger at the tray full of money. "We should use real hundreds."

"Real hundreds?" I was so tired, I didn't understand what she meant.

She grinned. "We could bring down one of the packets."

I stared at her, thinking this through. The idea of removing the money from its hiding place gave me a distinctly unsafe feeling, an irrational mixture of panic and fear. I shook my head.

"Come on. It'll be fun."

"No," I said. "I don't want to."

"But why not?"

"I don't think we should take the risk."

"What risk? We're just going to use it to play the game."

"I don't want to disturb it," I said. "It seems like it'd be bad luck."

"Oh, Hank. Don't be silly. When'll you have another chance to play Monopoly with real hundred-dollar bills?"

I started to answer her, but Jacob's voice interrupted me. He'd returned from the bathroom; neither of us had heard him approach. "It's hidden in the house?" he said. He was standing at the edge of the kitchen, looking tired and overfed. I frowned at Sarah.

"Some of it," she said. "Just a couple packets."

Jacob shuffled toward his chair. "So why don't we use it?" he asked.

Sarah didn't say anything. She poured my brother another glass of wine. They were both waiting for me to speak. And what could I say? There was no reason not to do it, just my own amorphous suspicion that it was wrong, that in dealing with the money we should be painstakingly rigorous, treating it as something potent and malevolent, like a gun or a bomb. I couldn't think of a way to express this, though, and even if I had, it would've come out sounding silly. It's just a game, they would've said; we'll return it when we're through.

"All right." I sighed, slouching back in my chair, and Sarah ran upstairs to get a packet.

. . .

Jacob was the little dog, Sarah the top hat. I was the racing car. The thrill of the hundred-dollar bills wore off with surprising celerity, so that soon they seemed just like the other denominations we were playing with—rectangles of colored paper, a little larger, a little thicker than the others, but nothing more. We were using them for imaginary transactions, and this cheapened them somehow, robbed them of their value. They ceased to feel real.

The game took several hours, so it was almost midnight before we finished. We quit when I went bankrupt. Sarah and my brother agreed to call it a draw, but Jacob would've won. He had more properties, more houses and hotels, and a great big, messy pile of money. It wouldn't have been long before he ran her out of business.

I put the game away while Sarah gathered all the hundred-dollar bills together and carried them back upstairs.

I didn't realize how drunk my brother was until he stood up. He heaved himself out of his chair and took two weak-kneed steps toward the counter, his face looking panicked, his arms held out rigidly before him. It was as though he'd suddenly been transformed into some sort of thick-bodied marionette and someone else was now controlling his movements, dragging him across the room by invisible strings. He rested one of his huge hands on the counter and stared down at it, as if he were afraid it might jump away when he turned his head. He gave a short giggle.

"Why don't you stay here tonight?" I said.

He looked around at the table and chairs, the dishwasher, the sink, the stove. "Stay here?"

"In the guest room. Upstairs."

Jacob frowned at me. He'd never spent the night at our house before, not in all the years we'd lived there, and it seemed like the idea of doing so now made him nervous. He started to say something, but I interrupted him before his words emerged.

"You can't drive home like this. You're too drunk."

"What about Sarah?" he whispered loudly, glancing toward the hallway.

"It's all right," I said. "She won't mind."

I helped him upstairs, feeling like a child beside his oversized body, pushing against its soft mass, straining to guide it forward. Every now and then he let out another little laugh.

I put him in the guest room, across the hall from our bedroom. He sat down on the bed and fumbled with his shirt. I crouched on the floor in front of him and started to untie his boots. The dog had followed us upstairs. He sniffed at each piece of furniture in the room, then climbed up onto the bed and curled himself into a tight, compact ball.

When I got the boots off, I looked up to find Jacob staring in bewilderment at the bed's headboard.

"It's all right," I said. "I'm putting you to sleep."

"It's my bed."

I nodded. "You're sleeping here tonight."

"It's my bed," he said again, with more insistence. He reached out to touch the headboard, and I realized what he meant. He meant that it was the bed he'd slept in as a child.

"That's right," I said. "Dad brought it over here just before he died."

Jacob glanced hazily around the room. Nothing else in it belonged to him.

"It's a new mattress, though," I said. "The old one was all worn out."

He didn't seem to understand me. "It's in the guest room now," he said.

He stared at the headboard for another moment or so, then lifted his feet from the floor and eased himself down onto his back. The bed rocked like a boat. The dog lifted his head, seemed to frown at us. I watched Jacob close his eyes. He appeared to fall asleep instantly, his breathing deepening within seconds to a snore. His face went slack, and his jaw fell open, so that I could see his teeth. They seemed too large, too wide and thick, for his mouth.

"Jacob?" I whispered.

He didn't answer. His glasses were still on, and I stood up to take them off. I pulled them from his ears, folded them shut, and set them on the table beside the bed. His face looked much older without the glasses, years older than it really was. I bent and kissed him lightly on the forehead.

Across the hall, the baby started to cry.

Jacob's eyes flickered open. "Judas kiss," he whispered hoarsely.

Still leaning over him, I shook my head. "No. I'm just saying good night."

He struggled to bring me into focus but didn't seem to manage it. "I'm spinning," he said.

"It'll stop. Just wait it out."

He smiled at that, seemed to fight down a giggle, then suddenly turned serious. "You kissed me good night?" he asked. His voice slurred a bit.

"Yes."

He stared up at me, blinking. Then he nodded. "Good night," he said thickly.

When he closed his eyes, I backed quietly out of the room.

Across the hall, I found Sarah just climbing into bed. She'd soothed Amanda, and the baby was making a soft gurgling sound as she fell asleep in her crib.

The money was stacked in a pile on my dresser. After I got into my pajamas, I went over and picked it up.

"That was stupid, Sarah," I said. "I can't believe you did it."

She stared at me from the bed. She looked surprised, hurt. "I thought it would be fun," she said. Her hair was pinned up in a bun, like a schoolteacher's. She was naked except for a pair of panties.

"We don't touch the money," I said. "We agreed about that."

"But it was fun. Admit it. You had fun."

I shook my head. "It's how we'll get caught, taking out the money."

"It's not like I took it out of the house."

"We aren't going to touch it again, not until we leave."

She frowned across the room at me. I could tell that she thought I was being too hard, but I didn't care.

"Promise?" I asked.

She shrugged. "Fine."

I brought the stack of money over to the bed and began to count it. I was still a little drunk, though, and I kept losing track of the numbers.

"He didn't take any," Sarah said finally. "I already checked it."

I froze, startled. I hadn't realized why I was counting it.

LYING in bed, waiting to fall asleep, we whispered back and forth at each other.

"What do you think will happen to him?" Sarah asked.

"To Jacob?"

I sensed her nod in the darkness. We were both on our backs. All the lights were out, and the baby was asleep in her crib. Sarah had forgiven me for lecturing her.

"Maybe he'll buy a farm," I said.

I felt her body go tense beside me. "He can't buy the farm, Hank. If he stays—"

"Not my father's farm. Just any farm. Someplace out west maybe, in Kansas, or Missouri. We could help him set it up."

Even as I spoke, I realized it would never happen. It had

been the wine that had allowed me to hope for it earlier that evening, but now I was sobering up, seeing things as they actually were rather than as I wished them to be. Jacob knew nothing about agriculture: he'd have just as much of a chance succeeding as a farmer as he would becoming a rock star or an astronaut. It was simply childishness on his part to keep on dreaming of it, a willful sort of naïveté, a denial of who he was.

"Maybe he'll travel," I tried, but I couldn't picture that either—my brother climbing on and off planes, dragging suitcases through airports, checking into expensive hotels. None of it seemed possible.

"Whatever he does," I said, "things'll be better for him than they are now, don't you think?"

I rolled over onto my side, draping one of my legs across Sarah's body. "Of course," she said. "He'll have one point three million dollars. How could things help but be better?"

"What's he going to do with it, though?"

"Just spend it. Like us. That's what it's for."

"Spend it on what?"

"On anything he wants. A nice car, a beach house, fancy clothes, expensive meals, exotic vacations."

"But he's so alone, Sarah. He can't just buy all that for himself."

She touched my face, a soft caress. "He'll find somebody, Hank," she said. "He'll be okay."

I was tired, so I tried to let myself believe her, but I knew she was probably wrong. The money couldn't change things like that. It could make us richer, but nothing more. Jacob was going to remain fat and shy and unhappy for the rest of his life.

Sarah's fingers moved up my face, a shadow in the darkness above me, and I shut my eyes against them.

"Everybody's going to get what they deserve," she said.

. . .

SOMETIME before morning I awoke to the sound of someone moving through the house. I rose onto my elbow, my eyes focusing instantly. Sarah was sitting beside me, her back against the headboard, nursing Amanda. An icy wind was rattling the windows in their frames.

"Someone's in the house," I said.

"Shhh," she whispered, not looking up from the baby. She reached out with her free hand and touched me on my shoulder. "It's just Jacob. He's using the bathroom."

I listened for a bit, listened to the walls creak against the wind, listened to Amanda softly cooing as she drew the milk from Sarah's body. Then I lay back down. After another minute or so, I heard my brother pad heavily back down the hallway to his room. He groaned as he lowered himself onto his bed.

"See?" Sarah whispered. "Everything's okay."

She kept her hand on my shoulder until right before I fell asleep.

6

We picked up Lou just after seven and drove into Ashenville, to the Wrangler. The Wrangler was one of two taverns in town, each an exact replica of the other. Years before, it had sported a western theme, but all that remained of that now was its name and the huge, graffiti-ridden skull of a longhorn steer slung up above the doorway. The building was long and narrow and dark, with a bar running down one wall and a line of booths down the other. In the rear, through a pair of swinging doors, was a big, open room. There was a pool table here, some pinball machines, and a broken-down jukebox.

Things were relatively quiet when we arrived. There was a handful of older men at the bar, sitting alone with bottles of beer. A few of them seemed to know Lou, and they grinned hello. A young couple was seated in one of the booths, leaning toward each other across the table and whispering fiercely, as if they were fighting but afraid to make a scene.

We went into the rear, and Jacob and Lou set themselves up for a game of pool while I bought the drinks. I got a boilermaker for Lou, a beer for Jacob, and a ginger ale for myself.

Jacob lost to Lou, and I bought another round. This happened three more times before some people came back and we had to give up the pool table. We went up front then and sat down in one of the booths. By now it was after eight, and the place was getting busier.

I continued to buy the drinks. I told Lou my ginger ale was scotch and soda, and he laughed, calling it an accountant's drink. He wanted to buy me a shot of tequila, but, smiling, I refused.

It was interesting, watching him get drunk. His face took on a deep redness, and his eyes went watery, their pupils slowly sinking beneath a flat, glassy sheen. He started to use the bathroom between every round, and by nine o'clock the meanness had begun to unshroud itself, the petty spitefulness, the essential Lou. At odd moments he seemed to forget that I was buying him his drinks: he'd begin to call me Mr. Accountant, start his winking routine with Jacob, his sneers and giggles. Then, just as quickly, he'd bounce back, slap me on the arm, and all three of us would be the greatest of friends again, coconspirators, a gang of gentlemen thieves.

Whenever a fresh drink arrived, he'd make a toast, the same one each time. "Here's to the little lady," he'd say. "Blessings on her downy head."

The tape recorder was in my shirt pocket. I reached up and scratched at it every minute or so, obsessively, as if it were some sort of talisman and I were touching it for luck.

After we'd been drinking for about an hour, I turned to Lou and asked, "Would you really've told the sheriff if I hadn't agreed to split the money?"

We were alone; I'd given Jacob my wallet and sent him up to the bar to buy another round. Lou pondered the question, his head bowed. "I needed the money, Hank," he said solemnly.

"You couldn't wait till the summer?"

"I needed it right away."

"Five months? You couldn't have held on for five more months?"

He reached across the table and took a sip of Jacob's beer. There was only a little left, but he didn't finish it. He smiled weakly at me. "I told you how I had some gambling debts?"

I nodded.

"Well, I lost some of Nancy's savings."

"How much?"

"See, I knew I could afford to lose because I had the money from the plane coming, so I put some big bets on a couple of long shots. I thought that even if I got just one, I'd be all right." He gave a little, nervous-sounding laugh. "I didn't get one, though. I lost it all."

"How much?" I asked again.

"Seventeen thousand. A little more. It was from her mother's will."

I was stunned, silenced. I couldn't imagine betting that much money on a horse. I watched him finish off Jacob's beer.

"We're broke, Hank. We don't have anything. Not to buy food, not to pay the rent, not anything till I get ahold of those packets."

"You're saying you would've told?"

"I needed the money. It didn't seem fair, your keeping it all this time when it's obvious no one's looking for the plane."

"I want to know if you would've told," I said, leaning across the table toward him.

"If I say no"—he smiled—"you might back out on your promise."

"My promise?"

"To split it up."

I didn't say anything.

"I need the money, Hank. I can't get by without it."

"But let's say you hadn't found out about Pederson. What would you've done then?"

Lou pursed his lips. "I guess I would've begged you," he said. He thought about this for a second; then he nodded. "I would've gotten down on my knees and begged."

The bar was crowded now, pulsing with voices and laughter. Clouds of cigarette smoke hung in the air, mixing with the sour smell of beer. I could see Jacob across the way, paying the bartender.

"You think that would've worked?" Lou asked.

I tried for a second to imagine him down on his knees before me, begging for the money. In many ways it seemed more threatening than the idea of him blackmailing me. It would've called on things I considered virtues—pity, charity, empathy—rather than simple fear, and thus, when I refused him, as I would've had to, it would've been a judgment not of him but of me. It was what he was probably going to do after we got the tape, I realized, and the thought of this gave me a tired feeling in my head.

"No," I said. "Probably not."

"Then I guess it's a good thing I found out about Pederson, isn't it?"

My brother was returning to the booth, so I didn't answer. I just pushed the empty glasses off to the side of the table and said, "Here come the drinks."

Lou reached out and touched my wrist. His fingertips were cold from holding Jacob's glass. "I had to get the money, Hank," he whispered quickly. "You understand that, don't you? It's nothing personal."

I stared down at his hand. It was gripping my arm like a claw, and I had to resist the temptation to pull myself free. "Yes," I said. It seemed like a small thing to give him. "I understand."

Around nine-thirty, Lou rose to his feet and headed off, a little unsteadily, to use the bathroom again. I watched him until he was safely out of earshot. Then I turned to Jacob.

"Can you tell when he's solidly drunk?"

My brother's nose was running; the skin above his lip was shiny with snot. "I guess."

"I want him drunk enough so that he's not thinking straight, but not so much that he slurs his words."

Jacob sipped at his beer. His glasses were fogged up, but he didn't seem to notice.

"When he looks like he's going to start slurring, stand up and say you want to head back to his house, that you've got a bottle of whiskey in the truck."

"I still don't think—" Jacob started, but I silenced him with a touch of my hand. Lou had emerged from the bathroom, swaying a bit. He stumbled against a barstool, and when the young man on it glanced over his shoulder, Lou loudly accused him of trying to trip him.

"You think that's funny?" Lou asked. "You think you're some kind of comedian?"

The young man, full bearded and twice Lou's size, stared in astonishment at him. "What's funny?" He was too surprised to be angry yet.

Lou hitched up his belt. "Tripping people coming back from the can. Sneaking up on them for laughs."

The young man turned all the way around to face him. The bar started to quiet.

"Sit down, Lou," someone said from one of the nearby stools. "You're gonna get yourself killed." A few people laughed.

Lou glanced around the bar. "Mocking me," he said. "I could've fallen and cracked my head." He pointed his finger at the young man. "You'd have gotten a kick out of that, wouldn't you? A big kick."

The young man didn't say anything. He stared down at Lou's finger.

"I'll give you a kick," Lou said. "You want a kick? I'll give you a good solid kick."

"Listen, buddy," the young man said. "I think maybe you've had a few too—"

"Don't buddy me," Lou said.

The young man started to climb off his stool. Simultaneously, Jacob stood up.

"You're not my buddy," Lou said.

Jacob, given his size and relative lack of sobriety, moved with surprising agility across the room. I watched from the booth as he rested his hand on Lou's shoulder. Lou turned, his scowl changing instantly to a beaming smile. "You're my buddy," he said to my brother. He glanced at the bartender. "He's my buddy," he shouted. Then he waved over toward me in the booth. "He's my buddy, too."

Jacob shepherded him back across the bar. I ordered another round of drinks.

IT WAS eleven o'clock before my brother stood up and suggested that we head back to Lou's house.

The dog was waiting for us in the cab of the truck, looking cold and dejected. He didn't seem to want to climb into the rear, so Jacob had to pick him up and shove him, whimpering, back through the torn plastic window. Lou urinated against the side of the building, a long, steady hissing in the darkness.

I drove. I'd bought a bottle of whiskey that afternoon at the liquor store, and now I told Jacob to take it out and offer it to Lou. Lou accepted gladly.

It was one of the coldest nights of the year. There were no clouds. The moon was just rising, a thick, white sliver, like a slice of cantaloupe, sitting cocked against the edge of the horizon. Above it hung a brilliant infinity of stars, high and bright in the deep blackness of the sky. The road out of Ashenville was empty of traffic, and Jacob's one functioning headlight, the left one, made it look narrower than it actually was. As we drove, the wind whipped through the cab, buffeting us, tugging at our jackets, and cracking the plastic window back and forth behind our heads like a bullwhip.

I turned off the lights before I reached the house so that I wouldn't wake Nancy. I parked at the bottom of the driveway.

"Well?" Jacob asked. He was on the passenger side. Lou was sitting between us, slouched over a little, one hand on the dashboard. Jacob had to lean forward to see me.

"Let's go inside," I said. "Bring the bottle."

"That's right," Lou said. "Bring the bottle." He slapped me on my leg. "You're okay. You know that? You're not half bad."

We climbed out, leaving the dog in the truck, and walked up the driveway to the house. Jacob and I went into the living room and sat on the couch while Lou used the bathroom. We could hear him urinating through the open doorway. It seemed to go on for several minutes.

The living room was down a step from the entranceway. It was wide and shallow, with a dark green shag carpet. There were two upholstered chairs in it, a black leather couch, an old-looking TV, and a long, low coffee table cluttered with magazines. It was nicer than I would've expected, but not by much.

Lou went into the kitchen after he finished peeing and got us some glasses. When he returned, Jacob poured the whiskey. I wasn't used to drinking hard liquor, especially not straight, and it burned my throat as it went down. The smell of it reminded me of my father kissing me good night, his head appearing suddenly above my bed, bending closer and closer but always stopping just before he touched my forehead, as if he were afraid to wake me. Some nights I didn't open my eyes, and there would only be the sweet fragrance of the alcohol on his breath to indicate his presence, along with the creak of the floorboards as he came forward, bowed toward me, and then retreated from the room.

Lou sat in one of the upholstered chairs, on the opposite side of the coffee table. Neither he nor Jacob seemed like they wanted to talk, and I couldn't think of a way to begin on my own. I kept glancing toward my brother, willing him to help me, but he didn't respond. His eyes were puffy from the liquor, so that he seemed like he was about to fall asleep.

It was several minutes before anyone spoke. Then Lou chuckled to himself and asked Jacob if he knew what you called a man with no arms and no legs in a swimming pool.

"Bob," Jacob said, sending them both into laughter.

They started talking about a man I didn't know, a friend of Lou's who'd lost his arm in an accident on a construction site last summer. He'd been feeding brush into a wood chipper and had gotten dragged into the machine. Lou and Jacob debated whether or not the man should blame himself for the accident—Lou thought he should, that it could only have happened out of carelessness or stupidity, but Jacob disagreed. The man was working in an auto supply store now. He'd told Lou that his arm had weighed ten and a half pounds. He knew this because that was how much lighter he was after the accident.

I sat there, quietly working at my drink, the tape recorder a tiny weight against my chest. Jacob and Lou seemed to forget about my presence, to talk as if I weren't there, and it gave me a glimpse of their friendship that I'd never had before. There was something about their dialogue—the sparse gruffness of their statements, the lengthy silences between responses—that reminded me of the conversations I used to overhear between our father and his friends. It was how I'd always imagined men were supposed to speak with one another, and to hear my brother do so now threw him suddenly into a different light, made him, for perhaps the first time in my life, seem more mature, more worldly, than I was.

When I finished my drink, Jacob refilled it.

They started arguing about one of their fishing spots, Devil's Lake, and how it had gotten its name. Jacob said that it was shaped like a head with two horns, but Lou didn't believe him. The whiskey was beginning to make me feel very warm, and when I noticed this, when I stopped and thought it through, a little spasm of panic shot across my body, like the trilling of an alarm bell. To be drunk in this situation was to fail, I knew; I needed to think clearly, to choose my words and actions with precision.

I set my glass down on the coffee table and, concentrating, tried to find an entry into their conversation, tried to think of a question or a statement, something subtle, a little verbal push to redirect things toward Pederson and the money. I strained and strained, but my mind refused to help me. It kept veering back toward the man who'd lost his arm, kept offering guesses about how heavy my own arms were, weighing them in my lap.

Finally, in desperation, I simply said, "What if I were to confess?"

It came out loud, almost a shout, surprising all three of us. Jacob and Lou turned to stare at me.

"Confess?" Lou asked. He grinned at me. He was drunk, and I think he must've thought I was, too.

"Could you imagine that?" I said. "Me confessing?"

"Confessing to what?"

"To taking the money, to killing Pederson."

He continued to smile at me. "You're thinking about confessing?"

I shook my head. "I just want to know if you can imagine me doing it."

"Sure," he said. "Why not?"

"Can you?" I asked Jacob. He was sitting slouched beside me, looking down at his hands.

"I guess," he managed. It came out fast, like a squeak.

"How?"

Jacob gave me a baleful stare. He didn't want to have to answer.

"You'd turn state's evidence," Lou said, smiling. "You'd rat on us so they'd let you off."

"But what would I say?"

"The truth. That you smothered him with his scarf."

I felt Jacob stiffen on the couch beside me. Lou's knowing about the scarf could mean only one thing—that Jacob had told him how I'd killed the old man. Lou might've guessed in the beginning, but once the issue had been raised, my brother hadn't held anything back. I noted this in my head, filed it away. It was something I could deal with later.

"Pretend you're me," I said to Lou. "Pretend Jacob's the sheriff and you've just come into his office to confess."

He gave me a suspicious look. "Why?"

"I want to hear what you think I'd say."

"I just told you. You'd say you smothered him with his scarf."

"But I want to hear you say it like you're me. I want you to act it out."

"Go ahead, Lou," Jacob prodded him. He glanced toward me, gave a mean little laugh. "Pretend you're an accountant."

Lou grinned at him. He took a swallow of whiskey, then stood up. He mimed knocking on a door. "Sheriff Jenkins?" he called. He made his voice sound high and shaky, like a nervous child's.

"Yes?" Jacob said, using the deep baritone he associated with authority.

"It's Hank Mitchell. I've got something I want to tell you."

"Come on in, Hank," Jacob boomed. "Have a seat."

Lou pretended to open the door. He walked in place for a moment, grinning stupidly, then sat down on the edge of his chair. He kept his knees primly together, his hands in his lap. "It's about Dwight Pederson," he started, and I reached up to scratch at my chest. There was a soft click as I pushed in the button, and then the tape recorder began to hum.

"Yes?" Jacob said.

"Well, he didn't die in an accident."

"What do you mean?"

Lou feigned glancing nervously around the room. Then he whispered, "I killed him."

There was a pause after that, while Lou waited for my brother to respond. I think Jacob was hoping that I'd stop it there, that all I wanted was that simple statement, but I needed something more. I needed him to say how he'd done it.

"You killed Dwight Pederson?" Jacob asked finally. He pretended to be shocked.

Lou nodded. "I smothered him with his scarf, then I pushed him off the bridge into Anders Creek. I made it look like an accident."

Jacob was silent. I could tell just by the way he was sitting that he wasn't going to say anything more, so I reached up and turned off the tape recorder. It seemed like we had more than enough: if a taped confession was going to frighten Lou into submission, then this ought to work as well as any other.

"All right," I said. "You can stop."

Lou shook his head. "I want to get to the part where you offer to testify against us." He waved at my brother. "Keep asking me questions, Jake."

Jacob didn't respond. He took a long swallow of whiskey, then wiped his mouth with the back of his hand. I removed the tape recorder from my pocket, rewound it to the beginning.

"What's that?" Lou asked.

"A tape recorder," I said. The machine made a soft thumping noise when it finished rewinding.

"A tape recorder?" my brother asked, as if confused.

I pressed the play button, turned up the volume with my

thumb, then set the machine down on the coffee table. There was a second or two's worth of hissing before Jacob's voice jumped out at us: "Yes?"

"Well, he didn't die in an accident," Lou's voice said.

"What do you mean?"

"I killed him."

"You killed Dwight Pederson?"

"I smothered him with his scarf, then I pushed him off the bridge into Anders Creek. I made it look like an accident."

I reached forward and pressed the stop button, then rewound the tape to the beginning.

"You recorded us?" Jacob said.

"What the fuck're you doing, Hank?" Lou asked.

"It's your confession," I said. I smiled at him. "It's you saying how you killed Dwight Pederson."

He stared at me in bewilderment. "That was you confessing," he said. "I was pretending to be you."

I leaned forward, pressed the play button, and the machine began to spin out their dialogue again. We all looked down at it, listening. I waited till it was finished, then I said, "Sounds more like your voice than mine, doesn't it?"

Lou didn't respond. He was drunk, and though he knew he was unhappy with what I'd done, it didn't seem like he could figure out exactly why.

"We're not going to split up the money till the summer," I said.

He appeared to be genuinely surprised by this statement. "You said we'd do it next weekend."

I shook my head. "We're going to wait till the plane's discovered, like we planned from the start."

"But I already told you, Hank. I need it now." He glanced toward Jacob for help. Jacob was staring down at the tape recorder, as if still trying to overcome his shock at its sudden appearance.

"I'll tell," Lou said. "I'll tell the sheriff about Pederson."

It was only now, I think, as he spoke these words, that he realized why I'd taped him. He sneered at me. "Nobody's going to believe that thing. It's obvious I'm just kidding around."

"If you and I both went to Sheriff Jenkins tomorrow and claimed that the other killed Dwight Pederson, who do you think he'd be more likely to believe? You?"

He didn't say anything, so I answered for him. "It'd be me, Lou. You can see that, can't you?"

"You fucking—" he started. He leaned forward and tried to grab the tape recorder from the table, but I was too quick. I snatched it away from him and slid it back into my shirt pocket.

"You aren't going to tell anyone anything," I said.

Lou stood up then, like he was going to come around the table and get me, and I stood up, too. I knew he wasn't a threat—he was smaller than me, and drunk—but I was still frightened enough by the idea of exchanging blows with him that I would've run to avoid it, would've sprinted straight across the room, up the step to the entranceway, and out the door. I'd gotten what I'd come for; now all I wanted to do was leave.

Lou scowled at me across the coffee table. Then he waved toward Jacob. "Grab him, Jake," he said.

Jacob jumped a little, sliding backward on the couch. "Grab him?"

"Sit down, Lou," I said.

"Come on, Jake. Give me a hand."

A short, heavy silence descended on the room while we waited to see what my brother would do. He cringed, seemed to pull back away from us, his head retracting into his shoulders like a turtle's. This was the moment he must've been dreading all evening, the point where he'd have to demonstrate his allegiance in a concrete way, where he'd have to choose, publicly, one of us over the other.

"The tape doesn't hurt you," he said, his voice sounding pathetically timid. "It's just to keep you from hurting him."

Lou blinked at him. "What?"

"He's not going to use it unless you tell on him. That seems fair, doesn't it?"

Jacob's words were like little pellets; they seemed to fly at Lou and bury themselves beneath his skin. Lou swayed a little on his feet, an empty look coming across his face. "You're in this together, aren't you?" he said.

Jacob was silent.

"Come on, Lou," I said. "Let's sit back down. We're still friends here."

"You set me up, didn't you? The two of you together." Lou's body went taut. Muscles I'd never seen before appeared on his neck, quivering. "In my own fucking house," he said. He closed his hands into fists, glanced around him as if searching for something to hit. "Let's pretend you're me," he said, mimicking my voice. He sneered at Jacob. "Jacob, you be the sheriff."

"I didn't know—" my brother started.

"Don't lie to me, Jake." Lou's voice dropped a notch, coming out hurt, betrayed. "You're just making it worse."

"Maybe Hank's right," Jacob said. "Maybe it's better if we wait till the plane's found."

"Did you know?"

"You can make it till then. I can help you out. I'll loan you—"

"You're gonna help me out?" Lou almost smiled. "How the fuck do you think you're gonna help me out?"

"Listen, Lou," I said. "He didn't know. It was all my idea."

Lou didn't even bother to look at me. He pointed at my brother. "I want you to tell me," he said. "Tell me the truth."

Jacob licked his lips. He glanced down at his glass, but it was empty. He set it on the table. "He promised he'd help me buy back my farm."

"Your farm? What the fuck're you talking about?"

"My dad's farm."

"I forced him to do it," I said quickly. "I told him he couldn't buy the farm unless he helped me trick you."

Again, Lou ignored me. It was as if I'd ceased to exist. "So you knew?" he asked Jacob.

My brother nodded. "I knew."

Very slowly, so that there was a certain majesty to the gesture, Lou raised his arm and pointed toward the door. He was expelling us, a king banishing a pair of traitors from his realm. "Get out," he said.

And this was exactly what I wanted to do. I thought that if we could leave, if we could just make it out to the truck before anyone said anything he couldn't take back in the morning, we'd be all right.

"Come on, Jacob," I said, but he didn't move. He was focused on Lou, his whole body leaning toward him, pleading for understanding.

"Can't you see—" he began.

"Get out of my house," Lou said, his voice rising toward a yell. The muscles on his neck reappeared, straining.

I picked up my jacket from the couch. "Jacob," I said.

He didn't move, and Lou began to scream. "Leave!" he shouted. He stamped his foot. "Now!"

"Lou?" a woman's voice called. We all froze. It was Nancy; we'd woken her up. Her voice seemed to come down out of the ceiling, as if it were the house itself that was speaking.

"Jacob," I said again, making it a command, and this time he rose to his feet.

"Lou?" Nancy called. She sounded angry. "What's going on?"

Lou backed away from us, out of the living room and into the entranceway. He stood at the bottom of the steps.

"They tricked me," he yelled.

"I have to go to work in the morning. You guys can't keep shouting like that."

"They made me confess."

"What?"

"They aren't going to give us the money."

Nancy still didn't understand him. "Why don't you go to Jacob's?" she asked.

Lou stood there a moment, swaying a little on his feet; then he turned suddenly, as if he'd come to some decision, and headed off down the hallway toward the bathroom. Jacob and I put on our jackets. I walked quickly toward the front door, and he followed right behind me. I wanted to leave before Lou had a chance to reappear.

"Lou?" Nancy called again.

I opened the door and was just about to step outside when I heard a noise off to my left. It was Lou. He hadn't gone to the bathroom after all; he'd gone to the garage and gotten his shotgun. He was carrying it now, jamming shells into its breech as he came.

"He's got a gun," Jacob said. He reached up and pushed at my back with his hand, urging me forward, and then, when I didn't move, rushed past me through the door. When he reached the walk, he broke into a run. I just stood there, watching Lou approach. He'd left the garage door open behind him, so that he came toward me out of a square of darkness, like a troll emerging from his cave. I was thinking that I could calm him down.

"What're you doing, Lou?" I asked. It seemed silly for him to be acting like this, like a thwarted child throwing a tantrum.

Nancy called his name again, her voice sounding as if she were already halfway back to sleep. "Lou?"

Lou ignored her. He stopped about five feet away from me, then raised the gun until it was leveled at my chest. "Give me the tape," he said.

I shook my head. "Put the gun down, Lou."

Behind me I heard Jacob opening the door to his truck.

There was a moment's pause, and then it slammed shut. *He's leaving me*, I remember thinking. *He's running away*. I waited for the cough of the engine turning over, waited for the crunch of the tires on the gravel as he pulled out of the driveway, but it didn't come. Instead I heard the heavy clumping of his footsteps returning toward me, and when I glanced back over my shoulder, I found him running up the driveway, his rifle held out in front of his chest. It was my older brother, finally, after all these years, coming to protect me.

But it was all wrong: so wrong, in fact, that at first I couldn't believe it was actually happening. An image floated up into my mind, absurdly, of Jacob playing army as a child: I saw him emerge from the cover of the south field, hesitate there like a real soldier, then scuttle toward the house, panting with the effort, a toy machine gun cradled in his arms, our uncle's World War II helmet balanced loosely on his head, bouncing forward and backward with every step, so that he had to keep reaching up and pushing it away from his eyes. He'd been coming to get me then, to capture me off the porch—a boys' game with make-believe weapons—and that was how he looked now, as if he were playing but pretending to be serious.

The sight of him, the sight of the rifle in his hands, sent a surge of terror through my body. It felt electric; my fingertips seemed to crackle with it. I held up my hand, waving him off, and he stopped at the foot of the walk, twenty feet away. I could hear his breath, a sawtoothed sound in the darkness. I turned back toward Lou, trying to fill the doorway with my body. I knew I couldn't let him see my brother, knew implicitly that if it reached the point where they stood facing each other with their guns, anything could happen. It would be out of my control.

"Give it to me, Hank," Lou said. His voice came out sounding remarkably controlled, and this hint of composure, tiny as it was, momentarily reassured me.

"Why don't we talk in the morning, Lou?" I said. "Everybody'll be calmer then, and we'll work things out."

He shook his head. "You're not going to leave until you give me the tape."

"Hank?" Jacob called from the foot of the walk. "You okay?"

"Go wait in the truck, Jacob."

Lou craned his neck to see outside, but I blocked his view. I stepped backward onto the porch, dragging the door shut behind me. I was trying to separate them, but Lou misinterpreted it. He thought I was running away, thought I was scared of him, and it gave him a burst of confidence. He took two quick steps forward, grabbed the edge of the door with his right hand, and yanked it open. He waved his gun in my face.

"I said you're not going to—" he started.

"Leave him alone, Lou," Jacob shouted.

Lou froze, startled, and we both turned to look. My brother was squinting down the barrel of his rifle, aiming it at Lou's head.

"Stop it, Jacob," I said. "Go back to the truck." But he didn't move. He was focused on Lou, and Lou was focused on him. I was being shoved off to the periphery, a prop in their drama.

"You gonna shoot me, Jake?" Lou asked, and then, together, they both began to yell, each trying to outshout the other: Jacob told him to leave me alone, to shut up, to put down the gun, that he didn't want to hurt him; and Lou started in about their friendship, about being tricked in his own house, about how much he needed the money, and how he was going to shoot me if I didn't give him the tape.

"Shhh," I kept saying, pleading now, and ignored by everyone. "Shhh."

In the midst of all this, I saw a light come on in one of the upstairs windows. I stared up at it, waiting for Nancy to appear, hoping that her voice, drifting down like an angel's from the sky above our heads, might stop this insanity, might silence their shouts and make them put down their guns. She didn't come to the window, though; she opened her bedroom door and ran down the hallway to the head of the stairs.

"Lou?" I heard her call. She was out of sight, but I could imagine how she looked from the sound of her voice—sleepy and bewildered, her hair tangled and matted, her face puffy around the eyes.

Instantly, Lou fell silent, and when he stopped yelling, my brother did, too. My ears were ringing from their shouting. The night seemed to settle around us, softly, in little pieces, like falling snow.

Nancy came down a few steps. I could see one of her feet now through the upper frame of the doorway. It was bare and very small. "What's going on?" she asked.

Lou's face was a brilliant red, his nostrils flared. He seemed to be having a hard time catching his breath. He was pointing his gun at the center of my chest, but he wasn't looking at me. He was looking at Jacob. "You fucking piece of shit," he said, very quietly. Then he glanced at me. "The two of you. Pretending to be my friends." He raised the gun until it was pointing at my face. "I ought to blow your fucking brains out."

"Come on, Lou," I said, keeping my voice low and calm. "We can talk this out." I didn't think he was going to shoot me; I thought it was just bluster, like a dog barking. Nancy's presence was a good thing; if we let her, I knew, she'd bring us out of this danger. Another few seconds and Lou would lower his gun. Then she'd take him inside, and it would all be over.

Nancy came down another step. I could see two feet and a shin now. "Put down the gun, baby," she said, and the softness of her voice was like a balm to me. I felt myself relax beneath its touch.

But Lou shook his head. "Go back to bed," he said. He pumped a shell into the shotgun's chamber, adjusted his aim at my face. "I'm just going to shoot these two pieces of—"

He didn't finish his sentence. There was an explosion behind me, a flash of blue light followed instantly by a sense of movement over my left shoulder. I ducked, shutting my eyes, and heard Lou's gun clatter to the tiled floor.

When I lifted my head, he'd disappeared from the doorway.

There was perhaps a second's worth of silence before Nancy began to scream. It was just long enough for me to make out the sound of the wind sighing though the branches of the trees above me, and then it was over, and there was only her voice. It filled the house, strained against the walls.

"Noooooo," she screamed. She went on and on, until she ran out of air, and then she began again. "Noooooo."

I knew what had happened: it was the absolute stillness behind me, and the utter horror which this stillness implied, that made it undeniable. My brother had shot Lou.

I stepped forward and up, across the porch and into the house, and found Lou lying on his back a few feet from the door. The bullet had hit him in the forehead, about an inch above his eyes. It had left a very small hole in front, but there was a large puddle of blood on the floor, working its way out across the entranceway, so I knew that the hole in back must be bigger. His face was absolutely expressionless, almost serene. His mouth was partly open, his teeth visible, his head tilted slightly back, so that it looked as if he were about to sneeze. His right hand was thrown flamboyantly out across the floor; his left was covering his heart. The shotgun was lying beside his shoulder.

He was dead, of course. There was no doubt about this: Jacob had killed him. And so, I thought to myself, just like that, in an instant, it was over—everything was going to be revealed now, all our secrets, all our crimes. We'd let things slip out of our control.

Nancy came down the stairs one step at a time. She was a big woman, larger than Lou. Her hair was shoulder length and dyed a peculiar, unabashedly artificial tint of orange. She was holding her hand over her mouth, her eyes locked on Lou's body. I watched her approach, feeling as if I were in some sort of trance. Everything seemed to be happening at a distance, as though I were observing it from behind a sheet of glass.

"Oh my God," she said, the words coming out at double speed, as if they'd been glued together. She kept repeating it, over and over again. "Oh my God oh my God oh my God."

She was wearing a Detroit Tigers T-shirt. It was extra-long, like a nightgown, and came down to her thighs. I could see her breasts moving beneath it, full and heavy, swinging a little each time she took a step.

I glanced back through the doorway at Jacob. He was still out on the walk, standing there like a statue, peering into the house. It seemed as if he were waiting for Lou to get up.

Nancy reached the bottom of the stairs, moved at a crouch across the entranceway, then stooped down beside Lou's corpse. She didn't touch him. She still had her hand over her mouth, and the sight of her like that sent a wave of pity through my body. I stepped forward, my arms held out to embrace her, but when she saw me coming, she jumped up and backed away toward the living room.

"Don't touch me," she said. Her legs were stocky beneath her T-shirt, pallid, like two marble pillars. She was beginning to cry a little; a pair of tears were moving in tandem down either side of her nose, as if in a race.

I tried to think of something soothing to say to her, but all I could come up with was a feeble lie. "It's okay, Nancy," I whispered.

She didn't react to this. She was staring past me, toward the doorway, and when I turned to see what she was looking at, I found Jacob standing there, the rifle cradled in his arms like a baby, a blank, mannequinish look pasted on his face.

"Why?" Nancy asked.

He had to clear his throat before he spoke. "He was going to shoot Hank."

The sound of my brother's voice pulled me out of my trance. If we could act together, I realized, the thought fluttering upward into consciousness on a pair of panicky wings, we could still salvage something from this horror: we could still save the money. It would simply be a matter of our agreeing to look at things in a certain way.

"He wasn't going to shoot anyone," Nancy said. She was staring down at Lou's body now. The puddle of blood was still growing, moving slowly out across the tiled floor.

"Nancy," I said softly, "it's going to be all right. We're going to work this out." I was trying to calm her down.

"You killed him," she said, as if in disbelief. She pointed her finger at my brother. "You shot him."

Jacob didn't say anything. His rifle was clenched tightly against his chest.

I took two steps toward Nancy, edging my way around the puddle of blood. "We're going to call the police," I said. "And we're going to tell them it was self-defense."

She glanced toward me, but not at me. It didn't seem like she understood.

"We're going to tell them that Lou was about to shoot him, that he was drunk, that he'd gone berserk."

"Lou wasn't going to shoot anyone."

"Nancy," I said. "We can still save the money."

She reacted to this statement as if it were a slap in the face. "You bastards," she hissed. "You shot him for the money, didn't you?"

"Shhh," I said. I made a quieting motion with my hand, but she started toward me, her fists clenched, her face distorted with rage. I backed away from her.

"You think I'm going to let you keep the money?" she said. "You fucking—"

I retreated all the way across the entranceway, past Lou's body, toward the door and my brother. She kept coming at me, yelling now, calling me names, shouting about the money. As she passed Lou's body, she stumbled against the shotgun, kicking it with one of her bare feet. It made a loud metallic noise as it slid across the tiles, and we all stared down at it.

There was a pause, while Nancy seemed to consider. Then she was bending to pick it up.

I stepped forward to grab it first, not to threaten her, only to keep her from getting it. We both got ahold of it, and there was a brief struggle. The gun was black and oily, and surprisingly heavy. I pushed, then pulled, then pushed again, and Nancy lost her grip. She stumbled back toward the stairs, fell against them, and, shrieking, lifted her arms to protect her head.

I realized with a shock that she thought I was going to shoot her.

"It's okay," I said quickly. I crouched down, began to lay the gun on the floor. "I'm not going to hurt you."

She started to back up the stairs.

"Wait, Nancy," I said. "Please."

She kept moving away, one step at a time, higher and higher, and I came after her, the gun in my hands.

"No," she said. "Don't."

"It's okay. I just want to talk."

When she got to the top of the stairs, she turned to the right and broke into a run. I sprinted after her, up the last few steps and then down the hallway. Her bedroom was at the very end. Its door was open, and there was a light on inside. I could see the foot of the bed.

"I'm not going to hurt you," I yelled.

She reached the door and tried to slam it shut, but I was right behind her. I caught it with my arm, forced it open. She backed away from me. The room was larger than I'd expected. There was a king-size water bed directly in front of us, pushed up against the wall. To the left was a little sitting area—two chairs and a table with a TV on it. There was a door behind the chairs, shut, which I assumed must've led to the bathroom. To the right, pressed up against the house's front wall, were two huge bureaus and a dressing table. There was a doorway there, too. It was open and led to a walk-in closet. I could see some of Nancy's dresses hanging inside.

"I just want to talk," I said. "Okay?"

Nancy fell backward against the bed and started crawling, crablike, across it. A sloshing sound came from the mattress, and the covers rose and fell with the rolling of the water beneath them.

I realized that I was pointing the shotgun at her. I took it in my left hand and held it out, away from my body, to show her that I wasn't going to use it. "Nancy—"

"Leave me alone," she cried. She reached the headboard and stopped, trapped. Her face was smeared with tears. She wiped at it with her hand.

"I promise I won't hurt you. I just want to—"

"Get out," she sobbed.

"We have to think about what we're doing. We have to calm down and—"

Her right hand shot out suddenly, reaching for the night table. At first I thought she was going to pick up the phone and call the police, so I stepped forward to snatch it away. Her hand wasn't moving toward the phone, though; it was moving toward the night table's drawer. She pulled it open, reached inside, fumbling blindly, in a panic, her eyes locked on me and the gun. A box of tissues fell out, landing on the floor with a hollow thump, and then, right behind it, came her hand. It was holding a small black pistol. She had it by the barrel.

"No," I said. I retreated toward the door. "Don't, Nancy."

She pulled the pistol toward her, worked her hand around to the grip. Then she raised it and aimed it at my stomach.

My mind was sending out a jumbled stream of contradictory orders, screaming at my body, telling it to leap forward and grab the pistol, to run away, to duck, to hide behind the door, but my body refused to listen. It acted on its own. My arms lifted the shotgun, and then my finger found the trigger, found its cold metal tongue, and pulled it backward.

The gun fired. Nancy's body was flung back against the headboard, and a tiny fountain of water sprang up at her side.

I stood there in shock. The spray of water made a sound like someone urinating when it landed on the bedspread. Nancy's body slumped over to the right, balanced for a second on the edge of the bed, then slipped with a thud to the floor. There was blood everywhere—on the sheets, the pillows, the headboard, the wall, the floor.

"Hank?" Jacob called. His voice sounded scared, shaky.

I didn't answer him. I was trying to absorb what had just happened. I took a step into the room, crouched down, set the gun on the floor.

"Nancy," I said. I knew she was dead, could tell just by the way she'd fallen from the bed, but the desire for this not to be true was overwhelming. I waited for her to answer me; the whole thing seemed like an accident, and I wanted to explain this to her.

"Hank?" Jacob called again. He was at the base of the stairs, but he sounded farther away. I had to strain to hear him.

"It's all right, Jacob," I yelled, though it wasn't, of course.

"What happened?"

I stood up and moved around the bed to get a better look at her. Her T-shirt was stained black with blood. It had hitched up a bit when she fell, so that now I could see her rear end. Water was sprinkling down off the bed onto her legs, making them glisten. She wasn't moving.

"You want me to come up?" Jacob called.

"I shot her," I yelled.

"What?"

"I shot her. She's dead."

Jacob didn't say anything. I listened for the sound of his feet on the stairs, but he didn't move.

"Jacob?"

"What?"

"Why don't you come up here now?"

There was a pause; then I heard him begin to climb. The water continued to shoot in a fine spray from the mattress. I picked up a pillow and set it on top of the leak. After a few seconds a little puddle started to form on the bedspread. There was the smell of urine in the air, an acidic tartness—Nancy had lost control of her bladder. The urine was mixing with the blood and the water on the floor, the whole mess seeping down into the carpet.

When I heard my brother's footsteps approach the doorway, I turned and said, "She had a pistol. She was going to shoot me."

Jacob nodded. He seemed to be making a conscious effort not to look at Nancy's body. He was still carrying his rifle. I could tell he'd been crying downstairs—his face was damp and his eyes red—but he'd stopped now.

"What should we do?" he asked.

I didn't know what to say. I still couldn't believe that I'd shot her. I could see her body lying there, could see the blood and smell the urine, but I couldn't connect all that to anything I'd done. I'd just raised the gun and pulled the trigger: it seemed like too simple an action to have resulted in all this carnage.

"I didn't mean to shoot her," I said to Jacob.

He glanced toward Nancy's body now, a quick, furtive movement, like a peck, then looked away. His face was extremely pale. He started toward the bed, as if to sit down on it, but I stopped him.

"Don't," I said. "It's broken."

He froze, shifting his weight from foot to foot. "I guess we should call somebody," he said.

"Call somebody?"

"The sheriff. The state police."

I stared across the room at the phone. It was sitting on the night table, above the open drawer. Nancy's body was slumped on the floor beneath it. Her hair was all wet now, a thick, dark clot. It was wound around her neck like a noose. Jacob was right, of course. The mess we'd made had to be cleaned up, and the police were the only people who could do this.

"They're not going to believe us," I said.

"Believe us?"

"That we shot them out of self-defense."

"No," he said. "They won't."

I edged my way around Nancy's body toward the night table.

"Will we tell them about the money?" Jacob asked.

I didn't answer him. An idea had come to me suddenly, a way to postpone for a few more minutes the exposure of our crimes.

"I'm going to call Sarah," I said. I tried to imply that this was a rational step, tried to make my voice come out sounding confident and resolute, but in reality there was no logic behind it. I simply wanted to speak with her, wanted to tell her what had happened and warn her of the storm that was about to engulf us.

I half-expected Jacob to argue with me, but he didn't, so I

picked up the phone. It was dark brown, the same color and style as the one in my office, and I found this oddly reassuring. When I started to dial, my brother turned and shuffled back across the room toward the doorway. I watched him disappear into the hall.

"Don't worry, Jacob," I called after him. "It's going to be okay."

He didn't answer me.

Sarah picked up on the third ring. "Hello?" she said. I could hear the dishwasher going in the background, which meant she was in the kitchen. She'd been waiting up for me.

"It's me," I said.

"Where are you?"

"At Lou's."

"Did you get him to say it?"

"Sarah," I said. "We shot them. They're both dead."

There was an instant's silence on the other end, like a skip on a record, and then, "What're you talking about, Hank?"

I told her what had happened. I took the phone and walked around to the other side of the bed while I talked, to get away from Nancy's body. I went to the window and looked out toward the road. I could see Jacob's truck, parked down at the base of the driveway. Everything was dark.

"Oh God," Sarah whispered when I finished, an echo of Nancy's cry. "Oh God."

I didn't say anything. I could hear her trying to catch her breath on the other end of the line, as if she were about to cry.

"What're you going to do?" she asked finally.

"I'm calling the police. We're going to turn ourselves in."

"You can't do that," she said. Her voice was quick, panicky, and it made me scared to hear it. I realized now why I'd called her: so that she might take control, fix what I'd broken—Sarah, my problem solver, my rock. But she was letting me down; she was just as bewildered by what had happened as I was.

"I don't have a choice, Sarah. This isn't something we can just walk away from."

"You can't turn us in, Hank."

"I won't involve you. I'll tell them you didn't know about any of it."

"I don't care about that. I care about you. If you give yourself up, they'll send you to jail."

"They're both dead, Sarah. I can't hide that."

"What about an accident?"

"An accident?"

"Why can't you make it look like an accident? Like with Pederson?"

I almost laughed, the idea seemed so absurd. She was flailing about, clutching at straws. "Jesus, Sarah. We shot them. There's blood everywhere. It's on the walls, the bed, the floor—"

"You said you shot Nancy with Lou's gun?"

"Yes."

"Then you can make it look like Lou killed Nancy, and Jacob killed Lou in self-defense."

"But why would Lou kill Nancy?"

Sarah didn't say anything, but I could sense her thinking over the phone, could feel it like a vibration. An image appeared in my mind of her pacing up and down through the darkened kitchen, the telephone pressed against her cheek, its cord wrapped tightly around her fist. She was regaining her composure; she was searching for a way out.

"Maybe he discovered she was cheating on him," she said.

"But why shoot her tonight? It's not like he found her in bed with someone. She was all alone."

There was a pause of perhaps ten seconds; then Sarah asked suddenly, "Did Sonny hear the shots?"

"Sonny?"

"Sonny Major. Are his lights on? Is he up?"

I looked out the window again. There was only darkness

down the road; Sonny's trailer was hidden behind it. "It doesn't look like it."

"You have to go get him."

"Get Sonny?" I had no idea what she was talking about.

"You have to make it look like Lou came home and found Nancy in bed with him."

I felt a dizzying wave of nausea rush over my body when she said this. It was all falling into place; she was making everything come together. Sonny was the only other person who knew about the money; if we killed him, it would just be us and Jacob. This was what I'd called her for, a solution to our trouble, but now that she'd found it for me, I didn't want it. It was too much.

"I can't shoot Sonny," I whispered. I could feel my back sweating, could feel beads forming along my shoulder blades.

"You have to," Sarah said, pleading now. "It's the only way it'll work."

"But I can't just drag him over here and kill him. He doesn't have anything to do with this."

"They'll send you to jail. Both you and Jacob. You have to save yourselves."

"I can't, Sarah."

"Yes, you can," she said, her voice rising. "You have to. It's our only chance."

I didn't say anything. My mind felt dull, numb, my thoughts viscous and unmanageable. I could see what she was saying: by killing Lou and Nancy, we'd taken two steps out over an abyss. We could either stop now, and fall into the pit beneath us, or take this third step and cross to safety. The idea shot through my mind, quickly, more wish than thought, that I didn't really have a choice. For one brief moment I allowed myself to believe it, that I'd lost control. It was a simple, easy feeling. Everything had already been determined for me—I was just following along now, handing myself over to my fate.

I let the feeling pass, and then I chose.

"This is bad, Sarah," I said. "It's evil."

"Please," she whispered. "Do it for me."

"I don't even know if he's home."

"You can go check. You have to at least check."

"And what about Lou?"

"Lou?"

"How do we explain Jacob's shooting Lou?"

Sarah answered me quickly, her voice breathless. "You tell the police you heard a gun go off as you were pulling out of the driveway. You thought Lou had surprised a burglar, so you stopped the truck and ran up to the house, Jacob with his rifle. As you came up the walk, Lou opened the door. He was drunk, enraged. He saw Jacob running toward him with the rifle, and he raised his shotgun at him. Then Jacob shot him in self-defense." She paused, and then—when I didn't respond immediately—said, "But you have to hurry, Hank. You're running out of time. They'll be able to tell if the shootings happen too far apart. They'll be able to tell who died first."

The urgency in her voice was contagious. I felt my pulse thump out from my chest into my arms and head. I started to move back toward the night table. The carpet was soaked with Nancy's blood. I had to walk along the edge of the wall to keep from getting it on my boots.

"Is Jacob okay?" Sarah asked.

"Yes," I said. "He was crying before, but I think he's all right now."

"Where is he?"

"He's downstairs. I think he's getting a drink."

"You have to talk to him. The police are going to question him. You have to make sure that he understands the story, that he doesn't break down and confess."

"I'll talk to him," I said.

"This is important, Hank. He'll be the weak link. If he breaks down, he'll send you both to jail."

"I know," I said. "I'll take care of him. I'll take care of everything."

Then I hung up the phone and ran downstairs.

I FOUND my brother in the living room, sitting on the couch. He'd unzipped his jacket and was drinking from a glass full of whiskey. His rifle was lying propped up against the foot of the stairs. I didn't look at Lou's body, just scanned it once as I passed through the entranceway, to make sure Jacob hadn't moved it, then stepped quickly down into the living room.

There was a woman's bathrobe draped across the arm of the couch. It was sky blue, silky. I picked it up and sniffed at it—a sweetish mix of perfume and tobacco. I unzipped my jacket and stuffed it inside.

"Are they coming?" Jacob asked.

"Who?"

"The police."

"Not yet."

"Did you call them?"

I shook my head. I saw a pack of Marlboro Lights sitting on the coffee table. Beside it were a lighter and a tube of lipstick. I scooped all three of them up and slid them into my jacket pocket. "I'm going to go get Sonny," I said. "We're going to make it look like Lou shot him and Nancy together."

I could see Jacob struggling to make sense of this. He frowned up at me, his forehead wrinkling, the glass of whiskey trembling a bit in his hand. "You're going to shoot Sonny, too?"

"We have to," I said.

"I don't think I want to do that."

"It's either that or go to jail. That's our choice."

Jacob was silent for a moment. Then he asked, "Why can't we run? Why can't we go get Sarah and the baby and the money and just drive off? We could head down to Mexico. We could—"

"They'd catch us, Jacob. They always do. They'd track us down and bring us back. If we want to save ourselves, this is how we have to do it." I was feeling panicky with the loss of time, jittery. It seemed like I could actually sense the two corpses cooling, draining, indelibly marking the chronology of their passing. I didn't want to have to argue with Jacob; I'd already made my decision. I turned and started toward the entranceway. "I'm not going to jail," I said.

I heard him stand up, as if to come after me. When he spoke, his voice came out high and tight, stopping me in midstride. "We can't kill all these people."

I turned to face him. "I'm going to save us, Jacob. If you let me, I'll be able to make it right."

His face took on a scared, frantic expression. "No. We have to stop."

"I'm just going to—" I began, but he didn't let me finish.

"I want to leave. I want us to run away."

"Listen to me, Jacob." I leaned forward and took his sleeve in my hand. I held it very lightly, just a small fold of red nylon between two of my gloved fingers, but it created a sudden, nearly palpable tension in the room. We both fell silent.

"I'm telling you how it's going to look," I said.

He met my eyes for the briefest of moments. He seemed to be holding his breath. I let go of his jacket.

"Lou comes home. He finds Nancy in bed with Sonny. She thought he was supposed to be out till late. He's drunk, violent; he gets his shotgun, and he shoots them both. We're just pulling out of the driveway. We hear the shots, think that he must've surprised a burglar. We run up to the house, you with your rifle from the truck. Lou opens the front door. He's gone berserk. He points the shotgun at us, and you shoot him."

Jacob was silent. I wasn't sure if he'd understood it all.

"It makes sense, doesn't it?" I asked.

He didn't answer.

"It'll work, Jacob. I promise. But we have to hurry."

"I don't want to be the one who shoots Lou," he said.

"All right. Then we'll tell them I shot him. It doesn't matter."

There was a long pause. I could hear the tap dripping in the kitchen.

"I just stay here and wait?" Jacob asked.

I nodded. "Put your gloves back on. And wash those glasses."

"You'll shoot him yourself?"

"That's right," I said, backing toward the door. "I'll shoot him myself."

SONNY lived in a house trailer, a tiny one, set up on cinder blocks about three quarters of a mile down the road from Lou's. There were sawhorses littered about the front yard, covered with snow, and the side of the trailer had S. MAJOR, CARPENTER painted on it in large, black letters. Below that was written HIGH QUALITY, LOW PRICE. Sonny's car, an old, rusted, and badly battered Mustang, was wedged into a gap in the snowbank lining the road.

I parked Jacob's truck alongside the car and left the engine running. Mary Beth was sound asleep on the front seat; he barely even lifted his head when I climbed out. I jogged up the shoveled path to the trailer and, very quietly, tried the door. It was unlocked; it opened with a faint squeak.

I stepped up and in, crouching through the low doorway. The trailer was dark, and once inside I had to wait for half a minute, holding my breath, while my eyes adjusted to the lack of light. I listened for sounds of movement around me, but there was nothing there.

I was in Sonny's kitchen. I could see a small countertop, a sink, a stove. By the window there was a card table with three chairs. The place was dirty, cluttered, and smelled stalely of fried food. I unzipped my jacket, careful not to make too much noise, took out Nancy's robe, and draped it over one of the chairs. I set the lighter and the cigarettes on the table.

I took my time moving across the kitchen toward the rear of the trailer. I placed a foot, paused, shifted my weight forward, paused, placed my other foot, and continued this all the way into the adjoining room, listening every instant for sounds of Sonny stirring.

The next room was a tiny sitting area—a couch, a coffee table, a TV set. I took out Nancy's lipstick and tossed it onto the couch. From where I was standing I could see, through an open doorway, the foot of Sonny's bed. Sonny was lying there. I could see the shape of his legs beneath the gray whiteness of the sheets.

I listened very closely, holding my body still, and, barely, made out the sound of his breathing. It was soft and low, just this side of a snore. He was sleeping deeply.

"Sonny," I called, my voice echoing against the trailer's walls. "Sonny!"

I heard an abrupt movement through the doorway, skin sliding across sheets. The legs pulled up and out of sight. I took a heavy step toward the bedroom.

"Sonny," I called. "It's Hank Mitchell. I need your help."

"Hank?" a voice came back. It was thick with sleep but a little edgy, too, a little scared.

I took another heavy step. A light came on in the bedroom, and, a second later, Sonny appeared through the doorway. He was a small man, wiry and stunted, like a little elf. He had brown, shoulder-length hair. He was naked except for a pair of white underpants, and in the dim light his skin looked pale, soft, like it'd be easy to bruise.

"Jesus, Hank," he said. "You scared the hell out of me."

He was holding a screwdriver. It was clenched in his right fist, like a knife.

"Jacob's hurt," I said. "He's puking blood."

Sonny gave me a blank look.

"We were drinking at Lou's, and he started puking blood."

"Blood?"

I nodded. "Now he's passed out."

"You want me to call an ambulance?"

"It'll be quicker if I bring him in myself. I just need you to help me lift him into the truck. Lou's too drunk to do it."

Sonny gave his eyes several rapid, exaggerated blinks, as if to clear them of tears. He stared for a moment at the screwdriver in his hand, then glanced around him, looking for a place to set it down. I could see that he wasn't really awake yet.

"Sonny," I said, forcing a note of panic into my voice. "We have to hurry. He's bleeding inside."

Sonny stared down at his underpants. He seemed surprised to be wearing them. "I have to put on some clothes."

"I've got to get back," I said. "You run over when you're dressed."

Without waiting for his answer, I turned and sprinted toward the front of the trailer. I ran outside and down the walk. I climbed into the truck and was just about to reverse it back up the road to Lou's when I saw Mary Beth sitting in the middle of Sonny's front yard. I opened my door and leaned out into the night. "Mary Beth," I whispered.

The dog sat up straight, ears erect.

"Come on." I made a clicking sound with my tongue.

The dog wagged his tail in the snow.

"Get in the truck," I pleaded.

He didn't move. I tried to whistle, but my lips were too cold. The dog stared at me.

I called his name one more time. Then I slammed shut the door and sped back up the road.

WHEN I got to Lou's, I found Jacob exactly as I'd left him. He was sitting on the leather couch, his hands still gloveless, sipping from his glass of whiskey.

I stood in the entranceway for a good ten seconds, absorbing the scene. He'd taken off his boots, too.

"What the fuck do you think you're doing?" I asked.

He looked up at me, startled. "What?" he said. He hadn't heard me come in.

"You were supposed to wash those glasses."

He held his glass up and stared into it. It was half full. "I wanted to wait till I finished."

"And I told you to put on your gloves, Jacob. You're leaving fingerprints."

He set his glass down on the coffee table. He wiped his hands on his pants, then glanced around the room for his gloves.

"We've got to clean up," I said. "It has to look like we weren't even here."

He found his gloves tucked inside his jacket pockets. He took them out and put them on.

"Your boots, too."

He bent forward to pull on his boots. "I can't tie them with my gloves on."

I waved my hand in the air. "Then take them off. We're running out of time."

He took off his gloves, tied his boots, put his gloves back on. When he finished, he rose to his feet, picked up the glasses from the table, and started off toward the kitchen.

"Where are you going?" I asked.

He stopped halfway across the room, blinking at me. "You told me to wash the glasses."

I shook my head. "Later. Sonny'll be here any second." I went over to the foot of the stairs and picked up Lou's shotgun. "Where does he keep his extra shells?"

Jacob stood there with the glasses held out in front of him. "In the garage."

"Come on. Show me."

He set the glasses down on the coffee table with a little clinking sound, then followed me out to the garage. There was an open cabinet there, just beyond the doorway, and on its floor was a cardboard box full of shells. I had Jacob show me how to load them into the gun. It held five shells in all. You had to pump a new one into the chamber each time you fired. I emptied the box of shells into my right-hand jacket pocket, and we went back inside.

When we got to the entranceway, I picked up my brother's rifle and held it out toward him. "Here," I said. "Take this."

Jacob didn't move. He stood there, about five feet from Lou's body, and stared at the rifle. He seemed undecided as to what he should do. "You told me you were going to shoot him."

I stepped forward, shaking the rifle. "Come on. You're just going to point it at him. We have to use Lou's gun to shoot him."

He hesitated. Then he reached out and took the rifle from me.

I went over to the front door, cracked it open, and peered outside toward Sonny's trailer. It was all lit up now.

"I'm going to wait for him on the porch," I said. "You stand in here. When you hear us talking, step outside and point your rifle at him. Don't say anything, and don't let him see inside. Just stand there and point the gun at him."

Jacob nodded.

I stepped out onto the porch and shut the door behind me.

. . .

It was another minute or so before I heard Sonny's car start. It revved twice; then the headlights flicked on, and it shot out onto the road, made a tight U-turn, and sped toward me. He parked at the top of the driveway, right next to the garage, shut off the engine, and came sprinting up the walk. He was almost to the door before he saw me standing there, waiting for him.

"Where is he?" he asked, out of breath. He was wearing a light brown winter parka with a big, fur-lined hood on it. His hair was still uncombed. He glanced down at the gun in my arms, then touched the corners of his eyes with his fingertips. They were watering from the cold. He stepped up onto the porch. With the door closed, the house looked perfectly normal. You couldn't tell what had happened.

"I had to—" Sonny started, but then, hearing the front door begin to open, he stopped. Jacob appeared through a crack in the doorway.

"You're all right?" Sonny asked, surprised.

Jacob didn't answer him. He squeezed his body out onto the porch and shut the door. Then he raised his rifle until it was pointing at the center of Sonny's chest. I stepped down onto the walk, in case Sonny tried to run back toward his car.

Sonny stared at Jacob's rifle for a moment. Then he glanced back toward me.

"Hank?" he said. He still hadn't caught his breath. He touched his eyes again.

I raised the shotgun until it was pointing at his stomach. The gun felt heavy in my hands, and its weight gave me a sudden sense of power. It felt exactly like it ought to, dense, potent, like something capable of killing. *This is craziness*, I thought to myself, briefly, and then I let go, slipping into it. All my fear, all my anxiety fell away: I felt capable of anything. I smiled at Sonny.

"What the fuck, Hank?" he said. "You think this is funny?"

"Take off your jacket," I said. I kept my voice very quiet.

He just stared at me.

"Come on, Sonny. Take it off."

He glanced from me to Jacob, then back to me again. He started to smile, but only got halfway. "This isn't funny, Hank. You woke me up."

I took a step forward and raised the gun until it was right in front of his face. "Do it," I said firmly.

Sonny's hands started to stray toward the zipper of his jacket. Then they stopped and fell back to his sides.

"Sonny," I said. "This is very important to me. I don't want to hurt you."

He glanced back at Jacob; then he looked for a bit into the barrel of the shotgun. "You woke me up," he said again.

I took another step forward. I touched the gun's barrel against his forehead. "Take off your jacket, Sonny."

He stepped back, staring at me. I tried to make my face into a stone, and, after a moment, it worked. He unzipped his jacket. Beneath it, he was wearing a blue flannel shirt and jeans.

"Take it," I said to Jacob.

Jacob stepped forward and took the jacket from Sonny. He folded it carefully over his arm. Sonny watched him do this. I watched Sonny.

"Now your boots," I said.

Sonny hesitated for about five seconds. Then he crouched down and took off his boots. He wasn't wearing any socks. His feet were small and bony, like a monkey's.

"The boots," I said to Jacob.

Jacob picked up Sonny's boots.

"Your shirt," I said.

Sonny tried out a little laugh. "Come on, Hank. Enough's enough. It's cold out." He wrapped his arms around his chest, glanced back at my brother. "Jacob?" he said. Jacob looked away.

"Take off your shirt, Sonny," I said.

He shook his head. "This is fucked, Hank. This isn't funny at all."

I stepped forward and hit him in the mouth with the shotgun. It was the strangest thing—I didn't consciously will it, it simply happened. I'd never struck anyone before in my life. Sonny took a step backward, but he neither fell down nor cried out. He gave me a dazed, vacant look.

"What?" he asked. His mouth was bleeding. He put his hand up to it and shut his eyes. He still seemed, on some level, to think that this was some sort of practical joke. When he opened his eyes, he looked at me as if he were expecting me to smile, to say that it was all right, that we were just fooling around.

"Take off your shirt," I said.

He took off his shirt and dropped it to the ground.

"Your pants."

"No, Hank," he started to plead.

Without thinking, I hit him again, this time in the side of the head. He fell to one knee. He rested there a moment, then got back up on his feet.

"Do it."

Sonny looked from me to Jacob. We were both pointing our guns at his chest. He took off his jeans.

"Your underpants," I said.

He shook his head. "This isn't a joke anymore, Hank. You've taken this too far." He was shivering now, from the cold, his whole body trembling.

"Don't talk, Sonny. If you talk, I'm going to hit you again."

He didn't say anything.

"Your underpants," I said.

He didn't move.

I lifted the shotgun until it was level with his face. "I'm

going to count to three. When I get to three, I'm going to shoot."

He still didn't move.

"One."

He glanced at Jacob. Jacob's hands were shaking so much that his rifle quivered in the air.

"Two."

"You're not going to shoot me, Hank," Sonny said. His voice came out raspy and unsure.

I paused but saw no way out. "Three."

Sonny didn't move.

I tightened my grip on the gun, aimed down the barrel at his face. "I don't want to do this, Sonny," I said. He was ruining my plan.

Sonny just stared at me. With each passing second he was gaining confidence. "Put the gun down," he whispered.

But then I had a revelation. I could shoot him here, I realized, he was undressed enough. It would look just as good: Lou discovered them, shot Nancy in her bed, then chased Sonny downstairs and killed him by the front door. It had the disorderly verisimilitude of reality.

I gave him one more chance. "Take them off," I said. My finger brushed lightly against the gun's trigger.

Sonny watched me, and his confidence seemed to waver. He licked at the blood on his lip. "What's this about, Hank?"

"Go inside now, Jacob," I said. I didn't want him to get any blood on his clothes. I took a deep breath, then climbed up onto the porch. I was going to edge around him toward the doorway, so that I'd be facing the road when I shot him.

Jacob cracked open the door and slipped into the house.

Sonny watched him disappear, and then, as if suddenly intuiting what I was about to do, dropped his hands to his sides. He slid his underpants down off his legs.

Naked, he looked tiny, like a boy. His shoulders were

hunched, skinny, his chest virtually hairless. He held his jeans over his crotch. I could tell just from his posture that I'd broken him. It was no longer a struggle for control: he was cowering, waiting to see what my next order might be.

"Drop them," I said.

Sonny let his jeans and underpants fall to the ground. He kept one hand over his groin, the other on his lips. His mouth was beginning to bleed in earnest now. There was blood all over his chin, and some of it had dripped down onto his chest.

"Put your hands on your head."

He put his hands on his head, exposing his groin. I pointed the shotgun at his chest.

"All right," I said. "Now turn around and open the door."

Very slowly, he spun around. I stepped forward, over his little pile of clothes, and pressed the gun's barrel into his spine. I sensed him stiffen, his back muscles clenching at the cold touch of the metal against his naked skin. It was like the tightening of a knot.

"Don't panic when you open the door, Sonny," I said. "Just stay calm, and everything'll be okay."

He dropped one of his hands, turned the knob, and pushed open the door.

After the darkness of the porch, there was something almost surreal about the brightly lit entranceway. It was like stepping up onto a stage. Lou's body was laid out across the tiles, his head thrown back, as if in laughter. The floor must've tilted a little toward the living room, because that's the way the blood had spread. It looked darker than it had before, almost black, and it glistened in the light.

The door swung away from Sonny, all the way around on its hinges until it banged into the wall. Jacob was standing off to the right, his rifle pointing down toward Lou's corpse; there was a startled expression on his face. He stared at us, waiting to see what we were going to do. Sonny didn't move, but I felt him inhale sharply, his back expanding against the barrel of the gun.

"Come on, Sonny," I said. "Just walk right by it."

I pushed him with the gun, forcing him to step forward into the house, his bare foot slapping down against the tiled floor. He stopped like that—one foot inside, one foot outside—bucking a little, like a mule. I pushed him again, harder this time, and suddenly he wasn't there. Jacob blocked the route to the garage, and Lou's body lay in front of the living room, so there was really only one place for Sonny to go. He ran straight up the stairs, taking them two at a time.

I sprinted after him.

When he reached the top, he turned to the right, and we raced down the hallway toward the master bedroom. I have no idea what drew him in that direction, to the exact spot where I wanted him most—perhaps he knew that they kept a pistol there, hidden away in the top drawer of the night table, or maybe it was simply the light seeping out through the half-open doorway, with its implication of refuge and protection—but it must've been an awful shock when he burst into the room and saw the ruin there, saw the blood and the water and heard my footsteps pounding so close behind him. He must've known then—if he still had any doubts after seeing Lou's body laid out across the entranceway—that I'd brought him over here to kill him.

His momentum carried him into the room, right up to the foot of the bed. I didn't see him look down at Nancy's body, but he must've seen it, must've caught at least a glimpse of it before he turned, his hands raised in a pair of fists, as if to strike me. His nakedness made him seem savage, like a caveman. His face was contorted, a horrible mixture of terror and rage and confusion. His chin was smeared with blood.

I was in the doorway, blocking his escape. I pumped the gun, and it ejected an empty shell—the one I'd killed Nancy with—onto the floor at my feet. Then, without pausing to think, I fired into Sonny's chest.

There was a kick against my body, a loud explosion, and a fresh spray of blood slapped wetly across the blankets.

Sonny was knocked onto the bed. He landed with a splashing sound, throwing a little wave of water off the edge of the mattress. His chest was a ragged mass of red and pink and white, but he was still alive. His legs were kicking, and he was trying to lift his head. He was staring at me, his eyes bulging from his head, showing more white than anything else. His right hand was clutching at the covers, pulling them toward his side.

I pumped the gun again, the empty shell falling to the carpet. Then I stepped forward and aimed down at his face. As I pulled the trigger, I saw him shut his eyes. The mattress literally exploded, showering the headboard and the wall behind it with water. I had to jump back to keep from getting it on my clothes.

From the safety of the doorway, I fired the last two shells into the ceiling above the bed. Then I reached into my pocket, put five new shells into the gun, and fired these indiscriminately around the room—at the armchairs off to the left, at the bathroom door, at the mirror above the dressing table.

I checked myself for spattered blood and reloaded the gun.

Descending the stairs, I fired once into the ceiling. When I got to the bottom, I turned and aimed out into the living room. I shot the leather couch, then the TV set, and finally the coffee table with our glasses on it.

I left one shell loaded in the gun.

I FOUND Jacob hiding in the bathroom. He was sitting on the closed lid of the toilet. His rifle was lying on the floor at his feet. Sonny's parka and boots were resting in his lap.

"All right," I said. I was standing in the doorway.

"All right?" Jacob asked. He didn't look up at me.

I took a deep breath. I felt shaky, high, a little out of control. I had the vague suspicion that I might not be thinking very well, and I tried now to slow things down. The hard part was over, I told myself; the rest was just a matter of us acting out our parts.

"It's finished," I said.

"He's dead?"

I nodded.

"Why'd you shoot so much?"

I didn't answer him. "Come on, Jacob. We have to get going."

"Did you have to shoot so much?"

"It's supposed to look like he's pissed. Like he's gone insane." I wiped my face with my hand. My gloves smelled of gunpowder; I realized I'd have to remember to hide them in the truck before we called the police. A string of water began to drip from the ceiling in the corner. It fell onto the ceramic toilet lid, making a sound like the ticking of a clock. It was from the water bed: it had already started soaking through the plaster.

Jacob removed his glasses. His face seemed off balance without them—the skin of his cheeks and jowls red and shiny, bloated to the point of distension, as if he were gout ridden, while up top his eyes seemed sunken, dim, weak looking.

"Aren't you afraid of later?" he asked.

"Later?"

"Guilt. Feeling bad."

I sighed. "We did it, Jacob. We had to do it, and we did it."

"You shot Sonny," he said, as if surprised by this.

"That's right. I shot Sonny."

"Dead," Jacob said. "In cold blood."

I didn't know what to say to that. I wanted to avoid thinking about what we'd done, knew implicitly that nothing good would come from self-analysis. Up to now I'd felt a comfortable sense of inevitability in all my actions, as if I'd merely been looking on, watching myself on film, thoroughly engaged in what was happening but harboring no illusion that I could alter even the most trivial of events. Fate, a voice seemed to whisper in my ear, and I let the reins slip from my hand. But now Jacob, with his questions, was eroding this. He was making me look back, see that the bloody water dripping down through the ceiling was there because I'd willed it into being. I pushed the thought away and immediately replaced it with an angry surge of resentment toward my brother, sitting there on the toilet, fat, passive, judging me while it was his own panic, his own rashness and stupidity that had trapped me into my crimes.

"None of this would've happened if you hadn't killed Lou," I said.

Jacob lifted his head, and I saw with a shock that he was crying. There were tear tracks running down his cheeks, and the sight of them filled me with regret: I shouldn't have spoken so harshly to him.

"I saved you," he said, his voice choking a little on the words. He turned his head to the right, trying to hide his face.

"Don't do this, Jacob. Please."

He didn't answer. His shoulders were shaking. He had one hand pressed against his eyes. The other one, the one that held his glasses, was resting on top of Sonny's boots in his lap.

"You can't fall apart now. We still have to deal with the police, the reporters—"

"I'm okay," he said. It came out like a gasp.

"We have to be composed."

"It's just . . . ," he started, but he couldn't find the words to finish. "I shot Lou," he said.

I stared down at him. He was making me scared. I was

beginning to see how, if we weren't careful, it could all unravel on us. "We have to get going, Jacob," I said. "We have to call it in."

He inhaled deeply, held it for a moment, then put his glasses back on, and struggled to his feet. His face was wet with tears, his chin shaking. I took Sonny's parka and boots from him and carried them out to the hall closet. The living room was a shambles. The coffee table was shattered, the TV imploded. Great, white, round hunks of stuffing protruded from the couch, like clouds, the way children draw them.

Jacob had forgotten his rifle in the bathroom, so I had to go get it for him. He followed me there and back like a dog. He was starting to cry again, and hearing him gave me a hollow pit in my stomach, a vertiginous sensation, as if I were falling off a building.

I opened the front door. "Go out to the truck," I said. "Call the police on the CB."

"The CB?" His voice sounded far away, like he wasn't really paying attention. I shivered. I could feel the cold air rising along the damp, sweaty skin of my back. I zipped up my jacket. Like my gloves, it smelled of gunpowder.

"It has to look like you're calling in scared," I said. "Like you saw me shoot him and, instead of going inside, ran back to the truck."

Jacob was staring down at Lou's body again, his face limp.

"Don't tell them too much, just that there's been a shooting. Tell them to send an ambulance, then get off."

He nodded but didn't move. His tears kept coming, seeping out the corners of his eyes one after the other and dropping down his face. They were dripping onto the front of his jacket, darkening the fabric.

"Jacob," I said.

He dragged his eyes upward, glanced over at me. He wiped his cheek with the back of his hand.

"We have to be alert now. We have to remember what we're doing."

He nodded again, took another deep breath. "I'm okay," he said. Then he started out the door.

I stopped him when he reached the porch. I was in the doorway, right where Lou had been standing when Jacob shot him. "Don't forget your rifle," I said. I held the gun toward him, and he took it. I was still out over the abyss, I realized. There was a fourth step to be taken before I could reach the other side.

As I watched him begin to pick his way down the icy walk, I brought the shotgun up against my body and pumped the last shell into its chamber.

Because he was my brother, I'd forgiven him for telling Lou about Pederson, and for lying to me about Sonny being in the car, but I couldn't forgive him for his weakness. That, I saw now, was a greater risk even than Lou's greed and stupidity. Jacob would break down when they questioned him tonight; he'd confess and turn me in. I couldn't trust him.

When he reached the end of the walk, I called his name. I was tired, exhausted with what I'd already done so far that evening, and this made it easier.

"Jacob," I said.

He turned around. I was standing in the doorway, with Lou's gun leveled at his chest.

It took him a moment to realize what was happening.

"I'm sorry," I said.

He tilted his head, like a giant parrot, confused.

"I didn't plan to do this, but I have to."

His body seemed to settle somehow, to freeze and solidify. He understood finally. "I'd never tell, Hank," he said.

I shook my head. "You'd fuck up, Jacob. I know it. You wouldn't be able to live with what we've done."

"Hank," he said, pleading now. "I'm your brother."

I nodded. I tightened my grip on the shotgun, raised it a little, adjusting my aim. But I didn't fire. I waited. It wasn't that I was wavering—I knew that I couldn't go back now, that it was as good as done—it was simply that I felt like I was forgetting something, skipping some crucial step. Something had to happen still.

Mary Beth appeared suddenly out of the darkness, making both of us jump, dog tags clinking together on his collar, his tail wagging madly. He went up to Jacob and pressed close against his legs, asking to be petted. Then he started toward me.

Jacob, when he saw me glance down at the dog, quickly raised his rifle and pulled the trigger. It made a clicking sound. The chamber was empty. There'd only been the one bullet in it, the bullet he'd loaded back on New Year's Eve, at the very beginning of all this, when we'd set off into the woods after the fox. My brother's face settled into a rueful smile. He seemed almost, but not quite, to shrug.

I fired the gun into his chest.

Before calling the police, I went inside to pee. The bathroom floor was covered with water. It dripped through the ceiling now at several points, like a miniature rain shower. The plaster was stained a light brown from it.

I picked up Sonny's clothes from the porch and carried them to the bedroom. I dropped them into the water beside the bed, then retrieved the pistol, dried it off with my jacket, and returned it to its drawer.

Downstairs again, I took the leftover shells and stuck them into Lou's pocket. I laid his gun on the floor beside his shoulder. His expression hadn't changed. The puddle of blood had spread to the edge of the living room and was dripping quietly onto its shag carpet.

Sonny had left his lights on, so I had to drive over there

quickly and turn them out. While I was there, I hung Nancy's robe in the trailer's bedroom closet and set her tube of lipstick on the sink in the bathroom.

As I drove back to Lou's, I looked for the dog, but he'd disappeared, scared off by the sound of the shotgun.

I called the police from Lou's driveway. I was brief on the radio, trying to sound panicked. I gave the address, said there'd been a shooting. I didn't answer the dispatcher's questions. "My brother," I said, forcing a sob into my voice. Then I clicked off the radio. I sounded good, I knew, convincing, and I felt a sudden infusion of confidence.

It's believable, I said to myself, it's going to work.

I took the tape recorder from my shirt pocket and played it one last time. It was eerie, sitting in the cab of the truck like that, listening to their voices go back and forth, and knowing they were dead. I stopped it before it was through, erased the whole thing, and hid the machine beneath the seat.

I waited in the truck for a while, then climbed out and went up the walk. I wanted to be by my brother when the ambulance arrived, crouching there, holding him in my arms.

I tried calling Mary Beth, but he didn't come. I stood on the walk for several minutes, shivering in the cold, listening for the sound of the dog's tags. I'd hidden my gloves with the tape recorder and was hoping that the wind would air the smell of gun smoke from my jacket.

I could just make out the ambulance's lights, far away across the fields but coming fast, flickering red and white off the horizon, when Jacob reached out and grabbed my ankle. His grip was tight, violent. I had to yank my leg twice to get it free.

A gurgling sound came out of his chest, very faint. As soon as I heard it, I realized that it had been going on for some time.

I stooped down beside him, just out of reach. His jacket was torn and soaked through with blood. I could see the lights coming closer. There were three sets of them—silent, no sirens, converging on Lou's house, two approaching from the east, still far away, and one from the south, which was closer.

Jacob tried to lift his head but couldn't. His eyes took a moment to find me; then they focused a little, faded, and focused again. His glasses were lying beside him on the walk.

I could hear the ambulance's engine now, racing.

"Help me," Jacob gasped.

He said it twice.

Then he lost consciousness.

7

The next morning, just after eight, I was sitting in an empty room on the second floor of the Delphia Municipal Hospital, watching myself on TV. First an announcer talked from the studio, reading something off a sheet of paper. The television was broken, so I couldn't hear what he was saying, but I knew that it was about what had happened the previous night because from the studio they cut to a shot of me, just a short one, perhaps five seconds, as I walked from a police car into the hospital. I was hunched over, hurrying, head down. I didn't look like myself, and this reassured me. I looked shaken, shocked, like I belonged there, on the news.

Next there was a reporter, a woman, talking into a microphone in front of Lou's house. She had on a heavy down jacket and thick yellow ski gloves. As she spoke, her long brown hair lifted itself an inch or so from her shoulders, trembling in the wind. Several police cars were parked behind her in the driveway. The yard was crisscrossed with tire tracks. Lou's front door was wide open, and I could see two men crouched inside the entranceway, taking pictures.

The woman talked for a bit, her face serious, grief-stricken. The announcer reappeared when she finished, and he seemed to say something consoling to her. Then the newsbreak was over.

There was a commercial next, and after that a cartoon.

Elmer Fudd chasing Daffy Duck. I turned away from the screen. I was sitting with Sarah and Amanda in what was once a two-bed, semiprivate room. For some reason it had been emptied of furniture. The beds were gone, the night tables, everything. Except for the two folding chairs Sarah and I sat in, the room was barren. The floor was light blue. I could see where the beds had stood; the tiles were a little darker there, two perfect rectangles against the wall, like shadows. There was a single small window, a slit in the side of the building, the same size and shape as the ones they used to have in castles, to shoot arrows through. It looked out onto the hospital's parking lot.

The television set hung on a bracket hooked into the ceiling. Though it gave me a sick feeling to look at it, I found it hard not to watch. It was the only thing in the room besides Sarah, and I didn't want to look at her. If I looked at her, I knew I'd start talking, and I didn't feel safe talking there.

We'd been put in the room as a courtesy, for our privacy. There were reporters down in the regular waiting room. I'd been up all night, had not eaten since the previous day. I was unshaven, dirty, shaky.

The FBI hadn't been called in. It was just the Fulton County Sheriff's Department. I'd spent two hours talking with them, and it had been fine. They were normal people, like Carl Jenkins, and they saw things exactly as Sarah and I had anticipated they would: Lou coming home drunk, finding Sonny and Nancy in bed together, getting his gun and shooting them; Jacob and I hearing the shots as we pulled away, Jacob running up to the house with his rifle, Lou opening the door, pointing his shotgun, two explosions ripping through the night.

The sheriff's deputies had treated me with great care and courtesy, like a victim rather than a suspect, mistaking my unconcealable distress over the possibility of Jacob's regaining consciousness for a brother's heartfelt grief.

Jacob was in his third hour of surgery.

Sarah and I sat in the room and waited.

Neither of us seemed to want to talk. Sarah tended Amanda. She nursed her, whispered to her, played little games with her. When the baby slept, Sarah closed her eyes, too, slouching forward in her folding chair. I watched the silent TV—cartoons, a game show, a rerun of "The Odd Couple." During commercials I went over to the window and stared down at the parking lot. It was a big lot, like a field of asphalt. The cars clustered around the building, leaving the far edge empty and forlorn looking. Beyond the parking lot was a real field, buried in snow. When the wind came up, it carried grains of this snow across the asphalt in little semi-transparent waves and threw them up against the hospital.

Sarah and I waited and waited. Doctors and nurses and policemen walked by outside the door, the clicking of their shoes echoing up and down the tiled hallway, drawing our eyes to their passing, but no one stopped to tell us anything.

Whenever the baby started to cry, Sarah hummed a little song to her, and she quieted down. After a while, I recognized the tune. It was "Frère Jacques." Listening to Sarah, I got it in my head, and then I couldn't get it out, even when she stopped.

Just after eleven, a sheriff's deputy came into the room. I was sitting in my chair, and I stood up to shake his hand. Sarah smiled and nodded, her arms wrapped around the baby.

"I don't want to impose at a time like this," the deputy began. Then he paused, as if he'd forgotten what he'd come to say. He stared up at the television, a Toyota commercial, and frowned. He wasn't one of the men I'd spoken to earlier. He looked too young to be a policeman, looked like a kid dressing up. His uniform was a little too big, his black shoes a little too shiny, the crease in his trooper's hat a little too perfect. When he frowned up at the TV, his whole face frowned, even his eyes. It was a perfectly round face, lightly freckled, a farm boy's face, flat and pale and moonlike.

"I'm real sorry about your brother," he started again. He glanced shyly at Sarah, taking in the baby in one swift glance, then turned back to the TV.

I waited, guarded.

"We have his dog," he said. "We found it at the crime site." He cleared his throat, pulled his eyes away from the TV, and gave me a hesitant look. "We were wondering if you wanted to look after it yourself."

He shifted his weight from one foot to the other. His shiny black shoes made a creaking noise.

"If you didn't," he said quickly, "if it's too much to think of right now, we can put it in the pound for a while." He glanced at Sarah. "Until things settle down."

I looked toward Sarah, too. She nodded at me.

"No," I said. "We'll take care of him."

The deputy smiled. He seemed relieved. "I'll drop him off at your house then," he said.

He shook my hand again before he left.

Forty minutes later a doctor came in to tell us that Jacob was out of surgery. He'd been moved to the intensive care unit and was listed in critical condition. The doctor told us that the blast from the shotgun had damaged both of Jacob's lungs, his heart, his aorta, three of his thoracic vertebrae, his diaphragm, his esophagus, his liver, and his stomach. He had a foldout chart to show Sarah and me where all these parts were in the body. As he listed off their names, he circled them with a red pen.

"We've done all we can for now," he said.

He gave Jacob a one-in-ten chance of surviving.

Later, when I was at the window again, Sarah turned to me and whispered, "Why didn't you check to see if he was alive?"

I could tell from her voice that she was on the edge of tears.

"If he lives . . . ," she said.

"Shhh." I glanced toward the door.

We watched each other for a moment, in silence. Then I turned back to the window.

JUST before three o'clock, a new doctor appeared. It was as if he'd snuck up on us; neither Sarah nor I heard him approach, he simply materialized in the doorway. He was tall and thin and good looking, with short gray hair and a white lab coat. Underneath his coat, he was wearing a red tie—bright red—and it made me think of blood.

"My name's Dr. Reed," he said.

He had a firm handshake, quick and tight, like a snake striking. He spoke rapidly, as if he were afraid he might be called off at any moment and wanted to get his say in before this happened.

"Your brother's regained consciousness."

I felt a surge of heat rush up my neck and into my face. I didn't look at Sarah.

"He's incoherent," the doctor said, "but he's calling your name."

I followed him out of the room, leaving Sarah sitting there with the baby. We walked down the hallway at a brisk clip. The doctor had long, efficient strides, and I had to break into a jog to keep up. We went to the elevators. Just as we arrived, one of them opened its doors for us, as if by magic. Dr. Reed pushed the fifth-floor button, a chime rang, and the doors slid shut.

"He's speaking?" I asked, slightly out of breath. I felt suspicious saying it and looked away.

The doctor was watching the numbers above the door. He held his clipboard clasped behind him in his hands. "Not really," he said. "He's drifting in and out of consciousness. All we've picked up is your name."

I closed my eyes.

"Normally I wouldn't let you in to see him," he said. "But to be frank, it may be your last chance."

The doors slid back, and we stepped out onto the fifth floor. The lighting was dimmer here. A group of nurses were whispering together behind a big counter right across from the elevators, and they glanced up when we appeared, looking at the doctor, not at me. I could hear soft beeping sounds coming from somewhere behind them.

Dr. Reed went over and spoke to one of them; then he came back and took me by the elbow, leading me quickly down the hall to the left. We passed several open doorways, but I didn't look inside them. I could tell which room was Jacob's. It was at the very end of the corridor, on the left-hand side. Carl Jenkins was standing outside it, talking to the deputy with the farm boy's face. They both nodded to me as the doctor led me inside.

My brother was lying in a bed just beyond the doorway. He looked huge beneath the covers, like a dead bear, but at the same time somehow depleted, as if he'd been drained and what was left now was merely his husk. His body was perfectly still. There were tubes everywhere, draped over the bed rail, trailing out haphazardly across the floor. Jacob was stuck full of them, like a puppet on a set of strings.

I went up to the bed.

There was an orderly on the other side, a very short, dark-haired young man, working at the tubing. He ignored my presence. A large boxlike machine with a tiny yellow video screen sat on a cart behind him, beeping steadily.

The room was large, a long rectangle, and had several other beds in it, hidden behind white curtains. I couldn't tell if they were occupied.

The orderly was wearing translucent rubber gloves. Through them, I could just make out the hair on the backs of his hands, black and wirelike, and pressed down close to the skin.

Dr. Reed stood at the foot of the bed.

"You can only stay a minute," he said. Then he turned to the orderly, and they whispered back and forth. While they talked, the doctor scribbled on his clipboard.

Holding my breath, I took my brother by the hand. It was cold, heavy, damp, like a hunk of meat. It didn't seem to belong to Jacob anymore. It was revolting. I had to grip it tightly to keep myself from throwing it away.

His eyes flickered at the pressure. When they opened a second later, they fell right on me. Then they didn't move at all. A set of tubes was stuck up his nose. His face was absolutely bloodless, so pale it seemed transparent. I could see the veins in his temples. His forehead was beaded with sweat.

He stared at me for a second, and then his lips moved, as if by reflex, into a smile. It wasn't Jacob's normal smile, it was unlike any I'd ever seen before. His lips stretched out straight across to either side of his face, so that he looked like a dog baring his teeth. His eyes didn't move at all.

"I'm here, Jacob," I whispered. "I'm right here."

He tried to respond but couldn't. He made a harsh, gasping sound at the back of his throat, and the machine's beeping increased its tempo. The doctor and the orderly glanced up from their discussion. Jacob shut his eyes. The beeping gradually slowed back down.

I continued to hold his hand for another minute or so, until the doctor asked me to leave.

Dr. Reed remained in the room with the orderly, so I made my way back to the elevator unaccompanied. Carl was at the opposite end of the hallway now, talking with a nurse. The farm boy had disappeared.

As I stepped into the elevator, I saw, out of the corner of my eye, Carl turn from the nurse and start to walk quickly toward me. Without thinking, I pressed the door-closed button. It was more from a simple desire to be alone than from any fear of him, but as soon as I did it, I recognized what it might look like—a guilty man's attempt to escape further interrogation. I jabbed my finger at the door-open button. It was too late, though; the elevator was already sliding slowly down its shaft.

When the doors opened again, I stepped out and turned to the left. I'd gone about ten feet before I realized that I was in the wrong place. In my hurry to avoid Carl, I'd pressed the third-floor button, rather than the second. It was the maternity ward; I recognized it from my visits to Sarah. I spun around, but by the time I returned to the bank of elevators, the one I'd arrived on had already shut its doors and disappeared.

There was a nurse's station directly across from the elevators, a long L-shaped counter, painted bright orange, just like the one on Jacob's floor. Three nurses were seated behind it. I'd seen them look up when I'd gotten off the elevator, and I could feel them staring at me now. I stood with my back to them, wondering if they knew who I was, if they'd seen me on TV or heard about me through the hospital's rumor mill. "That's the man whose brother was shot last night," I imagined them whispering, while they eyed me for signs of grief.

Somewhere down to the left a baby was crying.

The elevator on the right emitted its electric chime, and the doors slid open. Inside was Carl Jenkins. I blushed when I saw him but forced my voice to sound calm.

"Hello, Carl," I said, stepping forward.

He beamed at me. "What're you doing down here, Hank? You have another baby on me?"

I returned his smile, pressing the button for the second

floor. The doors slid shut. "Got so used to visiting Sarah, I punched the wrong button out of habit."

He laughed, short and soft, a polite chuckle. Then his face turned serious. "I'm real sorry about all this," he said. He was holding his hat in his hands, playing with the brim, and he stared down at it while he talked.

"I know," I said.

"If there's anything I can do . . ."

"That's awful kind of you, Carl."

The chime rang, the doors parted. We were at the second floor. I stepped outside. Carl held the doors open with his arm. "He say anything to you while you were in there?"

"Jacob?"

Carl nodded.

"No," I said. "Nothing."

I glanced up and down the hallway. There were two doctors off to the right, talking quietly together. To the left, I could hear a woman's laughter. Carl kept his arm across the doors.

"What were you three doing together last night, anyway?" he asked.

I looked closely at him, searching his face for some sign of suspicion. He'd been there when the deputies had asked the same question, and he'd heard my answer. The elevator tried to close, bucking his arm, but he held it back.

"We were celebrating the baby. Jacob took me out."

Carl nodded. He seemed to be waiting for something else.

"I didn't really want to go," I said. "But he was all excited about being an uncle, and I was afraid I'd hurt his feelings if I turned him down."

The elevator tried to close again.

"Did Lou say anything to Jacob before he shot him?"

"Say anything?"

"Did he swear at him, or call him names?"

I shook my head. "He just opened the door, raised his gun, and pulled the trigger."

Down the hallway, the doctors parted, and one of them started to walk toward us. His shoes squeaked against the tiled floor.

"Going down?" he called. Carl leaned his head out and nodded.

"What about that night when I saw you three over by the nature preserve?"

My heart jumped at the mention of our encounter there. I'd hoped that he'd forgotten that by now. "What about it?" I said.

"What were you three doing then?"

I couldn't think of anything to say to that, couldn't remember what, if anything, I'd told him at the time. I strained and strained, but my mind was too tired. The doctor was nearly upon us. "It was New Year's Eve," I said, trying to stall. It was all I could come up with.

"You guys were going out?"

I knew that this was wrong, but I couldn't come up with anything else, so I nodded slowly at him. Then the doctor was there, sliding past me into the elevator. Carl stepped back.

"Don't hesitate to call me if you need something, Hank," he said, as the doors slid shut. "You know I'd be glad to help any way I could."

THOUGH the doctors said I might as well leave, I stayed at the hospital for the rest of the afternoon. Jacob drifted in and out of consciousness, but I wasn't allowed to see him again. The doctors remained pessimistic.

Around five, as it was starting to get dark, Amanda began to cry. Sarah tried nursing her, then singing to her, then walking her around the room, but she refused to be quieted. Her crying got louder and louder. The sound of it gave me a headache, started to make the room seem smaller, and I asked Sarah to take her home.

She told me to come with them.

"You're not doing anything here, Hank," she said. "It's out of our hands now."

Amanda wailed and wailed, her tiny face red with the effort. I watched her cry, trying to think, but I was too tired. Finally, with a horrible wrenching feeling, as if something heavy were slipping from my grasp, I nodded to Sarah.

"All right," I said. "Let's go home."

I FELT a wonderful sense of release as I climbed into the car. All day long I'd been hoarding secrets way down inside myself, things I could say only to Sarah.

I could tell her now what had happened. Then I would go home, get something to eat, and fall asleep. And while I did that, while I slept, Jacob's torn body, in its battle for life, would decide my fate.

Sarah put the baby into her safety seat in back, then climbed behind the wheel. I sat beside her, slumped over, my body drooping, drained. My muscles ached with fatigue; I was nauseated with it. Outside, the sun had set; the sky was a deep navy blue, edging each second a little closer to black. Stars were coming out, one by one. There was no moon.

I rested my head against the window, letting its coolness keep me awake. I didn't begin to talk until we were out of the parking lot and on our way home. Then I told Sarah everything. I told her about the bar and the drinking, about the drive back to Lou's, and how we tricked him into confessing. I told her about Lou getting his gun, about Jacob shooting him, and me shooting Nancy. I told her about going to Sonny's trailer, about undressing him on the porch, and then chasing him up the stairs to the bedroom. She listened to me carefully, her head tilted toward me across the darkened seat.

Every now and then she nodded, as if to reassure me that she was paying attention. Her hands pulled the wheel back and forth, guiding the car home.

Amanda, strapped into her seat behind us, continued to cry.

When I reached the point where Jacob began to break down, I paused. Sarah glanced at me, her foot easing just perceptibly from the accelerator.

"He started crying," I said, "and I realized I had to do it. I realized he wasn't going to hold up, that when the police and the reporters arrived, he'd end up confessing."

Sarah nodded, as if she'd guessed this.

"There was no way he was going to pull himself together," I said. "So I shot him. I made the decision and I did it. And it felt right, too. The whole time I was doing it, I knew it was right."

I stared out the window, waiting for her response. We were passing the Delphia High School. It was a huge building, modern, brightly lit. There was something happening there tonight, a game or a play or a concert. Cars were pulling into the circular driveway. Teenagers congregated in loose groups at the edge of the pavement, cigarettes glowing. Parents streamed across the parking lot toward the big glass doors.

Sarah remained silent.

"But then," I said, "after I called the police and realized he was still alive, I was just frozen by it. Even if I could've thought of a way to finish him off, I wouldn't have done it."

I looked at Sarah.

"I didn't want him to die."

"And now?"

I shrugged. "He's my brother. It's like I'd forced myself to forget it, and then it came back and surprised me."

Sarah didn't say anything, and I shut my eyes, let my body tug me toward sleep. I listened to Amanda's crying, listened to the rhythm of it, how it came in waves. It seemed, gradually, to be moving farther away.

When I opened my eyes again, we were pulling into Fort Ottowa. A trio of boys popped up from behind a wall of shrubbery and launched a barrage of snowballs at our car. They fell short, skidding across the pavement before us, yellow in the headlights.

Sarah slowed the car. "If he lives, we'll both end up in jail."

"I wanted to do the right thing," I said, "but I couldn't figure out what it was. I wanted to protect us, and I wanted to save Jacob. I wanted to do both."

I glanced at Sarah for a response, but her face was expressionless.

"I couldn't, though," I said. "I had to choose one or the other."

Sarah dropped her voice to a whisper. "You did the right thing, Hank."

"Do you think so?"

"If he'd broken down, we'd be in jail right now."

"And do you think he would've broken down?"

I needed her to say yes, needed this simple reassurance, but she didn't offer it to me. All she said was, "He's your brother. If you thought he was a danger, then he probably was."

I frowned down at my hands. They were trembling a little. I tried briefly to make them stop, but they wouldn't obey me.

"Tell me the rest," Sarah said.

So I did. I told her about shooting Jacob, about driving back to Sonny's and turning out the lights. I told her about calling the police, and how my brother grabbed my ankle. As we pulled up into our driveway, I was describing my interview with the sheriff's deputies. Sarah eased the car into the garage, and we sat there—the engine off, the air growing cold around us—until I finished. Amanda continued to cry, her voice sounding merely tired now rather than angry, as it had before. I reached back and unstrapped her from her seat, then handed her to Sarah, who tried unsuccessfully to comfort her while I talked, by bouncing her on her lap, and kissing her on the face.

I told her about going to see Jacob.

"He smiled at me, like he understood," I said, not believing it. I looked at Sarah to see if she did, but she was making a face at Amanda. "Like he forgave me."

"He's probably in shock," Sarah said. "He probably doesn't even remember what happened yet."

"Will he remember later?" I wanted desperately to believe that he wouldn't; I clung to the idea. I wanted him to live and forget—about the money, the shooting, everything.

"I don't know."

"If he talks, we probably won't have much warning before they come and get us."

She nodded, then leaned her head down and kissed Amanda on her forehead. The baby was still crying, but quietly now, in little hiccoughs. Sarah whispered her name.

"We should get the money out of the house," I said, the words seeming to speed up on me as they came out, a thread of panic stitching them tightly together, squeezing out the spaces between them. "We should bury it somewhere, or take it—"

"Shhh," Sarah soothed. "It's all right, Hank. We're going to be okay."

"Why don't we just run?" I asked quickly, the idea coming to me as I spoke it.

"Run?"

"We could pack right now. Take the money and disappear."

She gave me a stern look. “Running would be a confession. It’s how we’d get caught. We’ve done what we’ve done; now we just have to wait and hope for the best.”

A car drove by on the street outside; Sarah watched it pass in the rearview mirror. When she spoke again, her voice came out very soft.

“The doctors think he’s going to die.”

“But I don’t want him to die,” I said, less because it was true than because it made me feel better to say it.

She turned and looked at me full in the face. “We can survive this, Hank, if we’re careful. We just can’t allow ourselves to feel guilty over what we’ve done, not for a single instant. It was an accident, the whole thing. We didn’t have a choice.”

“Jacob wasn’t an accident.”

“Yes, he was. From the moment Lou went out and got his gun, the whole thing became an accident. It ceased to be our fault.”

She touched Amanda’s cheek with her hand, and the baby, finally, fell silent. Without her crying, the car seemed suddenly to fill with space.

“What we’ve done is horrible,” Sarah said. “But that doesn’t mean we’re evil, and it doesn’t mean we weren’t right to do it. We had to save ourselves. Everything you did, every shot you fired, was in self-defense.”

She turned to look at me, pushing the hair out of her eyes with her hand, waiting for my response. And she was right, I realized. This was what we had to tell ourselves, that what we’d done was understandable, forgivable, that the brutality of our actions had stemmed not from our plans and desires but from the situation in which, through no fault of our own, we’d been trapped. That was the key: we had to envision ourselves not as the perpetrators of this tragedy but simply as two more unfortunates in its extensive cast of victims. It was the only way we’d ever be able to live with what we’d done.

“Okay?” Sarah whispered.

I stared down at Amanda, at the round dome of her head: my baby girl.

"Okay," I whispered back.

As we were climbing from the station wagon, the garage filled suddenly with light. A car had pulled into the driveway. I turned to squint at it.

"It's the police," Sarah said.

Hearing her say this, I felt my entire body shiver with exhaustion. If I panicked at all, it was purely intellectual. *Jacob's spoken,* whispered a voice in the back of my mind. *They've come to arrest you.* The thought flickered and danced through my skull, birdlike, but it didn't sink in, it didn't touch my depths. I was too tired to be moved like that; I was too near the end of what I could do.

The lights went out, and the police car took shape, a shadow in the driveway's darkness. The door opened.

I heard myself moan.

"Shhh," Sarah said. She reached toward me across the top of the car, her hand stretched out flat against the roof. "They're just here to tell you he died."

But she was wrong.

I forced myself down the driveway and found the deputy with the farm boy's face waiting for me by the car.

He'd come by to drop off Jacob's dog.

Inside, Sarah heated up the leftover lasagna. I ate it at the kitchen table, and she sat across from me. She put some of the lasagna into a bowl for Mary Beth, but he wouldn't eat any of it. He simply sniffed at it, then turned and walked out of the kitchen, whimpering. As I ate, I could hear him moving about the house.

"He's looking for Jacob, isn't he?" I asked.

Sarah looked up from her own lasagna. "Shhh, Hank," she said. "Don't."

I picked at my food. The sight of it made me think of my last dinner with my brother. I felt a wave of emotion at this, not so much sadness or guilt but rather some nameless surge of warmth, a tidal sense of movement within my chest. I was tired enough to cry, but I didn't want Sarah to worry.

She got up and took her dish to the sink.

Amanda started to wail again. We both ignored her.

The dog came into the kitchen, whimpering.

I stared at my food for a while; then I rested my head in my hands. When I shut my eyes, I saw the doctor's chart with the diagram of Jacob's body on it.

Sarah was running water in the sink.

There were red circles everywhere.

I WOKE up in the bedroom. I was sore, logy. My body felt leaden, as if it had been sewn to the mattress. I assumed that Sarah must've put me to bed, but I didn't remember. I was naked; my clothes were folded in a pile on a chair across the room.

Judging from the gray light filtering in from behind the shades, I decided it was morning. I didn't feel like turning to see the clock. I wasn't disoriented; I had no trouble remembering what had happened. There was a tender spot on the side of my rib cage, the beginning of a bruise, from where the shotgun had kicked me when I fired it.

Only gradually did I realize that the phone was ringing. I heard Sarah pick it up downstairs, heard the murmur of her voice. I couldn't make out what she was saying.

The dog was still whimpering, though he sounded far away now, like he'd been put out in the yard.

I started to drift off, still tired, but I was pulled back by the sound of Sarah climbing the stairs. Half asleep, my eyes just barely slitted open, I watched her come into the room.

I could tell by the way she moved that she thought I was still sleeping. She went first to the window, carrying Amanda to her crib. Then she came up beside the bed and began, very slowly, to undress. I watched her body through my eyelashes as she gradually unveiled it, taking off first her sweatshirt, then her bra, then her socks, then her jeans, then her underwear.

Her breasts were swollen with milk, but she'd already lost much of the weight she'd gained during her pregnancy. Her body was slim, compact, beautiful.

Amanda started to cry again, mimicking the sound of the dog beyond the window, a slow, soft, and melancholy whimpering.

Sarah glanced from me to the crib and back again. She seemed to hesitate; then she took off her earrings one at a time and set them down on the night table. They made a clicking sound when they touched the wood.

Naked, she slipped beneath the covers. She pressed her body tightly against my own, her right leg creeping up across my groin, her arm slipping around my neck. I lay perfectly still. Her skin was soft and powdered, and it made me feel unclean. She kissed me lightly on the cheek, then put her lips up to my ear.

I knew what she was going to whisper before she even began, but I waited for it, tense, as if it were a surprise.

"He's dead."

8

It took the media thirty-six hours to locate my house. I suppose they must've thought I lived in Ashenville rather than Delphia, or perhaps they held off for a bit out of some archaic sense of decorum, but by Sunday afternoon they'd arrived in full force. There were vans from each of the three Toledo television stations—channels 11, 13, and 24—as well as one from Channel 5 in Detroit. There were reporters and photographers from the Toledo *Blade*, the Detroit *Free Press*, the Cleveland *Plain Dealer*.

They were all surprisingly polite. They didn't knock on our door, didn't peer through our windows, didn't harass our neighbors. They simply waited until Sarah or I appeared, as we pulled either into or out of the driveway, then they clustered excitedly around the car taking pictures and shouting questions. We passed them with our heads down. I'm not sure what else they might've expected.

Their ranks gradually thinned in the following days. The television crews left first, that very night, then the newspaper reporters, one by one, drifting off to other, more pressing stories, until finally, a week later, the yard was suddenly empty, quiet; the dark oval scars of boot prints in the snow and the crumpled remains of coffee cups and sandwich wrappers along the curb were the only signs to remind us of their presence.

The funerals came and went in quick succession, one right upon the other—Nancy's on Tuesday, Sonny's on Wednesday, Lou's on Saturday, Jacob's on the following Monday. They were all held at St. Jude's, and I went to each of them.

The news media came to these, too, and I got to see myself on TV again. Each time I was astonished at how I appeared. I looked somber and mournful, limp with grief—more serious, more dignified than I'd ever felt in real life.

Jacob hadn't owned a suit, so I had to buy one for him to wear in his coffin. Though it seemed wrong in a way—he never would've worn it in real life—I was still pleased with its effect. The suit made him look young, even fit, a brown paisley tie knotted beneath his chin, a handkerchief sticking up crisply from the breast pocket of his jacket. The casket was closed for the funeral—all of them were—but I got to see him before the service. The undertaker had fixed him up; you couldn't have guessed how he'd died. His eyes were shut, and they'd put his glasses on. I stared down at him for a few seconds, then kissed him on the forehead and stepped back, allowing a young man with a white carnation in his lapel to come forward and screw shut the lid.

Sarah brought Amanda to Jacob's service, and the baby cried through the whole thing, whimpering softly against her mother's chest. Occasionally she broke into a sudden, startling wail, and the sound of it would echo off the low dome of the church, stretching itself out like a scream in a dungeon. Sarah jiggled her and rocked her, hummed songs to her and whispered in her ear, but nothing helped. She refused to be consoled.

The church was fairly full, though none of the mourners were Jacob's friends. They were people who'd known us growing up, people I was associated with through Raikley's, people who were simply curious. His only real friend had been Lou, and he was already buried, waiting for Jacob in the earth out behind the church.

The priest had asked me if I wanted to say a few words, but I declined. I said that I wasn't up to it, that I'd break down if I tried, which was probably true. He was understanding and did the eulogy himself, pretending, with a fair amount of success, that he'd known Jacob intimately and thought of him as a son.

After the service we walked out to the cemetery, where the grave was waiting, a rectangular hole in the snow.

The priest said a few more words. "The Lord giveth," he said. "The Lord taketh away. Blessed is the name of the Lord."

It started to snow a little as they lowered the coffin into the earth. I threw a handful of frozen clay in on top, and it landed with a hollow thud. A photo of me doing this showed up in the *Blade* that evening—me set off a few feet from the other mourners, dark suited, leaning over the open grave, the dirt falling from my hand, flecks of white drifting down through the air around me. It looked like something from a history book.

Sarah came forward and dropped a single rose on the casket, Amanda weeping in her arms.

As we were leaving, I turned to take one last look at the open grave. An old man with a backhoe was already preparing to fill it in, tinkering at his machine. A half dozen yards beyond him there was a woman playing hide-and-seek with two tiny boys among the tombstones. She jogged off and crouched behind a large marble cross, and the boys, giggling, came stumbling toward her through the snow, shouting with glee when they found her. She stood up to run to the next stone, but then, halfway there, saw me watching and froze. The two boys circled her, giddy with laughter.

I didn't want her to think that I was insulted by her lack of mourning, so I gave her a little wave. The boys saw me, and they waved back, hands high over their heads, like people departing on a cruise, but the woman whispered something to them, and—instantly—they stopped.

I could sense Sarah behind me, waiting to leave, could hear Amanda mewling in her arms. I didn't turn, though; I stood perfectly still.

It was the closest all that day I came to weeping. I don't know what it was—perhaps the two boys reminded me of myself and Jacob as children—but I got a shaking feeling, a tightness in my chest and head, a ringing in my ears. It wasn't grief, or guilt, or remorse. It was simply confusion: a sudden, nearly overwhelming wave of bewilderment over what I'd done. My crimes spread themselves out before me, and I could find no sense in them. They were inscrutable, foreign; they seemed to belong to someone else.

Sarah brought me back with a touch of her hand.

"Hank?" she said, her voice soft and concerned.

I turned slowly toward her.

"Are you okay?"

I stared at her, and she smiled calmly back at me. She was wearing a long, black woolen coat and a pair of winter boots. Her hands were tucked into thin leather gloves; a white scarf was wrapped around her neck. She looked startlingly pretty.

"Amanda's getting cold," she said, taking me by my arm.

I nodded and then, like a senile old man, allowed myself to be led back down the path to the car.

As we climbed inside, I heard the backhoe's engine rumble to life.

IN THE following days the world reached out to us. Neighbors dropped off casseroles on our doorstep, jars of homemade jam, loaves of fresh-baked bread, Pyrex containers full of soup. Acquaintances and coworkers called me up on the telephone, expressing sympathy. Strangers, moved by my story, wrote me letters, quoting psalms and self-help books on grief, offering advice and consolation. It was astonishingly generous, all this unsolicited solicitude, but it had a strangely unsettling effect on me, pointing as it did to an absence in my and Sarah's life that I hadn't really been conscious of before: we had no friends.

I couldn't exactly say how this had happened. We'd had friends in college; Sarah'd had whole troops of them. But somehow, after we'd moved to Delphia, they'd disappeared, and we hadn't replaced them with new ones. I didn't feel their lack—I wasn't lonely—I was simply surprised. It seemed like a bad sign, that we could exist all this time as a closed system, totally satisfying each other's needs, neither of us desiring any outside connection with the world. It seemed deviant, unhealthy. I could imagine what our neighbors would say if we were ever caught—how they weren't at all astonished, how we'd been so reclusive, so antisocial, so secretive. It was always loners who you heard about committing murders, and that this label might apply to us led me on to further considerations. Perhaps we weren't the normal people trapped in extraordinary situations that we'd been pretending to be. Perhaps we'd done something ourselves to create these situations. Perhaps we were responsible for what had happened.

I only half-believed this, if at all. In my mind, I could still go through the long succession of events that had culminated, ultimately, in Jacob's funeral and logically explain how each one had led inexorably to the next, how there'd been no alternatives, no branches in the path, no opportunities to turn back and undo what we'd already done. I'd shot Jacob because he was going to break down because I'd shot Sonny because I needed to cover up shooting Nancy because she'd been about to shoot me because Jacob had shot Lou because he'd thought Lou was going to shoot me because Lou was threatening me with his shotgun because I'd tricked him into confessing to Dwight Pederson's murder because Lou'd been blackmailing me because I didn't want to give him his share of the money till the summer because I wanted to make sure no one was looking for the plane . . .

It seemed as though I could keep working my way back like that forever, each cause's existence obviating the need for me to accept responsibility for its effect. But the mere fact that I felt the need to do this—and I was doing it frequently, obsessively, repeating it like a mantra in my head—seemed reason enough for worry. I was starting, just perceptibly, to doubt myself. I was beginning to question our motives.

WITHIN a week of Jacob's funeral, the public attention suddenly faded.

I returned to work that Monday, and my life immediately resumed its daily routine. Every now and then I'd overhear people in town talking about what had happened, and invariably they used words like *tragedy* and *shocking* and *horrible* and *senseless.* No one seemed to suspect a thing. I was above suspicion: there was no motive; even to speak of the possibility would've been cruel, tactless. After all, I'd lost my brother.

They found Nancy's robe and lipstick in Sonny's trailer. I saw an interview with one of her coworkers, and she said she thought the affair had been going on for quite some time. She didn't say why she thought this, and the reporter didn't ask her; her retroactive suspicion was enough. People talked about how belligerent Lou had been at the Wrangler that night, how he'd accused some kid of trying to trip him. They remembered him as being angry, combative, a drunk teetering on the edge of violence. And finally, to add the last note of credence to our story, the Toledo *Blade* published an article about Lou's gambling debts. His life had been falling apart, they said, disintegrating. He'd been a time bomb, a calamity waiting to happen.

The baby grew. She learned to roll over, which her mother claimed was precocious. Sarah started her job at the Delphia library again, part-time. She brought Amanda with her and laid her on the floor behind the checkout counter while she worked.

February slowly passed.

I KEPT putting off cleaning out Jacob's apartment. Finally, toward the end of the month, his landlord sent me a note at the feedstore, saying it had to be done by the first of March.

I continued to procrastinate right up to the twenty-ninth. It was a Monday, and I left work an hour early, swinging by the grocery store first to pick up some old boxes. I carried these, along with a thick roll of tape from Raikley's, over to the hardware store and climbed the steep flight of stairs to Jacob's room.

Inside, I found things exactly as I'd remembered them. There was the same smell, the same sordidness, the same disarray. The same dust motes floated through the air, the same empty beer bottles studded the floor, the same dirty sheets sat half stripped in a shapeless mound at the foot of the bed.

I began with his clothes, since that seemed the easiest. I didn't fold them, I simply jammed them into boxes. There wasn't that much: six pairs of pants—jeans and khaki dungarees—a half dozen flannel shirts, a bright red turtleneck, a large, hooded sweatshirt, a motley assortment of T-shirts, socks, and underwear. There was a single blue tie hanging from a hook, a picture of a bounding deer embroidered across its front; there were two pairs of sneakers and a pair of boots; there were hats and gloves, a black ski mask, a pair of bathing trunks, jackets for the different seasons. There were the gray slacks and the brown leather shoes he'd worn the morning he asked me to help him buy back the farm. Whenever I filled a box, I took it downstairs to my car and loaded it in the back.

From the clothes I moved to the bathroom—toiletries, towel, shaving kit, a plastic squirt gun, a stack of *Mad* magazines—and from the bathroom to the little alcove Jacob had used as a kitchen—two pots, a frying pan, a tray full of mismatched utensils, four glasses, a half dozen plates, a ragged-looking broom, and an empty can of Comet. Everything was greasy, grimy. I threw out the food—a can of ravioli, a box of Frosted Flakes, a putrid carton of milk, an unopened bag of chocolate donuts, a molding loaf of bread, three slices of American cheese, a shriveled apple.

I cleaned out the trash next—the beer bottles and old newspapers, the candy wrappers and empty bags of dog food. Then I moved to his bed. I stripped his sheets, wrapped his clock radio in a pair of thermal underwear, and stuffed it all into a box. I tossed his pillow over toward the door. Everything smelled faintly of Jacob.

The furniture in the apartment belonged to the landlord, so when I'd packed the sheets and pillow, there was nothing left to go through except his trunk. This was an old army footlocker—it'd been our uncle's during the Second World War, and he'd given it to Jacob on his tenth birthday. I was planning on just taking it downstairs unexamined, but then, at the last moment, I changed my mind, dragged it over to the bed, and swung open its lid.

The trunk's interior was surprisingly tidy. On the left, neatly folded and stacked, was an extra set of sheets and bath towels. They were from our parents' house; I recognized them immediately: powder blue towels, worn looking, monogrammed with our mother's initials. The sheets had little roses on them. On the right-hand side of the trunk there was a red tackle box, an old Bible, a fielder's glove, a box of bullets for Jacob's rifle, and a machete. The machete had belonged to the same uncle who'd given my brother the trunk; he'd brought it back from somewhere in the Pacific. It was long and menacing looking, with a thick, delicately curving blade and a light brown, wooden handle. It looked like something you might see in a museum, primitive and deadly.

Beneath the machete was a large, ancient-looking book.

Curious, I picked it up out of the trunk and sat down on the edge of Jacob's mattress. The sun had set since I arrived, and the apartment was dark. There was a light on in the bathroom, but that was all, so I had to strain to read the book's title. It was stamped in gold ink on the binding: *Farm Management from A to Z.*

I opened the cover, and on the inside, on the clean whiteness of the facing page, I found, written in pencil, our father's name. Beneath it, Jacob had scrawled his own name, in ink. I assumed that it must've been one of the trivialities granted to my brother in our father's will, a pathetic substitute for the promised farm itself. But when I began to flip through the pages, I saw that Jacob had treated this particular segment of his inheritance as anything but trivial. The book was heavily underlined, its margins clogged with scribbled notes. There were chapters on irrigation, drainage, equipment maintenance, fertilizers, grain markets, government regulations, shipping rates—all the things I'd told Jacob he'd never understand.

He'd been studying to be a farmer.

I flipped back toward the front of the book and checked its copyright date. It had been published in 1936, more than fifty years ago. There was no mention in its pages of pesticides or herbicides or crop dusting. The government regulations it discussed at such great length had been superseded several times over. My brother had been struggling through a uselessly outdated text.

I found a large, folded-up sheet of paper tucked into the back of the book. It was a diagram of our father's farm, drawn, from the looks of it, by Jacob himself. It showed where the barn was supposed to be, the machine shed, the grain bin. It showed the boundaries of the fields, with precise measurements from point to point and little arrows to indicate the drainage patterns. Paper-clipped to the diagram's top-right-hand corner was a photograph of our house, taken—I could tell by the lack of curtains in the windows—just before they knocked it down. Perhaps Jacob had driven out there to watch its demolition.

It's difficult for me to articulate exactly the way I felt, looking down at that photo, at that diagram and that book full of notes. First there was regret, I suppose, the simple wish that I'd been wise enough to leave the trunk alone, that I'd followed my original inclination and carried it down to the car with its contents undisturbed. I'd planned to be quick here, brutally efficient. I'd anticipated the danger my brother's possessions might hold for me and thus had set about my task with the greatest of care, treating the room as if it were booby-trapped, the most innocent of objects wired with little bombs of sorrow and regret. I'd almost pulled it off, too, had reached the very end before, careless with curiosity, I'd paused over the trunk. And now I was sitting here on the edge of Jacob's bed, the tears welling up in my eyes, the dark, empty apartment echoing with the staggered sound of my breathing, the soft precursors to my sobs of grief.

Grief: that's the closest I can come to describing what I felt. It was as though a tumor had blossomed suddenly in my chest, pushing aside my lungs, taking up the space they needed to breathe, so that I had to gasp out loud to fill them with air. I still believed what Sarah had said, that we'd done the right thing—the only thing we could do, which was to save ourselves—that if I hadn't shot Sonny and Jacob, we would've been caught and sent to jail. But at the same time I wished with all my heart that none of it had happened. I thought of the pain Jacob must've gone through, his body stuck full of tubes, his insides torn apart; I thought of his plans for the farm, his notes and diagrams; I thought of his coming to my rescue in the end, shooting his best friend to protect me, his brother; and everything was layered with grief.

Jacob, I realized, was an innocent, a child. No matter what Sarah said about accidents and self-defense and lack of choices, I was still to blame for what had happened to him—I was the murderer, there was no escaping that—it was my guilt, my sin, my responsibility.

For ten, maybe fifteen minutes I sat there, weeping into my hands. And then, without really wanting to—crying like that, I felt as good as I had in months; I felt virtuous, clean, as if I were being purged—I stopped. I fell silent as one falls silent after a bout of vomiting; my body, of its own accord, simply ceased to cry.

I waited for a moment, breathing deeply, to see what would happen next, but nothing did. It was getting late. I could hear someone walking back and forth in the apartment above my head. The floorboards creaked beneath the footsteps. Intermittently, from outside the window, there was the hush of cars moving up and down Main Street. A soft popping sound came from the steam in the radiator.

I wiped my face with my hand. I refolded the diagram and slid it back into the book. I set the book on the floor of the trunk and shut the lid. I'd rolled up my shirtsleeves to do the packing, and now I carefully rolled them back down, buttoning the cuffs.

I felt shaky, a little fragile, as if I hadn't eaten all day. I was conscious of the weight of my clothes pressing down on my body. My face was still moist from the tears, and I could feel my skin tightening a little as they dried. There was the taste of salt on my lips.

Before I even stood up, I knew how I was going to approach what had happened here tonight. I'd look on it as an anomaly, a parenthesis within my life, a tiny lacuna of despair into which I'd stumbled and then extracted myself. I would not tell Sarah about it, would keep it hidden, a secret. And when it happened again, as I knew it must, I'd repeat this process. Because even while I'd been weeping, even while I'd been sitting there gasping for air, I'd realized that it meant nothing, that it could not undo my crimes, could not even alter how I felt about them. What I'd done, I'd done, and the only way I could continue to function, the only way I could survive my brother's death, was to accept this. Otherwise, if I gave it the chance, my grief would deteriorate slowly into regret, my regret into remorse, and my remorse into an insidious desire for punishment. It would poison my life. I had to control it, discipline it, compartmentalize it.

After another minute or so, I rose to my feet and put on my jacket. I went into the bathroom and washed my face at the sink. Then I carried the footlocker and the box of sheets down to the street, locking Jacob's door behind me.

I left the boxes in the back of my car. I knew that if I took them out, it would be to throw them away, and I didn't feel like doing that just yet.

MARY BETH was the only one besides myself who seemed to mourn Jacob's absence. The dog went through a remarkable personality shift in the weeks following his arrival at my house. He became angry, a barker. He started to growl at us and would bare his teeth if we tried to pet him.

Sarah was worried about Amanda's safety, afraid the dog might attack her, so I decided we should keep him outside. Each morning as I left for work, I would tie him up by a piece of clothesline to the hawthorn tree in our front yard, and at night I'd stick him in the garage. This new routine seemed only to increase the dog's irritability. All day long he sat in the snow out front and barked at cars passing by, at the children waiting on the corner for the school bus, at the mailman making his rounds. Raw spots appeared on the skin beneath his collar from tugging at the rope. At night he would howl in the garage, over and over again for long stretches of time, and the sound would echo up and down the street. Among the children in the neighborhood, the rumor even sprang up that our house was haunted—that the nightly baying wasn't from the dog, it was from my brother's tortured ghost.

Amanda, as if it were infectious, also became short-tempered, loud, difficult to please or quiet down. She cried more than she used to, and there was a sharper edge to her voice now, as if she were complaining about real pain rather than mere discomfort. She became inflexibly attached to her mother and started to scream if she couldn't see her, or feel her touch, or hear her voice. Horribly enough, it was Jacob's bear that did the most to keep her calm. As soon as the man's voice within the toy's chest began to sing, she'd freeze, her whole body seeming to listen, to follow along with the tune:

Frère Jacques, Frère Jacques,
Dormez-vous? Dormez-vous?
Sonnez les matines. Sonnez les matines.
Ding, dang, dong. Ding, dang, dong.

I could quiet her down only at night, when it was dark and she was very sleepy.

After much debate, I sold Jacob's truck to the feedstore, and now, each morning when I drove in to work, I saw it parked there in the street, its rear end sagging down with sacks of grain.

A week after I cleaned out my brother's apartment, the sheriff came by my office. He asked me what I was going to do with Jacob's rifle.

"To tell the truth, I haven't really thought about it, Carl," I said. "I suppose I'll sell it."

He was sitting in the chair beside my desk. He was wearing his uniform and had his dark green police jacket on over it. His hat was in his lap. "I was guessing you might do that," he said. "And I was hoping you might let me put in the first bid."

"You want to buy it?"

He nodded. "I've been looking for a good hunting rifle."

The thought of him owning Jacob's gun gave me a distinctly unsafe feeling. It seemed like a piece of evidence somehow, and I didn't want him to have it. But I couldn't think of a way to put him off.

"I don't think it'll be a matter of bidding, Carl," I said. "You just offer me a price and it's yours."

"How's four hundred dollars sound?"

I gave my hand a little wave. "I'll give it to you for three hundred."

"You're not much of a bargainer, Hank." He smiled.

"I wouldn't want to overcharge you."

"Four hundred's a fair price. I know my guns."

"All right, then. Whatever you feel more comfortable with. But I'll give it to you for three."

He frowned. I could see that he wanted to pay less now but felt like he'd trapped himself into paying four hundred.

"How about I drop it off at your office tomorrow morning," I asked, "and you can just send me a check after you give it a closer look?"

He nodded slowly. "That sounds like a good plan."

We talked about other things then: the weather, Sarah, the baby. But when he rose to leave, he returned to the rifle. "You're sure you want to sell it?" he asked. "I wouldn't want to pressure you into it."

"Can't say I have much use for it myself, Carl. Never hunted in my life."

"Your father never took you hunting as a boy?" He seemed surprised.

"No," I said. "I've never even shot a gun."

"Not once?"

I shook my head.

He stood there before my desk, staring at me for several seconds. His hat was in his hands, and he was playing with the brim. For a moment it seemed like he might sit back down. "You'd know how to shoot one, though, wouldn't you?"

I thought about this, suddenly cautious. His voice had changed, become less casual. He wasn't asking the question just for conversation now; he was asking because he wanted to know the answer.

"I suppose," I said.

He nodded, standing there as if he expected something more. I looked away, staring down at my desk, at my hands spread out across it. In the bright light from my reading lamp, the hair on the backs of my fingers looked gray. I closed them into fists.

"How well did you know Sonny?" he asked, out of the blue.

I glanced up at him, my heart quickening in my chest. "Sonny Major?"

He nodded.

"Not that well. I knew who he was, he knew who I was. That's about all."

"Acquaintances."

"Yes," I agreed. "We'd say hello when we passed on the street, but we wouldn't stop to talk."

Carl took a second to absorb this. Then he put his hat on his head. He was about to leave.

"Why?" I asked.

He shrugged. "Just wondering." He gave me a little smile.

I believed him, could tell somehow that he was simply curious rather than suspicious: just as his feelings about my character had blinded him to the possibility of me killing Jacob and Sonny and Nancy, his feelings about Lou had made it hard to accept our story. He sensed, I think, that something was wrong with it, but he couldn't guess exactly what. He wasn't investigating; he was simply reviewing things, idly probing for missing pieces. I knew this, could see that he wasn't a threat. But still the conversation upset me. After he left, I went over and over everything I'd said, every gesture I'd made, searching for mistakes, subtle confessions of guilt. There was nothing there, of course, simply a vague aura of anxiety, growing more and more diffuse every time I tried to pin it down.

I told Sarah about selling the rifle to the sheriff but not about his questions.

THE NIGHT after Carl came by my office, Amanda kept us up late with her crying. We lay in bed with her, the lights out, the room dark, Sarah cuddling the baby in her arms while I wound and rewound Jacob's teddy bear. It was well after midnight before she fell asleep. Sarah and I both sat there in the silence that followed, as if stunned, terrified to move lest we startle the drowsing infant back awake. Our legs were touching beneath the blankets; I could feel Sarah's skin, a little patch of heat along my calf.

"Hank?" she whispered.

"What?"

"Would you ever kill me for the money?" Her tone was playful, joking, but within it, snaking deviously through her voice, I could hear an earnest note.

"I didn't kill them for the money," I said.

I sensed Sarah turning to glance at me through the darkness.

"I did it so we wouldn't get caught. I did it to protect us."

Amanda made a sighing sound, and Sarah rocked her back and forth. "Would you kill me to keep from getting caught, then?" she whispered. The earnest note had grown, pushing aside the playfulness.

"Of course not," I said, sliding down onto my back. I nestled into my pillow, making a show of it, trying to end the conversation. I was facing away from her.

"What if you knew you could get away with it, and that if you didn't, I'd turn you in?"

"You wouldn't turn me in."

"Let's say I had a change of heart. I wanted to confess."

I waited a moment; then I rolled over to face her. "What're you saying?"

Sarah was a dark shape outlined against the ceiling above me. "It's just a game. A hypothetical situation."

I didn't say anything.

"You'd go to jail," she said.

"I killed them for you, Sarah. For you and Amanda."

The bed made a creaking sound as she shifted her weight. I felt her leg move away from me. "You said you killed Pederson for Jacob."

I thought about that for a second. It was true, but it seemed like it wasn't. I tried to work my way around it.

"I couldn't do it," I said. "I'd just go to jail. You two are all I have." I reached out to touch her but brushed against Amanda instead. She woke up and started to cry.

"Shhh," Sarah said. We both listened, holding our bodies still, until the baby quieted down.

"Would you've thought you could kill Jacob before you did it?" Sarah whispered.

"That's different. You know that."

"Different?"

"I can trust you. I couldn't trust him." As soon as I said it, I realized how it sounded. It was only half what I meant, but I didn't say anything else. It seemed like I'd only make it worse by trying to take it back.

Sarah sat there thinking.

"You know what I mean," I whispered.

Just barely, I could see her nod. After a moment, she slipped out of bed and took Amanda to her crib. When she came back, she snuggled up close against me. I could feel her breath on my neck, and it made me shiver.

I debated for a bit before I spoke. Then I said, "Would you kill me?"

"Oh, Hank." She yawned. "I don't think I could kill anyone."

Outside, in the garage, as if he were much closer than he actually was, I heard the dog begin to howl. *Jacob's ghost*, I thought.

Sarah lifted her head and kissed me on my cheek.

"Good night," she said.

WEDNESDAY evening I came home from work and found three pieces of paper sitting on the kitchen table. They were photocopies of articles from the Toledo *Blade*. The first one was dated November 28, 1987, and its headline said:

DEADLY DUO KILLS SIX, KIDNAPS HEIRESS
Huge Ransom Demanded

The article told the story of Alice McMartin, the seventeen-year-old daughter of the Detroit millionaire Byron McMartin. On the evening of November 27, Alice was abducted at gunpoint from her father's estate in Bloomfield Hills, Michigan. The kidnappers, dressed as police officers, with badges, service revolvers, and truncheons, bluffed their way into the house shortly before 8:00 p.m. A security camera filmed them as they handcuffed six of the McMartins' household employees—four security guards, a maid, and a chauffeur—with their arms behind their backs before making them kneel with their faces against a wall. The kidnappers then took turns shooting their victims in the back of the head, using the security guards' own revolvers.

Byron McMartin and his wife discovered their daughter's absence, as well as the six corpses, when they returned home from a social function just after ten o'clock. The article quoted an unidentified source as saying that the kidnappers had left a ransom note behind, demanding as much as $4.8 million in unmarked bills.

The second article, like the first, came from the *Blade*'s front page. Its headline read:

HEIRESS' BODY ID'D BY FEDS
Father Loses Daughter, Ransom

This article was datelined "Sandusky, OH, Dec. 8," and it told how Alice McMartin's gagged and handcuffed corpse had been pulled out of Lake Erie three days before by a local fisherman. The body had apparently been in the water for some time, because the FBI needed the young woman's dental records to confirm her identity. She'd been shot in the back of the head before being dumped into the lake, probably within twenty-four hours of her abduction.

A ransom had been paid, the article said, after the FBI told Alice's father that it would help them catch the kidnappers.

The final article was from page 3 of the *Blade*.

It began:

FBI ID's McMARTIN KIDNAPPERS

Detroit, Dec. 14 (AP)—Using a security camera's film of the November 27 kidnapping of Alice McMartin, the daughter of the millionaire and former paper cup manufacturer Byron McMartin, during which six employees of the McMartin estate were murdered, the FBI has established the identity of two suspects and begun a nationwide manhunt for them.

The two men, identified as Stephen Bokovsky, 26, and Vernon Bokovsky, 35, both of Flint, Michigan, are brothers.

> The FBI, acting on a hunch that one or both of the kidnappers were former employees of Mr. McMartin, searched through thousands of personnel files, trying to match employee photographs with the grainy, low-quality images taken from the security camera. A match came when they opened the younger Bokovsky's file. He'd worked as a gardener on the McMartin estate in the summer of 1984.
>
> Vernon Bokovsky, the elder brother, was identified after FBI agents interviewed the brothers' parents, Georgina and Cyrus Bokovsky, of Flint. The two suspects reportedly stayed with their parents throughout the month of November. Cyrus Bokovsky, reached by phone, told a *Blade* reporter that he hasn't seen either of his sons since November 27, the night of the kidnapping.

Vernon had been paroled from the Milan Correctional Facility in 1986 after serving seven years of a twenty-five-year sentence for the 1977 murder of a neighbor in a dispute over the sale of a car. The FBI expressed confidence in their ability to track down and apprehend the suspects. "Now that we've ID'd them," one of the agents said, "it's only a matter of time before we bring them in. They can run all they want, but sooner or later, whether it's next week or next year, we'll get them."

The article ended with a quote from the same agent, expressing outrage at the brutality of the brothers' crime:

> "It was coldly methodical," Agent Teil said. "It's clear that these guys had planned it out with extreme care. They weren't killing out of panic. The thing you come away with after watching the film is how calm they were. They knew exactly what they were doing."
>
> Teil speculated that they murdered the six McMartin employees to eliminate the possibility of Stephen Bokovsky being recognized.

"They saw it as tying up loose ends," he said. "Fortunately for us they forgot about the camera."

I went back to the first article and read it again. Then I reread the other two articles. Included with the third one were three photographs. The first was a head-and-shoulders shot of Stephen Bokovsky. It was from his employee ID at the McMartin estate. He was small, dark haired, with a thin-lipped smile. His eyes were sunken and tired looking.

The second photo was of Vernon. It was a mug shot, from when he'd been in jail. He was bearded, intense, his jaw clenched tightly, as if he were in pain. He was much bigger than Stephen. They didn't look like brothers.

The third photo was a magnified image from the estate's security camera. It showed Stephen aiming down his arm at the back of a kneeling man's head.

I glanced around the kitchen. There was a pot on the stove, making bubbling sounds. It smelled like beef stew. Sarah was upstairs, with the baby. I could hear her, the low hum of her voice. It sounded like she was reading out loud. Her knitting was across from me on the table in a messy pile, the long needles pointing straight up into the air, like a booby trap.

I reread the articles again. When I finished, I went upstairs.

SARAH was in the bathroom, taking a bath with Amanda. She looked up when I came in, glancing quickly at the photocopies in my hand. I could tell that she was pleased with her discovery. Her face was radiant, triumphant. She grinned at me.

The bathroom was full of steam. I shut the door behind me and sat down on the closed lid of the toilet, loosening my tie.

Amanda was lying on her back in the warm water, smiling broadly, kept afloat by Sarah's thighs. Sarah was leaning forward, her hands clasped behind the baby's head. One of

Amanda's little feet was pressed up against her breast, denting it slightly.

Sarah was making up a story for Amanda. She paused only briefly when I arrived, then continued, picking up where she'd left off.

"The queen was very mad," she said, rocking the baby a little in the water. "She stormed out of the ballroom, casting angry looks from side to side. The king ran after her, his whole court following at a distance. 'Beloved!' he yelled. 'Forgive me!' He ran out into the street, glancing this way and that. 'Beloved!' he yelled. 'Beloved!' He sent his soldiers out to search the city. But the queen had disappeared."

Amanda giggled. She slapped one of her hands at the water, and it made a hollow clapping sound. She kicked her foot at Sarah's breast. Sarah giggled too.

I couldn't tell if the story was finished, so I waited a few moments before I spoke. I had the photocopies in my lap. They gave off a faint chemical smell in the moist air.

Sarah lifted her thighs, then dropped them, drawing a gasp from the baby. They were both pink from the water. The ends of Sarah's hair were limp and damp.

"You found them at the library?" I asked.

She nodded.

"I guess it has to be our money, doesn't it?"

She nodded again, bending forward to kiss the baby on her forehead. "Do you recognize one of them from the plane?" she asked.

I turned to the back page and stared at the photographs. "I can't really tell. His face was all chewed up."

"It's definitely our money."

"He'd have to be the younger one. He was small." I held the picture out toward her. "The other guy's big."

She didn't look at the photo. She was watching Amanda. "It's weird, their being brothers, isn't it?"

"What do you mean?"

"I mean you and Jacob."

I allowed myself to pursue that for a moment, but then I stopped. It wasn't something I really wanted to think about. I set the photocopies down on the edge of the sink.

"How'd you find them?" I asked.

She reached forward and pulled the plug on the drain. There was a rushing sound beneath the bathroom floor as the water began to make its way out. Amanda lay very still, listening.

"I just started going back through the old papers from the time you discovered the plane. I didn't have to go far. It was right there on the front page. When I saw it, I even remembered reading it."

"Me too."

"But it was just an article then. It didn't seem important."

"It changes things. Doesn't it?"

She glanced over at me. "How's that?"

"The way we talked ourselves into keeping it was that it was lost money—it didn't belong to anyone, no one was looking for it."

"And?"

"And now we know someone's looking for it. We can't say it isn't stealing anymore."

She stared up at me from the tub, her face confused. "It's always been stealing, Hank," she said. "It's just that before we didn't know who we were stealing from. Knowing where it's from doesn't make it any different."

She was right, of course. I saw it as soon as she said it.

"I think it's good we know where it came from," she said. "I was beginning to worry that it might be counterfeit, or marked. That we'd done all this and it was useless, we'd never be able to spend it."

"It might still be marked," I said. I felt my heart throb painfully at the idea—the bills were worthless; we'd killed them all for a bag full of paper. My mind reeled at the thought of it—all our struggle, all our terrible choices, coming now, like this, to nothing.

But Sarah waved it aside. "They demanded unmarked money. It says so in the article."

"Maybe that's why they shot her. Maybe they got the ransom and discovered—"

"No." She cut me off. "It says they killed her right away. They shot her before they even saw the money."

"Couldn't we tell by looking at it? Can't you hold it up to an ultraviolet light or something?"

"They wouldn't have given them marked bills. It'd be too much of a risk."

"It just seems like—"

"Trust me, Hank, all right? The bills aren't marked."

I didn't say anything.

"You're being paranoid. You're just looking for something to worry about."

A little whirlpool formed at the far end of the tub. We both watched it spiral. The drain made a loud sucking sound beneath it.

"It makes me want to go back to the plane," I said. "See whether or not it's him."

"Was he carrying a wallet?"

"I didn't even think to check."

"It'd be stupid to go back, Hank. It'd be just asking to get caught."

I shook my head. "I'm not going back."

Sarah lifted Amanda off her legs. The water was nearly gone from the tub. "Get a towel," she said.

I stood up, pulled a towel from the rack. I lifted the baby from Sarah's hands, swaddling her, and then brought her back to the toilet. When I sat down, I rested her on my knees, bouncing her a little. She started to cry.

"What scares me," I said, watching Sarah dry herself, "is that someone out there knows about the money."

"He's terrified, Hank. They have his name."

"The FBI said they're sure they'll catch him. He'll tell them about his brother disappearing with the money in a plane."

"And?"

"The connections are just under the surface, Sarah. It wouldn't be that hard for things to come together. Carl knows I heard a plane with engine trouble out by the nature preserve. He knows about Jacob and Lou and Sonny and Nancy getting shot. If they find the plane, and they know it's supposed to have four million dollars on it . . ." I trailed off. Hearing myself say these things, I felt an instant's flicker of panic, a tremor in the muscles at the back of my neck. I waved toward the photocopies on the sink. "It's like them forgetting about the security camera. We're bound to be overlooking something."

She dropped her towel into the clothes hamper. Her bathrobe was hanging from the back of the door; she took it down and put it on. Then she picked up Amanda from my lap.

"The connections only seem obvious to us," she said calmly. "No one else would see them." The baby slowly stopped crying.

I stood up. I was beginning to sweat beneath my suit, so I took off my jacket and draped it over my arm. My shirt was stuck to my back. "What if Jacob or Lou or Nancy left something behind, a diary or something. Or if one of them told somebody we don't know about . . ."

"We're okay, Hank," she soothed me. "You're letting yourself think too much." She stepped forward and hugged me with one arm, the baby—still whimpering a little—pressed tightly between our bodies. I let her rest her cheek against my own. Her skin smelled clean and damp and fresh.

"Think about how people see you," she said. "You're just a normal guy. A nice, sweet, normal guy. No one would ever believe that you'd be capable of doing what you've done."

SARAH'S birthday was Saturday, the twelfth of March. I wanted it to be a memorable one, not only because it was her thirtieth but also because of the money and the baby, so I got her two big gifts—both of which were well beyond my pre–duffel bag means.

The first was a condominium in Florida. Toward the end of February, I'd seen an advertisement in the paper announcing a government auction of property seized in drug raids. They listed all sorts of things that had to be sold—boats, cars, airplanes, motorcycles, satellite dishes, houses, condominiums, jewelry, even a horse farm—merchandise that could be purchased for less than 10 percent of its appraised value. It was on the following Saturday, March 5, in Toledo. I told Sarah that I had to work that day and drove into the city around nine, the hour it was scheduled to begin.

The address listed in the advertisement was a small warehouse, down by the port. Inside there were folding chairs lined up across the floor, facing a wooden podium. None of the actual merchandise was there—they simply had photographs of it, and long written descriptions, all pasted together in a catalog that they handed to you as you entered from the parking lot. There were about forty people already there when I arrived, all men, and a handful more came in after me.

The auction was late starting, so I had a half hour to sit and explore the catalog. I'd come to see if there was any nice jewelry, but, as I flipped through the glossy pages, I began to change my mind. The fourth item scheduled for bidding was a three-bedroom beachfront condominium in Fort Myers,

Florida. It had a deck, a hot tub, a solarium. There were color pictures of it, interior and exterior. It was white stucco, with a red-tiled roof, like a Spanish house. It was beautiful, luxurious, and I decided immediately that I was going to buy it for Sarah.

Its appraised value was listed as $335,000, but the bidding was set to start at $15,000. Sarah and I had a little over $35,000 saved up in the Ashenville bank, our nest egg for the move we'd been planning out of Fort Ottowa, and I decided, quite spontaneously, that I could spend $30,000 of it if I had to. I reasoned that if it came to the worst, and we still had to burn the hundred-dollar bills, I could sell the condo and probably even make a profit on it. I saw it as an investment—shrewd and calculating.

I'd never been to an auction before, so when it began, I watched to see how people bid. They simply raised their hands as a price was called out, and when someone finally won, a woman with a clipboard took him aside and wrote down some information.

There were only three other men besides myself who took part in the bidding for the condo. The price gradually climbed through the twenties. As it approached $30,000, I began to get nervous, thinking I wasn't going to get it, but then, suddenly, everyone else dropped out, and I ended up winning it for $31,000.

The woman with the clipboard took me off to the side. She was young, thin faced, with short, black hair. She had a name tag on, and it said Ms. Hastings. She spoke very quickly, in a hushed tone, explaining to me what I had to do.

She gave me a business card. I had to get a check for the full amount bid to the address listed on the card within the next week. I should allow ten working days after the receipt of my payment for them to process my papers. After that time, but not before then, I'd be able to come to the same address in person and receive my property—in this case the deed to the condominium. When she finished telling me this, and I'd filled out my name, address, and telephone number, she left me, moving on to the next person.

I sat back down in my chair, trying to sort through my feelings. I'd just committed myself to spending $31,000, nearly all of our savings. It seemed like a tremendously foolish thing to do. But then, in comparison to the money we had sitting on the floor beneath our bed, it was nothing. And I'd gotten a deal, too, had bought the place for less than a tenth of its appraised value. The longer I sat there, the more strongly this latter interpretation began to dominate my thoughts. I was a millionaire, after all, four times over; it seemed like I ought to start acting like one. By the time I got up to leave, I was feeling pleased enough with my purchase that there was a just perceptible jauntiness to my stride, and as I made my way to the exit, I even found myself wishing that I had a cane, so that I might twirl it as I walked.

My second gift to Sarah was a grand piano. This was something she'd always wanted, ever since she was little. She didn't know how to play, it had nothing to do with that; a piano simply represented to her, I think, the concrete embodiment of wealth and status, and as such it seemed fitting that I should give it to her now.

I shopped around, calling music stores from work, astonished at how much pianos cost. I'd had no idea; it was something I'd never even considered. I ended up finding one that had been marked down because there was an imperfection in its varnish, a large, hand-shaped stain on its lid. It cost me $2,400, virtually the balance of our account.

I had them deliver it to the house the morning of the twelfth. Sarah was working at the library, so she wasn't there when it arrived. It came in with its legs off, three men straining to carry it. I had them reassemble it in the living room. It looked absurd there, monstrous, dwarfing the rest of the furniture, but I was pleased with it. It was something special, something she'd like, and I knew it would look better in our next house.

I taped a little red bow to a sheet and draped it across the piano. I'd saved the page from the catalog with the condominium on it, and I put this next to the bow. Then I sat down and waited for her to return.

SARAH seemed much more impressed with the piano than the condo, perhaps because it was a physical presence in the room, concrete, undeniable, something whose keys she could touch and make a sound, rather than a mere picture of an object thousands of miles away. It was an actuality, whereas the condo remained nothing more than a promise.

"Oh, Hank," she said as soon as she saw it, "you've made me so happy."

She tapped out "When the Saints Go Marching In," the only song she knew. She opened the lid and looked at the strings. She pressed the pedals with her feet, ran her hands across the keys. She tried to sound out "Frère Jacques" for Amanda but couldn't seem to get it right, and each time she made a mistake the baby would begin to cry.

Later that night—after the unveiling of the gifts; after a special dinner of cornish hens and stuffing and green beans and mashed potatoes, all of which I cooked myself; and after two bottles of wine—we made love on top of the piano.

It was Sarah's idea. I was nervous that it might collapse beneath our weight, but she took off her clothes and jumped right up onto its lid, reclining there on her elbows with her legs spread wide.

"Come on." She smiled at me.

We were both a little drunk.

I stripped out of my own clothes and slowly, listening all the time for the warning creak of a collapsing leg, climbed up on top of her.

It was a remarkable experience. The piano's hollow chamber echoed our own sighs and moans back up at us, returning them subtly altered—adding a peculiar resonance and fullness, embedding within them the soft choral vibrations of its tautly stretched wires.

"This is the beginning of our new life," Sarah whispered in the middle of it, her mouth pressed up tight against my ear, making her breath sound like a scuba diver's, deep and passionate and strangely distant.

As I nodded in response, I banged my knee down on the piano's lid, and the whole thing seemed to moan for a moment, a long, mournful echo seeping up through the wood, making it vibrate, so that it trembled against our naked bodies.

When we finished, Sarah got a bottle of furniture polish from the hall closet and wiped away our sweat.

MONDAY, on my lunch break, I made a quick visit to the cemetery. I walked from spot to spot, reading headstones—Jacob's, my parents', Pederson's, Lou's, Nancy's, Sonny's.

It was a cloudy afternoon, gray and overcast, the sky hanging low above the ground, pressing down like a tarp. The view was desolate, empty. Beyond the church and the low scattering of tombstones, there was nothing but the horizon, and it was miles away. A bouquet of flowers was resting beside the Pederson plot, chrysanthemums—yellows and reds—their vivid colors looking garish in the dim light, more like splashes of paint from a passing vandal than the sincere symbols of grief they were meant to be. Inside St. Jude's, someone was practicing the organ. I could hear the sound coming faintly through the brick wall, the same low, throbbing sequence of notes repeated over and over again.

It hadn't snowed since the last rush of funerals, nothing more than the brief flurry the day Jacob was buried, and the fresher of the graves stood out along the cemetery's floor, a handful of large, black rectangles, each one slightly sunken.

When I was little I'd pictured death as an animated pool of water. It looked just like a puddle, a little darker maybe, a little deeper than usual, but when you walked by, it would reach up with two liquid arms and pull you into itself, swallowing you down. I have no idea where I got this image, but I held on to it for a long time, probably until I was ten or eleven years old. It may've been something my mother had told me once, the way she had of explaining it to children. If this were true, then Jacob must've held the same idea.

The fresh graves looked like puddles.

Before leaving, I stood for a few minutes beside our family plot. Jacob's name had been chiseled onto the marker, right beneath our father's. The blank spot in the stone's bottom-right-hand corner was waiting for me, I knew, and it was a nice feeling to realize that—unless I were to die within the next few months—it would never be filled in. I was going to be buried a long way from here, under a different name, and thinking this gave me an instant's rush of happiness. It was the best I'd felt since the shootings, the most confident in our course: for perhaps the first and only time, what we'd gotten seemed worth the price we'd paid. We were escaping our lives. That cube of granite had been my fate, my destination, and I'd broken away from it. In a few months, I'd set out into the world, free from everything that had formerly bound me. I would re-create myself, would chart my own path. I would dictate my destiny.

THURSDAY evening I returned from work and found Sarah in the kitchen, crying.

At first I wasn't sure. All I noticed was a stiffness, a strained formality, as if she were angry with me. She was standing at the sink washing dishes. I came in, still in my suit and tie, and sat down at the table to keep her company. I asked her some questions about her day, and she answered them in monosyllables, short little grunts from deep in her throat. She wasn't looking at me; her head was tucked down against her chest, watching her hands working at the dishes in the soapy water.

"You okay?" I asked finally.

She nodded, not turning around, her shoulders hunched forward, making her back look round. The plates clinked together in the sink.

"Sarah?"

She didn't answer, so I got up and came to the counter. When I touched her on the shoulder, she seemed to freeze, as if in fright.

"What's the matter?" I asked, and then, leaning forward to catch her eye, I saw the tears rolling slowly down her face.

Sarah wasn't a crier; I could count the number of times I'd seen her in tears on the fingers of one hand. They appeared only in the wake of major tragedies, so my first reaction to her weeping was one of panic and fear. I thought immediately of the baby.

"Where's Amanda?" I asked quickly.

She continued to work at the dishes. She turned her face off to the side, made a sniffling sound. "Upstairs."

"She's all right?"

Sarah nodded. "She's sleeping."

I reached forward and turned off the water. In the absence of its rushing, the kitchen took on a sudden silence, and it seemed to add a peculiar weight to the moment, which frightened me.

"What's going on?" I asked. I slid my arm along her back until I had her in a half embrace. She stood there rigid for a second, her hands draped over the edge of the sink, as if they'd been broken at the wrists, then she let herself fall toward me, let a sob work its way raggedly up through her chest. I hugged her with both arms.

She cried for a while, returning my embrace, her wet hands dripping soapy water down my neck and onto the back of my suit.

"It's all right," I whispered. "It's all right."

When she quieted down, I brought her over to the table.

"I can't work at the library anymore," she said, sitting down.

"They fired you?" I couldn't imagine how she could possibly be fired from the library.

She shook her head. "They asked me not to bring Amanda anymore. People were complaining about the noise." She wiped at her cheek with her hand. "They said I can come back after she's outgrown her crying."

I leaned forward and took her by the hand. "It's not like you really need the job right now."

"I know. It's just . . ."

"We've got enough money without it." I smiled.

"I know," she said again.

"It doesn't really seem like it's worth crying over."

"Oh, Hank. I'm not crying over that."

I looked at her in surprise. "What're you crying for?"

She wiped at her face again. Then she shut her eyes. "It's complicated. It's all sorts of things put together."

"Is it about what we've done?"

My voice must've come out strange—nervous maybe, or scared—because she opened her eyes at the sound of it. She looked directly at me, as if she were appraising me. Then she shook her head.

"It's nothing," she said. "It's just me being tired."

THAT weekend a thaw arrived.

Saturday the temperature rose to fifty degrees, and everything, the whole world, began to melt in a sudden dripping, sliding, oozing rush. Large, perfectly white clouds floated across the sky throughout the afternoon, pushed gently northward by the moist touch of a southerly wind. The air smelled deceptively of spring.

Sunday was even warmer; the thermometer eased its way up into the lower sixties, accelerating the melting. By late morning, the ground had begun to reappear in small squares and slashes the size of footprints, dark against the dirty whiteness of the retreating snow, and in the evening, when I went out to untie the dog and put him in the garage, I found him sitting in an inch-deep puddle of mud. The earth was unveiling itself.

I had trouble falling asleep that night. Water dripped loudly from the eaves beyond the window with an incessant ticktock sound. The house creaked and moaned. There was a sense of movement in the air, of things breaking free, coming undone.

I lay in bed and tried to trick my body into fatigue, consciously relaxing muscles, forcing my breathing to slow and deepen, but every time I shut my eyes, a vivid image of the plane floated up before me. It was lying on its belly in the orchard, its wings and fuselage free of snow, its metal skin glinting brightly in the sunshine, like a beacon, attracting the eye. Looking down at it in my head, I could sense it waiting, could feel its impatience. It was yearning to be found.

ON WEDNESDAY of that week, a strange thing happened to me. I was sitting at my desk, working on an account discrepancy, when I heard Jacob's voice out in the lobby.

It wasn't his voice, of course, I knew that, but its tone and pitch were so eerily familiar that I couldn't resist rising from my chair, walking quietly over to my door, opening it, and peeking out.

There was a fat man there, a man I'd never seen before. He wasn't a customer; he'd merely come inside to ask for directions.

He didn't look at all like Jacob. He was old, balding, with a thick, drooping mustache, and as I watched him speak, watched the unfamiliar gestures of his hands, the way his face moved above his mouth, the illusion that he was using Jacob's voice gradually disappeared. It started to sound a little too throaty, a little too rough. It was an old man's voice.

But then I shut my eyes, and it instantly became my brother's once again. I stood there very still, focusing my whole mind on the sound of it, and, listening, I felt an irresistible surge of sadness and loss rise up within myself. It was overwhelming, stronger than anything I'd ever felt before, so powerful that it had an actual physical effect on me, like a wave of nausea. I bent forward slightly at the waist, as if I'd been hit in the stomach.

"Mr. Mitchell?" I heard.

I opened my eyes, straightened my body. Cheryl was standing behind the checkout counter, staring at me with an expression of grave concern. The fat man stood in the center of the lobby, his right hand touching the corner of his mustache.

"Are you all right?" Cheryl asked. She seemed as if she were about to come running toward me.

I tried quickly to recall the past few moments in my mind, to see if I'd made some sort of sound standing there, a groan, or a gasp, but everything was blank. "I'm fine," I said. I cleared my throat, smiled toward the fat man. He gave me a friendly nod, and I returned it.

Then I stepped back into my office and shut the door.

THAT evening I read an article in the paper about a giant confidence game that had been operating lately in the Midwest, bilking millions of dollars from unsuspecting investors.

A fake advertisement would be placed in the local paper, announcing a government sale of goods seized in drug raids. People would bid on this merchandise sight unseen, apparently believing that since the government was running the auction nothing fraudulent could be occurring. The con men would have several confederates mixed in with the crowd, to help artificially raise the bidding. Their victims would make payments by check, assuming that they'd bought things at less than 10 percent of their appraised value, then show up two weeks later to find that their purchases were nonexistent, simply photographs in a catalog.

I took this news with remarkable calm. My check had cleared the day before; I'd gone by the bank to see. My account balance was listed as $1,878.21. I'd given away $31,000, virtually our entire savings, but I couldn't force myself to believe it. It seemed like too horrible a thing to have happened so quietly. A calamity had struck, undoubtedly one of the worst I'd ever encountered, but it had arrived with such little fanfare, a tiny article in the middle of the paper, that I had trouble accepting it. I needed something more, needed to be woken from my sleep late at night by the ringing of the phone, needed the sound of sirens in the distance, needed a sudden flash of pain in the center of my chest.

I surprised myself, in fact, by feeling more reassurance than grief. As long as I maintained the image of the duffel bag in my mind, I could make the $31,000 seem inconsequential, a minor mistake, an unfortunate lapse in judgment. And I found the idea of someone stealing it, rather than my merely losing it, strangely comforting. There were men out there who were just as bad as me, even worse, a whole gang of them traveling the country and robbing innocent people of their savings. It made what I'd done seem a little more explicable, a little more natural. It made it seem easier to understand.

There was a tremor of fear, too, of course—I can't deny that—a cold, little kernel of terror mixed in with my reassurance. The safety net that I'd strung up to aid our descent into crime, the idea of burning the packets at the first sign of trouble, had been swept away. We could never relinquish the money now, no matter what might happen in the future, because without it we had nothing. My last illusion of freedom had been stripped from me—I realized this with perfect lucidity—and it was this thought that lay at the core of my fear. I was trapped: from here on out, all my decisions about the money would be dictated by its indispensability; they would become choices of necessity rather than desire.

When I'd finished studying the article, I tore it out of the paper and flushed it down the toilet. I didn't want Sarah to know until we were safe and far away.

LATE that night, while I was untying Mary Beth from his tree to take him into the garage, I noticed that the raw spots beneath his collar had grown dramatically worse. They were open sores now, bleeding, oozing runny streams of pus. Mud was plastered into the surrounding fur.

Seeing this, I felt a burst of compassion for him. I knelt beside him on the wet ground and tried to loosen his collar a notch, but as soon as I touched him, he tucked his head, and, very quickly, very neatly, like someone pruning a branch off a bush, bit me on my wrist.

I jumped up, shocked, and he cowered before me in the mud. I'd never been bitten by a dog before, and I wasn't sure how I ought to react. I considered kicking him, stomping into the house and leaving him to spend the night out in the yard but then decided against it. I wasn't really angry, I realized; I merely felt like I ought to be.

I carefully inspected my wrist. The sun was set, and the yard was dark, but just by the way it felt, I could tell that the dog hadn't broken the skin. It was only a nip, a sort of slap rather than a closed-fisted blow.

I watched Mary Beth lie down in the mud and begin to lick at his paws. Something, I knew, had to be done about him. He was sick, unhappy, like an animal in the zoo, tied up all day, imprisoned during the night.

The front light flicked on, and Sarah leaned out the door. "Hank?" she called.

I turned toward her, still holding my wrist in my hand.

"What're you doing?" she asked.

"The dog bit me."

"What?" She hadn't heard.

"Nothing," I said. I bent down and carefully took Mary Beth by his collar. He let me do it. "I'm putting him in the garage," I said to Sarah.

THURSDAY night, late, I opened my eyes and sat up in bed, my body literally shaking with an irrational, panic-filled sense of urgency. Deep in the depths of sleep, I'd devised a plan, and now I turned to wake Sarah and tell her.

"Sarah," I hissed, shaking her shoulder.

She rolled away from my hand. "Stop it." She groaned.

I turned on the light and pulled her toward me. "Sarah," I whispered, staring down at her, waiting for her eyes to open. When they did, I said, "I know how to get rid of the plane."

"What?" She glanced toward Amanda's crib, then blinked up at me, her face still half asleep.

"I'm going to rent a blowtorch. We'll take it out into the woods and cut the plane into little pieces."

"A blowtorch?"

"We'll bury the pieces in the woods."

She stared at me, trying to grasp what I was talking about.

"It's the last piece of evidence," I said. "Once it's gone, we'll have nothing left to worry about."

Sarah sat up in bed. She brushed her hair from her face. "You want to cut up the plane?"

"We have to do it before someone discovers it." I paused, thinking. "We can do it tomorrow. I'll take the day off. We'll call around to find a place that rents—"

"Hank," she said.

There was something about her voice that made me stop and look at her. Her face was frightened. Her arms were folded tightly across her chest.

"What's wrong?" I asked.

"Listen to yourself. Listen to how you sound."

I stared blankly at her.

"You sound crazy. We can't take a blowtorch out into the woods to cut up the plane. That's insane."

As soon as I heard her say this, I realized that she was right. It suddenly seemed absurd, as if I'd been talking in my sleep, babbling like a child.

"We've got to calm down," she said. "We can't let things get to us."

"I was only—"

"We've got to stop this. What we've done, we've done. Now we just have to live our lives."

I tried to touch her hand, to show her that everything was all right, that I was in control, but she pulled away.

"If we keep on like this," she said, "we'll end up losing everything."

Amanda made a short crying sound, then stopped. We both glanced toward the crib.

"We'll end up confessing," Sarah whispered.

I shook my head. "I'm not going to confess."

"We're so close, Hank. Somebody'll find the plane soon, there'll be a big commotion, and then people'll start to forget. As soon as that happens, we'll be able to leave. We'll just take the money and leave."

She shut her eyes, as if to picture us leaving. Then she opened them again.

"The money's right here." She patted the bed with her hand. "Right beneath us. It's ours if we can keep it."

I stared at her. The light on the night table made a little golden cloud out of her hair, so that it looked like she had a halo.

"But don't you feel bad sometimes?" I asked.

"Bad?"

"About what we've done?"

"Of course," she said. "I feel bad all the time."

I nodded, relieved to hear her admit this.

"We have to live with it, though. We have to treat it just like any other grief."

"But it's not just like any other grief. I killed my brother."

"It wasn't your fault, Hank. You didn't choose to do it. You have to believe that." She reached forward to touch my arm. "It's the truth."

I didn't say anything, and she pressed down on my arm, pinching my skin.

"Do you understand?" she said.

She stared at me, squeezing my arm until I nodded. Then she glanced at the clock. Her head slipped away from the light, and her halo disappeared. It was 3:17 in the morning. I was fully awake now; my thoughts were clear. In my mind, I repeated her words: *It wasn't your fault.*

"Come here," she said. She held out her arms for a hug. I leaned forward into her body, and when she got a grip on me, she dragged me slowly toward the mattress.

"Everything's going to be all right," she whispered. "I promise." She waited a moment, as if to make sure that I wasn't going to try to sit up again; then she rolled away and turned out the light.

As we lay there in the darkness, Mary Beth began to howl.

"I'm going to shoot him," I said. "I'm going to put him out of his misery."

"Oh, Hank." Sarah sighed, already halfway into sleep. She was lying a few inches to my right, the sheets growing cool in the gap between us. "We're all through with shooting now."

Sometime before daybreak, winter returned. A wind came up from the north, and the air turned cold.

Friday morning, as I made my way out across the farm country in to work, it started to snow.

9

THE SNOW continued to fall throughout the morning and into the afternoon—heavy, incessant, as if it were being thrown from the sky. The customers brought it into Raikley's, brushing it from their shoulders and stamping it from their boots, so that it collected on the tiles before the door, melting into little puddles. Everyone seemed excited by it, even giddy: the suddenness of its arrival, the rapidity with which it fell, the ghostly silence that it draped across the town. There was a manic quality to the voices I heard drifting into my office from the lobby, a holidaylike tone, an extravagant friendliness and good cheer.

For me, though, the storm acted not as a stimulant but as a sedative. It calmed and reassured me. Ignoring my work, I spent much of the morning sitting at my desk, staring out the window. I watched the snow fall on the town, softening the contours of the cars and buildings, blocking out the colors, making everything white, uniform, featureless. I watched it fall on the cemetery across the road, erasing the black rectangles of Jacob's and Lou's and Nancy's and Sonny's graves. And when I closed my eyes, I pictured it falling in the nature preserve, drifting quietly down through the stunted trees of the orchard, and slowly, flake by flake, burying the plane.

I accepted Sarah's logic—eventually the wreck had to be discovered. It had to be found and then forgotten, so that we could leave and begin our new lives. But I knew, too, that the longer it took to surface, the safer we would be. I prayed silently: *Let no one connect the shootings with the money on the plane. Let no one remember the one when they think of the other.*

While I watched the storm, I daydreamed about where we'd go and how we'd live. I doodled on a pad—miniature sailboats, Concorde jets, the names of foreign countries. I imagined myself making love with Sarah on an island beach, pictured myself surprising her with expensive presents from native bazaars: exotic perfumes, tiny statues of ivory and wood, jewels of every size and color.

All day the snow continued unabated, filling in the morning's footprints, drifting back across the freshly plowed road.

ABOUT a half hour before closing, I got a call from Sheriff Jenkins.

"Howdy, Hank. You busy?"

"Not really," I said. "Just tidying things up for the weekend."

"Think you could pop over to my office real quick? I got somebody here you might be able to help."

"And who's that?"

"A man by the name of Neal Baxter. He's from the FBI."

WALKING across the street through the snow, I thought, *This has nothing to do with what I've done. They wouldn't call me over to arrest me; they'd come to Raikley's and get me themselves.*

Carl's office was in the town hall, a squat, two-story, brick building with a short flight of concrete steps leading up to its double doors. I paused at the foot of these steps, beside the aluminum flagpole, and tried quickly to gather myself together. I brushed the snow from my hair. I unbuttoned my overcoat and straightened my tie.

Carl met me in the entranceway. It seemed as though

he'd been waiting for me there. He was smiling; he greeted me like an old friend. He took me by the arm and led me off to the left, toward his office.

He had two offices really, a large outer one and a smaller inner one. His wife, Linda, a short woman with a pretty face, was working in the outer one, typing at a desk. She smiled at me as we came in, and whispered hello. I smiled back. Through the open doorway beyond her, I could see a man sitting with his back to me. He was tall and crew cut and dressed in a dark gray suit.

I followed Carl into the inner office, and he shut the door behind us, blocking out the sound of Linda's typing. There was very little in the tiny room—a wooden desk, three plastic chairs, a row of filing cabinets along the wall opposite the window. Two pictures were propped up on top of the cabinets: one of Linda holding a cat in her lap; another of the entire Jenkins clan—children, grandchildren, cousins, nephews, nieces, in-laws—all crowded together on a lawn in front of a yellow house with blue shutters. The desk was clean, orderly. A little American flag in a plastic stand sat beside a tin can full of yellow pencils and a stone paperweight without any papers to weigh down. Behind the desk, hanging from a wall, was a glass-doored gun cabinet.

"This is Agent Baxter," Carl said.

The man rose from his chair, turning to face me. He leaned forward to shake my hand, wiping his own along the side of his pant leg before he did so. He was lean, broad shouldered, with a square face and a flat nose, like a boxer's. His handshake was short, firm, decisive, and he held my eye while Carl introduced us. I found him strangely familiar for some reason, as if he resembled a movie star, or an athlete, but I couldn't exactly place it; the resemblance was too vague, just the bare trace of a memory. He was polished; there was a glow about him, a sheen of calm competence.

We sat down, and Carl said, "You remember earlier this winter, when I saw you out by the nature preserve?"

"Yes," I said, a fistlike ball of panic forming at the center of my chest.

"Didn't Jacob say you guys had heard a plane with engine trouble a few days before?"

I nodded.

"Why don't you tell Agent Baxter what you heard?"

I could see no way to avoid it, no way to lie or evade the question, so I did exactly as Carl asked. I dragged up Jacob's story and laid it out for the FBI man. "It was snowing," I said. "Hard, like today, so we weren't really sure, but it sounded like an engine coughing on and off. We pulled over to the edge of the road to listen, but we didn't hear anything more—no crash, no engine, nothing."

Neither Carl nor Agent Baxter spoke.

"It was probably just a snowmobile," I said.

Agent Baxter had a little black book open in his lap. He was taking notes. "Do you remember the date?" he asked.

"We saw the sheriff on New Year's Eve. It happened a few days before that."

"You said it was near where I saw you?" Carl asked. "Out by Anders Park?"

"That's right."

"Which side were you driving on?"

"The south side. Near the center."

"By the Pederson place?"

I nodded, my heartbeat rising, forcing its way up into my temples.

"Would you be willing to take us out there?" Agent Baxter asked.

I gave him a confused look. "To the nature preserve?"

"We'd have to go in the morning," Carl said. "After the storm passes."

My overcoat was dripping melted snow onto the floor. I

started to take it off but stopped myself when I saw how my hands trembled once they were free from my lap.

"What's going on?" I asked.

There was a short silence while the two lawmen seemed to debate who should speak, and what exactly ought to be revealed. Finally Agent Baxter, with just the slightest, the most subtle of movements, gave Carl a little shrug.

"The FBI's looking for a plane," Carl said.

"This is all confidential, of course," the agent said.

"I'm sure Hank understands that."

The FBI man sat back in his chair, crossing his legs. His shoes were shiny and black, their leather spattered with little water spots from walking through the snow. He gave me a long, penetrating look.

"Last July," he said, "an armored car was robbed as it was leaving the Chicago Federal Reserve Bank. From the start we suspected that it was an inside job, but nothing came of it until this past December, when the car's driver was arrested for raping an old girlfriend. After his lawyer told him that he might get twenty-five years, he jumped on the phone to us, saying he wanted to turn state's evidence."

"He handed over his friends," I said.

"That's right. He was mad anyway because they took off after the heist without giving him his share, so he fingered them, and we got his charges reduced to a misdemeanor."

"And you caught the robbers?"

"We traced them to Detroit, their hometown, and set up a surveillance team outside their apartment."

"A surveillance team? Why didn't you just arrest them?"

"We wanted to make sure we got the money, too. There was no evidence to indicate that they'd even tapped into it yet. They both had jobs and were living together in a rathole apartment down by the stadium, so we assumed the money was hidden somewhere, that they were waiting to make sure no one was looking for them. Unfortunately, our surveillance was sloppy, and the suspects bolted. We caught one of them the next day trying to cross into Canada, but the other one disappeared. We'd almost given up on him when an informant called my partner and told him that the suspect was about to take off in a small plane from an airfield outside of Detroit. We rushed over there and arrived just in time to see the plane lift off from the ground."

"You couldn't follow it?" I asked.

"There was no reason to."

"They knew where he was going," Carl said. He seemed very pleased by this idea. He sat back in his chair and grinned at the FBI man. Agent Baxter ignored him.

"My partner's informant gave us the suspect's destination. It was another small airfield, this one just north of Cincinnati." The agent paused, staring at me, his face collapsing into a frown. "Unfortunately, the plane never arrived."

"Maybe he went somewhere else."

"It's possible, but doubtful. For various reasons, we consider our informant's word to be virtually incontestable."

"They think he crashed on the way," Carl said. "They're covering his route, going over it town by town."

"Was the money on the plane?" I asked.

"We assume so," the agent said.

"How much?"

Agent Baxter glanced toward Carl. Then he looked at me. "Several million dollars."

I let out a low whistle and raised my eyebrows, feigning disbelief.

"We wanted to head out around nine tomorrow morning," Carl said, "after the weather clears. Can you make it then?"

"I didn't see a plane go down, Carl. I just heard an engine."

They stared at me, waiting.

"I mean, I really don't think we'd find anything out there."

"We realize it's a long shot, Mr. Mitchell," Agent Baxter said. "But we've reached the point in our investigation where all we have are long shots."

"It's just that I can't show you anything. I didn't even get out of the car. You could simply drive along Anders Park Road and see everything I did."

"We'd still appreciate it if you came. You'd be surprised at what you might remember once you got there."

"Is nine o'clock bad for you?" Carl asked. "We can make it earlier if you want."

I felt my head shake, as if of its own volition.

Carl grinned at me. "I'll treat you to a cup of coffee when we get back."

As I got up to leave, Agent Baxter said, "I don't think I can put too much emphasis on the confidentiality of all this, Mr. Mitchell. The whole thing's something of an embarrassment to the Bureau. We'd be very disappointed if the press were to get ahold of it somehow."

Carl interrupted before I could respond. "Press, hell," he said. "There's four million dollars sitting in those woods. Word gets out, and we'll have a goddamn treasure hunt on our hands."

He laughed and threw me a parting Lou-like wink. Agent Baxter smiled icily.

SARAH already had dinner prepared when I got home.

"A robbery?" she said, when I told her what had happened. She shook her head. "No way."

I was sitting across from her at the kitchen table, watching her serve herself a leg of barbecued chicken. I already had one on my plate. "What do you mean, no way?"

"It doesn't make sense, Hank. The kidnapping made sense."

"This isn't a guess, Sarah. It's not a theory. I talked to a man from the FBI, and he told me where it's from."

She frowned down at her plate, pushing at her rice with her fork, mixing it into her peas. The baby was on the floor beside us, lying in her Portacrib. She looked like she always did lately, like she was about to cry.

"He's searching for a plane full of money," I said. "You can't tell me there's more than one of those around here."

"It's hundred-dollar bills, Hank. If it were an armored car, there'd be other denominations. There'd be fifties and twenties and tens."

"You aren't listening. I just told you, I talked to him myself."

"It's old money. If it were coming out of a Federal Reserve bank, it'd be new. They burn old bills there and replace them with fresh ones."

"So you're telling me he's lying?"

She didn't seem to hear me. She was biting at her lip, her head turned toward the baby. Suddenly she gave me an excited look. "Did he show you his badge?"

"Why would he show me his badge?"

She dropped her fork onto her plate, pushed back her chair, and ran from the room.

"Sarah?" I called after her, bewildered.

"Wait," she yelled over her shoulder.

As soon as she left the room, the baby began to cry. I hardly even looked at her. I was trying to devise a way to get the money back into the plane without leaving any tracks. I scraped at my chicken with my knife, tearing strips of meat from the bone.

Amanda increased her volume, her body tightening like a fist, her face flooding a dark crimson.

"Shhh," I whispered. I stared down at my slowly cooling food. I'd have to go during the night, I realized, right after dinner, before it stopped snowing. I'd have to do it in the dark. I'd keep three packets, just enough to cover what I'd lost on the condominium, and give everything else back.

Sarah returned a moment later, carrying a sheet of paper. She sat down with an exultant look on her face, her cheeks flushed with it, the paper held out toward me like a gift.

I took it from her, recognizing it immediately. It was the photocopy of the article about the kidnapping.

"What?" I said.

She grinned at me. "It's him, isn't it?" She leaned down and touched Amanda's face with the back of her hand. The baby stopped crying.

I examined the piece of paper. It was the third article, the one with the photographs. I studied them left to right—first the younger brother, then the older, then the freeze-frame of the younger one executing the security guard.

"He's looking for his brother," Sarah said.

My eyes strayed back to the center picture and for one brief, intense instant, I was flooded with a sense of recognition. There was something familiar about the man's eyes, about the way his cheeks sloped down toward his mouth, the way he held his head on his shoulders. But then, just as quickly, it was gone, overwhelmed by his other features—his beard and thick hair, the stockiness of his frame, the mug-shot frown on his face.

"You're saying it's Vernon," I said. "The older one." I laid the piece of paper on the table between us.

She nodded, still smiling. Neither of us had eaten any of our food yet. It was cold now, the sauce on the chicken growing viscid. I scrutinized the photo, willing myself to recognize Agent Baxter in Vernon Bokovsky's features. I concentrated, squinting, and briefly managed to make him appear, but again it was only for a second. The photo was several years old. It was blurry, grainy, heavily shadowed.

"It's not him," I said. "The guy I met today was skinnier." I pushed the article back across the table toward Sarah. "He had a crew cut, and no beard."

"Maybe he's lost weight, Hank. Maybe he cut his hair and

shaved his beard." She looked from me to the article, then back again. "You can't tell me it's impossible."

"I'm just saying that it doesn't seem like it's him."

"It's got to be him. I know it."

"He seemed like an FBI guy, Sarah. He had that professional look, like a movie star. Poised, perfectly groomed, a nice dark suit . . ."

"Anybody can do that," she said impatiently. She slapped her hand at the article. "He impersonated a cop to kidnap the girl. Why wouldn't he fake being an FBI agent to get back the ransom?"

"But it'd be such a risk. He'd have to go through every town from here to Cincinnati, show up in all these different police stations, each of which would probably have his face tacked up somewhere on a poster. It'd be like he was asking to get caught."

"Put yourself in his shoes," Sarah said. "Your brother takes off in a plane with all that money and disappears. You think he's crashed, but you wait and wait, and nothing's reported. Wouldn't you go out and try to find him?"

I thought about it, staring across the table at the photos.

"You couldn't just give it up. You'd have to at least try and get it back."

"He's thinner," I said quietly.

"Think about what we've already done to keep the money. What he's doing is nothing compared to that."

"You're wrong, Sarah. You're just making this up."

"Would the real FBI try to find a plane like this? Send an agent in a car all the way across the state? Wouldn't they just issue some sort of announcement?"

"They don't want it leaked to the press."

"Then they'd call on the phone. They wouldn't send an agent."

"Why wouldn't the kidnapper call, then? It'd be safer. There'd be less chance of getting caught."

She shook her head. "He wants to be there. He wants to be able to control things, convince people with the way he's dressed, the way he acts. Like he convinced you. He can't do that on the phone."

I thought back over my interview with Agent Baxter, searching for clues. I pictured him wiping his palm on his pant leg before he shook my hand, like it was clammy with sweat. I remembered how insistent he'd been about confidentiality, keeping the story away from the press.

"I don't know . . ."

"You have to use your imagination, Hank. You have to picture him with more hair, with a beard."

"Sarah." I sighed. "Does it even matter?"

She picked up her fork and poked at her chicken. "What do you mean?" Her voice was hesitant with suspicion.

"If we were to decide that he was really the kidnapper, would it change what I did tomorrow?"

She cut off a square of chicken and put it into her mouth. She chewed slowly, pausing between bites, as if she were afraid it might be poisoned. "Of course," she said.

"Let's say we agree that he's really an FBI agent."

"But we don't."

"Just hypothetically. For the sake of argument."

"All right," she said. Her fork was poised over her plate. I could tell that she was waiting to contradict me.

"What would I do?"

"You'd take him to the plane."

"If I were going to take him to the plane, I'd have to go back tonight and return the money."

She set her fork down on her plate. It made a clinking sound when it hit. "Return the money?"

"They know it's on the plane. There's no excuse for any of it to be missing."

She stared across the table at me, as if waiting for something more. "You can't give it back," she said.

"We'd have to, Sarah. I'd be the only one they'd suspect. As soon as we left town, they'd know."

"But after all you've done? You'd just let it go?"

"After all we've done," I corrected her.

She ignored me. "You wouldn't have to put the money back, Hank. If you guided him to the plane, you'd be beyond suspicion. There'd be no tracks in the surrounding snow, so it'd look like no one had been there. He'd find the five hundred thousand and just assume that his informant was wrong, that the pilot had left the rest behind somewhere."

I pondered that. It seemed to make sense. It was a risk, but no more of a risk than sneaking back to return the money would be.

"Okay," I said. "Let's say that if we decide he's really from the FBI, I'll brave it out and take him to the plane."

She nodded.

"Now what'll I do if we decide he's actually the kidnapper?"

"You won't go."

"Because?"

"Because he's a murderer. He killed all those people—the guards and the chauffeur and the maid and the girl. You'll call Carl and make up an excuse. You'll say that the baby's sick and you have to take her to a doctor."

"I'm a murderer, too, Sarah. Being a murderer doesn't necessarily mean anything."

"As soon as he sees the plane, he'll shoot you both. That's why he wants you to go, so he can get rid of all the witnesses."

"If I don't go, Carl'll take him by himself."

"And?"

"And, by your logic, if they find the plane, this guy'll shoot him."

She thought about that. When she spoke, her voice was low and ashamed sounding. "That wouldn't be such a bad thing for us," she said. "Any violence he does will only help cover up our involvement with the plane. It'll push us off to the edge."

"But if we were sure it was Vernon, it'd be like we were setting Carl up. It'd be just as bad as shooting him ourselves."

"They're the only two people who can threaten us. They're the only ones who can tie you to the plane."

"Wouldn't you feel bad, though? If Carl were killed like that?"

"It's not like I'm asking you to shoot him, Hank. I just want you to stay away."

"But if we know . . ."

"What do you want to do? You want to warn Carl?"

"Doesn't it seem like we ought to?"

"And what would you say to him? How would you explain your suspicions?"

I frowned down at my plate. She was right: there was no way I could warn him without revealing my knowledge of the plane's cargo.

"He might not even shoot him," Sarah said. "We're just guessing about that. He might just take the money and disappear."

I didn't really believe this, and I don't think she did either. We both picked at our food.

"You don't have a choice, Hank."

I sighed. It had come down to that again—our telling ourselves that we didn't have a choice. "It's a moot point anyway," I said.

"What do you mean?"

"I mean we won't know if it's him until after it's over."

Sarah stared down at Amanda, thinking this through. The baby's arms were extended stiffly into the air, one pointing toward me, the other toward her mother. It looked as if she were trying to hold our hands, and, for a moment, I was tempted to reach out and touch her. I resisted, though; I knew it would only make her cry.

"We can call the FBI office in Detroit," Sarah said. "We can ask for an Agent Baxter."

"It's too late; they'll be closed by now."

"We can call in the morning."

"I'm meeting them at nine. They won't be open before that."

"You can stall them for a bit. I'll call from here, and then you can run over to your office and call me to find out."

"And if there's no Agent Baxter?"

"Then you won't go. You'll tell Carl that I just called, that the baby's sick and you have to go home."

"And if there is one?"

"Then you'll go. You'll take them to the plane."

I frowned. "It's a risk either way, isn't it?"

"But at least something's going to happen. The waiting's over; it's all going to come out now."

The baby let out a short yelp, an exploratory sound. Sarah reached down and touched her hand. My dinner sat before me, cold and uneaten.

"We'll leave soon," Sarah said, as if she were comforting Amanda rather than me. "We'll leave and everything'll be all right. We'll take our money and change our names and disappear, and everything'll be all right."

Sometime after midnight, I opened my eyes to the sound of Amanda waking up. She always signaled the onset of a nocturnal crying spell with several minutes of quiet gurgling—a choking babbling mixed with little hiccoughs. She was doing it now, building up from a soft undertone, something close to the idling of a car's engine, toward what I knew would momentarily be a sudden, window-rattling shriek of distress.

I slipped from beneath the covers, padded barefoot across

the room, and scooped her out of her crib. Sarah was lying on her stomach in the bed, and as I snuck away, she reached out her hand, pulling my empty pillow toward her chest.

I rocked the baby in my arms.

"Shhh," I whispered.

She was too far along to be comforted so easily, though; she let me know this with a single avian squawk, like an extended burp, and I took her quickly across the hall into the guest room, to keep her from waking her mother. I climbed onto the bed there, pulling the comforter around us.

I'd come to enjoy these late-night sessions with Amanda. They were our sole form of bodily contact; during the day she'd begin to shriek as soon as I touched her. Only at night could I hold her in my arms, or stroke her face, or kiss her softly on the forehead. Only at night could I soothe her, quiet her, make her fall asleep.

I was pained by her constant crying; it weighed on me like a feeling of guilt. Whenever she was left alone with me, she immediately started to weep. Our pediatrician, though he seemed hesitant to say when it might end, claimed that it was just a phase, a brief period of increased sensitivity to her environment. I understood this and trusted his opinion, but still—despite my efforts not to—I couldn't help letting it affect my feelings for her. I was developing a cruel ambivalence around her, so that while I was filled with both warmth and pity in her presence, I was also faintly repulsed, as if her crying were symbolic of some budding character flaw, an innate pettiness and irritability, a judgment of me, a refusal to accept my love.

At night, for some reason, all this disappeared. She accepted me, and I was flooded with love for her. I'd tuck my head down close to her face and inhale the soft, soapy fragrance of her body. I'd cuddle her against my chest, let her hands grip at my skin, explore my nose, my eyes, my ears.

"Shhh," I said now, and whispered her name.

The room was cold, its corners sunk in shadow. I'd left the door open, and through it I could see the hallway. Its bare white wall seemed to glow in the darkness.

Very slowly, Amanda began to quiet. She twisted her head back and forth on her neck, her hands opening and closing in rhythm with her breathing. She pressed her feet up against my ribs.

Twice now, I'd dreamed that she could talk. Both times she was in her Portacrib by the kitchen table, eating with a fork and knife. She babbled nonsense, her voice surprisingly deep and throaty, her eyes staring straight in front of her, as if she were talking into a TV camera. She made lists: lists of colors—blue, yellow, orange, purple, green, black; lists of cars—Pontiac, Mercedes, Chevrolet, Jaguar, Toyota, Volkswagen; lists of trees—sycamore, plum, willow, oak, buckeye, myrtle. Sarah and I listened in stunned silence while she lay there before us, smiling, the words literally tumbling from her lips. Then she listed names—Pederson, Sonny, Nancy, Lou, Jacob . . . When she got to Jacob, I stood up and slapped her in the face. Both times that's how the dream ended—I woke up with the slap—and each time I was left with the inescapable feeling that if I hadn't struck her, she would've kept reciting names, spitting them out, one after the other. The list would never have ended.

As she quieted down, I began to hear the house. The snow had passed, and a wind had come up. The walls creaked with it, a boatlike sound. When it gusted, it made the windows shake. Shivering, I pulled the comforter more tightly around us, supporting Amanda's weight within its folds.

I knew that I could take her back into the bedroom now, that she was about to fall asleep, but for some reason I didn't want to. I wanted to stay there for a while yet, with her quiet in my arms.

This was Jacob's bed. The thought came unbidden, a surprise, and following right behind it was an image of him lying there, drunk, and of me bending over him to kiss him good night. Without thinking, I held the quilt to my nose and inhaled, trying to believe that I could smell him in it, though of course I couldn't.

Judas kiss, he'd whispered.

Outside, on the street, a snowplow passed, thudding and scraping. I glanced down at Amanda. She was limp in my arms, as if she were sleeping deeply, but her eyes were still open. I could see them shining in the darkness, like glass marbles.

When I looked forward to the approaching morning, I got a hard knot in my stomach. I couldn't escape the feeling that no matter what I decided to do, it would probably be a mistake.

The best solution, I realized suddenly, the utterly ruthless one, would be simply to take the money and run. I could abandon Sarah and Amanda, just head off into the night, alone. I could start up a different life from scratch, change my name, create a new identity. I closed my eyes and pictured myself purchasing a new car, something foreign and sporty and brightly colored, not worrying about financing or loans or payment schedules, simply counting out the money from my wad of hundred-dollar bills into the startled salesman's hand. I imagined myself driving off in this new car, living out of a suitcase, buying new clothes when the old ones got dirty, moving from hotel to hotel—expensive ones with pools and saunas and weight rooms and king-size beds—all the way across the country in a giant zigzag, moving on as soon as I grew tired of a place, westward or southward or eastward or northward, any direction I felt like as long as it was somewhere new, as long as it was away from here where I was now, home, Ohio, where I'd always been.

And why not? If I could kill my own brother, then I must be capable of anything. I must be evil.

Above me, in the attic, the wind made a moaning sound. I glanced down at Amanda, at the soft glimmer of her eyes.

I could kill her. I could wrap her in the quilt and smother her. I could take her by her ankles and beat her against the wall. I could squeeze her head between my hands until it popped. And I could kill Sarah, too, could sneak across the hallway and strangle her in her sleep, could suffocate her with her pillow, could smash in her face with my fists.

I pictured all of this in my mind, one image following quickly after the other. I could do it, I realized. If I could imagine it, if I could plan it out, then I could do it. It'd simply be a matter of my mind telling my hands what to do. Nothing was beyond me.

There was a rustling sound in the hall, and when I looked up, Sarah was in the doorway. She was wearing her robe, tying its belt in a loose knot as she stood there. Her hair was pinned back with a barrette.

"Hank?"

I gazed up at her, mute. The bloody images slowly slipped from my head, dreamlike, leaving little, shallow pools of guilt behind, like puddles after a rainstorm.

Of course not. The thought rippled through my mind, drifting down to its very depths and returning changed, an echo of the original. *I love them both so terribly.*

I bent my head and brushed Amanda's eyelashes with my lips. "She's having trouble falling asleep," I whispered.

Sarah stepped into the room, the floorboards creaking beneath her. She climbed up onto the bed with me, and I opened the quilt, enclosing her within it, my arm circling down around her waist. She wrapped her legs around my own, resting her head against my shoulder, so that it was just above Amanda's.

"You have to tell her a story," she said.

"I don't know any stories."

"Then you have to make one up."

I thought for a moment, but my mind was blank. "Help me," I whispered.

"Once upon a time there was a king and a queen." She paused, waiting for me to pick up.

"Once upon a time," I began, "there was a king and a queen."

"A beautiful queen."

"A beautiful queen"—I nodded—"and a very wise king. They lived in a castle by a river, and it was surrounded by fields."

I trailed off, at a loss.

"Were they rich?"

"No. They were just normal. They were like all the other kings and queens."

"Did the king fight in battles?"

"Only when he had to."

"Tell a story about one of his battles."

I thought for nearly a minute. Then I got an idea that seemed, as I lay there in the darkness, like it might be clever.

"One day," I said, "the king was out walking in the forest and he stumbled upon an old wooden box. At first he thought it was a coffin. It was shaped like one, and its lid was nailed shut, but it wasn't buried, it was just lying in the grass. And it was heavier than a coffin would be. When the king tried to pick it up, he strained his back."

"What was in it?" Sarah asked, but I ignored her.

"The king went home, and he told the beautiful queen about the box. 'Queen,' he said . . ."

"Beloved," Sarah whispered.

"Beloved?"

"That's what they call each other. Beloved."

" 'Beloved,' the king said, 'I found a heavy box in the forest. Come help me carry it home.' So she did, and they brought it back to the castle, and the king called two of his dukes into the throne room to help him pry off the lid."

"And there was a witch inside," Sarah said.

"No. It was full of gold. Gleaming bars of gold."

"Gold?" she prompted me, but I hesitated. I was realizing that it might not be so clever after all.

"How much gold?"

"A lot," I said. "More than they ever would've dreamed of owning."

"And were they excited?"

"They were more frightened than excited. They realized that the neighboring kings and queens would be jealous of them now, and would attack with their armies to steal the treasure. They'd have to recruit an army of their own and dig a new moat before letting anyone know about the gold. Otherwise they'd lose not only it but their whole kingdom, too. So the king warned the two dukes not to speak of what they'd seen, and as a reward for their silence, he promised them each a portion of the treasure."

I paused, to see if she'd caught on yet. She hadn't, though: she was lying very still, waiting for me to continue.

"Days passed, and the king began to dig his new moat. But then, quite suddenly, he started to hear distressing rumors in his court, rumors about the gold. The queen heard the rumors too, and she came to see him. 'Something must be done about the dukes, Beloved,' she said."

"Oh, Hank." Sarah sighed, her voice sounding pained.

"The king agreed, and they decided to kill the dukes. But since they couldn't simply execute them without confirming the court rumors, they organized a jousting tournament and arranged for the dukes to die during the contest, apparently accidentally, one run through with a lance, the other trampled by his horse."

"Was one of them the king's brother?"

I started to shake my head, but then I stopped. "Yes."

"And was the money safe then?"

"The gold."

"Was the gold safe? Did they build the moat and recruit their army?"

"No. Right after they murdered the dukes, their neighbors appeared with their armies and arrayed them on the fields around the castle."

I fell silent. When I glanced down, I saw that Amanda was staring directly at me. She'd been listening to my voice. The room was dark and cold, but we were warm together beneath the quilt.

I felt Sarah's hand slide across my stomach toward the baby, and watched her as she stroked the infant's forehead with her fingertips. "How does it end?" she asked. Her head was heavy against my shoulder, like a stone.

"The king went off alone to think. When he returned, he found the queen on the battlement of their castle. He was worn out with keeping his secret. His face was pale; his lips trembled when he bent to kiss her hand. 'Perhaps, Beloved,' he said, 'we shouldn't have opened the box. Perhaps we should've left well enough alone.' "

"The queen kisses the king on his forehead," Sarah said, lifting herself so she could kiss me on my forehead. "She says, 'Beloved, it's too late to question things like that. The armies are arrayed for battle.' She waves her arm out over the edge of the battlement, toward the campfires which dot the fields for as far as the eye can see."

"When was the time to question things?"

"In the beginning, Beloved. Before the box was opened."

"But we didn't do it then. We didn't know what we know now."

She craned back her head, trying to see my face in the darkness. "Would you really give it up? If there was a way you could?"

I was silent for a moment. When I spoke, I didn't answer

her question. I simply whispered, "I should've turned it in right from the start."

Sarah didn't respond to that, she just snuggled closer. The baby had fallen asleep, a soft warmth against my chest.

"It's too late now, Hank," Sarah whispered. "It's too late."

10

EARLY the next morning, even before the sun appeared, the snow began to melt. It took its leave in the same manner it had arrived—with a wild, headlong rush, as if the whole storm had been an embarrassing error on nature's part, a regrettable mistake that it wished to erase and forget as rapidly as possible. The temperature jumped into the upper forties, and a heavy mist rose from the ground, hiding the dawn. Groaning and hissing and dripping, the snow dissolved quickly into slush, and the slush even more quickly into water, so that by eight o'clock, when I drove into town, I was hindered not by ice on the roads but by mud.

Carl was in his office, alone, reading the paper.

"You're awful early, Hank," he said, when he looked up and found me standing in his doorway. "We aren't going to head off till nine."

His voice was loud in the empty office, cheery. As usual, he seemed absurdly pleased to see me, as if he were lonely and glad for the company. He poured me a cup of coffee, offered me a donut, and then we both sat down, his big wooden desk filling the space between us.

"I was planning on swinging by the feedstore real quick," I said, "but I forgot my key."

"They let you have a key?" Carl grinned. He had a mustache of powdered sugar on his upper lip.

I nodded. "My face inspires trust in people."

He studied my face, taking me more seriously than I'd intended. "Yes," he said. "That's probably true." He wiped the sugar off his lip, glanced out the window across the street toward Raikley's.

"I'm going to have to wait till Tom gets in," I said. "That'll be around nine, so I might hold you guys up for a few minutes."

He was still looking out at the feedstore, a slight frown on his lips. "That's all right," he said. "We can wait."

Beyond the window, the street was wet, slushy. A light rain had begun to fall.

"You really think there's a plane out there?" he asked.

I tilted my head, as if debating. "I doubt it. I think we would've heard a crash if it'd been a plane."

Carl gave a slow nod. "I imagine."

"I'm sort of sorry I even reported it in the first place. I'd hate to waste this guy's time on a false alarm."

"I don't think he minds. He seems fairly desperate, driving all over the state like this."

We fell silent for a moment. Then I asked, "Did he show you a badge or anything?"

"A badge?"

"I always wondered if they look like they do in the movies."

"And how's that?"

"You know, bright and silver with the big F-B-I stamped across the center."

"Sure they do."

"You saw his?"

He had to consider for a second. Then he shook his head. "No, but I've seen them before." He winked at me. "I'm sure he'd show it to you, if you asked him."

"No," I said. "I was just curious. I'd feel silly asking."

We both returned to our coffee. Carl took another bite from his donut, glancing down at the newspaper, and I stared out the window, watching as a pickup truck moved slowly past, a wet dog huddled up against the back of the cab. Inevitably it made me think of Mary Beth, caused a picture of him—cold and uncomfortable, tied by a short length of rope to the hawthorn tree in my front yard—to appear for a moment in my mind.

A strange thing happened then, as soon as this image took shape. Right there, not even trying, just sitting in Carl's office with the cup of coffee in my hands, a half-eaten donut perched on the desk before me, the room stuffy and overwarm, I thought of a plan. I thought of a way to make things right.

I turned from the window, my eyes straying up above Carl's head, toward the gun cabinet on the wall behind him.

"You think you could loan me a gun?" I asked.

He looked up from his paper, blinking. He had powder on his lip again. It made him look childish, unreliable. "A gun?"

"A pistol."

"What would you want with a pistol, Hank?" He seemed genuinely surprised.

"I've decided to put Jacob's dog down."

"You want to shoot him?"

"He hasn't really been able to adapt to Jacob's absence. He's just gotten meaner and meaner, so that now I don't think I can trust him around the baby." I paused, slipping in a lie. "He bit Sarah the other day."

"Bad?"

"Bad enough to give us a good scare. She's making me keep him out in the garage now."

"Why not just take him to a vet? Pete Miller'll put him down for you."

I pretended to consider this, but then, sighing, shook my head. "I have to do it on my own, Carl. The dog was Jacob's best friend. If it has to be done, he would've wanted me to do it myself."

"You ever shoot a dog before?"

"I've never shot anything before."

"It's a horrible feeling, Hank. It's one of the worst things in the world. If I were you, I'd take him to Pete."

"No," I said. "I wouldn't feel right doing that."

Carl frowned.

"It'd only be for a day, Carl. I'll do it this afternoon, and have it back to you by the time you leave tonight."

"You even know how to use a gun?"

"I'm sure you could show me whatever I need to know."

"You'll just take him out in a field somewhere and shoot him?"

"I thought I'd do it near our old place. Bury him there, too. I figure that's what Jacob would've wanted."

He considered for a moment, his face serious, frowning. "I guess I could loan you one for a day," he said.

"It'd be a big help, Carl."

He spun his chair around so that he was facing the gun cabinet. "You wanted a pistol?"

I nodded, standing up so I could get a better view. "How about that one?" I pointed at a black revolver hanging from a peg in the cabinet's bottom-right-hand corner. It looked like the one he wore on his belt.

Carl took a key ring from his pocket, unlocked the glass-paneled door, and removed the gun. Then he sat down, opened his bottom desk drawer, and took out a small cardboard box full of bullets. He flipped open the pistol's cylinder and showed me how to load it.

"You just aim along the barrel and squeeze the trigger," he said. "Don't jerk it, pull it easy." He handed the gun across the desk to me, along with two bullets. "The cylinder'll advance automatically. There's no safety or anything like that."

I set the bullets down on the desk, side by side.

"It's my old pistol," Carl said.

I hefted it in my hand. It had a dense, compact feel, like a fist of iron. It was cool and oily to the touch.

"It's like the one you carry now?" I asked.

"That's right, just older. Probably older than you even. I got it when I first took office."

We both sat back down. I placed the gun on the edge of the desk, beside the bullets. The bullets were smaller than I'd expected, with shiny silver jackets and gray conical heads. They didn't look like they belonged with the gun. They weren't sinister enough; they lacked the pistol's threatening quality, its overt potential for violence. They looked harmless, like toys. I leaned forward and picked one of them up. Its skin had the same oily surface as the gun.

"I'll probably want to take a couple of practice shots before I actually do it," I said.

Carl stared at me.

"You think I could have a few more?"

He opened the drawer again to take out the box. "How many?"

"How many does it hold?"

"Six."

"How about four more, then?"

He removed four bullets from the box and rolled them one at a time across the desk. I collected them in my hand.

Beyond the window, I saw Tom Butler appear, stoop shouldered against the misting rain, a bright orange poncho clinging to his body. He was unloading something from the trunk of his car.

"There's Tom," I said. I stood up, checked my watch. It

was ten minutes till nine. "I should be able to finish by five after. Can you wait till then?"

Carl waved his arm at me. "Take your time, Hank. We're in no rush."

I started toward the door, but he stopped me.

"Wait," he said, and I turned, startled. He held out his hand. "Let me have the gun."

He picked up the bag of donuts and emptied it out onto the desk. There were three donuts inside, two powdered and one chocolate. The chocolate one rolled slowly across the desk's wooden surface, balanced for an instant on its edge, and then fell with a soft slap to the floor at my feet. I bent over to retrieve it. When I stood up, Carl was wrapping the pistol in the paper bag.

"You don't want to get it wet," he said.

I took it from him, nodding. The bag was pink and white, with blue lettering. LIZZIE'S DONUTS, it said, the words folding themselves slantwise across the pistol's butt.

"You'll be careful, won't you?" he asked. "Hate to loan you a gun and have you accidentally shoot yourself with it."

"I'll be careful," I said. "I promise."

AS I WAS making my way down the town hall steps, I caught sight of Agent Baxter up the street, just climbing from his car. I paused on the sidewalk, waiting for him to approach.

He strode toward me, his body erect, his head held up against the rain. His feet, bootless, cut straight through the piles of slushy snow scattered across the sidewalk. I watched him come, searching his face for similarities to the picture of Vernon Bokovsky. I scanned the close-set eyes, the small, flat nose, the low, squarish forehead, tried to draw in a beard along his jawline, to lengthen his hair and add weight to his cheeks, but I only had a second to do it. Then he was right in front of me, returning my gaze with a directness that unnerved me, made me feel awkward and suspicious. I looked away.

"Good morning, Mr. Mitchell," he said.

Confronted with his presence, I had an instant's tremor of panic. He was dressed exactly like the day before—a dark suit; an overcoat; black, shiny shoes. His head was bare, his hands gloveless. He had that same confident air about him that I'd found so intimidating on our first meeting, and beside him—dressed in my old jeans, a flannel shirt, my oversized parka—I felt like a hick, a country bumpkin fresh from the fields.

The panic passed, however, almost as quickly as it had come. I looked at the man before me, his crew cut slick with rain, his skin raw looking from the cold, and I realized that the walk, the handshake, the practiced formality, were nothing but a show. He was cold and uncomfortable, and he was going to be miserable when he got out into the woods.

"The sheriff's inside," I said. "I've just got to run a quick errand across the street before we go." I waved my arm toward the feedstore. Tom Butler was standing outside its front door, a damp cardboard box clenched beneath one of his arms. He was searching his pockets for his keys. The poncho, all folds and billows, hindered him like a shroud.

As I started out into the street, the agent called me back.

"Hey," he said. "What's in the bag?"

I turned halfway toward him. He was standing before me on the sidewalk, the barest hint of a smile on his face. I glanced down at the bag. I was holding it clasped against my chest, the paper molded into the damp, unmistakable shape of a pistol.

"The bag?"

"I'd kill for a donut right now."

I smiled at him, relief rushing through my body like a drug. "They're inside," I said. "I just borrowed the bag so my camera wouldn't get wet."

He eyed the bag. "Camera?"

I nodded, the lie seeming to maintain itself of its own accord, without any conscious thought on my part. "I'd loaned it to the sheriff."

I started to turn back toward the road but then stopped myself. "Want me to take your picture?" I asked.

Agent Baxter retreated a step toward the doors above him. "No. That's okay."

"You sure? It's no problem." I started to unwrap the bag.

He backed another step away from me, shaking his head. "It'd just be a waste of your film."

I shrugged, retightening the paper. I put the bag back against my chest. "Your choice," I said.

Turning to cross the street, I caught sight of my reflection in the rain-smeared window of a parked car. Above my shoulder I could see Agent Baxter continuing on up toward the town hall's big wooden doors.

Before I'd even fully thought it out, I'd called his name.

"Vernon," I said.

His reflection, murky and dim on the wet glass, paused as it pushed at the doors. He turned his head halfway toward me. It was an ambiguous gesture; it allowed me to see in it whatever I wanted.

"Hey, Vernon," I yelled, waving across the street at Tom, who was just disappearing into Raikley's. I jogged out into the road. Tom turned to stare at me, the cardboard box still clamped beneath his arm. He waited for me, holding open the door.

"You call me Vernon?" he asked.

I brushed the rain from my parka, stomped my boots on the rubber mat, and gave him a confused look. "Vernon?" I shook my head. "I said, 'Wait, Tom.' "

When I glanced back across the street, the town hall steps were empty.

. . .

My office was dim, the blinds drawn, but I didn't turn on a light. I went straight to my desk and took the pistol from the bag. It was covered with donut crumbs.

The clock on my wall said 9:01.

I shined the gun against my pant leg, removing the crumbs. Then I loaded the bullets.

When the clock flipped to 9:02, I picked up the phone to call Sarah.

The line was busy.

I put down the phone. I tried jamming the pistol into my jacket's right-hand pocket, but it was too big to fit: its butt protruded and its weight made the parka hang at an odd angle on my body.

I took off my jacket, unbuttoned my shirt, and slid the pistol into my waistband, barrel first, fiddling with it until it felt secure. It was in the center of my belly, sharp and cold against my skin, its grip pointing to the right. Its weight there gave me a peculiar charge, a little burst of excitement, making me feel like a gunslinger in a movie. I buttoned up my shirt but left it untucked, so that it covered the gun. Then I put my parka back on.

The clock changed to 9:03.

I dialed home again. Sarah answered on the first ring.

"It's him," I said.

"What do you mean?"

I told her quickly about the badge, about how he hadn't wanted his picture taken, and how I'd called his name on the street. She listened quietly, not once questioning any of my deductions, but even so, as soon as I started to speak, I felt my sense of certainty begin to seep away. There were alternative explanations for everything that had occurred, I realized, all of which were just as plausible, if not more so, than the idea that Agent Baxter was an impostor.

"I called the FBI," Sarah said.

"And?"

"And they said he was on field duty."

It took me a second to absorb this. "They have an Agent Baxter?"

"That's what they said."

"You asked for Neal Baxter?"

"Yes. Agent Neal Baxter."

I stood there for a moment, frozen, the phone clamped against my face. I was shocked; I hadn't expected this at all.

"What do you think that means?" I asked.

Even over the phone I could sense her shrugging. "Maybe it's just a coincidence."

I tried to force myself to believe this, but it didn't work.

"Baxter's not that uncommon a name," she said.

I could feel the pistol digging into my gut. It felt alive, like it was kneading my stomach. I repositioned it with my hand.

"He might've even known there was a Neal Baxter," she said. "He might've picked the name on purpose."

"So you're saying it's him?"

"Think about what you just told me, Hank. About him not having a badge and all."

"I didn't say he didn't have a badge. All I said was that he didn't show one to Carl."

Sarah didn't respond to this. Behind her, in the background, I could hear Jacob's teddy bear singing.

"Just tell me," I prodded her.

"Tell you what?"

"If you think it's him."

She hesitated, and then, "I do, Hank. I really do."

I nodded but didn't say anything.

"Do you?" she asked.

"I did," I said. I walked from my desk to the window. I lifted the blind and peeked out at the day. Everything was cloaked in mist. The cemetery's gate looked black in it, like a net, the tombstones beyond it gray and cold and indistinct.

"I guess I still do," I said.

"So you're coming home?"

"No. I'm going."

"But you just said—"

"I got a pistol, Sarah. I borrowed it from Carl."

There was silence on the other end, and I could feel her thinking. It was as if she were holding her breath.

"I'm going to protect him," I said. "I'm going to make sure he doesn't get hurt."

"Who?"

"Carl. If it's Vernon, and he pulls a gun, I'm going to shoot him."

"You can't do that, Hank. That's insane."

"No," I said. "It isn't. I've thought it out, and it's the right thing to do."

"If it's Vernon, it's important for us that he escapes. That way no one else will know how much money was on the plane."

"If it's Vernon, he's going to kill him."

"That's not our problem. We don't have anything to do with that."

"What're you talking about? We have everything to do with it. We know what Vernon's going to try and do."

"It's just a guess, Hank. We don't know for sure."

"I can stop him if I go."

"Maybe, maybe not. A pistol's not like a shotgun. It's a lot easier to miss with. And if you miss, he'll kill you both."

"I'm not going to miss. I'm going to stay right up next to him the whole time. I'll be too close to miss."

"He's a murderer, Hank. He knows what he's doing. You wouldn't have a chance against him."

The bear continued to sing behind her, its voice slow now, shaky. I pushed the gun farther down into my belt. I didn't want to listen to her, wanted just to go, but her words settled into my mind like tiny seeds, sprouting pale shoots of doubt. I began to waver. I tried to revive my determination by imagining how it would feel to draw the pistol from beneath my coat, to crouch down like a cop on TV, aim at Vernon's chest, and pull the trigger, but what I saw instead was everything that could go wrong—the gun snagging on my shirt; my boots slipping in the snow; the gun not firing, or firing wide, or high, or down into the ground at my feet, and then Vernon turning on me with his wooden smile.

I realized with a shock that I was scared of him.

"You have to think of the baby, Hank," Sarah said. "You have to think of me."

My dilemma seemed simple: I could either go with them or stay away. To go would be the braver choice, I knew, the nobler one, but also the riskier. If it was really Vernon who was waiting across the street, then he was probably planning on shooting both Carl and me. By going home, I'd escape that. I'd leave Carl to his fate, whatever that might be, and save myself.

I stood there pondering these two alternatives. Sarah was silent, waiting for me to speak. My left hand was in my pocket; I could feel some coins in there, my car keys, a little penknife that had belonged to my father. I pulled out one of the coins. It was a quarter, a bicentennial one.

If it comes up heads, I thought to myself, *I'll go.*

I tossed the coin into the air, caught it in my palm.

It was heads.

"Hank?" Sarah said. "Are you there?"

I stared down at the quarter with a pit of fear in my stomach. I'd wanted it to be tails, I realized, had been praying for it with all my heart. I debated flipping it again, going for two out of three, but I knew it didn't really matter. I'd just keep doing it until I got what I wanted. It was only a trick to soothe my conscience, a way to escape responsibility for my cowardice. I was too scared to go.

"Yes," I said. "I'm here."

"You're not a policeman. You don't know anything about guns."

I didn't say anything. I flipped the coin over in my palm so that the tails side was facing up.

"Hank?"

"It's all right," I said quietly. "I'm coming home."

I CALLED Carl and told him that the baby was vomiting, that Sarah was in a panic.

He was full of concern. "Linda's here now," he said. "She's done some nursing in her time. I'm sure she'd be willing to drive out with you if you need some help."

"That's awful nice of you, Carl, but I don't think it's that serious."

"You sure?"

"Positive. I just want to get her to a doctor to be safe."

"You head straight home then. I'm sure we can manage on our own. You didn't really see anything anyway, did you?"

"No. Nothing at all."

"You said you heard it on the south side? By the Pederson place?"

"Just a little ways past it."

"All right, Hank. Maybe I'll give you a call when we get back, let you know how it went."

"I'd like that."

"And I hope everything's okay with the baby."

He was about to hang up. "Carl?" I said, stopping him.

"What?"

"Be careful, okay?"

He laughed. "Careful of what?"

I was silent for several seconds. I wanted to warn him, but I couldn't think of a way to do it. "Just the rain," I said finally. "It's supposed to get colder later. The roads'll ice up."

He laughed again, but he seemed touched by my concern. "You be careful, too," he said.

I COULD see Carl's truck from my window—it was parked in front of the church—so I waited there, hidden behind the blinds, to watch them leave. They appeared almost immediately, walking side by side. Carl had on his dark green police jacket and his forest ranger's hat. The rain was falling in a thick mist now, forming puddles in the gutter and adding a rawness to the day, a cold, aching feeling, which I could sense even through the window.

Carl's truck was like a normal pickup, except it had a red-and-white bubble light on its roof, a police radio hooked to the underside of its dashboard, and a twelve-gauge shotgun hanging from a rack on the rear window. It was dark blue, with the words ASHENVILLE POLICE written in bold white letters on its side. I watched as he climbed in behind the wheel, then leaned across the seat to unlock the agent's door. I heard the engine start, saw them put on their seat belts, then watched the windshield wipers begin to slide back and forth, clearing the glass of rain. Carl removed his hat, smoothed his hair once with his hand, and put the hat back on.

I stood there, crouching beside the window in my darkened office, until they pulled out onto the road and headed off toward the west, toward the Pederson place and the nature preserve, toward Bernard Anders's overgrown orchard and the plane that lay within it as if in the hollow of a hand, awaiting, while the rain freed it from its veil of snow, their imminent arrival.

Before the truck disappeared down Main Street, its brake lights flashed once, as if in farewell; then the mist fell in behind them, leaving just the town beyond my window, its cold and empty sidewalks, its drab storefronts, with the rain running over everything, beading and pooling, and hissing as it fell.

. . .

I DROVE home.

Fort Ottowa was quiet. It was like entering a cemetery—the winding roads, the empty lawns with their mounds of dirt, the tiny, cryptlike houses. The children were all inside, hiding from the rain. Occasional lights dotted the windows; televisions flickered bluely behind drawn curtains. As I made my way through the neighborhood, I could picture Saturday-morning cartoons; card tables littered with jigsaw puzzles and board games; parents in bathrobes sipping mugs of coffee; teenagers upstairs sleeping late. Everything seemed so safe, so normal, and when I reached my own house, I was relieved to see that—at least from the outside—it looked exactly like all the others.

I parked in the driveway. There was a light on in the living room. Mary Beth was sitting beneath his tree in the rain, Buddha-like, his fur plastered wetly to his body.

I got out of the car and went into the garage. There was a small shovel hanging from a hook on the wall there, and I was just reaching up to pull it down when Sarah opened the door behind me.

"What're you doing, Hank?" she asked.

I turned toward her with the shovel. She was standing in the doorway, a step up from the garage. Amanda was in her arms, sucking on a pacifier. "I'm going to shoot the dog," I said.

"Here?"

I shook my head. "I'm going to drive him out to Ashenville. To my dad's old farm."

She frowned. "Maybe this isn't the best time to do that."

"I told Carl I'd return his pistol to him by this afternoon."

"Why not wait till Monday? You can have a vet do it then, and you won't need the gun."

"I don't want a vet to do it. I want to do it myself."

Sarah shifted Amanda from her right arm to her left. She

was wearing jeans and a dark brown sweater. Her hair was tied back in a ponytail, like a girl's. "Why?" she asked.

"It's what Jacob would've wanted," I said, not sure if this was actually the truth or merely a continuation of the lie I'd told Carl earlier.

Sarah didn't seem to know how to respond to this. I don't think she believed me. She frowned down at my chest.

"The dog's miserable," I said. "It's not fair to him, keeping him out there in the cold."

Amanda turned to look at me when I spoke, her round head swiveling on her neck like an owl's. She blinked her eyes, and her pacifier fell out of her mouth, bouncing down the step into the garage. I came forward and picked it up. It was damp with her saliva.

"I'll be back in an hour or so. It won't take that long."

I held out the pacifier to Sarah, and she took it from me, grasping it between two of her fingers. Our hands didn't touch.

"You aren't going by the nature preserve, are you?" she asked.

I shook my head.

"You promise?"

"Yes," I said. "I promise."

She watched from the front window as I untied Mary Beth and led him toward the car. Jacob's things were still loaded in the back, and when the dog got inside, he began to sniff at the boxes, his tail wagging. I climbed in behind the wheel. Sarah was holding Amanda up to the window, waving the infant's tiny hand back and forth.

I could see her mouth moving in an exaggerated fashion. "Bye-bye," she was saying. "Bye-bye, doggy."

Mary Beth slept the whole way out to the farm, curled up in a ball on the backseat.

The weather didn't change. A fine drizzle fell from the sky, dissolving into the mist. Houses materialized around me as I drove, ghostlike beside the road, surrounded by barns and silos and outbuildings, their colors bleached, their eaves dripping, old cars parked haphazardly about their yards. The ground had already begun to appear in places, dark, muddy clumps rising like gloved fists through the snow; in some fields there were whole lines of them, marching parallel into the distance, the remnants of last year's furrows, their termini hidden by the fog.

When I reached the farm, the dog refused to climb out of the car. I opened the door for him, and he backed away from me, growling and baring his teeth, his hair rising along his neck. I had to drag him out by the clothesline.

He shook himself when he hit the ground, stretched, then jogged off ahead of me into the field.

I followed him, holding the rope in my left hand and the shovel in my right. The pistol was holstered beneath my belt.

The snow was melting rapidly, but it was still deep enough in places to rise up over my boots. It was heavy and wet, like white clay, and difficult to move through. My pant legs grew dark with its moisture, clinging to my calves so that I looked like I was wearing knickers and knee socks. The drizzle drifted down from the sky, falling lightly on my head and shoulders and sending a chill across my back.

I flipped up the collar on my parka. Mary Beth moved in a zigzag course before me, sniffing at the snow. His tail was wagging.

We headed out into the center of the field, toward the spot where my father's house had once stood. His windmill was off to the left, barely visible in the mist, its blades dripping water into the snow.

I stopped near where I thought our front stoop should've been and dropped the clothesline and the shovel to the ground. I stepped on the rope with my boot, to keep the dog from running away. Then I removed the pistol from my waistband.

Mary Beth started to jog back toward the road but only got about ten feet away before the clothesline went taut and he had to stop. Beyond him, our tracks were dark and round in the snow, two wobbly lines connecting us with the station wagon at the edge of the road. There was an ominous quality to the view; the fog seemed to deny us retreat, to form a thick gray-white wall just beyond the car, imprisoning us in the muddy field. It was like a drawing from a book of fairy tales, full of hidden threat and terror, and I got a peculiar feeling looking at it, something close to fear.

Carl could be dead right now, I knew. I wanted to believe that he wasn't, that, having spent the morning walking aimlessly around the woods, they were already heading back toward town, but my mind wouldn't let me. Against my will, I kept picturing the wreck. The snow would've melted from it: it would be impossible to miss. I could see it in my head, could see the crows, the wizened trees. I could see Vernon very calmly—so that the gesture seemed perfectly innocuous—pulling a pistol from beneath his jacket and shooting Carl in the head. I could see Carl falling, could see his blood in the snow. The birds would fly up at the sound of the shot. Their cries would echo off the side of the orchard.

I bungled the shooting of the dog, transformed what I'd planned to be an act of mercy into one of torture.

I got behind him and aimed at the back of his neck, but he spun toward me just as I pulled the trigger. The bullet hit him in the lower jaw, breaking it so that it hung down from his head at a grotesque angle. He fell onto his side, whimpering. His tongue was severed; blood poured from his mouth.

When he tried to rise to his feet, I fired again, in panic. This time I hit him in the rib cage, just below the shoulder.

He rolled over onto his side in the snow, his legs jerking out straight and freezing like that, rigid against the ground. His chest heaved in and out with a deep bubbling sound. For a moment I thought that it would be enough, that he was going to die, but then he started to struggle upward again, and a frightening sound emerged from his throat, something closer to a scream than a bark. It went on and on and on, rising and dipping in volume.

I stepped forward and straddled his body. I was sweating now, my hands slick with it, trembling. I placed the gun's barrel against the top of his head. I shut my eyes, my stomach rising into my throat, and pulled the trigger.

There was a sharp crack, a muffled echo, and then silence.

The rain increased slightly, growing into full-size drops, riddling the snow.

Mary Beth's body was outlined in blood, a large, pink circle around his head and shoulders. It gave me a guilty feeling to look at it. I thought of my father, how he'd refused to slaughter animals on his farm, persisting in this compunction year after year despite the disdain and derision it had earned him among his neighbors. And now I'd violated his taboo.

I stepped away from the dog, wiped my face with the back of my sleeve. The mist hung all about me, blocking out the world.

I picked up the shovel and started to dig. The ground was soft on top, wet and muddy, but this only lasted for about ten inches; then it was as if I were attempting to dig through a slab of concrete. The shovel's blade made a ringing sound each time I brought it down; the earth was frozen solid. I used my boots, kicking at the dirt, but nothing happened: I could go no deeper. If I was going to bury the dog here—which I had to, there was no way I could carry his bloody corpse back to the car—it would have to be in a ten-inch grave.

I grabbed Mary Beth by his legs and dragged him into the

hole. Then I scraped the dirt back over him. There was barely enough to cover his body; I had to finish the job with snow, piling it up until I'd built a little mound. It was something that wouldn't last, I knew. If an animal didn't dig it up by the spring, then George Muller, the man who owned the farm now, would uncover it when he plowed the field. I felt a pang of remorse over this, imagining what Jacob would've thought if he could've seen how inadequate it was. I'd failed my brother even here.

I CRIED on the way home, for the first time since Jacob's apartment. I'm not sure even now what prompted it. It was a little bit of everything, I suppose—it was Carl and Jacob and Mary Beth and Sonny and Lou and Nancy and Pederson and my parents and Sarah and myself. I tried to stop, tried to think of Amanda, and how she'd never know about any of it, how she'd grow up, surrounded by all the benefits of our crimes without any of the pain, but it seemed impossible to believe, a fantasy, the happy-ever-after ending of a fairy tale. We'd romanticized the future, I realized, and this added a further weight to my grief, a sense of futility and waste. Our new lives were going to be nothing like we'd imagined: we were going to lead a hard, fugitive existence, full of lies and subterfuge and the constant threat of getting caught. And we'd never escape what we'd done; our sins would follow us to our graves.

I had to pull over onto the edge of the road before I entered Fort Ottowa and wait for my tears to run their course. I didn't want Sarah to know that I'd been crying.

BY THE time I returned to the house, it was almost noon. I hung the shovel on its hook in the garage, then went inside. I was muddy, cold. My face felt bloated from weeping, my hands weak and shaky.

Sarah called out to me from the living room.

"It's me," I yelled. "I'm home."

I heard her stand up to come greet me, but then the phone began to ring, and she went into the kitchen instead.

I'd just finished taking off my boots when she leaned her head out into the hallway. "It's for you, Hank," she said.

"Who is it?" I whispered, moving toward her.

"He didn't say."

I remembered how Carl had promised to telephone me when he returned from the nature preserve, and I felt a surge of relief. "Is it Carl?"

She shook her head. "I don't think so. He would've asked about the baby."

She was right, and I knew it, but I still allowed myself to hope. I went into the kitchen and picked up the phone, expecting to hear his voice.

"Hello?" I said.

"Mr. Mitchell?"

"Yes?"

"This is Sheriff McKellroy, of the Fulton County Sheriff's Department. I was wondering if you'd be able to come on into Ashenville for a bit, so that we could ask you a few questions."

"Questions?"

"We could send a cruiser if you wanted, but it'd be easier if you could just drive in yourself. We're kind of strapped for manpower right now."

"Can I ask what this is all about?"

Sheriff McKellroy hesitated, as if unsure what he should say. "It's about Officer Jenkins. Carl Jenkins. He's been shot."

"Shot?" I said, and the horror and regret in my voice were genuine. Only the surprise was counterfeit.

"Yes. Murdered."

"Oh, my God. I can't believe it—I saw him just this morning."

"Actually, that's what we'd like to talk—"

Someone on the other end interrupted the sheriff, and I heard him put his hand over the phone. Sarah stood across the kitchen, watching me. The baby was beginning to cry a little in the other room, but she ignored her.

"Mr. Mitchell?" McKellroy's voice returned.

"Yes?"

"Did you meet a man named Neal Baxter yesterday afternoon?"

"Yes," I said. "From the FBI."

"Did he show you any identification?"

"Identification?"

"A badge? A picture ID?"

"No. Nothing like that."

"Could you describe him for me?"

"He was tall. Maybe six-four or so. Broad shouldered. Black hair, cut short. I can't remember what color his eyes were."

"Do you remember what he was wearing?"

"Today?"

"Yes."

"An overcoat. A dark suit. Black leather shoes."

"And did you see his car?"

"I saw it this morning. I saw him climb out of it."

"Do you remember what it looked like?"

"It was blue, four doors, like a rental car. I didn't see the plates."

"Do you know the make?"

"No," I said. "It was a sedan, kind of boxy, like a Buick or something, but I didn't notice the specific make."

"That's all right. We'll probably show you some pictures when you get in, and maybe we'll be able to identify it from that. Can you come right away? We're at the town hall."

"I still don't understand what happened."

"It's probably best if you just wait till you get here. Do you need us to send a cruiser?"

"No. I can drive myself."

"And you'll come quick?"

"Yes," I said. "I'll leave right now."

II

I TOOK the pistol out of the car before I left and put it in the garage. It didn't seem like something I'd want to have with me when I spoke with the police.

The rain was still falling, an icy drizzle, but I could tell that it was going to stop soon. The sky was lighter; the air was growing colder. The fields alongside the road were quilted brown and white.

Ashenville was abuzz with activity. Two television crews—one from Channel 11 and one from Channel 24—were busy assembling their cameras on the sidewalk. Several police cars were pulled up in front of the town hall. The street was crowded with gawkers.

I parked a little ways down the block.

There was a policeman standing at the foot of the town hall steps, and at first he wouldn't let me by. Then one of the wooden doors opened above us, and a short, pudgy man leaned out.

"You Hank Mitchell?" he asked.

"Yes."

He held out his hand, and I climbed up the steps to shake it. "I'm Sheriff McKellroy," he said. "We spoke on the phone."

He led me inside. He was very small, and he waddled

when he walked. He had a wan, pasty face, and short, colorless hair that smelled strongly of hair tonic, as if he'd come here directly from a barbershop.

Carl's office was packed with policemen. They all seemed very busy, as if they were under some sort of deadline. No one looked up when we came in. I recognized one of the deputies from when Jacob had been shot. He was the one with the farm boy's face, the one who'd dropped off Mary Beth at my house. He was at Linda's desk, talking to someone on the phone.

"Collins!" Sheriff McKellroy yelled. "Take Mr. Mitchell's statement."

One of the policemen stepped forward, a tall man, older looking than McKellroy, with a lean, grizzled face and a cigarette in his mouth. He escorted me back out into the hallway, where it was quieter.

The idea of giving a statement to the police made me nervous, but it turned out to be a remarkably simple affair. I just told him my story, and he wrote it down. There was no interrogation, no third degree. He didn't even seem particularly interested in what I had to say.

I started almost three months earlier, at the end of December. I told him how I'd heard a plane with engine trouble out by the nature preserve, how I'd mentioned it to Carl, and how—since there'd been nothing in the news about a missing airplane—he'd said it was probably a false alarm.

"I didn't think anything about it," I said, "until yesterday afternoon, when Carl called me over as I was leaving work. There was a man from the FBI in his office, and he was looking for a missing plane."

"That was Agent Baxter?" Collins asked.

"That's right. Neal Baxter."

He wrote this down. "Did he say why he was searching for the plane?"

"He said it had a fugitive in it."

"A fugitive?"

"Someone the FBI was looking for."

"He didn't say who?"

I shook my head. "I asked, but they wouldn't tell me."

"They?"

"He and Carl."

"So Officer Jenkins knew?"

"I think so. That's what it seemed like."

He scribbled this down. Then he flipped to a clean page in the notebook. "You met them again this morning?"

"That's right. We'd planned to go out around nine o'clock to look for the plane, but my wife called just as we were leaving and said that our daughter was throwing up. So I went home instead."

"And that was the last you saw of either Officer Jenkins or Agent Baxter?"

I nodded. "They drove off, and I went home."

Collins scanned his pad, rereading what I'd told him. He underlined something, then closed the notebook.

"Can you tell me what's going on?" I asked.

"You haven't heard?"

"Just that Carl's been murdered."

"He was shot by this man who was looking for the plane."

"Agent Baxter?"

"That's right."

"But why?"

Collins shrugged. "All we know is what you and Mrs. Jenkins have told us: Officer Jenkins left town with Baxter around nine-fifteen. Just after eleven o'clock, Mrs. Jenkins looked out her window here and saw Baxter pull up, alone, in her husband's truck. He parked it across the street, walked back to his own car, and drove away. She called her house, thinking that her husband might've been dropped off there, but got no answer, so she decided to drive out to the nature preserve herself and see what was going on. When she arrived at the park, she found their tracks in the snow and just followed them in. They went on for about a half mile through the trees and stopped beside the wreckage of a small plane. That's where she found her husband's body."

"Linda found him herself?" I asked, horrified by the thought of this.

He nodded. "Then she ran back to the road and called us on the radio."

"But why would he have shot Carl?"

Collins seemed to debate for a second. He slid his pen into his shirt pocket. "Baxter didn't mention anything to you about some missing money?"

"No." I shook my head. "Nothing."

"Mrs. Jenkins said he told her husband there was four million dollars on the plane."

"Four million dollars?" I stared incredulously at him.

"That's what she claims."

"So he shot Carl for the money?"

"We aren't sure—Baxter may have been lying. He said it came from an armored-car robbery in Chicago last July, but we can't find any record of that. All we know is that it had something to do with the plane. Beyond this, it's anyone's guess."

Collins left me, to show my statement to Sheriff McKellroy. I wasn't sure if I could go yet—the sheriff had said that I might have to look at some pictures to identify Vernon's car—so I just stuck around. They'd brought some folding chairs into Carl's outer office, and I took one and sat down by the window. The farm boy nodded hello when I came in with Collins, but after that no one paid me any attention. Someone had brought in a police radio, which hissed and sputtered in the corner. There was a large map tacked up on the wall, and sometimes Sheriff McKellroy would go over and draw a line on it.

They were hunting for Vernon, I knew, tracking him down.

Outside, the crowd had grown. People were pulling up in cars. Both of the TV crews were filming interviews—Channel 11 with a state policeman, Channel 24 with Cyrus Stahl, Ashenville's octogenarian mayor. The weather was clearing, and the town had taken on a festive air. People were talking in large groups. Some children had gotten out their bikes and were racing up and down the street. Little boys peered inside the parked police cars, their hands cupped to the windows.

The rain had stopped, and a wind had sprung up from the north, gusting now and then in cold little shocks of air that made the flag above the town hall snap and flutter, its lanyard clanking hollowly against the aluminum pole, like the distant tolling of a bell. The flag had been dropped to half-mast, in mourning for Carl.

I'd been sitting there for almost an hour and was staring out the window in a daze when the room behind me seemed to explode in a rush of movement.

"Where's Mitchell?" I heard the sheriff yell. "He go home?"

I turned around and found one of the deputies pointing at me. "He's right here."

Collins and the farm boy were picking up their hats and jackets and striding toward the door. Everyone seemed to be talking at once, but I couldn't focus on what they were saying.

"Collins," Sheriff McKellroy yelled. "Sweeney. Take Mr. Mitchell with you. Have him ID the body."

"The body?" I said.

"You mind?" the sheriff asked from across the room. "It'd be a big help."

"Mind what?"

"We got a guy that fits the description you gave of Baxter, but we need a positive ID." He pointed toward Collins and the farm boy, who were waiting in the doorway. "They'll take you," he said.

I picked up my jacket and started toward the door but then stopped in midstride. "Would it be all right if I called my wife?" I asked McKellroy. "Just to let her know where I am?"

"Of course," he said, giving me an understanding look. He evicted a deputy from Linda's desk and sat me down there.

I picked up the phone and dialed home.

Linda had a picture of herself and Carl on her desk, and I turned away from it, toward the window, though not quickly enough to avoid having to wonder where she was right now. Probably at home, I thought. She'd never forget what she'd seen this morning—her husband lying in the snow, dead—and it gave me a tired feeling to think this, a numbness in my heart.

Like this morning, Sarah answered on the first ring.

"It's me," I said. "I'm at the police station."

"Is everything okay?"

"Carl's dead. The guy from the FBI shot him."

"I know," she said. "I heard about it on the radio."

"But it sounds like they caught him. They're taking me out now to make sure it's the same guy."

"Taking you where?"

"I don't know. I think he might be dead."

"Dead?"

"They said 'body.' They want me to ID the body."

"They killed him?"

"I'm not sure. That's what it sounds like."

"Oh, Hank," she whispered. "That's perfect."

"Sarah," I said quickly, "I'm at the police station." I glanced around the room to see if anyone was listening.

Collins and the farm boy stood by the door, their hats in their hands. They were both watching me, waiting for me to finish.

Sarah fell silent. I could hear the radio playing in the background, a man's high-pitched voice, selling something. "Do you know when you'll be home?" she asked.

"Probably not for a little while."

"I'm so relieved, Hank. I'm so happy."

"Shhh."

"We're going to celebrate tonight. We're going to ring in our new life together."

"I have to say good-bye now, Sarah. We can talk when I get home."

I set down the phone.

THE FARM boy drove, and I rode beside him in the front seat. Collins sat in back. We headed south out of town, speeding, our lights flashing. The temperature was dropping now, and the roads had spots of ice on them. The air seemed to grow clearer by the moment, the views wider and crisper. Every now and then a tatter of bluish sky appeared between the swiftly moving clouds above us.

"Did Sheriff McKellroy say 'body'?" I asked the farm boy.

He nodded. "That's right."

"So Baxter's dead?"

"Dead as a doornail," Collins said from the backseat, his voice sounding almost gleeful. "Shot full of holes."

"Perforated," the farm boy said.

"Like a sieve."

They both grinned at me. They seemed excited, like two boys on a field trip.

"He was killed down near Appleton," Collins said, "at the entrance to the Turnpike there. He ran into a pair of state troopers, shot one of them in the leg, and then the other one blew him away."

"Four shots," the farm boy said.

"Three to the chest. One to the head."

The farm boy glanced across the seat at me. "Does that bother you?" he asked with sudden seriousness.

"Bother me?"

"Having to go ID him if he's been shot. The blood and everything."

"Head shots can be pretty ugly," Collins said. "It'll be best if you just give him a quick glance. Try to think of it as meat, like you're looking at a pile of ground—"

The farm boy interrupted him. "His brother was shot," he said quickly.

Collins fell silent.

"Remember a couple months ago? That guy out here that came home and found his wife in bed with his landlord? The one that went crazy?"

"That was your brother?" Collins asked me. "The gambler?"

The farm boy shook his head. "His brother was the other guy. The one that got shot coming to the rescue."

I could actually feel the mood in the car shift downward. It was as if we'd driven into a shadow. The farm boy leaned forward and turned the cruiser's heat up a notch. There was a warm push of air against my face.

"I'm sorry, Mr. Mitchell," Collins said. "I didn't know."

I nodded. "It's all right."

"How's that dog?" the farm boy asked. He glanced in the mirror at his partner. "His brother had a real nice dog. Mr. Mitchell adopted it."

"What kind of dog?" Collins asked. They were both working together, trying to revive their good spirits.

"It was a mutt," I said. "Part German shepherd, part Lab. But I had to put him down."

Neither of them said anything. The farm boy fiddled with the radio.

"He didn't adapt very well to my brother's absence. He got mean. He bit my wife."

"Dogs are like that," Collins said. "They get attached. They feel grief just like us."

After that no one said anything for the rest of the trip. The farm boy concentrated on the driving. Collins sat smoking in the back. I stared out the window at the road.

VERNON had been shot at a tollbooth, trying to get onto the Ohio Turnpike just north of Appleton. As he'd pulled up to take his ticket, his car had slid on a little patch of ice and banged into the one in front of him. There were a pair of state troopers on the other side of the median, and when they saw the accident, they came over to help. Even then, if Vernon had stayed calm, he might've gotten away. He'd changed his blue car for a red one sometime after leaving Ashenville and had put on a parka and a wool hat to cover his crew cut, so he didn't look like the man the troopers were searching for. But he panicked when he saw them coming, climbed out of his car, and pulled a gun.

It took us a while to get through to the tollbooth. The entrance ramp had been blocked off, and there was a state trooper rerouting traffic, waving it on down the road to the west. There were five or six police cars parked at odd angles across the little plaza. An ambulance was just leaving as we arrived, its lights flashing.

There wasn't much around the exit—a pair of gas stations, a boarded-up Dairy Queen, a convenience store. It was farm country, flat and featureless.

We pulled off onto the edge of the road, then got out and walked toward the tollbooth. Vernon's car, a cherry red Toyota hatchback, was sitting there with its door hanging open. The area around it had been roped off with bright yellow tape. There were state troopers everywhere, but no one seemed to be doing anything. The car Vernon had rear-ended had been driven away.

I could see a body lying beside the Toyota. It was covered with a silver blanket.

We ducked under the tape and made our way through the milling policemen to the corpse. The farm boy and I crouched down beside it, and he flipped back the blanket. Collins stood behind me.

"That him?" he asked.

It was Vernon. He'd been shot in the side of the head, just above the ear. I could see the entry hole, a black puncture, no larger than a dime. There was blood everywhere—on Vernon's face, the blanket, the pavement, even his teeth. His shirt collar was pink with it. His eyes were open, round with surprise, staring straight up at the sky. I had to resist the temptation to reach down and shut them.

"Yeah," I said. "That's the guy."

The farm boy flipped back the blanket, and we stood up.

"You okay?" he asked. He touched me on my elbow, turned me away from the corpse.

"I'm fine," I said, and then, surprising myself, felt my face begin to grin. I had to concentrate to stop, had to clench my teeth together and tighten my jaw. It was the relief that did it—I was startled by its strength—it eclipsed my sadness over Carl's murder, made his death seem almost worthwhile, expedient, the sort of price one might expect to pay for a bag full of treasure. For the first time since the night we decided to take the packets, I felt absolutely secure. Sarah had been right, it was perfect: now there was no one left to connect us to the money. Everyone was dead—Vernon and his brother and Carl and Lou and Nancy and Jacob and Sonny and Pederson. Everyone.

And the money was ours.

Collins went off to radio Sheriff McKellroy and tell him

that I'd identified the body while the farm boy fell into conversation with some of the state troopers. I started to return to the car—it had gotten cold out, and I wanted to sit down—but then changed my mind and remained where I was. I was curious to see if they'd found the bag of money yet and thought that if I hung around I might hear about it. I moved off toward the tollbooth and stood there, just beyond the yellow tape, with my hands in my pockets, trying to look inconspicuous.

A red-haired policeman began to take pictures. He pulled back the blanket and photographed Vernon's body. He photographed the Toyota, the tollbooth, the blood on the pavement—everything from several different angles. Although the weather was continuing to clear, the day was still dark, and he used a flashbulb on his camera. It went off again and again in rapid cadence, little explosions of light, like sun bouncing off a mirror.

After a few minutes, a news crew pulled up in a yellow van. CHANNEL THIRTEEN was written diagonally across its side in large red letters, and below it, in black, ACTIONNEWS. They had a Minicam with them, and they started filming the crime scene with it. They tried to get a shot of Vernon's body, but one of the troopers ordered them away.

A dark brown car arrived right after the van, and two men climbed out of it. I could tell they were from the FBI as soon as I saw them. They looked like Vernon had—tall and lean, short haired and hatless. They were both wearing overcoats, unbuttoned over dark suits and sedate ties. They had black shoes on their feet, black leather gloves on their hands. Hovering all around them—both in the way they moved and in the gestures they used when they spoke to the troopers—was that same coolly professional air, that same sense of icy precision and control, which Vernon had so successfully imitated when we'd been introduced. And it intimidated me now exactly as it had then; my chest went tight, my heart sped up, my back began to sweat.

The horrible fear that I'd overlooked something, that I'd left some clue, some incriminating trace of myself within the crime, drifted, draftlike, into my thoughts. If I were to be caught, I realized with a chill, these would be the men who'd do it.

I watched them walk over to Vernon's body and crouch down beside it. They uncovered him and began checking his pockets, pulling them inside out. One of them took Vernon by the chin and turned his head back and forth, as if he were examining his face. When he let go of it, he wiped his hand on the silver blanket, murmuring something to his partner. His partner shook his head.

From Vernon's body they proceeded to an inspection of the Toyota, and from there to a brief conference with one of the state troopers. After about a minute or so, the trooper called over the farm boy and introduced him to the two agents. They talked for a few seconds; then the farm boy turned to point in my direction.

"Mr. Mitchell?" one of the agents called. He started walking toward me. "Hank Mitchell?"

"Yes?" I said, stepping forward to meet him. "I'm Hank Mitchell."

He reached into his jacket and pulled out his wallet. He flipped it open to show me his shield. It gave me an anxious feeling, watching him do this, like I was being arrested. "My name's Agent Renkins," he said. "I'm from the Federal Bureau of Investigation."

I nodded, staring at the badge.

"My partner and I were wondering if you'd mind driving back into town with us, so you could tell us what you know about all this."

"I've already gone over it once with the police," I said. "Couldn't you get my statement from them?"

"We'd prefer to hear it for ourselves. You can appreciate that, can't you?" He gave me one of Vernon's fake smiles.

I didn't answer; it was clear that I didn't have a choice. The other agent came up to join us. He had a black plastic garbage bag clamped beneath his arm.

"We're parked over here," Renkins said, pointing toward their car. Then he turned and led me away.

I RODE in the backseat. Renkins drove, and his partner, Agent Fremont, sat beside him. The two men looked virtually identical from the rear—their shoulders were the same width, their heads rose to the same height above the car's seat, and their hair grew out in exactly the same tint of dark brown, covering their identically round scalps to the same depth and thickness.

There was only one variation between them, though it was a dramatic one. Fremont's ears were much too large for his head. I couldn't help staring at them as we pulled away from the toll plaza; they were huge, convoluted ovals, stiff looking and astonishingly white, and they had an extremely personable effect on me. They made him instantly likable. He must've been teased about them when he was little, I thought, remembering Jacob's childhood and how he'd been tormented for his weight, and I felt a wave of pity for the man.

It was a remarkably different sensation, sitting in the rear of the agents' car, than it had been sitting in the front of the cruiser. It was just a normal car, like a traveling salesman might own—black vinyl interior, little ashtrays on the doors, a cheap-looking tape deck in the dashboard—but, alone in the backseat, I had the definite sensation that I was in their custody, that I was under their control. It was a feeling I hadn't had in the cruiser.

We headed toward Ashenville, moving at right angles along the perpendicular farm roads, first north, then east, then north again, and I told them my story. They kept a tape recorder running as I spoke, but they seemed relatively uninterested in what I had to say. They asked no questions; they didn't glance back at me when I paused or nod encouragement to move me along. They sat impassively before me, staring out the windshield at the road. We retraced the route I'd driven with Collins and the farm boy earlier that afternoon, passed the same landmarks, the same houses, the same farms. The only difference was that it was clear now, the air pale and dry. The sun, approaching the end of its slow arc to the west, glinted brightly off of distant rooftops.

As I talked, I decided that the agents' silence could mean only one of two things. Either they'd already accepted my story and were merely listening now as a formality or they'd discovered something damning in their investigation of the crime site, some contrary evidence that wiped everything I was saying aside, and they were simply waiting for me to finish, allowing me to dig myself further and further into my falsehood before unmasking me for what I was: a liar, a thief, a murderer. I lingered as I neared the close of my tale, pausing and repeating myself, fearful to discover which of these possible alternatives would confront me.

But then, unavoidably, I reached the end.

Fremont punched a button on the tape recorder, stopping it. Then he turned to look at me.

"There's only one problem with your story, Mr. Mitchell."

A tightness settled into my stomach when he said this. I looked out at the passing fields, forcing myself to wait before I spoke. Off in the distance I could see a scarecrow, dressed in black, hanging from a pole. He had a straw hat on, and from this far away, at first sight, he looked like a real man.

"A problem?" I asked.

Fremont nodded, his elephantine ears moving up and down like paddles beside his head.

"The man whose corpse you identified back there—he wasn't from the FBI."

The relief I felt at these words was so intense that it had an actual physical effect on me. Over the entire surface of my body, my pores opened, and I began to sweat. It was a strange, even horrible sensation, like losing control of one's bladder, a sudden slipping, a dizzying loss of control. It made me want to giggle, but I suppressed it. I wiped my forehead with my hand.

"I don't understand," I said. My voice came out hoarser than I would've liked. Fremont didn't seem to notice.

"His name was Vernon Bokovsky. That plane you heard with engine trouble back in December was carrying his brother. It crashed in the nature preserve."

"He was looking for his brother?"

Fremont shook his head. "He was looking for this." He lifted the plastic bag from between his feet. I leaned forward to get a better look. It gave me a thrill to see it; it was knowing something secret.

"A garbage bag?" I said.

"That's right." Fremont grinned. "Full of some very expensive trash." He opened the bag, shaking it so I could see the money.

I stared at it, counting to ten in my head, trying to look speechless with surprise. "Is it real?" I asked.

"It's real." Fremont stuck a black-gloved hand into the bag and pulled out one of the packets. He held it up before my face. "It's ransom," he said. "Bokovsky and his brother were the guys who kidnapped that McMartin girl last November."

"The McMartin girl?"

"The heiress. The one they shot and dumped in the lake."

I kept my eyes on the money. "Can I touch it? I'm wearing gloves."

The two agents laughed. "Sure," Fremont said. "Go ahead."

I stretched out my hand, and he set the packet in it. I stared down at it, weighing it in my palm. Renkins watched me in the rearview mirror, a friendly smile on his face.

"It's heavy, isn't it?" he asked.

"Yes," I said. "It's like a little book."

We were approaching Ashenville now. I could see it rising from the horizon, a low mound of buildings clustered tightly around the crossroads. It looked fake, illusory, like the city of Oz.

I handed the packet to Fremont, and he dropped it back into the bag.

Ashenville had returned to normal in my absence. The TV crews had left, the crowds had disappeared, and now the town looked exactly like it would've on any other Saturday afternoon, empty, sleepy, a little run-down around the edges. The only thing that remained as a reminder of its recent tragedy was the flag, fluttering limply at half-mast.

Renkins parked in front of the town hall, and we climbed out onto the sidewalk to say good-bye.

"I'm sorry you had to get dragged into all this," Fremont said. "You've been very cooperative." We were standing at the base of the town hall's steps. There was only one police car left.

"I still don't really understand what happened," I said.

Renkins grinned at me. "I'll tell you what happened," he said. "Two brothers kidnapped a girl outside of Detroit. They shot seven people, including the girl, and escaped with a ransom of four point eight million dollars. One of the brothers crashed a plane into that park. The other came out to find him, pretending to be a federal agent. When he saw the plane, he shot Officer Jenkins."

His smile deepened.

"And then a state trooper shot him."

"There's four point eight million dollars in that bag?" I asked, as if I were ready to believe it.

"No," Renkins said. "That's five hundred thousand."

"Where's the rest?"

He shrugged, glanced at Fremont. "We're not sure."

I gazed off at the town. There were two birds fighting over something in the gutter up the block. They screeched loudly at each other and took turns trying to fly away with it, but it was too big, neither of them could lift it. I couldn't tell what it was.

"So there are four point three million dollars out there, just floating around?"

"It'll turn up," Fremont said.

I looked at him, closely, but his face was absolutely expressionless. Renkins was staring up the street at the birds.

"What do you mean?" I asked.

"We had the money for two hours before Mr. McMartin had to take it to the drop site. We couldn't mark it—we were afraid the kidnappers would detect the markings and kill the girl, so we put together a task force of twenty agents, and they wrote down as many of the serial numbers as they could." He smiled at me, like he was letting me in on a joke. "We ended up recording just under five thousand of them, one out of ten of the bills."

I didn't say anything. I simply stared at him, struck dumb. I couldn't really bring myself to grasp what he was saying.

"We'll track it down," he said. "It's just a matter of waiting for the numbers to turn up. You can't go around passing hundred-dollar bills without eventually sticking in someone's memory."

"The money's marked," I said slowly. I looked down at my feet, frowning, trying not to react to this news, trying to appear calm, distant, uninvolved. I concentrated my whole mind on my boots, forced myself to think up names for their color, occupying all my energies on this task, knowing implicitly that I'd collapse if I allowed myself to try to lift the full weight of Fremont's revelation.

"That's what it amounts to," he said. "Marked money."

"Crime doesn't pay," Renkins said.

Tan, I thought, *oatmeal*. With a strain I managed *amber*.

But the knowledge slipped in around the words, waterlike, seeping through the cracks. The money was marked.

Fremont offered me his hand. I forced myself to take it, struggled to match its firmness. Then I repeated the ritual with Renkins.

"Our knowing about the serial numbers," he said, "that's confidential, of course. It's the only way we'll be able to catch whoever else is involved in this."

Fremont nodded. "So if you talk to the press . . ."

"Yes," I said, "I understand."

"If we need you, you'll be around?" Renkins asked.

"Of course," I said. I gestured across the street toward Raikley's. "I work over there."

They both glanced at the feedstore. "We probably won't have to bother you," Renkins said. "It seems pretty cut-and-dried."

"Yes," I said weakly.

Sepia, I thought. *Terra-cotta. Adobe.*

"I'm just sorry you had to get mixed up in all this. It's a tragedy, the whole fucking thing."

He gave my shoulder a parting pat, and then they turned, one after the other, walked up the town hall steps, and disappeared through the double doors.

I watched my feet make their way toward the curb. They shuffled out into the street, then moved across it to the other side. My car was there, a little ways down the block, and my boots guided me around its rear end, stopping when they reached the door. Magically, my hand emerged from my jacket pocket, holding the keys. It unlocked the door, pulled it open, and my body bent at the waist, my head ducking forward, as I dropped into the seat.

And it was only then, safe in my car with the door shut firmly behind me, that I let my mind slip free, allowed it to settle on Fremont's words, absorb them like a sponge, swelling with their import.

The money was worthless.

My first reaction, one that had even begun to trickle out while I was standing there with Fremont and Renkins on the sidewalk, was an overwhelming wave of despair. The bloodied corpses of Pederson and Nancy and Sonny and Jacob all rushed forward to confront me—four lives I'd ended with my own hands to protect my hold on the bag of money, money that was nothing now, simply stacks of colored paper.

Fatigue followed directly behind despair, like rain from a cloud. It was my body's reaction to the horror of what I'd done—a bonenumbing tiredness, a feeling of surrender and acceptance. I sank in the seat, my head falling forward on my chest. I'd been living for almost three months beneath a tangled knot of strain, a knot that had just been loosened, severed even, in one sharp stroke. There was some relief in that at least—for now it was truly over. I could go home and burn the money, the final fragment of damning evidence, the last loose end.

Move.

The thought flickered through my despair and fatigue, a warning from some deep corner of my mind, some frontier outpost that was still planning, still cautious, still carrying on the fight, unaware that the war was over.

If Fremont or Renkins were to glance out Carl's window, it whispered, *they'd see you sitting here in a daze. It might set them thinking. Start the car. Drive away.*

The voice had strength to it, the strength of caution. It was a voice I'd been listening to with care for nearly three months, and, automatically, as if conditioned, I listened to it now, too. My hand rose, inserting the key in the ignition.

But then I stopped.

On the street corner behind me, perhaps fifty feet away, was a phone booth, the sinking sun glinting off its Plexiglas sides.

Drive away, the voice said. *Now.*

I scanned the street. Across the intersection, in front of the church, a woman moved down the sidewalk with a little girl in a stroller. She was talking, and the child was twisting around in her seat to watch her. They were dressed brightly, in matching yellow parkas. I recognized them—they were Carla and Lucy Drake, the daughter and granddaughter of Alex Freedman, the owner of Freedman's Dry Cleaning. I'd gone to high school with Carla; she'd been in Jacob's class, three years ahead of me. I watched her now as she and her daughter made their way up the walk to St. Jude's and disappeared inside.

The voice persisted, a tone of urgency creeping in: *Drive away*.

I ignored it. I had a view of Carl's office window, but the sun was glinting off it like a mirror. Fremont and Renkins were invisible behind it.

I glanced back at the phone booth, then scanned the street one last time. It was empty.

I climbed quickly from the car.

SARAH answered on the third ring.

"Hello?" she said.

I paused, a long, weighty moment. Sitting in the car, I'd thought that telling her immediately would help somehow, would diffuse the grief I felt pressing down on my heart, allow me to shift some of it onto hers. I'd wanted her to know, so that I could soothe her, could tell her that it would be all right, because by doing so, I knew that I would soothe myself, too. But as soon as I heard her voice, I realized that I couldn't do this over the phone; I had to be there; I had to be able to touch her while I talked.

"Hi," I said.

"Are you still at the police station?" she asked.

"No. I'm out on the street. On a pay phone."

"We can talk then?"

"We can talk."

"I saw all about it on the news."

I could hear the excitement in her voice, the relief. She thought it was over, she thought we were free. It was how I wanted to feel.

"Yes," I said.

"It's done now, isn't it? We're the only ones that know." She sounded elated. I was half-expecting her to laugh.

"Yes," I said again.

"Come home, Hank. I want to start our celebration. I've planned it out."

Her voice was rich with joy. It stabbed at me like a knife.

"We're millionaires now," she said. "Starting from this very moment."

"Sarah—"

She cut me off. "I don't think you'll care, Hank, but I did something stupid."

"Stupid?"

"I went out and bought a bottle of champagne."

I shut my eyes, pressed the receiver against the side of my face. I knew what she was going to tell me; I could see it coming.

"I used some of the money," she said. "One of the hundred-dollar bills."

I felt no surprise, no rush of panic. It was as if I'd known from the very beginning, from the very moment I'd pushed the duffel bag out of the plane, that this would happen. It seemed just; it seemed deserved. I rested my forehead against the side of the phone booth, the Plexiglas cold and smooth along my skin.

"Hank?" she said. "Hon? Are you mad?"

I tried to speak, but my throat was clogged, and I had to clear it first. I felt drugged, half asleep, dead.

"Why?" I said. My voice came out very small.

"Why what?"

"Why did you use the money?"

She was immediately defensive. "It just seemed like the right way to start things off."

"You promised not to touch it."

"But I wanted to be the first one to spend it."

I was silent, struggling to find a way through this. "Where?" I asked finally.

"Where?"

"Where did you buy the champagne?"

"That's how I was smart. I didn't buy it around here. I went all the way out by the airport and bought it there."

"Where by the airport?"

"Oh, Hank. Don't be mad."

"I'm not mad. I just want to know where."

"A place called Alexander's. It's a little package store on the highway, right before you get to the airport's access road."

I didn't say anything. I was thinking, my mind moving slowly, painfully around the situation, searching for an escape.

"I was good, Hank. You would've been proud of me. I said the bill was a birthday present, that I hadn't wanted to break it, but the banks were closed and my sister had just been proposed to, so it was worth it."

"You brought Amanda with you?"

Sarah hesitated. "Yes. Why?"

I didn't answer her.

"It's no big deal," she said. "The cashier hardly even seemed to notice. He just took the bill and gave me my change."

"Was there anyone else besides the cashier in the store?"

"What do you mean?"

"Customers? Employees?"

She thought for a second. "No, just the cashier."

"What did he look like?"

There was a pause on the other end.

"Hank," she said. "He didn't even notice."

"What did he look like?" I asked again, raising my voice.

"Come on. He doesn't know me. It's no big deal."

"I'm not saying it's a big deal. I just want to know what he looked like."

She sighed, as if exasperated. "He was big," she said. "Black hair, a beard. He had wide shoulders and a thick neck, like a football player."

"How old?"

"I don't know. Young. Probably midtwenties. Why?"

"Don't spend any more of it before I get back," I said, forcing a little laugh, trying to make it sound like a joke.

She didn't laugh. "Are you coming home now?"

"In a bit."

"What?"

"In a bit," I said more clearly. "I've got a few things to take care of here. Then I'll be home."

"Are you mad, Hank?"

"No."

"Promise me you aren't."

I lifted my head and stared off across the intersection. Carla and Lucy Drake had reemerged from the church. They were moving down the opposite side of the street now, their faces hidden beneath their yellow hoods. The little girl seemed asleep. Neither of them sensed me watching them.

"Hank?" Sarah asked.

I sighed, a tired sound. "I promise you I'm not mad," I said.

Then we said good-bye.

THERE was a directory hanging from a wire beneath the phone. I looked up Alexander's in it and called the number. A young man's voice answered.

"Alexander's."

"Yes," I said. "What time do you close tonight?"

"Six o'clock."

I checked my watch. It was 4:52.

"Thank you," I said.

I WAS halfway back to my car when I thought of something else, the first vestige of a plan. I stopped in midstride and returned to the phone booth.

I looked up the state police in the directory.

A woman answered. "State Police."

"Hello," I said, deepening my voice to disguise it, in case they taped their calls. "I'd like to report a suspicious person."

"A suspicious person?"

"A hitchhiker. I picked him up outside of Ann Arbor, and while we were driving south he pulled out a machete, started sharpening it right there in my front seat."

"Pulled out what?"

"A machete, a big knife. I told him to get out after that, and he did, no problem, but then I started thinking, maybe the kid's dangerous, so I decided I ought to call you, just to be safe."

"Did he threaten you with the machete?"

"No, nothing like that. I asked him to leave, and he left. I just thought maybe you might want to check him out."

"Where did you drop him off?"

"Outside of Toledo, right near the airport. He made a joke about hijacking a plane with the machete."

"On Airport Highway?"

"Yes. Outside a convenience store."

"Can you describe him, please?"

"He was young, maybe eighteen or so. Thin. Kind of weird looking, like he was sleepy or drugged out . . ."

"Caucasian?"

"Yes. Red hair, pale skin, freckles. He was wearing a gray sweatshirt, the kind with a hood on it."

"Height?"

"Average. Maybe six feet, a little less."

"And may I have your name?"

"I'd rather not," I said. "I live in Florida. I'm on my way back there now. I'd prefer not to get involved in anything up here."

"I understand," the woman said, her voice clipped, officially precise. "Thank you for calling. I'll have the dispatcher alert our patrolmen."

I SPENT the next twenty minutes sitting in my car, right there on Main Street. St. Jude's rang the hour, a little melody of bells, then five heavy strokes. The sun closed in on the western horizon, the sky around it taking on a pinkish tint. It had turned into a stunning afternoon, the air so crystalline it seemed like it wasn't there. Objects—the cars lining the street, the storefronts, the parking meters, the church steeple—seemed more clearly defined than usual, as if they had thin, black lines drawn around their edges.

The town was quiet, abandoned looking.

I knew there was a 90 percent chance that the bill Sarah had used was untraceable. Perhaps this should've been enough for me, but it wasn't. I thought about it, debated it in my head. If only one of the bills had been marked, or ten of them, or even a hundred, I think I might've acted differently, I might've just let it go. There were five thousand of them, though, one out of ten, and that was too much. I couldn't take the risk.

Fremont and Renkins came down the town hall steps shortly after five. They didn't notice me; they walked off to the right, up the sidewalk, Fremont talking in an animated manner, Renkins nodding emphatically to everything he said. They climbed into their car and pulled out, heading east, toward Toledo. Renkins drove.

I waited until my watch said five-ten. Then I started my own car, eased it away from the curb, and, also heading east, the setting sun large and red in my rearview mirror, made my way carefully out of town.

It was a thirty-minute drive to the airport.

12

IT STAYED farm country until right before I hit the airport. Then the highway broadened to four lanes, and buildings started to pop up—convenience stores, video arcades, taverns, cheap hotels, pool halls, fast-food restaurants—growing denser and taller and brighter the farther east I went. Traffic thickened, cars exiting and entering, blinkers flashing. This was the edge of Toledo, a long boulevard of neon and fluorescent light reaching out like a tentacle from the city's core.

Alexander's was a dingy-looking store, bunkerlike, with low, concrete walls and a flat roof. Iron bars crisscrossed its windows, and a sign flashed BEER on and off in pink and blue letters above its door. There was only one car in its tiny lot, a black, mud-spattered Jeep, sitting out near the road.

I drove past, then circled back.

There was a greenhouse a hundred feet beyond Alexander's. It was closed for the weekend, dark. I pulled into its gravel lot and parked facing the street, to facilitate my getaway.

Across the highway, running parallel to the road, was a chain-link fence topped with a double coil of razor wire. Beyond it lay the airport. I could just make out the control tower in the distance, could see the slow spiral of its spotlight through the night sky, and, below it, the vague red-and-green glow of the runways.

I climbed out, walked around to the rear of my station wagon, and swung open the tailgate. Jacob's trunk was there; it'd been the last thing I loaded when I cleaned out his apartment. Quickly, I lifted its lid and reached inside, my hand moving over the stack of bath towels, the tackle box, and the fielder's mitt, groping for the cool, metallic edge of the machete's blade.

It was off to the right, exactly where I'd left it. I took it out and set it on the bumper. Then I began searching through the other boxes. I found Jacob's ski mask in the first one I opened, his hooded sweatshirt in the second.

I exchanged my jacket for the sweatshirt. It was much too big for me—the sleeves hung down to my fingertips and the hood draped itself across my face like a monk's cowl—but that was exactly what I wanted: it would cover my hair and forehead, disguising my features long enough for me to enter the store and make sure that it was empty. Then I could put on the ski mask.

I slid the machete up my right-hand sleeve, handle first. Its point rested in the center of my palm, a sharp pinprick of pain. I jammed the ski mask into my pants pocket, swung the tailgate shut with my hip. Then I headed off toward the store.

It was quarter till six, and the sun had just disappeared. Drivers were switching on their headlights.

As I entered the parking lot in front of Alexander's, a plane thundered overhead, shaking the air, a huge mass of steel less than a hundred feet above me. Its landing lights threw a moment's glare onto the asphalt, like a flashbulb popping, then it was gone, shooting across the highway, its engines whining as they decelerated, its flaps coming down, its wheels stretching toward the ground. I watched it until it landed.

When I pushed open the store's front door, a bell rang above my head, alerting the cashier to my presence. He was sitting behind a counter off to the left, reading a newspaper.

There was a radio playing beside him, tuned to an evangelical station, its volume turned up high.

"You got to be careful what you listen to," a man's voice said from the radio. "Just like there's the word of God, there's also the word of Satan. And it sounds the same. It sounds exactly the same."

The cashier glanced up at me, nodded, then returned to his paper. He was exactly as Sarah had described him: large, muscular, bearded. He was wearing jeans and a white T-shirt, and he had a tattoo on his arm, black and green, of a bird in flight.

I moved past him and into the store's center aisle. I kept my right arm clamped against my side as I walked, holding the machete in place. The store was longer than it was wide, and by the time I reached its rear, I was safely out of sight.

I pulled off the hood and looked around.

The back wall was lined with sliding glass doors, behind which sat cans of soda and beer, tubs of ice cream, boxes of frozen food.

I walked quickly to the left, then back to the right, scanning the other two aisles. They were empty; there was no one else in the store.

The radio continued to preach, reading now from the Bible: " 'There is great gain in godliness with contentment; for we brought nothing into the world, and we cannot take anything out of the world; but if we have food and clothing, with these we shall be content.' "

Beyond the refrigerated display case, in the far-right-hand corner of the building, was a door. It was cracked partway open, its interior lost in darkness. I assumed that it led to a storeroom.

" 'But as for you, man of God, shun all this; aim at righteousness, godliness, faith, love, steadfastness, gentleness. . . .' "

At the end of the center aisle, there was a gigantic display of red wine. There were six green-glass gallon jugs lined up along the floor, in two rows of three. On top of these bottles was a sheet of cardboard, and on top of the cardboard another six jugs of wine. There were five levels in all, a total of thirty jugs. They rose up to just below my chin.

" 'I charge you to keep the commandment unstained . . .' "

I took out the ski mask and pulled it over my head. It smelled of my brother, of his sweat, and at first it made me gag, so that I had to breathe through my mouth.

"That's the Bible. The Word of God. Once I had a listener call in . . ."

I slid the machete out of my sleeve.

" 'Who wrote the Bible?' she asked me . . ."

When I turned to head back down the aisle to the front of the store, I was remarkably calm, and this calmness seemed to feed on itself, growing stronger and stronger with each passing moment, like panic might in a similar situation.

The cashier was reading his paper. He was sitting on a stool, with his arms resting on the counter. He was a good six inches taller than I and probably outweighed me by ninety pounds. It made me wish that I'd brought Carl's pistol. I had to stand in front of him for several seconds before he looked up. Then he just stared. He seemed neither frightened nor surprised. Very slowly, he closed his newspaper.

I gestured threateningly at him with the machete, nodded toward the cash register.

He reached across the counter and turned down the radio. "What the fuck do you think you're doing?" he asked.

"Open the register," I said. The words came out sounding hoarse, nervous. It was how his voice should've sounded.

He smiled. He wasn't as young as I'd thought at first; close up, he looked like he might even be older than I was.

"Get out of my store," he said calmly.

I stared at him, bewildered. The stench of Jacob's sweat in

the ski mask was making me dizzy. I realized that things weren't going to happen like I'd planned, and it gave me a sinking feeling, a hard little pip of nausea in my stomach.

"You gonna chop me up?" he asked. "You gonna kill me with that thing?" His voice began to rise in anger.

"All I want is the money."

He scratched at the tattoo on his arm, then took his beard in his hand and lifted it toward his nose, thinking. "I'll give you this one chance," he said. He waved toward the door. "You run now, and I'll let you go."

I didn't move. I just stood there, speechless.

"Either run or stay," he said. "That's your choice."

I lifted the machete, held it up over my head like I was going to hit him. I felt foolish doing it: I could tell that it didn't look real. I waved it in the air. "I don't want to hurt you," I said, meaning it as a threat, but it came out sounding like I was begging. "I've killed people. I'm a murderer."

He smiled at me. "You're staying?"

"Just give me the money."

He climbed off his stool and, almost casually, made his way around the counter. I retreated into the center of the store, the machete held out in front of my chest. He walked toward the door, so that for a moment I thought he was going to leave, but then he pulled a set of keys from his pocket and twisted shut the lock. He turned his back on me to do it, as if to emphasize how little he feared me.

"Come on," I said. "Quit screwing around."

He slid the keys back into his pocket and took a step toward me. I retreated into the center aisle. I held the machete in both hands, straight out in front of me. I was trying to look threatening, trying to regain control of the situation, but I knew that it wasn't working.

"Anything I do to you now," he said, his voice laced with a sudden malice, "will be in self-defense. That's how the police'll see it. You came in here with that knife, threatened me, tried to steal what's mine. You've put yourself outside the protection of the law."

He came toward me slowly, grinning. He seemed to be enjoying himself. I continued to back away.

"I gave you a chance to run because I knew it was the Christian thing to do. But you wouldn't leave. So now I'm going to make sure, no matter what happens to you once the police arrive, that you'll never do this again. I'm going to teach you some respect for other people's property."

He was in the aisle now, stalking me. I was about ten feet away from him. I held the machete in my right hand and waved it again, but he didn't seem to notice. He was staring at the shelf to his right, as if searching for something. I watched as he reached up and pulled down a can of peas. He hefted it in his hand, and then, very calmly, without any hurry to the motion whatsoever, reared back and threw it at me. It hit me in the chest, hard, with a loud cracking sound, just below my left nipple. I stumbled backward, gasping. It felt like he'd broken one of my ribs.

"This is a rare opportunity," he said. "There aren't many situations where you can hurt someone as bad as I'm going to hurt you and get away with it."

I had no idea how to handle this. He was supposed to have just given me the money. Then I was going to make him lie down on the floor and count to a hundred while I ran off to my car.

"I'll even be congratulated for this," he said. "Taking a bite out of crime. They'll call me a hero."

I continued backing down the aisle. I assumed that the building had an exit in the rear, probably through the storeroom I'd noticed earlier. I thought that if I could just hold him off till I got there, I could make a break for it, could get outside and sprint for my car.

He reached up again, pulled down a jar of olives from one of the shelves, and threw it at me. It hit me in the shoulder this time, then fell to the floor, shattering at my feet. A dull, tingling ache spread down my arm, and my fingers, as if of their own accord, opened, dropping the machete. It landed in the olives. I had to pick it up with my left hand.

"That's enough," I said. "I'll go now. You can keep the money."

He laughed, shaking his head. "You missed your chance. The door was open, and now it's shut."

At the end of the aisle, something caught my arm. Without taking my eyes off the cashier, I tried to jerk it free. I looked back, quickly, and saw the display of red wine, the huge column of jugs. There was a large staple in the sheet of cardboard that divided the third tier of bottles from the fourth, and it was on this that my sweatshirt had become hooked.

I glanced toward the cashier. He was six feet away. Another step and he would've been able to reach out and grab me. In a panic, I yanked my arm away from the staple, but instead of freeing myself, I simply pulled the sheet of cardboard out of the display. The bottles it had supported balanced there for an instant, like in a magic trick, trembling, and then began to fall. The whole display came apart before my eyes, the jugs hitting the floor one after the other in a loud, prolonged crash.

There was a brief silence in the store, a pause through which the preacher's voice found its way toward us down the aisle. "And is there a difference," he asked, "between a sin of *o*mission and a sin of *co*mmission? Is one punished with more vengeance in the fires of Hell than the other?"

The tiles at my feet were red-black with wine. Shards of glass lay scattered about, like jagged islands. I stepped back from the mess, retreating all the way to the rear wall, watching as the puddle spread out across the floor.

The cashier made a whistling sound, shaking his head. "Now who do you think's going to pay for that?" he asked.

We both stared down at the shattered bottles. The sheet of cardboard hung from my arm, swaying. I tore it free and dropped it to the floor. My fingers were still tingling, and my chest ached each time I took a breath. I wanted to begin working my way toward the storeroom, but my legs wouldn't move. They held me there, pressed up against the icy door of the cooler, paralyzed.

The cashier stepped forward, moving around the edge of the puddle. He paused at the far side, no more than three feet away, turned his back to me, and stooped down to retrieve a funnel-shaped hunk of glass from the wreckage. It was in the center of the puddle, and he had to lean forward on his toes to reach it.

He was getting it to use as a weapon, I knew. When he stood up, he was going to cut me.

I glanced toward the storeroom. I was fairly confident that I could make it there if I sprinted. The cashier was off balance, in a crouch; I'd catch him by surprise. And when I pushed away from the cooler, that's what I thought I was going to do—I thought I was going to run. But I didn't. Instead, without planning to, I found myself stepping toward him. My hands grasped the machete like a baseball bat. I lifted it over my head, my eyes locked on the back of his neck. Then I brought it down with all my strength.

It was only as I did it, only as I heard the blade hiss through the air above me, that I realized it was what I'd yearned to do all along.

He seemed to sense the blow coming. He started to rise, twisting his body to the right. This was the side I hit him on, the machete coming down at an angle, striking him just below the chin, its blade burying itself into his throat. It cut deep, but not nearly as deep as I'd hoped. Brutal as it sounds, I'd wanted to chop off his head in a single stroke, ending it in an instant. I didn't have the strength, though, or the blade wasn't sharp enough, because it sank about two inches in, then stopped. I had to jerk it free as he collapsed to the floor.

There was another silence, another pause.

The radio echoed through the store: "And Christ said, '*Eli, Eli, lama sabachthani?*' That is to say, 'My God, my God, why hast thou forsaken me?' "

The cashier was lying on his stomach, with his hands tucked in at the sides of his chest, as if he were about to do a push-up. There was a tremendous amount of blood, much more than I would've expected, more even than I would've thought his body could contain. It came out of his neck in thick cords, rhythmically, mixing with the pool of wine.

I'd severed his carotid artery.

"And so if our Savior in the moment of his passing was brought to the point of questioning God, what is to keep us, mere mortals, flawed individuals that we are, from questioning Him likewise?"

I stood there, watching him bleed. I held the machete away from my body, to keep it from dripping on my pants. I could see that it was simply a matter of waiting now, and I was relieved by this. I felt too drained, too sluggish, to hit him again.

"Something goes wrong in your life. You get sick, you lose your job, and you say, 'Where is the Lord's hand in this?' "

I stepped forward, into the puddle, switching the machete from my right to my left hand. Blood continued to surge from the man's wound, but his body was very still. Although I didn't think he was dead yet, I was sure that he was close to it, approaching the boundary, slipping beyond its edge. I thought to myself, quite clearly, *You're watching him die*.

But then a surprising thing happened. Very slowly, as if he were being pulled from above by a set of strings, he climbed to his hands and knees.

I was too shocked to step back. I stayed right beside him,

watching in astonishment, my body bent forward at the waist, my head tilted to the side.

Somehow, in an awkward, disjointed series of movements, he struggled onto his feet. He stood there, stooped over, his hands on his thighs, a thick stream of blood still pulsing from the gash in his neck. His T-shirt was soaked a deep red with it, and it clung to his body. I could see the shape of his nipples through the fabric. His face was perfectly white.

"You say, 'Either the Lord has forsaken me or He is purposefully sending hardship my way.' And you see no reason why you might deserve this. You're righteous, you're faithful, you're loving, you're steadfast, you're gentle, and yet the Lord chooses . . ."

I took a step back from him, toward the cooler, and he raised his head. He stared at me, his eyes blinking very rapidly. His breathing made a watery sound in his chest; his lungs were filling with blood. He put his hands on his throat.

I took another step backward. I knew that I should hit him again, kill him, knew that this would be the humane thing to do, but I didn't feel like I had the strength to raise the machete. I felt spent, finished.

He tried to speak: his mouth opened and closed. There was no sound, though, simply the gurgling in his chest. And then, very slowly, as if he were moving underwater, he pulled his left hand away from his throat and extended it to the shelf at his side. He wrapped his fingers around the neck of a ketchup bottle sitting there, and, more shoving it than throwing it, propelled it toward me through the air.

It hit me in the leg. It didn't hurt; it bounced off, cracking into three nearly equal pieces on the floor. I stared down at it, another tint of red.

"And you say, 'The Lord moves in mysterious ways? What does that mean to me?' You say, 'Isn't that some sort of cop-out? Some sort of escape clause for when things go bad and you preachers have no explanation?' You say, 'Where is

Responsibility? Where is Justice?' You're angry and you feel you deserve an answer . . ."

He put his hand back up to his throat. The blood pumped out between his fingers, but more weakly now.

When he fell, he did so in stages, hesitating for an instant between each one, like an actor overplaying his part. He dropped to his knees first, landing on a shard of glass from one of the jugs, crushing it with a horrible grinding sound beneath his weight. He paused, settled back on his rear end, paused again, then sank sideways to the floor. His head banged into the base of the shelf, bouncing off it at an awkward angle, his hands falling away from his throat.

All of this happened in slow motion.

"Let's say that someone tells you, 'The Lord giveth. The Lord taketh away.' What does that mean to you?"

I stared down at him, counting in my head as I had with Pederson on the edge of the nature preserve. I counted to fifty, breathing once between each number. As I watched, the blood slowly stopped pulsing from his neck.

I stuck the machete through my belt, like a pirate. Then I pulled off the ski mask. The air felt cool against my face, soothing, but the smell of Jacob's body remained stuck in my nostrils. It seemed to cling to my cheeks, like grease. I took off the sweatshirt, dragging it over my head. My back was drenched with perspiration. I could feel it running down in little rivulets along my spine, soaking into the waistband of my underpants.

"Or they say, 'A man's mind plans his way, but the Lord directs his steps . . .' "

I wanted to check the cashier's pulse, but the thought of touching his wrist gave me a loose, sick feeling in my stomach, so I let it go. He was dead. I could tell that just from the amount of blood on the floor—it was a huge puddle, spreading out along the rear of the store and seeping down the center aisle. Mixed with the wine and ketchup and shattered glass, it looked surreal, ghoulish, like something from a nightmare.

"Or they say, 'The Lord has made everything for its purpose, even the wicked for the day of trouble . . .' "

I stood there, listening to the preacher's voice. He was in a studio somewhere, and it sounded like there were people with him, offering up an occasional "Amen!" or "Glory!" or "Hallelujah!" And then there were hundreds, maybe thousands of people all across the region—Ohio, Michigan, Indiana, Illinois, Kentucky, West Virginia, Pennsylvania—sitting in their homes, driving in their cars, listening. Each of them was connected to the others, and all of them were connected to me, simply by the sound of this man's voice.

And they don't know, I thought. *They don't know about any of this.*

Very slowly, I felt myself begin to calm down. My pulse slackened; my hands stopped shaking. I'd almost ruined everything by coming here, but now I'd saved it. We were going to be all right.

I lifted my shirt to look at my chest. It was already starting to bruise, a deep purple flower blossoming across my rib cage.

"Let me talk to you about *fate*, Brothers and Sisters. What does that word mean to you? If I say to you that you are *fated* to die someday, is there one among you who would question me? Of course not. And yet if I were to say to you that you are *fated* to die on one particular day, at one particular hour, and in one particular way, you would shake your head and say that I was a fool. And yet that is what I do say to you, I say . . ."

I shook myself, as if from a stupor, walked quickly down the center aisle to the front of the building, leaned over the counter, and clicked off the radio. There was a SORRY, WE'RE CLOSED sign hanging from the front door, and I flipped it so that it was facing out. I wanted to turn off the lights, too, and spent nearly a minute searching for the switch before finally giving up on the idea and returning to the back of the store.

Without the preacher's voice, the building had an ominous silence to it. Every noise I made echoed back at me from the shelves of food, sounding furtive, rodentlike.

I took the cashier by his feet and started to drag him toward the darkened storeroom. He was lighter than I would've thought, drained of blood, but it was still a difficult task. His body was cumbersome, awkward, and the floor was treacherous with blood.

My chest throbbed every time I moved.

The storeroom was tiny, a narrow rectangle. There was a mop in it, a bucket, some cleaning supplies on a shelf. In its very rear were a sink and a dirty-looking toilet. The smell of disinfectant was heavy in the air. There was no exit. If I'd run there, I would've been trapped.

I dragged the cashier in, feet first, but had to stop midway to untangle his arms from the narrow doorway. I laid them across his chest, like a corpse in a coffin, then pulled him the rest of the way in, propping his legs up against the toilet so that there'd be enough space to shut the door. I took his wallet, his watch, and his key ring and put them in my pocket.

Once the body was safely hidden, I walked back through the puddle to the front of the building. I went behind the counter and rang open the cash register. The hundred-dollar bill was in the bottom of the drawer, beneath the till. It was the only one there. I folded it in half and slipped it into the front pocket of my jeans.

There was a stack of paper bags on the counter. I grabbed one, shook it open, and emptied the rest of the register into it—bills, change, everything.

As I was shutting the drawer, my eyes searching the surrounding shelves for other items a drifter might steal, a car pulled into the lot. The sight of it literally paralyzed me, froze me in place, my hand hanging in midair above the register. I watched as it rolled up to the edge of the building, its headlights shining through the front windows.

The sweatshirt and ski mask were sitting before me on the counter. I picked up the sweatshirt and started to put it on, but the arms were all tangled, and I couldn't get it over my head. Finally I just gave up and held it out in front of my chest, as if hoping to hide behind it.

The headlights went out, and the engine shut off. A woman climbed from the car.

I took the machete from my belt and set it on the counter, covering it with the cashier's newspaper.

You could see the puddle of blood and wine from the front door, could stare right down the center aisle to the rear of the store. I'd tracked it forward on my boots, too: my footprints trailed across the floor to the counter, looking painted on the tiles, like the kind they have at dance schools, a bright, shiny red, perfect and precise, their edges still glistening with wetness. I stared at them from the counter, a queasy flutter seizing hold of my chest. I realized that I wasn't thinking, that I was being careless. I was leaving clues behind.

As the woman approached the front door, another plane flew overhead, roaring in on its descent to the airport, its engines making the building tremble. She turned to stare at it, ducking a little, instinctively, at the sound. She was old, probably in her late sixties, and elegantly dressed—a dark fur coat, pearl earrings, black high-heeled shoes, a tiny black purse. Her face, despite a thick layer of rouge, had a definite paleness to it, as if she'd been sick recently. Her expression was tight, firm, like she was late for something and rushing to make up time.

She tried the door, found it locked, held her black-gloved hand up to the glass to peer inside. Her eyes fell immediately on me, standing frozen behind the counter. She made an elaborate show of checking her watch. Then she held up two fingers. I watched her mouth form the words "Two . . . minutes . . . till . . . six!"

I shook my head at her. "Closed," I yelled.

A voice was whispering madly in my skull, high-pitched, frantic: *Let her go*, it said. *She'll remember nothing. It looks as if you're closing up, as if you're ready to leave. Let her go.*

I rested my hands on the counter and shook my head again, willing her to climb back into her car.

She rattled the door.

"I just need a bottle of wine," she yelled through the glass. I heard her, but from a distance. Her voice reminded me of someone I knew, though I couldn't decide exactly who.

"We're closed," I yelled.

She rapped at the glass with her fist. "Please."

I looked down at my hands, checking them very slowly, finger by finger, to make sure that they were free of blood. When I looked back up, she was still there. She was going to make me do it, I realized; she wasn't going to leave.

She rattled the door again. "Young man!"

I knew what I was going to do, saw how it would end. The past three months had conditioned me for it, trained me, and now the weight of all that had come before seemed to eliminate any other possibility, render it impotent, a mere half measure where nothing but the most extreme would suffice. I'd just spent three hours talking with the police. If she were able to describe what I was wearing, they'd know right away who it was. And then I'd be caught; I'd be sent to jail. I recognized the horror of it, realized that it would be the worst thing I'd ever done—worse even than killing my brother—that it would be something I'd regret for the rest of my life, and yet, of my own free will, I chose to do it. I was scared, nervous, trapped. I'd just killed a man with a machete. There was blood on my pants and boots, and every time I took a breath it smelled of Jacob.

I stepped out from behind the counter.

"A single bottle of wine," she yelled through the glass.

I unlocked the door with the cashier's keys. I pulled it open, glancing at her car to make sure she was alone. It was empty.

"I'll be extremely brief," she said, sounding slightly out of breath. "I simply need a dinner wine, to bring as a gift."

She stepped inside, and I closed the door behind her, twisting the lock shut with a click. I put the keys back into my pocket.

She turned to look at me. "You do sell wine?"

"Of course," I said. "Wine, beer, champagne . . ."

She waited for me to go on, but I didn't. I stood there, smiling, my body between her and the door. Now that I'd made my decision, I was remarkably calm. It was the same way I'd felt with Sonny, like I was slipping into a groove, acting out a role.

"Well? Where is it?" She hadn't noticed the bloody boot tracks yet.

"We have to make a deal, first."

"A deal?" she asked, confused. She looked at me then, really looked, assessing me for the first time, taking in my face, the expression of my eyes. "I don't have time for jokes, young man," she said, her head assuming an imperious tilt, like a hawk's.

"I knocked over a rack of red wine." I pointed toward the rear of the store.

She peered down the center aisle at the puddle. "Dear me," she said.

"My mop's up on a shelf in the storeroom, and I have to climb a ladder to get it. I need someone to hold the ladder for me."

She stared at me again. "You're asking me to hold the ladder?"

"I'm doing you a favor, letting you in like this."

"A favor?" She snorted. "You were closing up early, trying to sneak home before you were supposed to. I don't imagine your boss would look upon this as any great favor."

"All you have to do is hold—"

The woman tapped at her watch. "It was two minutes before six. A favor! I never heard of such a thing."

"Look," I said. "I can't clean that up without a mop. And I can't get to the mop without your help."

"Whoever heard of storing a mop on a shelf?"

"I'm asking for a very small amount of your time."

"I'm dressed for dinner. Look at me! I can't be holding ladders for people when I'm dressed like this."

"What if I give you the wine for free?" I asked. "Any bottle you choose, on the house. All you have to do is come back to the storeroom and hold the ladder for me."

She hesitated, her face wrinkling with thought. Beyond the window, cars zipped by, one after the other, a steady stream of lights.

"You said you had champagne?"

I nodded.

"Dom Pérignon?"

"Yes," I said. "Of course."

"Then that's what I want."

"All right," I said. "That's what you'll get." I stepped back over to the counter and picked up the newspaper, folding it over the machete. Then I returned to the woman and took her by her elbow.

"If we go down the far aisle, we can avoid the puddle."

She allowed herself to be guided forward. Her heels clicked loudly against the tiled floor. "I won't be mussed, will I? I won't do this if it involves touching anything dirty."

"It's all very clean," I soothed her. "It's simply a matter of steadying the ladder."

We were heading down the far aisle. My eyes moved along the shelves we passed, noting items at random—bread, croutons, salad dressing, toilet paper, Kleenex, sponges, canned fruit, rice, crackers, pretzels, potato chips.

"I don't have much time," she said. She brushed at her fur coat, glanced quickly at her wrist. "I'm already late."

I was still holding her by the elbow. The machete was in my left hand. I could feel its blade through the paper.

"I'll be up and down the ladder, find your champagne, and like that"—I took my hand away from her arm and snapped my fingers—"you'll be out of here."

"This is the most extraordinary situation," she said. "I can't recall anything like it."

I returned my hand to her elbow, and she looked up at me.

"You know I won't be coming back here again," she said. "This is the last time I'll ever grace this establishment. That's what forcing customers into awkward situations does, young man. It alienates them. It puts them off."

I nodded, barely listening. Without sensing its approach, I'd suddenly become extremely nervous. I could feel my blood pulsing through my head, thickly, as if my veins were too small for it. We were nearing the end of the aisle. The puddle had spread all the way to the wall, blocking off the doorway. There were boot prints around its edge and drag marks from the cashier's body. The woman stopped short when she saw it, stomping her foot.

"I'm not walking through that."

I tightened my grip on her arm, moving my body to her rear. I pushed her forward toward the storeroom.

"What on earth are you doing? Young man?"

I stuck the newspaper-wrapped machete beneath my arm and then, gripping her with both hands, half-carried, half-pushed her into the dark red puddle. She made light, high-kneed steps, trying to dance her way through, her feet going tap, tap, tap on the tiles.

"This is outrageous," she said, her voice rising to a low shriek.

There was a pause while I fumbled with the doorknob. Looking down, I saw her shoes, stained from the puddle. They were very tiny, like a child's.

"I . . . will . . . not . . . stand . . . being . . . ," she sputtered, trying to free herself from my grip. I had a solid hold on her jacket, though, a fistful of fur, and I refused to let her go.

". . . manhandled . . . by . . . a . . . common . . ."

I got the door open, slid my hand to her back, and pushed her inside. With my other hand, I shook the machete free from its disguise. The newspaper fluttered down into the puddle.

She was surprisingly stable on her feet. She seemed to sense the body in front of her before she actually realized what it was and regained her balance with two quick steps, one landing beside the cashier's head, the other beside his chest.

She started to turn toward me, her mouth opening in protestation, but then her eyes were pulled downward by the horribly familiar form of the obstruction at her feet.

"Dear God," she said.

I'd planned on doing it quickly, as quickly and cleanly as possible, just hitting her from the rear, hard, and leaving, but the sound of her voice stopped me. I realized with a shock who it reminded me of. It was Sarah—the exact same tone and pitch, only raised a bit by age; the same firmness riding beneath the words, the same self-confidence and resolution. I thought to myself, *This is how Sarah will sound when she's old.*

The woman took advantage of my hesitation to turn on me, and the expression on her face—a mixture of fear, disgust, confusion—jarred me into an even longer pause.

"I don't . . . ," she began, but then fell silent, shaking her head. The room was dark; the only light came from the open doorway, where I was standing. My shadow covered the woman to her waist. I held the machete out in front of me, as if to ward her off.

"What is this?" she asked, her voice shaking a little but still sounding remarkably calm. I watched her as she carefully repositioned her feet, turning so that she could face me directly. She straddled the cashier's corpse, putting one foot on either side of his stomach. The hem of her fur coat bunched up a little, resting against his body.

I knew that I ought to kill her, that the longer I spent there, the more danger I'd be in, but a lifetime's training in the proper social behavior of responding when one is addressed overrode that knowledge. Automatically, without thinking, I answered her question.

"I killed him," I said.

She glanced down at the cashier's face, then back up at me.

"With that?" she asked, gesturing toward the machete.

I nodded. "Yes. With this."

We stared at each other then, for perhaps ten or fifteen seconds, though it seemed like much longer. We were each waiting for the other to initiate something.

I tightened my grip on the machete. My mind sent out an order to my arm—clear, precise, direct. *Hit her*, it said. But my arm remained in front of me, motionless.

"What kind of a man are you?" the woman asked finally.

The question took me by surprise. I stared at her, thinking. It seemed important that I answer her sincerely. "I'm just normal," I said. "I'm like anyone else."

"Normal? Only a monster would be capable of . . ."

"I've got a job. A wife, a baby girl."

She averted her eyes when I said this, as if it were something she didn't want to hear. She noticed that her coat was resting on the cashier's body, and she tried to reposition it, but it was too long. She glanced back up at me.

"But how could you do this?"

"I had to."

"Had to?" she asked, as if the idea were absurd. She eyed

the machete with disgust. "You *had* to kill him with that thing?"

"I stole some money."

"Surely you could've taken it without killing him. You could've . . ."

I shook my head. "Not from him. I found it in a plane."

"A plane?"

I nodded. "Four million dollars."

She was confused now. I'd lost her. "Four million dollars?"

"It was ransom. From a kidnapping."

She frowned at that, as if she thought I was lying. "What does that have to do with him?" she asked angrily, pointing down at the cashier. "Or me?"

I tried to explain. "My brother and I killed someone to keep him from finding out about the money. And then my brother shot his friend to protect me, and I shot his friend's girlfriend and their landlord to protect my brother, but then he started to break down, so I had to shoot him to protect myself, and then the kidnapper . . ."

She stared at me, and the fear in her face made me stop, made me realize how I must sound, like I was insane, a psychopath.

"I'm not crazy," I said, trying to make my voice come out rational, calm. "It all makes sense. It all happened one thing after the other."

There was a long moment of silence. It was broken finally by the roar of another plane flying over. The whole building echoed with the sound of its engines.

"I tried to make you leave," I said, "but you kept knocking on the door. You wouldn't listen."

The woman clicked open her purse. She reached up, pulled off her earrings, and dropped them inside, one at a time.

"Here," she said, holding it toward me.

I stared down at it. I didn't understand what she wanted me to do.

"Take it," she said.

I reached out with my left hand and took the bag.

"I didn't do it for the money," I said. "I did it to keep from getting caught."

She didn't say anything. She didn't know what I was talking about.

"It's like those old stories about people selling their souls. I did one bad thing, and it led to a worse thing, and on and on and on, until finally I ended up here. This is the bottom." I waved the machete toward the cashier. "This is the worst thing. It can't go any farther."

"No," the woman said, seizing on this last statement as if she thought it might save her life. She straightened herself up. "It won't go any farther."

She started to reach her hand toward me, and I stepped backward, shifting my weight.

"We'll stop it here," she said. "Won't we?"

She tried to catch my eye, but I looked away, down at the cashier's corpse. It was staring up at the ceiling.

"Let's stop it here," she said. She stepped forward, hesitantly, sliding her foot along the tiles, as if she were on a frozen pond, testing the slickness of the ice.

I could still hear Sarah in her voice, riding just below the surface. I tried to block it out but couldn't. The purse was in my left hand and the machete in my right, held motionless before me.

"I'm going to help you do it," she said.

She was right beside me now, edging around my body toward the open doorway behind me, moving slowly, carefully, as if I were some small wild animal that she was afraid to startle into flight.

"It's going to be okay," she said.

She took another shuffling step and was in the doorway. I turned to watch her.

For a moment, I actually thought I was going to let her go. I was going to let her finish it for me, was going to place myself in her hands.

But then her back was to me. She was tiptoeing into the puddle, the store opening itself up before her, and whatever it was that had been holding me back was gone. I stepped out after her, raised the machete above my head, and swung for her neck. Like the cashier, she sensed it coming just before it hit. She started to turn and lift her hand, made a short squeaking sound in her throat, as if, absurdly, she were trying to suppress a laugh, and then the blade hit her, knocking her to the left. She bounced off the shelves there, dragging down some cans of soup behind her as she fell.

There were none of the cashier's melodramatic death throes. She simply collapsed into the puddle, bleeding, and was dead. The soup cans rolled across the tiles with a tiny metallic sound, which, when they finally stopped, deepened the silence of the store.

Everything was very still.

It was close to seven o'clock before I reached home. I parked out in the driveway, and—with a caution rising from the proximity of my neighbors' windows—left the machete and the woman's fur coat in the car.

As I came up the front walk, I smelled the sharp, comforting odor of burning wood. Sarah had a fire going in the fireplace.

I took off my boots on the porch and carried them inside.

The entranceway was dark, the door to the living room shut tight. Down the hall I could hear Sarah moving about in the kitchen. There was the soft suction sound of the refrigerator being opened, then the clinking of glasses. She flashed by the open doorway, dressed in her robe, her hair down. She smiled toward me as she passed.

"Wait," she yelled. "Don't come in till I tell you."

The kitchen light flicked out, and I heard her move into the living room. I stood very still in the darkened entranceway, listening, my boots in one hand, the paper bag full of money in the other. I could tell from the sound of her voice that she was excited, happy. She thought that we were free now, free and rich, and she'd planned a celebration. I couldn't imagine how I was going to tell her otherwise.

"All right," she yelled. "Come in."

I stepped forward, nearly silent in my stocking feet, tucked the paper bag beneath my left arm, and slid open the door.

"Voilà!" Sarah said triumphantly.

She was lying on the floor, propped up on her elbows. She'd taken off her bathrobe and picked up the bearskin rug from the hearth. It was wrapped around her body, like a blanket, and she was naked beneath it. Her hair, draped seductively over her face, hid her expression, but I could tell just from the way she held her head that she was smiling at me. On the floor by her elbow was the bottle of champagne. Beside it sat two glasses.

All the lights were off; the room was illuminated solely by the logs burning in the fireplace, the reflection of which trembled off of the mirror on the opposite wall, making it seem to shake slightly, as if someone were pounding his fist against the outside of the house. The front curtains were pulled shut.

I saw the duffel bag before I saw the money. It was standing by the entrance to the kitchen, buckled over, empty. The money was on the floor. It had been meticulously laid out, packet by packet, to form a seamless green surface across the carpet. Sarah was lying on top of it.

"This is the plan," she said huskily, through her mask of

hair. She lifted the bottle toward me. "We're going to get a little drunk, and then I'm going to fuck you on the money."

The mock sexy baritone of her voice failed her on the last few words, and, suddenly shy, she finished with a giggle. "We've made our bed," she said, gesturing with her hand toward the money, "and now we're going to sleep on it."

I didn't move from the doorway. I still had my hat and parka on. There was a long pause, while she waited for me to say something. I didn't; my mind was blank, numb.

"Do you want to eat something first?" she asked, her voice taking on a note of concern. "Have you had dinner yet?"

She sat up a little, the rug slipping down her shoulder, revealing one of her breasts.

"There's some cold chicken in the fridge," she said.

I slid the door shut behind me, then turned back toward her. I didn't know how to tell her; I was waiting for an opening. I felt as if I were about to do something very cruel.

"Where's Amanda?" I asked, unable to think of anything else to say.

Sarah flicked the hair away from her face. "Upstairs," she said, "sleeping." And then, after a pause, "Why?"

I shrugged.

She sat up a little more, leaned back on her hand. She gave me a long, inquisitive look. "Hank?" she said. "What's wrong?"

I came into the room, edging my way around the money, and sat down behind her on the piano bench. I leaned forward to drop my boots to the floor, but then decided against it and placed them in my lap instead, resting them on the bag of money. It made a crackling sound beneath their weight. The boots were stained black around their soles. They stank of wine.

"Have you been drinking?" Sarah asked. She had to spin

around to see me, and as she did so, she sat all the way up, crossing her legs.

I gave her a slow shake of my head. "The money's marked," I said.

She just stared at me. "You're drunk, Hank. I can smell it." She pulled the rug up around her shoulders, covering her breast. Her left knee stuck out down below, hard and pale in the firelight, like marble.

"It's marked," I said again.

"Where did you go? A bar?"

"If we spend it, we'll get caught."

"You reek, Hank. You smell like Jacob." Her voice rose on this last statement, becoming angry. I was ruining her celebration.

"I haven't had anything to drink, Sarah. I'm perfectly sober."

"I can smell it."

"It's on my boots and pants," I said. I held the boots out toward her. "They're soaked with wine."

She stared first at my boots, then at the dark splash marks on my jeans. She didn't believe me. "And where were you that they got like that?" she asked, her voice taking on a litigious tone.

"Out by the airport."

"The airport?" She looked at me like I was lying. She still didn't get it.

"The money's marked, Sarah. They'll track us down if we spend it."

She stared up at me, the set, angry look slowly slipping from her face. I could see her shuffling the pieces about in her head, could see them, one by one, falling into place.

"The money's not marked, Hank."

I didn't answer; I knew I didn't have to. She understood now.

"How can it be marked?" she asked.

In my head I was silently going over everything I'd done after killing the woman, checking things off one by one. I felt tired, stupid, like I was forgetting something crucial.

"You're being paranoid," she said. "If it were marked, they would've said so in the paper."

"I talked to the FBI men. They told me themselves."

"Maybe they suspect you took it. Maybe they're just trying to scare you."

I smiled sadly at her and shook my head.

"They would've said something in the paper, Hank. I'm sure of it."

"No," I said. "It's their trap. It's how they plan on catching whoever's taken it. They copied down the serial numbers before they paid the ransom, and now the banks are looking for them. As soon as you start spending it, they'll track you down."

"They couldn't have done that. There were forty-eight thousand bills. It would've taken them forever."

"They didn't copy them all. Just five thousand of them."

"Five thousand?"

I nodded.

"So the rest are still good?"

I could see where she was heading, and I shook my head. "There's no way to tell the good from the bad, Sarah. Every time we went out and spent a bill, there'd be a one-in-ten chance that it was marked. We couldn't risk it."

The firelight threw quick, flickering shadows across her face while she considered this. "I could get a job at a bank," she said. "I could steal the list of numbers."

"You wouldn't find it at a normal bank. It'd only be at a Federal Reserve bank."

"Then I could get a job at one of those. There's one in Detroit, isn't there?"

I sighed. "Stop it, Sarah. It's over. You're just making it harder."

She frowned down at the mattress of money. "I already spent one," she said. "I spent one tonight."

I reached into my front pocket and took out the hundred-dollar bill. I unfolded it and held it toward her.

She stared at it for several seconds. Then she looked down at my boots.

"You killed him?"

I nodded. "It's all over, Beloved."

"How?"

I told her how I'd done it, how I'd called the police about the hitchhiker, how the cashier had come after me when I tried to rob him, and how I'd hit him with the machete. I lifted my shirt to show her my bruise, but she couldn't see it in the dim light. She interrupted me before I got to the woman.

"Oh God, Hank," she said. "How could you have done this?"

"I didn't have a choice. I had to get the money back."

"You should've just let it go."

"He would've remembered you, Sarah. He would've remembered the baby, and your story about the money. They would've tracked us down."

"He didn't know who—"

"You were on TV at Jacob's funeral. He would've described you, and someone would've remembered. They would've put it all together."

She thought about that for a few seconds. The rug had slipped down her shoulder again, but she ignored it.

"You could've brought five twenties to the store," she said, "asked him to return the hundred-dollar bill, said that your wife had spent it, and that it had sentimental value."

"Sarah," I said, losing my patience, "I didn't have time to

get five twenties. I would've had to come all the way back here. I had to get there before he closed."

"You could've gone to the bank."

"The bank wasn't open."

She started to say something more, but I didn't let her.

"It doesn't matter," I said. "It's already done."

She stared at me, her mouth still open to speak. Then she shut it and nodded.

"Okay," she whispered.

Neither of us spoke for the next minute or so. We were both thinking about where we were, and what we were going to do next. A log collapsed in the fireplace, sending up a shower of sparks and a tiny, just perceptible wave of heat. I could hear the clock ticking on the mantelpiece.

Sarah picked up one of the packets, held it in her hand. "At least we weren't caught," she said.

I didn't say anything.

"I mean, it's not the end of the world." She forced a smile at me. "We're just right back where we started. We can sell the condo, sell the piano . . ."

At the mention of the condo, I felt a sharp pain in the center of my chest, as if I'd been hit by an arrow. I touched my sternum with my fingertips. I'd forgotten all about the condominium, had forced it from my mind.

Sarah continued. "We did bad things, but only because we had to. We were trapped into them, each one led us on to the next."

I shook my head, but she ignored me.

"The important thing," she said, "the thing that really matters, is that we didn't get caught."

She was trying to turn things around, trying to put them in the best possible light. It was how she dealt with tragedies; I recognized it immediately. Usually it was something I admired—her doing it made it easier for me, too—but now it seemed too simple, like she was taking it all too lightly, forgetting what we'd done. Nine people had been murdered. I'd killed six of them myself. It seemed impossible, but it was true. Sarah was trying to hide from it, trying to obscure the fact that they were dead because of us, because of the plans we'd made along the way, because of our greed and fear. She wanted to avoid what would follow from this admission, wanted to escape the damage we both knew it was going to do to our lives. We couldn't escape, though; I understood that even then.

"We can't sell them back," I said.

She glanced up at me, as if she were surprised to hear me speak. "What?"

"I got the piano on sale." I reached behind me and touched its keyboard, pressing down one of its keys, a high one. It made a plinking sound. "They won't take it back."

She shrugged this off. "We can put an ad in the paper and sell it ourselves."

"I didn't buy a condominium," I said, shutting my eyes. When I opened them she was staring at me, confused.

"It was a scam. I got ripped off. They stole my money."

"I—" she started. "What are you talking about?"

"It was a fake auction. They took my check and cashed it. The condo doesn't exist."

She shook her head, opened her mouth to speak, then shut it, then opened it again.

Finally she said, "How?"

I readjusted the boots in my lap, lining them up. They felt stiff now; the blood had dried. "I don't know."

"Did you tell the police?"

I smiled at her. "Come on, Sarah."

"You just let them take it?"

I nodded.

"All our savings?"

"Yes," I said. "Everything."

She put her hand up to her face, touched the back of it to

her forehead. She was still holding the packet. "We'll be stuck here now," she said, "won't we? We'll never be able to move."

I shook my head. "We've got our jobs. We can start to save again."

I was trying to console her, but even as I spoke, I began to feel the full weight of her words. In a single day we'd gone from being millionaires to virtual penury. We had $1,878 in the bank; it was nothing. Any day now we'd have to start dipping into it—for our monthly payments on the house and cars, for our phone bill, electric bill, gas bill, water bill. We'd have to pay off our credit cards. We'd have to buy food and clothes. From here on out, everything was going to be a struggle, a constant battle to make ends meet. We were poor; we were what I'd sworn all my adult life we'd never be: we were like my parents.

We wouldn't be able to leave Fort Ottowa either; by the time we saved up enough money for a move, we'd be worrying about Amanda's education, or a new car, or my retirement. We were going to stay here forever, and we'd never be able to purge the house of what we'd done. Its rooms, and their awful freight of memories, would always be there, waiting to ambush and accuse us. The floor beneath our bed would never cease to be the place where we hid the duffel bag, the guest room where Jacob spent his last night, the kitchen where we packed the baby pouch, the piano where we tried to baptize our new life together with a drunken act of love.

We weren't simply returning to where we'd begun, as Sarah had tried to claim. We'd lost all that, had given it up that very first day without even realizing it, and now we'd never, no matter how long we lived, be able to get it back.

"We've still got the money," Sarah said. She held the packet out toward me.

"It's just paper. It's nothing."

"It's our money."

"We have to burn it."

"Burn it?" she asked, as if surprised. She lowered the packet into her lap, readjusted the rug around her shoulders. "We can't burn it. Some of it's still good."

"I've got to get rid of my boots, too." I held them up to the light, turning them around in the air. "How should I get rid of my boots?"

"I'm not going to let you burn the money, Hank."

"And the bottle of champagne you bought, and his wallet and watch and keys."

She didn't seem to hear me. "We can run with it," she said. "We can just get out and spend as we go. We can leave the country, go to South America, Australia, somewhere far away. We can live like outlaws, like Bonnie and Clyde." She trailed off, staring down at the packets spread out around her. They looked shiny in the firelight. "Some of it's still good," she whispered.

"A purse, too," I said. "And a fur coat."

"Maybe if we wait long enough, they'll forget about the numbers. We could keep it till we're old."

"How can I get rid of a fur coat?"

Her gaze returned to me, focusing sharply on my face. "A fur coat?"

I nodded, feeling a little dizzy. I hadn't eaten since that morning. My body was so tired and hungry that it ached. I probed at the bruise on my rib cage, trying to see if anything was broken.

"Where did you get a fur coat?"

"An old woman," I said. "She came in while I was there."

"Oh, God. Oh, Hank."

"I'd taken off my mask. I tried to make her go away, but she wouldn't leave."

Upstairs, directly above our head, the baby began to cry.

I stared across the room at the fire. My mind felt unfocused, anchorless, like I couldn't trust it. For some reason I started to think of the pilot in the plane, Vernon's brother, and the pull I'd felt toward his corpse that first day, that inexplicable urge to touch it. Then I thought about Alexander's, and how, just before I left, when I tried to mop up my boot prints from the floor, the blood seemed to get redder and redder as I smeared it, losing all hint of blackness, moving closer and closer to pink. Next came an image of Jacob, standing in the snow in his red jacket, his nose bleeding, crying over Dwight Pederson's body. And as that last picture, the one of my brother, melted away within my mind, I felt a shiver of foreboding. There were going to be more than just monetary debts coming due now, I realized. There were going to be things I'd have to account for to myself, explain and rationalize, things I'd have to live with that would make the loss of the money seem almost inconsequential.

We've nothing left, I thought to myself, the words rising unbidden in my head. *We've nothing left.*

"Oh, God," Sarah whispered again.

I set my boots down on the piano bench, rose to my feet, and edged my way carefully around the blanket of bills to the fireplace. She turned to watch me.

"Hank," she said.

I pulled open the fire screen and, with a quick movement, threw the paper bag full of money onto the burning logs.

"Let's keep the money," she said. "We can keep it and see what happens."

The bag caught quickly, contracting in upon itself, like a fist. As it began to dissolve into flame, the coins started to fall out one by one, plopping musically to the cement floor beneath the logs. One of them, a blackened quarter, rolled lazily out across the hearth. I flicked it back inside with my foot.

"Hank," she said. "I'm not going to let you burn it."

Amanda raised her volume, screaming now, her cries echoing down the stairs. We both ignored her.

"We have to, Sarah. It's the last piece of evidence."

"No," she pleaded, with a tremor in her voice, as if she were close to tears. "Don't."

I crouched down before the fire. I could feel its heat on my face, opening my pores. "I promised you I'd burn it if things got out of hand," I said. "Didn't I?"

She didn't answer.

I reached out behind me across the floor until I felt one of the packets. I picked it up and, forcing myself not to look at it, tossed it onto the logs. It took a while to burn; the paper was too densely packed. It just smoked around the edges a bit, the ink going black, giving the flames a greenish tint. I reached back for another packet and tossed it in on top of the first. It was going to take a long time to burn them all, I realized. And then I'd have to get rid of the ashes, bury them in the backyard or flush them down the toilet. And the boots, and the ski mask, and the sweatshirt, and the purse, and the fur coat, and the machete, and the woman's jewelry, and the cashier's watch and wallet and keys.

I heard a rustling sound behind me. She was picking up the money.

Amanda was still crying, but it seemed more distant now, just background noise, like traffic passing outside a window.

I turned to look at Sarah. She was sitting folded in upon herself, the bearskin wrapped around her body, so that she looked like an old squaw. She was staring past me, toward the fire.

"Please," she said.

I shook my head. "We have to, Sarah. We don't have a choice."

She lifted her face to me, and I saw that she was crying, her skin shiny with tears, a thin strand of hair pasted across her cheek. As I watched, the rug fell from her shoulders, revealing her lap. She'd collected about twenty packets there, as if she hoped to save them from the flames.

"But what'll we have without it?" she said. Her voice caught on the words and ended with a sob.

I didn't answer her. I just leaned forward and, very slowly, pried her hands away from the money. Then I took the packets one by one out of her lap and set them in the flames.

"We'll be all right," I said, lying to soothe her. "You'll see. We'll be just like we used to be."

It took me four hours to burn the money.

THE FRONT page of Sunday's *Blade* was dominated by the story of Carl's murder. There were pictures of the plane, the bag full of money, Vernon's corpse. There was nothing about Alexander's, though; the bodies weren't discovered until a little after five that morning, so it had to wait until the evening news.

The old woman's name was Diana Baker. She'd just dropped her son off at the airport and was on her way to a dinner party in Perrysburg. When she didn't show up at the party, her host called her house, and then, having received no answer, the police. A passing patrolman noticed her car in Alexander's parking lot early the next morning. He stopped to investigate, peered through the store's front window, and saw the bloody smear marks I'd left on the floor when I tried to mop up my footprints.

Besides the son, who was a lawyer in Boston, the old woman had a daughter and four grandchildren. Her husband had died seven years before, though her obituary didn't say how. The cashier's name was Michael Morton. He had parents in Cincinnati but no brothers or sisters, no wife or children.

The state police released a composite sketch of a suspect based on the description I'd given them over the phone. It looked exactly like you would've expected, like a young, addicted drifter, a derelict. The woman's son ran ads in all the major Florida papers begging whoever had called the police that night to come forward with more information, and lots of people did, adding further murk to the investigation. Once the cashier and the old woman were buried, the story stopped making the news.

After I burned the money, I flushed the ashes down the toilet. I still have the rest of the stuff—the duffel bag and the machete and the ski mask and the sweatshirt, the old woman's purse and jewelry and fur coat, the cashier's watch and wallet and keys. I'd planned to go out into the woods somewhere once the ground thawed and bury it all in a big hole full of lye, but it's been five and a half years now, and I haven't done it yet, so I doubt I ever will. I keep everything stored away up in the attic, hidden in Jacob's trunk. It's dangerous, I know, foolish, but if it ever reached the point where people were knocking on our door with a search warrant, I'd just as soon have them find something decisive, so that it would all be over quickly.

A few months after the killings, I saw in the paper that Byron McMartin had filed suit against the Federal Bureau of Investigation for negligence in his daughter's death, but I never heard what happened with the case.

Sarah and I had another baby two years ago, a boy. In a fit of what I can only call penance, I suggested that we name him after my brother, and Sarah, still groggy from the pain of labor, surprised me by agreeing. There are times when I regret it, but not as often as you might think. We call him Jack rather than Jacob.

It was in June, six weeks after her brother's birth, that Amanda had her accident. We'd set up a little plastic wading pool in the backyard for her, and somehow, in the time it took me to go inside the house, use the bathroom, and return, she managed to fall face down in the water in such a way that she couldn't get back up. She was unconscious when I found her, her hands and lips blue, her body cold to the touch. I yelled for Sarah to call an ambulance, then started pushing on

Amanda's chest and breathing into her mouth like I'd seen people do on TV, and by the time the paramedics arrived, I'd managed to revive her.

The paramedics took her to the hospital, where she remained for the next two weeks. There was some brain damage, hypoxia, though the doctors weren't sure how much. They recommended that she spend some time down in Columbus, at a clinic for head injuries—promising us that it would speed her recovery—but our insurance wouldn't cover it. When word got out in Ashenville about our trouble, St. Jude's started raising money to help us. They ended up collecting six thousand dollars, enough for a one-month stay at the clinic. Everyone who donated signed a giant get-well card, which they gave us with the check. Both Ruth Pederson's and Linda Jenkins's names were on the card.

It's hard to tell what good the clinic did, but the doctors all seemed pleased with the results. Even now, though it's clear to Sarah and me that Amanda will be damaged for life, they still speak of a young body's resiliency, of similar cases with sudden, almost miraculous recoveries. They say we should never give up hope, but Amanda's physical maturation has slowed to the point of stasis; she still looks like the two-and-a-half-year-old I pulled from the pool that afternoon, still has the same thin arms and legs, the same large, round skull waiting impatiently for the body beneath it to begin to grow. Her speech hasn't developed, her coordination is poor, her bowel and bladder control erratic. She's still attached to Jacob's bear and won't go anywhere without it. Sometimes she wakes in the middle of the night and winds it up, so that I'll surface suddenly from a deep sleep to the sound of "Frère Jacques" drifting into our bedroom from the darkness across the hall. Amanda sleeps in what used to be the guest room, in Jacob's old bed.

Sarah takes a surprisingly fatalistic attitude toward the

accident. She's hinted several times now that she believes it's a form of punishment, a way of paying for our crimes, and in the way she hovers over Jack, I can tell she thinks something might happen to him, too, unless we're vigilant and protect him.

I still work at the feedstore, in the same position. I've had some raises over the years, but just enough to keep up with inflation. Sarah's back at the library, full-time now, because we need the money. Amanda's accident used up the small amount of savings we'd managed to accrue.

You'll want to know how we spend our days, I suppose, how we manage to live with what we've done. Sarah and I never discuss the money or the murders; even when we're alone together we pretend that none of it ever happened. There are times when I want to talk, of course, but never to Sarah. It's to strangers I want to speak, people who could, perhaps, offer me an objective opinion about what I've done. It's not an urge to confess—I feel nothing like that—but rather a desire to go through things step by step with someone impartial, so that they might help me discover where I first began to go wrong, help me pinpoint that one moment after which everything became inevitable.

The children will never know about any of it, and there's some solace in that.

There are days during which I manage not to think of our crimes at all, but these are few and far between. Other times, when I do think of them—of me standing in Alexander's with the machete raised above my head, or in Lou's doorway with the shotgun in my hands—they seem unreal, like they never really happened. I know in my heart that they did, though, know exactly what I'm capable of, know it in a way that you probably never could, not unless you've been there, immersed in a similar situation, making your own fateful choices.

For a while I used to have dreams where I let the old

woman escape, let her run out the door to her car and drive away, but that's stopped now.

Since we never talk about it, I don't really know how Sarah feels. All I have are hints, like her agreeing to name our son after my brother, or the time I found her sitting on Jacob's trunk in the attic, lost in thought, the old woman's fur coat draped across her knees, its collar matted with dried blood. I imagine she feels much like I do—that we're not so much living now as simply existing, moving from one day to the next with a hollow, bewildered feeling, trying all the time, but never with much success, not to remember what has happened.

When things get especially bad, I force myself to think of Jacob. I picture him as he was the day he took me out to our father's farm. He's in his gray flannel slacks, his leather shoes, his bright red jacket. His hairless head looks cold without a hat, but he doesn't seem to notice. He's spinning on his heels, pointing out where our barn used to be, the tractor shed and grain bins. In the distance, when the wind blows, I can hear the creak of our father's windmill. I return to this moment again and again because it always makes me weep. And when I weep, I feel—despite everything I've done that might make it seem otherwise—human, exactly like everyone else.